The proceeds from the sale of this book will be used to support the mission of Library of America, a nonprofit organization that champions the nation's cultural heritage by publishing America's greatest writing in authoritative new editions and providing resources for readers to explore this rich, living legacy.

American Christmas Stories

EDITED AND WITH AN INTRODUCTION BY

Connie Willis

The Library of America Collection

Contents

Introduction

BY CONNIE WILLIS

I LOVE CHRISTMAS. I never complain about the crush at the mall or the stores starting to decorate before Halloween—or Labor Day—or having to buy presents. I like buying presents and going caroling and watching *Love Actually* and *White Christmas*. I like bubble lights and snow and Starbucks eggnog lattes—pretty much everything about the holiday season, in fact, except fruitcake and saccharine Hallmark TV movies.

And among all the things I love about Christmas, one of the best is its stories. Even though I'm primarily known for science fiction, I've written nearly a score of Christmas stories and novellas, and one of my family's treasured traditions is reading our favorite stories aloud, Valentine Davies's novelization of *Miracle on 34th Street* every night at dinner through Advent and George V. Higgins's "The Impossible Snowsuit of Christmas Past" on Christmas Eve while sitting in front of the fire.

The first time my daughter saw *The Muppet Christmas Carol*, she raced home from the movie theater to read Dickens's novella to her younger cousins, and I still spend way too much of December reading Dickens's *The Chimes* and Jean Shepherd's *A Christmas Story* and David Sedaris, and, as I clean up the post-holiday mess and face the bleak despairs of January, W. H. Auden's "For the Time Being."

Many of the stories my family and I have read are American stories, though I never really thought about it—Christmas is such a universal holiday—and when I was asked to help edit this collection, I had to look up the nationality of many of the authors. (I'd thought Christopher Morley was British and was convinced Saki was American.)

I'd also never thought about the history of the American Christmas story, and how it had come to exist, which turned out to be a fascinating story in itself.

Neither the Pilgrims nor the Puritans approved of Christmas, that pagan,

Papist, raucous holiday, and by 1659, they'd outlawed Christmas and imposed a fine of five shillings for anyone caught celebrating it. Even worse, as relations between the colonists and the British deteriorated and the Revolutionary War approached, what little of Christmas there was, was deemed an English holiday and therefore unpatriotic. Not at all a promising beginning, and certainly nothing to write stories about.

Nevertheless, as they say, Christmas persisted, thanks largely to immigrants from Germany, the Netherlands, Central Europe, and Scandinavia who were coming to the colonies (and then the newly formed United States), bringing their Christmas traditions from back home with them— the Dutch custom of hanging up stockings, the German Christmas tree, the Moravian Christmas star, midnight mass and mistletoe and cookies and Father Christmas, all of which began working their way into the American observance of Christmas and then into American stories. Early American holiday stories by Washington Irving and Nathaniel Hawthorne were basically accounts of English Christmases transplanted to New York and New England, but as the holiday evolved, so did the stories.

In 1812, when Washington Irving wrote the revised and expanded second edition of his *History of New York*, he added two wholly new passages describing Saint Nicholas "riding jollily among the tree tops, or over the roofs of the houses" in a wagon, dropping presents for children down chimneys, smoking a pipe, and "laying his finger beside his nose." In 1823 an anonymous poem titled "A Visit from St. Nicholas," more commonly known as "The Night Before Christmas," appeared in the Troy, New York, *Sentinel*. Clement C. Moore later claimed authorship, though a compelling case has been made that the author was actually Major Henry Livingston, Jr., a good friend of Washington Irving's.

Whoever wrote it, the poem repeated Irving's mention of the pipe, flying vehicle (now a sleigh), and children's gifts, and added other details—reindeer, a sack full of toys, and "visions of sugarplums," though no one then nor since has ever had a clear idea of what exactly a sugarplum is.

"The Night before Christmas," along with tales about Christmas festivities in England in Irving's *Sketch Book* (1819–20) and accounts of American Christmases by Hawthorne, James Fenimore Cooper, and, later, Harriet Beecher Stowe, began to shape the image of a distinctly American holiday, though American Christmas stories remained thin on the ground for most of the first half of the nineteenth century.

Then, in the 1860s, three pivotal things happened. The first was the Civil War, which separated three million men and boys from their homes and brought grief and loss to the families of more than six hundred thousand of them. To the soldiers, Christmas became a treasured memory, and to the people back home, a time of remembering loved ones far away from home and longing for when the family could celebrate the holiday together again. The first chapter of Louisa May Alcott's *Little Women*, with its loving portrayal of a wartime Christmas—the girls' father away at the front and the family suffering deprivation but cheerfully making the best of things—is a perfect example of the feelings of sadness and longing the war produced.

The second thing to happen was the appearance of a number of pictures depicting Christmas. A pair of engravers, Currier and Ives, who specialized in "engravings for the people"—inexpensive enough for the average family to own—produced a set of hand-colored prints depicting ice-skating on frozen ponds, sleigh rides through snowy landscapes, and jolly homecomings.

At the same time, Thomas Nast, a political illustrator most famous for popularizing the symbols of the Democratic donkey and the Republican elephant, began drawing a series of Civil War–themed cartoons for *Harper's Weekly* that included a depiction of Santa Claus. In one of the cartoons, he showed a jolly, rotund Santa, dressed in the stars of the Union flag, delivering presents to the troops. In others he portrayed Santa riding in his sleigh and going down a chimney, and, in one of his most affecting illustrations, bringing Christmas to a praying woman and a homesick soldier separated by war. Thomas Nast's cartoons of Santa Claus gave Christmas a face, Currier and Ives's engravings gave it a setting, and together they brought the image of Christmas into focus for Americans.

Lastly, Charles Dickens came to the States in 1867, on a speaking tour during which he read *A Christmas Carol* to American audiences for the first time. Dickens was a gifted speaker with an already devoted following, but this wasn't just any speaking tour, and *A Christmas Carol* wasn't just any story. It had everything—humor, pathos, drama, redemption, unforgettable characters, and a truly happy ending. It also had ghosts, which had been a Christmas tradition since the Middle Ages, and great lines, like "Bah, humbug!" and "God bless us, every one!" It was the embodiment of everything a Christmas story should be, and Dickens's American audiences loved it.

The coming together of *A Christmas Carol*, Nast's cartoons, and Currier and Ives's prints had the effect of touching a match to tinder. The celebrating of Christmas—and the writing about it—ignited, and soon Christmas stories by Americans were appearing everywhere. Louisa May Alcott wrote nearly a score of them, Kate Douglas Wiggins brought out a collection of Christmas tales, and so did Henry Van Dyke. Stories like "The Birds' Christmas Carol" and "The Other Wise Man" and "The Gift of the Magi" became instant classics, and nearly every American author, from *The Red Badge of Courage*'s Stephen Crane to *Pollyanna*'s Eleanor Porter, decided to take a crack at writing one.

This was not necessarily a good thing. Many of the stories produced in the years following the Civil War were preachy, sentimental, and/or weepily tragic, and when Hans Christian Andersen came along with his "The Little Match Girl," three-hanky stories taking "a poor girl or boy and letting them freeze somewhere under a window behind which there is usually a Christmas tree that throws its radiant splendor upon them," as Maxim Gorky described them, became omnipresent and came close to killing off the genre altogether.

Luckily, not everyone was writing treacly tragedies. Mark Twain was looking at the more cheerful side of Christmas, William Dean Howells was laughing at its excesses, and other authors were taking a clear-eyed look at the social issues surrounding the holiday.

And the stories were no longer confined to Currier-and-Ives country. As the nation expanded, so did the stories' landscapes. Kate Chopin wrote stories set in the South and Willa Cather the Southwest. Bret Harte told rough-edged tales of Christmas on the frontier, and Jack London set his stories in the midst of the Klondike gold rush. Author James Nicoll once said that "English doesn't borrow from other languages; it follows them down dark alleys to beat them unconscious and rifle their pockets for new vocabulary." The American Christmas story in the late nineteenth and early twentieth centuries did the same thing, grabbing traditions and tales from everybody and everywhere: the farm and the city and a whole new group of immigrants, this time from Ireland, Poland, Russia, Portugal, and Italy.

In the meantime, African American authors began relating their Christmas experiences, experiences vastly different from those of white Americans and marred by racism, cruelty, and the feeling of being outsiders, stories that have expanded and enriched the American Christmas story.

By the 1920s, the Christmas story was as firmly established and as quintessentially an American tradition as the Christmas tree (stolen from Germany) and Santa Claus (swiped from the Netherlands). It was also omnipresent. Christmas stories were appearing weekly during the lengthening holiday season in *Harper's Bazaar*, *Vanity Fair*, *Women's Home Companion*, and a host of other magazines, and there was a constant demand for new stories to fill their pages.

Many of the stories were truly awful. H. L. Mencken railed against stories in which "the deserving poor" were force-fed Christmas dinner and unwanted sermons, John Kendrick Bangs's hero struggled to come up with a story idea that hadn't already been done to death, and Dorothy Parker complained about the ever-present "story of the snowbound train" with its Scrooge-ish millionaire and the golden-haired child who reforms and redeems him. "Words are powerless to convey the loathing I have for that story," she said, and she was right. There were lots of them.

But there was gold amid the dross, with stories by Sherwood Anderson and Edna Ferber and Fannie Hurst. Damon Runyon's "Three Wise Guys" was published in *Collier's* and F. Scott Fitzgerald's "A Short Trip Home" came out in *The Saturday Evening Post*.

Still, it was obvious new blood was needed, and anthology editors began looking for stories in less traditional venues, including pulp magazines like *Weird Tales*, *Black Mask*, *True Detective*, and *Astounding*. There they found science fiction authors examining the possibilities of time travel and considering what Christmas in the future—or in space—might be like and fantasy writers exploring the worlds of myths and fairy tales and putting new twists on the traditional Yuletide ghost story. They found horror writers delving into the frightening side of the holidays—and of the emotions they can arouse in us; mystery authors writing detective stories with Christmas settings; and authors like Mary Roberts Rinehart, Ray Bradbury, John Collier, and Arthur C. Clarke to add to the canon.

Through the ensuing decades, the Christmas story continued to evolve and expand, absorbing customs and cultures and events like the Blob. Moves to the cities and suburbs brought shifts in customs and attitudes, and stories began to be less about happy families gathered around the Christmas tree and more about drunken office parties and urban alienation. World War II revived many of the same feelings the Civil War had, and fears of the atomic bomb issued in darker, more cynical stories.

Other groups of new writers—Hispanic, Asian American, Puerto Rican—began telling *their* stories, and even corporations, a favorite villain in Christmas stories, had something to contribute to the holiday. Montgomery Ward created "Rudolph the Red-Nosed Reindeer," Coca-Cola produced an updated Santa Claus whose image was to become almost as iconic as Thomas Nast's, and Macy's and Gimbel's department stores provided the settings for *Miracle on 34th Street* and *Elf*.

Today's American Christmas is a hopelessly tangled mishmash of religious holiday, national holiday, historical holiday, and, as Ralphie in *A*

Christmas Story, the classic movie made from Jean Shepherd's novel *In God We Trust, All Others Pay Cash*, puts it, the holiday "around which the entire kid year revolved." The American Christmas story is also becoming increasingly international, with authors like Nalo Hopkinson, who does not self-identity as an American, bringing new memories and traditions into the mix of American stories. Christmas, and the stories about it, incorporate classic traditions, ethnic customs from all over, brand new refinements, and everything from the Rockettes to regifting, from Christmas pageants to ugly sweaters, from nostalgia to existential angst. Plus: Christmas newsletters, Secret Santas, department store windows, laser yard decorations, Kwanzaa, community productions of the *The Nutcracker*, luminarias, e-cards, angels, and "Grandma Got Run Over by a Reindeer." Far too much for any one short story collection—or a dozen, for that matter—to capture in its pages.

But *American Christmas Stories* comes as close as humanly possible to doing just that. It includes stories from the American Christmas story's earliest years (Louisa May Alcott's "Kate's Choice" and J. B. Moore Bristor's "Found After Thirty-Five Years—Lucy Marshall's Letter") to modern stories from disparate backgrounds and cultures (Jose R. Nieto's "Ixchel's Tears" and Leo Rosten's "Mr. K*A*P*L*A*N and the Magi") to stories from the day after tomorrow (Ray Bradbury's "The Gift" and Raymond E. Banks's "Christmas Trombone").

There are stories that will make you laugh (Robert Benchley's "Christmas Afternoon" and Thomas M. Disch's "The Santa Claus Compromise") and stories that will make you think (W.E.B. Du Bois's "The Sermon in the Cradle" and Grace Paley's "The Loudest Voice") and stories that will make you cry (Jacob Riis's "The Kid Hangs Up His Stocking" and Christopher Morley's "The Tree That Didn't Get Trimmed.")

There are old standbys (Mark Twain's "A Letter from Santa Claus," William Dean Howells's "Christmas Every Day," and Edna Ferber's "No Room at the Inn") and familiar authors (Stephen Crane, Shirley Jackson, Katherine Anne Porter, and John Updike), plus some you've never heard of. And a couple of hidden treasures *nobody's* ever heard of, like Pauline E. Hopkins's "General Washington" and Mary Agnes Tincker's "From the Garden of a Friend."

My favorites? That's hard—there are so many great stories. If I had to pick, though, I'd guess my shortlist would have to include Langston Hughes's wistful "One Christmas Eve" and George V. Higgins's "The Impossible Snowsuit of Christmas Past," which perfectly captures both the nostalgia and loss which are so much a part of Chritmas, and Amy Tan's very short piece about a different kind of Christmas dinner, which somehow manages to capture, in its few hundred words, an entire novel's worth of cultural pressures and generation gaps. And the love that's capable of reconciling them.

My favorite of all is probably Pete Hamill's "The Christmas Kid." It's got baseball in it—and Brooklyn and World War II and a school Christmas pageant, pathos and humor and drama—and a happy ending. It embodies everything a Christmas story should be.

Just as *American Christmas Stories* embodies what an anthology of American Christmas stories should be. It's a book that shows just how the modern American Christmas story came to be—and at the same time it's a perfect candidate to read aloud from on Christmas Eve.

I hope you enjoy it as much as we've enjoyed putting it together. And a very merry—and very American—Christmas to all of you!

December 2020

Postscript: After the table of contents had been finalized, Library of America editors selected their favorite Christmas "novelette" by Connie Willis for inclusion in this anthology.

American Christmas Stories

BRET HARTE

How Santa Claus Came to Simpson's Bar

IT HAD BEEN RAINING in the valley of the Sacramento. The North Fork had overflowed its banks and Rattlesnake Creek was impassable. The few boulders that had marked the summer ford at Simpson's Crossing were obliterated by a vast sheet of water stretching to the foothills. The up stage was stopped at Grangers; the last mail had been abandoned in the *tules*, the rider swimming for his life. "An area," remarked the "Sierra Avalanche," with pensive local pride, "as large as the State of Massachusetts is now under water."

Nor was the weather any better in the foothills. The mud lay deep on the mountain road; wagons that neither physical force nor moral objurgation could move from the evil ways into which they had fallen, encumbered the track, and the way to Simpson's Bar was indicated by broken-down teams and hard swearing. And farther on, cut off and inaccessible, rained upon and bedraggled, smitten by high winds and threatened by high water, Simpson's Bar, on the eve of Christmas day, 1862, clung like a swallow's nest to the rocky entablature and splintered capitals of Table Mountain, and shook in the blast.

As night shut down on the settlement, a few lights gleamed through the mist from the windows of cabins on either side of the highway now crossed and gullied by lawless streams and swept by marauding winds. Happily most of the population were gathered at Thompson's store, clustered around a red-hot stove, at which they silently spat in some accepted sense of social communion that perhaps rendered conversation unnecessary. Indeed, most methods of diversion had long since been exhausted on Simpson's Bar; high water had suspended the regular occupations on gulch and on river, and a consequent lack of money and whiskey had taken the zest from most illegitimate recreation. Even Mr. Hamlin was fain to leave the Bar with fifty dollars in his pocket,—the only amount actually realized of the large sums won by him in the successful exercise of his arduous profession. "Ef I was asked," he remarked somewhat later,—"ef I was asked to pint out a purty little village where a retired sport as did n't care for money could exercise hisself, frequent and lively, I 'd say Simpson's Bar; but for a young man with a large family depending on his exertions, it don't pay." As Mr. Hamlin's family consisted mainly of female adults, this remark is quoted rather to show the breadth of his humor than the exact extent of his responsibilities.

Howbeit, the unconscious objects of this satire sat that evening in the listless apathy begotten of idleness and lack of excitement. Even the sudden splashing of hoofs before the door did not arouse them. Dick Bullen alone paused in the act of scraping out his pipe, and lifted his head, but no other one of the group indicated any interest in, or recognition of, the man who entered.

It was a figure familiar enough to the company, and known in Simpson's Bar as "The Old Man." A man of perhaps fifty years; grizzled and scant of hair, but still fresh and youthful of complexion. A face full of ready, but not very powerful sympathy, with a chameleon-like aptitude for taking on the shade and color of contiguous moods and feelings. He had evidently just left some hilarious companions, and did not at first notice the gravity of the group, but clapped the shoulder of the nearest man jocularly, and threw himself into a vacant chair.

"Jest heard the best thing out, boys! Ye know Smiley, over yar,—Jim Smiley,—funniest man in the Bar? Well, Jim was jest telling the richest yarn about—"

"Smiley 's a —— fool," interrupted a gloomy voice.

"A particular —— skunk," added another in sepulchral accents.

A silence followed these positive statements. The Old Man glanced quickly around the group. Then his face slowly changed. "That's so," he said reflectively, after a pause, "certingly a sort of a skunk and suthin of a fool. In course." He was silent for a moment as in painful contemplation of the unsavoriness and folly of the unpopular Smiley. "Dismal weather, ain't it?" he added, now fully embarked on the current of prevailing sentiment. "Mighty rough papers on the boys, and no show for money this season. And tomorrow's Christmas."

There was a movement among the men at this announcement, but whether of satisfaction or disgust was not plain. "Yes," continued the Old Man in the lugubrious tone he had, within the last few moments, unconsciously adopted,—"yes, Christmas, and to-night 's Christmas eve. Ye see, boys, I kinder thought—that is, I sorter had an idee, jest passin' like, you know—that may be ye 'd all like to come over to my house to-night and have a sort of tear round. But I suppose, now, you would n't? Don't feel like it, may be?" he added with anxious sympathy, peering into the faces of his companions.

"Well, I don't know," responded Tom Flynn with some cheerfulness. "P'r'aps we may. But how about your wife, Old Man? What does *she* say to it?"

The Old Man hesitated. His conjugal experience had not been a happy one, and the fact was known to Simpson's Bar. His first wife, a delicate, pretty little woman, had suffered keenly and secretly from the jealous suspicions of her husband, until one day he invited the whole Bar to his house to expose her infidelity. On arriving, the party found the shy, *petite* creature quietly engaged in her household duties, and retired abashed and discomfited. But the sensitive woman did not easily recover from the shock of this extraordinary outrage. It was with difficulty she regained her equanimity sufficiently to release her lover from the closet in which he was concealed and escape with him. She left a boy of three years to comfort her bereaved husband. The Old Man's present wife had been his cook. She was large, loyal, and aggressive.

Before he could reply, Joe Dimmick suggested with great directness that it was the "Old Man's house," and that, invoking the Divine Power, if the case were his own, he would invite whom he pleased, even if in so doing he imperilled his salvation. The Powers of Evil, he further remarked, should contend against him vainly. All this delivered with a terseness and vigor lost in this necessary translation.

"In course. Certainly. Thet 's it," said the Old Man with a sympathetic frown. "Thar 's no trouble about *thet*. It 's my own house, built every stick on it myself. Don't you be afeard o' her, boys. She *may* cut up a trifle rough,—ez wimmin do,—but she 'll come round." Secretly the Old Man trusted to the exaltation of liquor and the power of courageous example to sustain him in such an emergency.

As yet, Dick Bullen, the oracle and leader of Simpson's Bar, had not spoken. He now took his pipe from his lips. "Old Man, how 's that yer Johnny gettin' on? Seems to me he did n't look so peart last time I seed him on the bluff heavin' rocks at Chinamen. Did n't seem to take much interest in it. Thar was a gang of 'em by yar yesterday,—drownded out up the river,—and I kinder thought o' Johnny, and how he 'd miss 'em! May be now, we 'd be in the way ef he wus sick?"

The father, evidently touched not only by this pathetic picture of Johnny's deprivation, but by the considerate delicacy of the speaker, hastened to assure him that Johnny was better and that a "little fun might 'liven him up." Whereupon Dick arose, shook himself, and saying, "I 'm ready. Lead the way, Old Man: here goes," himself led the way with a leap, a characteristic howl, and darted out into the night. As he passed through the outer room he caught up a blazing brand from the hearth. The action was repeated by the rest of the party, closely following and elbowing each other, and before the astonished proprietor of Thompson's grocery was aware of the intention of his guests, the room was deserted.

The night was pitchy dark. In the first gust of wind their temporary torches were extinguished, and only the red brands dancing and flitting in the gloom like drunken will-o'-the-wisps indicated their whereabouts. Their way led up Pine-Tree Cañon, at the head of which a broad, low, bark-thatched cabin burrowed in the mountain-side. It was the home of the Old Man, and the entrance to the tunnel in which he worked when he worked at all. Here the crowd paused for a moment, out of delicate deference to their host, who came up panting in the rear.

"P'r'aps ye 'd better hold on a second out yer, whilst I go in and see thet things is all right," said the Old Man, with an indifference he was far from feeling. The suggestion was graciously accepted, the door opened and closed on the host, and the crowd, leaning their backs against the wall and cowering under the eaves, waited and listened.

For a few moments there was no sound but the dripping of water from the eaves, and the stir and rustle of wrestling boughs above them. Then the men became uneasy, and whispered suggestion and suspicion passed from the one to the other. "Reckon she 's caved in his head the first lick!" "De-coyed him inter the tunnel and barred him up, likely." "Got him down and sittin' on him." "Prob'ly bilin suthin to heave on us: stand clear the door, boys!" For just then the latch clicked, the door slowly opened, and a voice said, "Come in out o' the wet."

The voice was neither that of the Old Man nor of his wife. It was the voice of a small boy, its weak treble broken by that preternatural hoarseness which only vagabondage and the habit of premature self-assertion can give. It was the face of a small boy that looked up at theirs,—a face that might have been pretty and even refined but that it was darkened by evil knowl-edge from within, and dirt and hard experience from without. He had a blanket around his shoulders and had evidently just risen from his bed. "Come in," he repeated, "and don't make no noise. The Old Man 's in there talking to mar," he continued, pointing to an adjacent room which seemed to be a kitchen, from which the Old Man's voice came in deprecating accents. "Let me be," he added, querulously, to Dick Bullen, who had caught him up, blanket and all, and was affecting to toss him into the fire, "let go o' me, you d—d old fool, d' ye hear?"

Thus adjured, Dick Bullen lowered Johnny to the ground with a smothered laugh, while the men, entering quietly, ranged themselves around a long table of rough boards which occupied the centre of the room. Johnny then gravely proceeded to a cupboard and brought out several articles which he deposited on the table. "Thar 's whiskey. And crackers. And red herons. And cheese." He took a bite of the latter on his way to the table. "And sugar." He scooped up a mouthful *en route* with a small and very dirty hand. "And terbacker. Thar 's dried appils too on the shelf, but I don't admire 'em. Appils is swellin'. Thar," he concluded, "now wade in, and don't be afeard. *I* don't mind the old woman. She don't b'long to *me*. S'long."

He had stepped to the threshold of a small room, scarcely larger than a closet, partitioned off from the main apartment, and holding in its dim recess a small bed. He stood there a moment looking at the company, his bare feet peeping from the blanket, and nodded.

"Hello, Johnny! You ain't goin' to turn in agin, are ye?" said Dick.

"Yes, I are," responded Johnny, decidedly.

"Why, wot's up, old fellow?"

"I'm sick."

"How sick?"

"I've got a fevier. And childblains. And roomatiz," returned Johnny, and vanished within. After a moment's pause, he added in the dark, apparently from under the bedclothes,—"And biles!"

There was an embarrassing silence. The men looked at each other, and at the fire. Even with the appetizing banquet before them, it seemed as if they might again fall into the despondency of Thompson's grocery, when the voice of the Old Man, incautiously lifted, came deprecatingly from the kitchen.

"Certainly! Thet's so. In course they is. A gang o' lazy drunken loafers, and that ar Dick Bullen 's the orneriest of all. Did n't hev no more *sabe* than to come round yar with sickness in the house and no provision. Thet 's what I said: 'Bullen,' sez I, 'it 's crazy drunk you are, or a fool,' sez I, 'to think o' such a thing.' 'Staples,' I sez, 'be you a man, Staples, and 'spect to raise h—ll under my roof and invalids lyin' round?' But they would come,—they would. Thet 's wot you must 'spect o' such trash as lays round the Bar."

A burst of laughter from the men followed this unfortunate exposure. Whether it was overheard in the kitchen, or whether the Old Man's irate companion had just then exhausted all other modes of expressing her contemptuous indignation, I cannot say, but a back door was suddenly slammed with great violence. A moment later and the Old Man reappeared, haply unconscious of the cause of the late hilarious outburst, and smiled blandly.

"The old woman thought she 'd jest run over to Mrs. McFadden's for a sociable call," he explained, with jaunty indifference, as he took a seat at the board.

Oddly enough it needed this untoward incident to relieve the embarrassment that was beginning to be felt by the party, and their natural audacity returned with their host. I do not propose to record the convivialities of that evening. The inquisitive reader will accept the statement that the conversation was characterized by the same intellectual exaltation, the same cautious reverence, the same fastidious delicacy, the same rhetorical precision, and the same logical and coherent discourse somewhat later in the evening, which distinguish similar gatherings of the masculine sex in more civilized localities and under more favorable auspices. No glasses were broken in the absence of any; no liquor was uselessly spilt on floor or table in the scarcity of that article.

It was nearly midnight when the festivities were interrupted. "Hush," said Dick Bullen, holding up his hand. It was the querulous voice of Johnny from his adjacent closet: "O dad!"

The Old Man arose hurriedly and disappeared in the closet. Presently he reappeared. "His rheumatiz is coming on agin bad," he explained, "and he wants rubbin'." He lifted the demijohn of whiskey from the table and shook it. It was empty. Dick Bullen put down his tin cup with an embarrassed laugh. So did the others. The Old Man examined their contents and said hopefully, "I reckon that 's enough; he don't need much. You hold on all o' you for a spell, and I 'll be back"; and vanished in the closet with an old flannel shirt and the whiskey. The door closed but imperfectly, and the following dialogue was distinctly audible:—

"Now, sonny, whar does she ache worst?"

"Sometimes over yar and sometimes under yer; but it 's most powerful from yer to yer. Rub yer, dad."

A silence seemed to indicate a brisk rubbing. Then Johnny:

"Hevin' a good time out yer, dad?"

"Yes, sonny."

"To-morrer's Chrismiss,—ain't it?"

"Yes, sonny. How does she feel now?"

"Better. Rub a little furder down. Wot 's Chrismiss, anyway? Wot 's it all about?"

"O, it 's a day."

This exhaustive definition was apparently satisfactory, for there was a silent interval of rubbing. Presently Johnny again:

"Mar sez that everywhere else but yer everybody gives things to everybody Chrismiss, and then she jist waded inter you. She sez thar 's a man they call Sandy Claws, not a white man, you know, but a kind o' Chinemin, comes down the chimbley night afore Chrismiss and gives things to chillern,—boys like me. Puts 'em in their butes! Thet 's what she tried to play upon me. Easy now, pop, whar are you rubbin' to,—thet 's a mile from the place. She jest made that up, did n't she, jest to aggrewate me and you? Don't rub thar. . . . . Why, dad!"

In the great quiet that seemed to have fallen upon the house the sigh of the near pines and the drip of leaves without was very distinct. Johnny's voice, too, was lowered as he went on, "Don't you take on now, fur I 'm gettin' all right fast. Wot 's the boys doin' out thar?"

The Old Man partly opened the door and peered through. His guests were sitting there sociably enough, and there were a few silver coins and a lean buckskin purse on the table. "Bettin' on suthin,—some little game or 'nother. They 're all right," he replied to Johnny, and recommenced his rubbing.

"I 'd like to take a hand and win some money," said Johnny, reflectively, after a pause.

The Old Man glibly repeated what was evidently a familiar formula, that if Johnny would wait until he struck it rich in the tunnel he 'd have lots of money, etc., etc.

"Yes," said Johnny, "but you don't. And whether you strike it or I win it, it 's about the same. It 's all luck. But it 's mighty cur'o's about Chrismiss,—ain't it? Why do they call it Chrismiss?"

Perhaps from some instinctive deference to the overhearing of his guests, or from some vague sense of incongruity, the Old Man's reply was so low as to be inaudible beyond the room.

"Yes," said Johnny, with some slight abatement of interest, "I 've heerd o' him before. Thar, that 'll do, dad. I don't ache near so bad as I did. Now wrap me tight in this yer blanket. So. Now," he added in a muffled whisper, "sit down yer by me till I go asleep." To assure himself of obedience, he disengaged one hand from the blanket and, grasping his father's sleeve, again composed himself to rest.

For some moments the Old Man waited patiently. Then the unwonted stillness of the house excited his curiosity, and without moving from the bed, he cautiously opened the door with his disengaged hand, and looked into the main room. To his infinite surprise it was dark and deserted. But even then a smouldering log on the hearth broke, and by the upspringing blaze he saw the figure of Dick Bullen sitting by the dying embers.

"Hello!"

Dick started, rose, and came somewhat unsteadily toward him.

"Whar 's the boys?" said the Old Man.

"Gone up the cañon on a little *pasear*. They're coming back for me in a minit. I 'm waitin' round for 'em. What are you starin' at, Old Man?" he added with a forced laugh; "do you think I 'm drunk?"

The Old Man might have been pardoned the supposition, for Dick's eyes were humid and his face flushed. He loitered and lounged back to the chimney, yawned, shook himself, buttoned up his coat and laughed. "Liquor ain't so plenty as that, Old Man. Now don't you git up," he continued, as the Old Man made a movement to release his sleeve from Johnny's hand. "Don't you mind manners. Sit jest whar you be; I 'm goin' in a jiffy. Thar, that 's them now."

There was a low tap at the door. Dick Bullen opened it quickly, nodded "Good night" to his host, and disappeared. The Old Man would have followed him but for the hand that still unconsciously grasped his sleeve. He could have easily disengaged it: it was small, weak, and emaciated. But perhaps because it *was* small, weak, and emaciated, he changed his mind, and, drawing his chair closer to the bed, rested his head upon it. In this defenceless attitude the potency of his earlier potations surprised him. The room flickered and faded before his eyes, reappeared, faded again, went out, and left him—asleep.

Meantime Dick Bullen, closing the door, confronted his companions. "Are you ready?" said Staples. "Ready," said Dick; "what 's the time?" "Past twelve," was the reply; "can you make it?—it 's nigh on fifty miles, the round trip hither and yon." "I reckon," returned Dick, shortly. "Whar 's the mare?" "Bill and Jack 's holdin' her at the crossin'." "Let 'em hold on a minit longer," said Dick.

He turned and re-entered the house softly. By the light of the guttering candle and dying fire he saw that the door of the little room was open. He stepped toward it on tiptoe and looked in. The Old Man had fallen back in his chair, snoring, his helpless feet thrust out in a line with his collapsed shoulders, and his hat pulled over his eyes. Beside him, on a narrow wooden bedstead, lay Johnny, muffled tightly in a blanket that hid all save a strip of forehead and a few curls damp with perspiration. Dick Bullen made a step forward, hesitated, and glanced over his shoulder into the deserted room. Everything was quiet. With a sudden resolution he parted his huge mustaches with both hands and stooped over the sleeping boy. But even as he did so a mischievous blast, lying in wait, swooped down the chimney, re-kindled the hearth, and lit up the room with a shameless glow from which Dick fled in bashful terror.

His companions were already waiting for him at the crossing. Two of them were struggling in the darkness with some strange misshapen bulk, which as Dick came nearer took the semblance of a great yellow horse.

It was the mare. She was not a pretty picture. From her Roman nose to her rising haunches, from her arched spine hidden by the stiff *machillas* of a Mexican saddle, to her thick, straight, bony legs, there was not a line of equine grace. In her half-blind but wholly vicious white eyes, in her pro-truding under lip, in her monstrous color, there was nothing but ugliness and vice.

"Now then," said Staples, "stand cl'ar of her heels, boys, and up with you. Don't miss your first holt of her mane, and mind ye get your off stirrup *quick*. Ready!"

There was a leap, a scrambling struggle, a bound, a wild retreat of the crowd, a circle of flying hoofs, two springless leaps that jarred the earth, a rapid play and jingle of spurs, a plunge, and then the voice of Dick some-where in the darkness, "All right!"

"Don't take the lower road back onless you 're hard pushed for time! Don't hold her in down hill! We 'll be at the ford at five. G' lang! Hoopa! Mula! GO!"

A splash, a spark struck from the ledge in the road, a clatter in the rocky cut beyond, and Dick was gone.

Sing, O Muse, the ride of Richard Bullen! Sing, O Muse of chivalrous men! the sacred quest, the doughty deeds, the battery of low churls, the fear-some ride and grewsome perils of the Flower of Simpson's Bar! Alack! she is dainty, this Muse! She will have none of this bucking brute and swaggering, ragged rider, and I must fain follow him in prose, afoot!

It was one o'clock, and yet he had only gained Rattlesnake Hill. For in that time Jovita had rehearsed to him all her imperfections and practised all her vices. Thrice had she stumbled. Twice had she thrown up her Roman nose in a straight line with the reins, and, resisting bit and spur, struck out madly across country. Twice had she reared, and, rearing, fallen backward; and twice had the agile Dick, unharmed, regained his seat before she found her vicious legs again. And a mile beyond them, at the foot of a long hill, was Rattlesnake Creek. Dick knew that here was the crucial test of his ability to perform his enterprise, set his teeth grimly, put his knees well into her flanks, and changed his defensive tactics to brisk aggression. Bullied and maddened, Jovita began the descent of the hill. Here the artful Richard pretended to hold her in with ostentatious objurgation and well-feigned cries of alarm. It is unnecessary to add that Jovita instantly ran away. Nor need I state the time made in the descent; it is written in the chronicles of Simpson's Bar. Enough that in another moment, as it seemed to Dick, she was splashing on the overflowed banks of Rattlesnake Creek. As Dick expected, the momentum she had acquired carried her beyond the point of balking, and, holding her well together for a mighty leap, they dashed into the middle of the swiftly flowing current. A few moments of kicking, wading, and swimming, and Dick drew a long breath on the opposite bank.

The road from Rattlesnake Creek to Red Mountain was tolerably level. Either the plunge in Rattlesnake Creek had dampened her baleful fire, or the art which led to it had shown her the superior wickedness of her rider, for Jovita no longer wasted her surplus energy in wanton conceits. Once she bucked, but it was from force of habit; once she shied, but it was from a new freshly painted meeting-house at the crossing of the county road. Hollows, ditches, gravelly deposits, patches of freshly springing grasses, flew from beneath her rattling hoofs. She began to smell unpleasantly, once or twice she coughed slightly, but there was no abatement of her strength or speed. By two o'clock he had passed Red Mountain and begun the descent to the plain. Ten minutes later the driver of the fast Pioneer coach was overtaken and passed by a "man on a Pinto hoss,"—an event sufficiently notable for remark. At half past two Dick rose in his stirrups with a great shout. Stars were glittering through the rifted clouds, and beyond him, out of the plain, rose two spires, a flagstaff, and a straggling line of black objects. Dick jingled his spurs and swung his *riata*, Jovita bounded forward, and in another moment they swept into Tuttleville and drew up before the wooden piazza of "The Hotel of All Nations."

What transpired that night at Tuttleville is not strictly a part of this record. Briefly I may state, however, that after Jovita had been handed over to a sleepy ostler, whom she at once kicked into unpleasant consciousness, Dick sallied out with the bar-keeper for a tour of the sleeping town. Lights still gleamed from a few saloons and gambling-houses; but, avoiding these, they stopped before several closed shops, and by persistent tapping and judicious outcry roused the proprietors from their beds, and made them unbar the doors of their magazines and expose their wares. Sometimes they were met by curses, but oftener by interest and some concern in their needs, and the interview was invariably concluded by a drink. It was three o'clock before this pleasantry was given over, and with a small waterproof bag of india-rubber strapped on his shoulders Dick returned to the hotel. But here he was waylaid by Beauty,—Beauty opulent in charms, affluent in dress, persuasive in speech, and Spanish in accent! In vain she repeated the invitation in "Excelsior," happily scorned by all Alpine-climbing youth, and rejected by this child of the Sierras,—a rejection softened in this instance by a laugh and his last gold coin. And then he sprang to the saddle and dashed down the lonely street and out into the lonelier plain, where presently the lights, the black line of houses, the spires, and the flagstaff sank into the earth behind him again and were lost in the distance.

The storm had cleared away, the air was brisk and cold, the outlines of adjacent landmarks were distinct, but it was half past four before Dick reached the meeting-house and the crossing of the county road. To avoid the rising grade he had taken a longer and more circuitous road, in whose viscid mud Jovita sank fetlock deep at every bound. It was a poor preparation for a steady ascent of five miles more; but Jovita, gathering her legs under her, took it with her usual blind, unreasoning fury, and a half-hour later reached the long level that led to Rattlesnake Creek. Another half-hour would bring him to the creek. He threw the reins lightly upon the neck of the mare, chirruped to her, and began to sing.

Suddenly Jovita shied with a bound that would have unseated a less practised rider. Hanging to her rein was a figure that had leaped from the bank, and at the same time from the road before her arose a shadowy horse and rider. "Throw up your hands," commanded this second apparition, with an oath.

Dick felt the mare tremble, quiver, and apparently sink under him. He knew what it meant and was prepared.

"Stand aside, Jack Simpson, l know you, you d—d thief. Let me pass or—"

He did not finish the sentence. Jovita rose straight in the air with a terrific bound, throwing the figure from her bit with a single shake of her vicious head, and charged with deadly malevolence down on the impediment before her. An oath, a pistol-shot, horse and highwayman rolled over in the road, and the next moment Jovita was a hundred yards away. But the good right arm of her rider, shattered by a bullet, dropped helplessly at his side.

Without slacking his speed he shifted the reins to his left hand. But a few moments later he was obliged to halt and tighten the saddle-girths that had slipped in the onset. This in his crippled condition took some time. He had no fear of pursuit, but looking up he saw that the eastern stars were already paling, and that the distant peaks had lost their ghostly whiteness, and now stood out blackly against a lighter sky. Day was upon him. Then completely absorbed in a single idea, he forgot the pain of his wound, and mounting again dashed on toward Rattlesnake Creek. But now Jovita's breath came broken by gasps, Dick reeled in his saddle, and brighter and brighter grew the sky.

Ride, Richard; run, Jovita; linger, O day!

For the last few rods there was a roaring in his ears. Was it exhaustion from loss of blood, or what? He was dazed and giddy as he swept down the hill, and did not recognize his surroundings. Had he taken the wrong road, or was this Rattlesnake Creek?

It was. But the brawling creek he had swam a few hours before had risen, more than doubled its volume, and now rolled a swift and resistless river between him and Rattlesnake Hill. For the first time that night Richard's heart sank within him. The river, the mountain, the quickening east, swam before his eyes. He shut them to recover his self-control. In that brief interval, by some fantastic mental process, the little room at Simpson's Bar and the figures of the sleeping father and son rose upon him. He opened his eyes wildly, cast off his coat, pistol, boots, and saddle, bound his precious pack tightly to his shoulders, grasped the bare flanks of Jovita with his bared knees, and with a shout dashed into the yellow water. A cry rose from the opposite bank as the head of a man and horse struggled for a few moments against the battling current, and then were swept away amidst uprooted trees and whirling drift-wood.

The Old Man started and woke. The fire on the hearth was dead, the candle in the outer room flickering in its socket, and somebody was rapping at the door. He opened it, but fell back with a cry before the dripping, half-naked figure that reeled against the doorpost.

"Dick?"

"Hush! Is he awake yet?"

"No,—but, Dick?—"

"Dry up, you old fool! Get me some whiskey *quick*!" The Old Man flew and returned with—an empty bottle! Dick would have sworn, but his strength was not equal to the occasion. He staggered, caught at the handle of the door, and motioned to the Old Man.

"Thar 's suthin' in my pack yer for Johnny. Take it off. I can't."

The Old Man unstrapped the pack and laid it before the exhausted man. "Open it, quick!"

He did so with trembling fingers. It contained only a few poor toys,— cheap and barbaric enough, goodness knows, but bright with paint and tinsel. One of them was broken; another, I fear, was irretrievably ruined by water; and on the third—ah me! there was a cruel spot.

"It don't look like much, that 's a fact," said Dick, ruefully. . . . . "But it 's the best we could do. . . . . Take 'em, Old Man, and put 'em in his stocking, and tell him—tell him, you know—hold me, Old Man—" The Old Man caught at his sinking figure. "Tell him," said Dick, with a weak little laugh,— "tell him Sandy Claus has come."

And even so, bedraggled, ragged, unshaven, and unshorn, with one arm hanging helplessly at his side, Santa Claus came to Simpson's Bar and fell fainting on the first threshold. The Christmas dawn came slowly after, touching the remoter peaks with the rosy warmth of ineffable love. And it looked so tenderly on Simpson's Bar that the whole mountain, as if caught in a generous action, blushed to the skies.

1872

LOUISA MAY ALCOTT

Kate's Choice

"WELL, WHAT DO YOU think of her?"

"I think she's a perfect dear, and not a bit stuck up with all her money."

"A real little lady, and ever so pretty."

"She kissed me lots, and don't tell me to run away, so I love her."

The group of brothers and sisters standing round the fire laughed as little May finished the chorus of praise with these crowning virtues.

Tall Alf asked the question, and seemed satisfied with the general approval of the new cousin just come from England to live with them. They had often heard of Kate, and rather prided themselves on the fact that she lived in a fine house, was very rich, and sent them charming presents. Now pity was added to the pride, for Kate was an orphan, and all her money could not buy back the parents she had lost. They had watched impatiently for her arrival, had welcomed her cordially, and after a day spent in trying to make her feel at home they were comparing notes in the twilight, while Kate was having a quiet talk with mamma.

"I hope she will choose to live with us. You know she can go to any of the uncles she likes best," said Alf.

"We are nearer her age than any of the other cousins, and papa is the oldest uncle, so I guess she will," added Milly, the fourteen-year-old daughter of the house.

"She said she liked America," said quiet Frank.

"Wonder if she will give us a lot of her money?" put in practical Fred, who was always in debt.

"Stop that!" commanded Alf. "Mind now, if you ever ask her for a penny I'll shake you out of your jacket."

"Hush! she's coming," cried Milly, and a dead silence followed the lively chatter.

A fresh-faced bright-eyed girl of fifteen came quietly in, glanced at the group on the rug, and paused as if doubtful whether she was wanted.

"Come on!" said Fred, encouragingly.

"Shall I be in the way?"

"Oh! dear, no, we were only talking," answered Milly, drawing her cousin nearer with an arm about her waist.

"It sounded like something pleasant," said Kate, not exactly knowing what to say.

"We were talking about you," began little May, when a poke from Frank made her stop to ask, "What's that for? We *were* talking about Kate, and we all said we liked her, so it's no matter if I do tell."

"You are very kind," and Kate looked so pleased that the children forgave May's awkward frankness.

"Yes, and we hoped you'd like us and stay with us," said Alf, in the lofty and polite manner which he thought became the young lord of the house.

"I am going to try all the uncles in turn, and then decide; papa wished it," answered Kate, with a sudden tremble of the lips, for her father was the only parent she could remember, and had been unusually dear for that reason.

"Can you play billiards?" asked Fred, who had a horror of seeing girls cry.

"Yes, and I'll teach you."

"You had a pony-carriage at your house, didn't you?" added Frank, eager to help on the good work.

"At grandma's,—I had no other home, you know," answered Kate.

"What shall you buy first with your money?" asked May, who *would* ask improper questions.

"I'd buy a grandma if I could," and Kate both smiled and sighed.

"How funny! We've got one somewhere, but we don't care much about her," continued May, with the inconvenient candor of a child.

"Have you? Where is she?" and Kate turned quickly, looking full of interest.

"Papa's mother is very old, and lives ever so far away in the country, so of course we don't see much of her," explained Alf.

"But papa writes sometimes, and mamma sends her things every Christmas. We don't remember her much, because we never saw her but once, ever so long ago; but we do care for her, and May mustn't say such rude things," said Milly.

"I shall go and see her. I can't get on without a grandmother," and Kate smiled so brightly that the lads thought her prettier than ever. "Tell me more about her. Is she a dear old lady?"

"Don't know. She is lame, and lives in the old house, and has a maid named Dolly, and—that's all I can tell you about her," and Milly looked a

little vexed that she could say no more on the subject that seemed to interest her cousin so much.

Kate looked surprised, but said nothing, and stood looking at the fire as
if turning the matter over in her mind, and trying to answer the question
she was too polite to ask,—how could they live without a grandmother?
Here the tea-bell rang, and the flock ran laughing downstairs; but, though
she said no more, Kate remembered that conversation, and laid a plan in
her resolute little mind which she carried out when the time came.

According to her father's wish she lived for a while in the family of each
of the four uncles before she decided with which she would make her home.
All were anxious to have her, one because of her money, another because
her great-grandfather had been a lord, a third hoped to secure her for his
son, while the fourth and best family loved her for herself alone. They were
worthy people, as the world goes,—busy, ambitious, and prosperous; and
every one, old and young, was fond of bright, pretty, generous Kate. Each
family was anxious to keep her, a little jealous of the rest, and very eager to
know which she would choose.

But Kate surprised them all by saying decidedly when the time came,—

"I must see grandma before I choose. Perhaps I ought to have visited her
first, as she is the oldest. I think papa would wish me to do it. At any rate,
I want to pay my duty to her before I settle anywhere, so please let me go."

Some of the young cousins laughed at the idea, and her old-fashioned,
respectful way of putting it, which contrasted strongly with their free-and-
easy American speech. The uncles were surprised, but agreed to humor her
whim, and Uncle George, the eldest, said softly,—

"I ought to have remembered that poor Anna was mother's only daughter, and the old lady would naturally love to see the girl. But, my dear, it will
be desperately dull. Only two old women and a quiet country town. No fun,
no company, you won't stay long."

"I shall not mind the dulness if grandma likes to have me there. I lived
very quietly in England, and was never tired of it. Nursey can take care of
me, and I think the sight of me will do the dear old lady good, because they
tell me I am like mamma."

Something in the earnest young face reminded Uncle George of the sister he had almost forgotten, and recalled his own youth so pleasantly that
he said, with a caress of the curly head beside him,—

"So it would, I'm sure of it, and I've a great mind to go with you and 'pay
my duty' to mother, as you prettily express it."

"Oh, no, please don't, sir; I want to surprise her, and have her all to my-self for a little while. Would you mind if I went quite alone with Nursey? You can come later."

"Not a bit; you shall do as you like, and make sunshine for the old lady as you have for us. I haven't seen her for a year, but I know she is well and comfortable, and Dolly guards her like a dragon. Give her my love, Kitty, and tell her I send her something she will value a hundred times more than the very best tea, the finest cap, or the handsomest tabby that ever purred."

So, in spite of the lamentations of her cousins, Kate went gayly away to find the grandma whom no one else seemed to value as she did.

You see, grandpa had been a farmer, and lived contentedly on the old place until he died; but his four sons wanted to be something better, so they went away one after the other to make their way in the world. All worked hard, got rich, lived splendidly, and forgot as far as possible the old life and the dull old place they came from. They were good sons in their way, and had each offered his mother a home with him if she cared to come. But grandma clung to the old home, the simple ways, and quiet life, and, thank-ing them gratefully, she had remained in the big farm-house, empty, lonely, and plain though it was, compared to the fine homes of her sons.

Little by little the busy men forgot the quiet, uncomplaining old mother, who spent her years thinking of them, longing to see and know their chil-dren, hoping they would one day remember how she loved them all, and how solitary her life must be.

Now and then they wrote or paid her a hasty visit, and all sent gifts of far less value to her than one loving look, one hour of dutiful, affectionate companionship.

"If you ever want me, send and I'll come. Or, if you ever need a home, remember the old place is here always open, and you are always welcome," the good old lady said. But they never seemed to need her, and so seldom came that the old place evidently had no charm for them.

It was hard, but the sweet old woman bore it patiently, and lived her lonely life quietly and usefully, with her faithful maid Dolly to serve and love and support her.

Kate's mother, her one daughter, had married young, gone to England, and, dying early, had left the child to its father and his family. Among them little Kate had grown up, knowing scarcely any thing of her American re-lations until she was left an orphan and went back to her mother's peo-ple. She had been the pet of her English grandmother, and, finding all the aunts busy, fashionable women, had longed for the tender fostering she had known, and now felt as if only grandmothers could give.

With a flutter of hope and expectation, she approached the old house after the long journey was over. Leaving the luggage at the inn, and accompanied by faithful Nurse, Kate went up the village street, and, pausing at the gate, looked at the home where her mother had been born.

A large, old-fashioned farm-house, with a hospitable porch and tall trees in front, an orchard behind, and a capital hill for blackberries in summer, and coasting in winter, close by. All the upper windows were curtained, and made the house look as if it was half-asleep. At one of the lower windows sat a portly puss, blinking in the sun, and at the other appeared a cap, a regular grandmotherly old cap, with a little black bow perked up behind. Something in the lonely look of the house and the pensive droop of that cap made Katy hurry up the walk and tap eagerly at the antique knocker. A brisk little old woman peered out, as if startled at the sound, and Kate asked, smiling, "Does Madam Coverley live here?"

"She does, dear. Walk right in," and throwing wide the door, the maid trotted down a long, wide hall, and announced in a low tone to her mistress,—

"A nice, pretty little girl wants to see you, mum."

"I shall love to see a young face. Who is it, Dolly?" asked a pleasant voice.

"Don't know, mum."

"Grandma must guess," and Kate went straight up to the old lady with both hands out, for the first sight of that sweet old face won her heart.

Lifting her spectacles, grandma looked silently a minute, then opened her arms without a word, and in the long embrace that followed Kate felt assured that she was welcome to the home she wanted.

"So like my Anna! And this is her little girl? God bless you, my darling! So good to come and see me!" said the old lady when she could speak.

"Why, grandma, I couldn't get on without you, and as soon as I knew where to find you I was in a fidget to be off; but had to do my other visits first, because the uncles had planned it so. This is Dolly, I am sure, and that is my good nurse. Go and get my things, please, Nursey. I shall stay here until grandma sends me away."

"That will never be, deary. Now tell me every thing. It is like an angel coming to see me all of a sudden. Sit close, and let me feel sure it isn't one of the dreams I make to cheer myself when I'm lonesome."

Kate sat on a little stool at grandma's feet, and, leaning on her knee, told all her little story, while the old lady fed her hungry eyes with the sight of the fresh young face, listened to the music of a loving voice, and felt the happy certainty that some one had remembered her, as she longed to be remembered.

Such a happy day as Kate spent talking and listening, looking at her new home, which she found delightful, and being petted by the two old women, who would hardly let Nursey do any thing for her. Kate's quick eyes read the truth of grandma's lonely life very soon; her warm heart was full of tender pity, and she resolved to devote herself to making the happiness of the dear old lady's few remaining years, for at eighty one should have the prop of loving children, if ever.

To Dolly and madam it really did seem as if an angel had come, a singing, smiling, chattering sprite, who danced all over the old house, making blithe echoes in the silent room, and brightening every corner she entered.

Kate opened all the shutters and let in the sun, saying she must see which room she liked best before she settled. She played on the old piano, that wheezed and jangled, all out of tune; but no one minded, for the girlish voice was as sweet as a lark's. She invaded Dolly's sacred kitchen, and messed to her heart's content, delighting the old soul by praises of her skill, and petitions to be taught all she knew. She pranced to and fro in the long hall, and got acquainted with the lives of painted ancestors hanging there in big wigs or short-waisted gowns. She took possession of grandma's little parlor, and made it so cosey the old lady felt as if she was bewitched, for cushioned arm-chairs, fur foot-stools, soft rugs, and delicate warm shawls appeared like magic. Flowers bloomed in the deep, sunny window-seats, pictures of lovely places seemed to break out on the oaken walls, a dainty work-basket took its place near grandma's quaint one, and, best of all, the little chair beside her own was seldom empty now.

The first thing in the morning a kiss waked her, and the beloved voice gave her a gay "Good-morning, grandma dear!" All day Anna's child hovered about her with willing hands and feet to serve her, loving heart to return her love, and the tender reverence which is the beautiful tribute the young should pay the old. In the twilight, the bright head always was at her knees; and, in either listening to the stories of the past or making lively plans for the future, Kate whiled away the time that used to be so sad.

Kate never found it lonely, seldom wished for other society, and grew every day more certain that here she could find the cherishing she needed, and do the good she hoped.

Dolly and Nurse got on capitally; each tried which could sing "Little Missy's" praises loudest, and spoil her quickest by unquestioning obedience to every whim or wish. A happy family, and the dull November days went by so fast that Christmas was at hand before they knew it.

All the uncles had written to ask Kate to pass the holidays with them, feeling sure she must be longing for a change. But she had refused them all, saying she should stay with grandma, who could not go anywhere to join other people's merry-makings, and must have one of her own at home. The uncles urged, the aunts advised, and the cousins teased; but Kate denied them all, yet offended no one, for she was inspired by a grand idea, and carried it out with help from Dolly and Nurse, unsuspected by grandma.

"We are going to have a little Christmas fun up here among ourselves, and you mustn't know about it until we are ready. So just sit all cosey in your corner, and let me riot about as I like. I know you won't mind, and I think you'll say it is splendid when I've carried out my plan," said Kate, when the old lady wondered what she was thinking about so deeply, with her brows knit and her lips smiling.

"Very well, dear, do any thing you like, and I shall enjoy it, only don't get tired, or try to do too much," and with that grandma became deaf and blind to the mysteries that went on about her.

She was lame, and seldom left her own rooms; so Kate, with her devoted helpers, turned the house topsy-turvy, trimmed up hall and parlors and great dining-room with shining holly and evergreen, laid fires ready for kindling on the hearths that had been cold for years, and had beds made up all over the house.

What went on in the kitchen, only Dolly could tell; but such delicious odors as stole out made grandma sniff the air, and think of merry Christmas revels long ago. Up in her own room Kate wrote lots of letters, and sent orders to the city that made Nursey hold up her hands. More letters came in reply, and Kate had a rapture over every one. Big bundles were left by the express, who came so often that the gates were opened and the lawn soon full of sleigh-tracks. The shops in the village were ravaged by Mistress Kate, who laid in stores of gay ribbon, toys, nuts, and all manner of queer things.

"I really think she's lost her mind," said the postmaster as she flew out of the office one day with a handful of letters.

"Pretty creter! I wouldn't say a word against her, not for a mint of money. She's so good to old Mrs. Coverley," answered his fat wife, smiling as she watched Kate ride up the village street on an ox-sled.

If grandma had thought the girl out of her wits, no one could have blamed her, for on Christmas day she really did behave in the most singular manner.

"You are going to church with me this morning, grandma. It's all arranged. A close carriage is coming for us, the sleighing is lovely, the church all trimmed up, and I must have you see it. I shall wrap you in fur, and we will go and say our prayers together, like good girls, won't we?" said Kate, who was in a queer flutter, while her eyes shone, her lips were all smiles, and her feet kept dancing in spite of her.

"Anywhere you like, my darling. I'd start for Australia tomorrow, if you wanted me to go with you," answered grandma, who obeyed Kate in all things, and seemed to think she could do no wrong.

So they went to church, and grandma did enjoy it; for she had many blessings to thank God for, chief among them the treasure of a dutiful, loving child. Kate tried to keep herself quiet, but the odd little flutter would not subside, and seemed to get worse and worse as time went on. It increased rapidly as they drove home, and, when grandma was safe in her little parlor again, Kate's hands trembled so she could hardly tie the strings of the old lady's state and festival cap.

"We must take a look at the big parlor. It is all trimmed up, and I've got my presents in there. Is it ready, Doll?" asked Kate, as the old servant appeared, looking so excited that grandma said, laughing,—

"We have been quiet so long, poor Dolly don't know what to make of a little gayety."

"Lord bless us, my dear mum! It's all so beautiful and kinder surprisin', I feel as ef merrycles had come to pass agin," answered Dolly, actually wiping away tears with her best white apron.

"Come, grandma," and Kate offered her arm. "Don't she look sweet and dear?" she added, smoothing the soft, silken shawl about the old lady's shoulders, and kissing the placid old face that beamed at her from under the new cap.

"I always said madam was the finest old lady a-goin', ef folks only knew it. Now, Missy, ef you don't make haste, that parlor-door will bust open, and spoil the surprise; for they are just bilin' over in there," with which mysterious remark Dolly vanished, giggling.

Across the hall they went, but at the door Kate paused, and said with a look grandma never forgot,—

"I hope I have done right. I hope you'll like my present, and not find it too much for you. At any rate, remember I meant to please you and give you the thing you need and long for most, my dear old grandma."

"My good child, don't be afraid. I shall like any thing you do, and thank you for your thought of me. What a curious noise! I hope the fire hasn't fallen down."

Without another word, Kate threw open the door and led grandma in. Only a step or two—for the old lady stopped short and stared about her, as if she didn't know her own best parlor. No wonder she didn't, for it was full of people, and such people! All her sons, their wives and children, rose as she came in, and turned to greet her with smiling faces. Uncle George went up and kissed her, saying, with a choke in his voice, "A merry Christmas, mother!" and everybody echoed the words in a chorus of good-will that went straight to the heart.

Poor grandma could not bear it, and sat down in her big chair, trembling, and sobbing like a little child. Kate hung over her, fearing the surprise had been too much; but joy seldom kills, and presently the old lady was calm enough to look up and welcome them all by stretching out her feeble hands and saying, brokenly yet heartily,—

"God bless you, my children! This *is* a merry Christmas, indeed! Now tell me all about it, and who everybody is; for I don't know half the little ones."

Then Uncle George explained that it was Kate's plan, and told how she had made every one agree to it, pleading so eloquently for grandma that all other plans were given up. They had arrived while she was at church, and had been with difficulty kept from bursting out before the time.

"Do you like your present?" whispered Kate, quite calm and happy now that the grand surprise was safely over.

Grandma answered with a silent kiss that said more than the warmest words, and then Kate put every one at ease by leading up the children, one by one, and introducing each with some lively speech. Everybody enjoyed this and got acquainted quickly; for grandma thought the children the most remarkable she had ever seen, and the little people soon made up their minds that an old lady who had such a very nice, big house, and such a dinner waiting for them (of course they had peeped everywhere), was a most desirable and charming grandma.

By the time the first raptures were over Dolly and Nurse and Betsey Jane (a girl hired for the occasion) had got dinner on the table; and the procession, headed by Madam proudly escorted by her eldest son, filed into the dining-room where such a party had not met for years.

It would be quite impossible to do justice to that dinner: pen and ink are not equal to it. I can only say that every one partook copiously of every thing; that they laughed and talked, told stories, and sang songs; and when no one could do any more, Uncle George proposed grandma's health, which was drunk standing, and followed by three cheers. Then up got the old lady, quite rosy and young, excited and gay, and said in a clear strong voice,—

"I give you in return the best of grandchildren, little Kate."

I give you my word the cheer they gave grandma was nothing to the shout that followed these words; for the old lady led off with amazing vigor, and the boys roared so tremendously that the sedate tabby in the kitchen flew off her cushion, nearly frightened into a fit.

After that, the elders sat with grandma in the parlor, while the younger part of the flock trooped after Kate all over the house. Fires burned everywhere, and the long unused toys of their fathers were brought out for their amusement. The big nursery was full of games, and here Nursey collected the little ones when the larger boys and girls were invited by Kate to go out and coast. Sleds had been provided, and until dusk they kept it up, the city girls getting as gay and rosy as Kate herself in this healthy sport, while the lads frolicked to their hearts' content, building snow forts, pelting one another, and carousing generally without any policeman to interfere or any stupid old ladies to get upset, as at home in the park.

A cosey tea and a dance in the long hall followed, and they were just thinking what they would do next when Kate's second surprise came.

There were two great fireplaces in the hall: up the chimney of one roared a jolly fire, but the other was closed by a tall fire-board. As they sat about, resting after a brisk contra dance, a queer rustling and tapping was heard behind this fire-board.

"Rats!" suggested the girls, jumping up into the chairs.

"Let's have 'em out!" added the boys, making straight for the spot, intent on fun.

But before they got there, a muffled voice cried, "Stand from under!" and down went the board with a crash, out bounced Santa Claus, startling the lads as much as the rumor of rats had the girls.

A jolly old saint he was, all in fur, with sleigh-bells jingling from his waist and the point of his high cap, big boots, a white beard, and a nose as red as if Jack Frost had had a good tweak at it. Giving himself a shake that set all the bells ringing, he stepped out upon the hearth, saying in a half-gruff, half-merry tone,—

"I call this a most inhospitable way to receive me! What do you mean by stopping up my favorite chimney? Never mind, I'll forgive you, for this is an unusual occasion. Here, some of you fellows, lend a hand and help me out with my sack."

A dozen pair of hands had the great bag out in a minute, and, lugging it to the middle of the hall, left it beside St. Nick, while the boys fell back into the eager, laughing crowd that surrounded the newcomer.

"Where's my girl? I want my Kate," said the saint, and when she went to him he took a base advantage of his years, and kissed her in spite of the beard.

"That's not fair," whispered Kate, as rosy as the holly-berries in her hair.

"Can't help it,—must have some reward for sticking in that horrid chimney so long," answered Santa Claus, looking as roguish as any boy. Then he added aloud, "I've got something for everybody, so make a big ring, and the good fairy will hand round the gifts."

With that he dived into his bag and brought out treasure after treasure, some fine, some funny, many useful, and all appropriate, for the good fairy seemed to have guessed what each one wanted. Shouts of laughter greeted the droll remarks of the jolly saint, for he had a joke about every thing, and people were quite exhausted by the time the bottom of the sack was reached.

"Now, then, a rousing good game of blind man's buff, and then this little family must go to bed, for it's past eleven."

As he spoke, the saint cast off his cap and beard, fur coat, and big boots, and proceeded to dance a double shuffle with great vigor and skill; while the little ones, who had been thoroughly mystified, shouted, "Why, it's Alf!" and fell upon him en masse as the best way of expressing their delight at his successful performance of that immortal part.

The game of blind man's buff that followed was a "rouser" in every sense of the word, for the gentlemen joined, and the children flew about like a flock of chickens when hawks are abroad. Such peals of laughter, such shouts of fun, and such racing and scrambling that old hall had never seen before. Kate was so hunted that she finally took refuge behind grandma's chair, and stood there looking at the lively scene, her face full of happiness as she remembered that it was her work.

The going to bed that night was the best joke of all; for, though Kate's arrangements were peculiar, every one voted that they were capital. There were many rooms, but not enough for all to have one apiece. So the uncles and aunts had the four big chambers, all the boys were ordered into the great playroom, where beds were made on the floor, and a great fire blazing that the camping out might be as comfortable as possible. The nursery was devoted to the girls, and the little ones were sprinkled round wherever a snug corner was found.

How the riotous flock were ever got into their beds no one knows. The lads caroused until long past midnight, and no knocking on the walls of paternal boots, or whispered entreaties of maternal voices through key-holes, had any effect, for it was impossible to resist the present advantages for a grand Christmas rampage.

The girls giggled and gossiped, told secrets, and laid plans more quietly; while the small things tumbled into bed, and went to sleep at once, quite used up with the festivities of this remarkable day.

Grandma, down in her own cosey room, sat listening to the blithe noises with a smile on her face, for the past seemed to have come back again, and her own boys and girls to be frolicking above there, as they used to do forty years ago.

"It's all so beautiful I can't go to bed, Dolly, and lose any of it. They'll go away to-morrow, and I may never see them any more," she said, as Dolly tied on her night-cap and brought her slippers.

"Yes, you will, mum. That dear child has made it so pleasant they can't keep away. You'll see plenty of 'em, if they carry out half the plans they have made. Mrs. George wants to come up and pass the summer here; Mr. Tom says he shall send his boys to school here, and every girl among them has promised Kate to make her a long visit. The thing is done, mum, and you'll never be lonely any more."

"Thank God for that!" and grandma bent her head as if she had received a great blessing. "Dolly, I want to go and look at those children. It seems so like a dream to have them here, I must be sure of it," said grandma, folding her wrapper about her, and getting up with great decision.

"Massy on us, mum, you haven't been up them stairs for months. The dears are all right, warm as toasts, and sleepin' like dormice, I'll warrant," answered Dolly, taken aback at this new whim of old madam's.

But grandma would go, so Dolly gave her an arm, and together the two old friends hobbled up the wide stairs, and peeped in at the precious children. The lads looked like a camp of weary warriors reposing after a victory, and grandma went laughing away when she had taken a proud survey of this promising portion of the rising generation. The nursery was like a little convent full of rosy nuns sleeping peacefully; while a pictured Saint Agnes, with her lamb, smiled on them from the wall, and the firelight flickered over the white figures and sweet faces, as if the sight were too fair to be lost in darkness. The little ones lay about promiscuously, looking like dissipated Cupids with sugar hearts and faded roses still clutched in their chubby hands.

"My darlings!" whispered grandma, lingering fondly over them to cover a pair of rosy feet, put back a pile of tumbled curls, or kiss a little mouth still smiling in its sleep.

But when she came to the coldest corner of the room, where Kate lay on the hardest mattress, under the thinnest quilt, the old lady's eyes were full of tender tears; and, forgetting the stiff joints that bent so painfully, she knelt slowly down, and, putting her arms about the girl, blessed her in silence for the happiness she had given one old heart.

Kate woke at once, and started up, exclaiming with a smile,—

"Why, grandma, I was dreaming about an angel, and you look like one with your white gown and silvery hair!"

"No, dear, you are the angel in this house. How can I ever give you up?" answered madam, holding fast the treasure that came to her so late.

"You never need to, grandma, for I have made my choice."

1872

MARK TWAIN

A Letter from Santa Claus

Palace of St. Nicholas,
In the Moon,
Christmas Morning.

M Y DEAR SUSIE CLEMENS:
I have received & read all the letters which you & your little sister have written me by the hand of your mother & your nurses; & I have also read those which you little people have written me with your own hands—for although you did not use any characters that are in grown people's alphabets, you used the character which *all* children, in all lands on earth & in the twinkling stars use; & as all my subjects in the moon are children & use no character but that, you will easily understand that I can read your & your baby sister's jagged & fantastic marks without any trouble at all. But I had trouble with those letters which you dictated through your mother & the nurses, for I am a foreigner & cannot read English writing well. You will find that I made no mistakes about the things which you & the baby ordered in your *own* letters—I went down your chimney at midnight when you were asleep, & delivered them all, myself—& kissed both of you, too, because you are good children, well trained, nice-mannered, & about the most obedient little people I ever saw. But in the letters which you dictated, there were some words which I could not make out, for certain, & one or two small orders which I couldn't fill because we ran out of stock. Our last lot of kitchen furniture for dolls had just gone to a very poor little child in the North Star, away up in the cold country above the Big Dipper. Your mama can show you that star, & you will say, "Little Snow Flake (for that is the child's name), I'm glad you got that furniture, for you need it more than I." That is, you must *write* that, with your own hand, & Snow Flake will write you an answer. If you only spoke it, she wouldn't hear you. Make your letter light & thin, for the distance is great & the postage very heavy.

There was a word or two in your mama's letter which I couldn't be certain of. I took it to be "trunk full of doll's clothes?" Is that it? I will call at your kitchen door about nine oclock this morning to inquire. But I must not see anybody, & I must not speak to anybody but you. When the kitchen door-bell rings, George must be blindfolded & sent to open the door, & then he must go back to the dining room or the china closet & take the cook with him. You must tell George he must walk on tip-toe and not speak—otherwise he will die some day. Then you must go up to the nursery & stand on a chair or the nurse's bed, & put your ear to the speaking tube that leads down to the kitchen, & when I whistle through it, you must speak in the tube & say, "Welcome, Santa Claus!" Then I will ask whether it was a trunk you ordered or not? If you say it was, I shall ask you what *color* you want the trunk to be. Your mama will help you to name a nice color, & then you must tell me every single thing, in detail, which you want the trunk to contain. Then when I say "Good bye & a Merry Christmas to my little Susie Clemens!" you must say, "Good bye, good old Santa Claus, & thank you very much—& please tell that little Snow Flake I will look at her star to-night & she must look down here—I will be right in the west bay-window; & every fine night I will look at her star & say, I know somebody up there, & *like* her, too." Then you must go down in the library, & make George close all the doors that open into the main hall, & everybody must keep still for a little while. I will go to the moon & get those things, & in a few minutes I will come down the chimney which belongs to the fire-place that is in the hall—if it is a trunk you want, because I couldn't get such a thing as a trunk down the nursery-chimney, you know.

People may talk, if they want to, till they hear my footsteps in the hall—then you tell them to keep quiet a little while till I go back up the chinmey. Maybe you will not hear my foot steps at all—so you may go now & then & peep through the dining room doors, & by & by you will see that thing which you want, right under the piano in the drawing room—for I shall put it there. If I should leave any snow in the hall, you must tell George to sweep it into the fireplace, for I haven't time to do such things. George must not use a broom, but a rag—else he will die some day. You must watch George, & not let him run into danger. If my boot should leave a stain on the mar-ble, George must not holy-stone it away. Leave it there always in memory of my visit; & whenever you look at it or show it to anybody you must let it remind you to be a good little girl. Whenever you are naughty, & somebody points to that mark which your good old Santa Claus's boot made on the marble, what will you say, little Sweetheart?

Good-bye, for a few minutes, till I come down to the world & ring the kitchen door-bell.

Your loving
Santa Claus,

Whom people sometimes call "The Man in the Moon."

1875

J. B. MOORE BRISTOR

Found After Thirty-Five Years—Lucy Marshall's Letter

A TRUE STORY FOR CHRISTMAS

"WANT ANY WHITEWASHING DONE m'am?" asked Alfred Nelson, as he stood for a moment before a small Virginia house.

"If you can do good work you might undertake this room," answered an elderly woman; "Mrs. Marshall is out this morning, but I heard her say she only wanted an experienced hand, as the last man who did it made it look badly. Do you make a business of whitewashing?"

"I do whatever I can," was the answer. "My wife was cook in the hotel, and lifting heavy things helped to bring on a cancer, the doctor says. She can't do anything now, and I have to pay a woman to take care of my three children."

Mrs. Marshall soon came in, and hearing Alfred's story, engaged him at once. She was a stranger in Virginia, having gone there after her marriage, which was a most unsuitable and unhappy one. Her husband had fine chances in life, but drank secretly, managing the habit so that it was hardly suspected in the church to which he belonged, its effects being felt by his family, to whom his laziness and drowsiness brought poverty. The house in which they lived, a plain brick, tastefully painted in Lucas' softest gloss shades, was mortgaged and now offered at Sheriff's sale. It had only two rooms down stairs, and three—one a mere cupboard in size—above, yet if the law had allowed Lucy Marshall the poor boon of quiet possession to herself, and liberty to work for her little ones in peace, undisturbed by Henry Marshall, she would have been thankful. Progress in some things has been made, but men are not far advanced in just-treatment of women.

Mrs. Marshall was warm-hearted and felt for those who had been in bondage, and still suffered from ties that had been cruelly rent by so-called "owners." There were many colored people in the place, and she tried to help them. As she sat down to her work she asked Alfred if he had always been free.

"No, indeed," was his answer; "I lived in N——, and was sold away from my mother when I was six years old, about thirty-six years ago." A shudder of horror passed through Mrs. Marshall as she asked:

"Did your mother see you taken away? How did it happen?"

"I was playing in the street, when my master came up and said:

"Alfred, do you see that man on horseback?"

"I said yes, and he told me to go with him. He took me out of the place and I never saw or heard of any of my people again."

"Thirty-five years," repeated Mrs. Marshall. "Your mother is most likely dead or sold away, but some one of your family might be there. Have you ever written to ask?"

"Yes, but I got no answer."

"It it worth trying again. I will write for you at any time, mind, and for any one else freely." She urged him that the letter should be written and sent there, but he did not seem much interested; in fact he had no change at that moment. Mrs. Marshall would have offered it on what would be due him when the work was done, or given it, but she saw he chewed tobacco from time to time. Thrifty and managing herself, she felt less like offering, and after saying paper and envelope would be given, and the letter prepared at any time, she urged no more, her own perpetually recurring worries drawing off her attention. Alfred did his work and left. Spring, which only brought sadness to Mrs. Marshall, came and went, then summer and fall. December set in and things were darker than before. They were often on short allowance of food, though she turned everything to account, selling the plants in her neat garden raised from seeds and cuttings and accepting an offer at the lowest wages to review holiday books only during the illness of one of the editorial staff of a city paper.

The day was not very cold, and there was no fire save a small one lighted long enough to make a cup of coffee fresh and fragrant in the ideal pot that shone like silver. Then Lucy untied the parcels that had come by express, and turned over the tinted pages of some of Randolph's new books. In dainty bas relief was the "World's Christmas Hymn." Turning over the illustrations her eyes fell on the words:

> "The people are perplexed and saying,
>   How long? how long?
> And on my hand I bowed my head;
> There is no peace on earth, I said,
>   For hate is strong,

And mocks the song
Of peace on earth, good will to men!

Then pealed the bells more loud and deep;
God is not dead, nor doth he sleep;
The wrong shall fall,
The right prevail
With peace on earth, good will to men."

But to her the words seemed a mockery just then. Why had her life been so? Why had she been brought to this place? She thought of those who had suffered in it more than she. If her heart quivered with anguish and was wild with rage and grief when brutal Henry Marshall threatened if she left him to take from her the infant that lay in the cradle, and hide him from her, how had other mothers felt whose children had been torn from them, and sold to slavery worse than death? Would not a people that tolerated slavery, and now the rum traffic, legalize any outrage for gold? Mechanically she turned over other volumes, reading passages here and there. "The Appearance of Our Lord to Men before His Birth in Bethlehem," By Doctor Baker, who in Georgia remained at his post, standing loyal when those around him were false. She read over that page which speaks of Christ's having in almost every instance of healing, touched those whom he cured. "He laid his hand upon every one of them," is written of the multitude he healed. This was a type of human help and sympathy. But in those dreary years what had she known? And of all sufferers I think few receive less sympathy than the drunkard's wife. That men and women are now wakening to earnest efforts in temperance work is not so much from sympathy as their interest and fear. The nation did not rise in righteous indignation and put down slavery. Men waited till it became a political necessity, an absolute war measure, without which they could not conquer the foe. And not until the people see and realize that prohibition means economy in expense, low taxation, good times and prosperity, will it be carried. Meanwhile how long will be the heartache of weary wives and mothers.

"I have often found," said Lucy Marshall sadly to herself, "that in moments of deepest despair, it is a good thing to try and help others. The year will close most sadly to me. Can I brighten it to some one else? When my work is done I shall go to-night to some of the cabins and offer to write for them."

That afternoon as she read Mrs. Prentiss' "Flower of the Family," remem-

bering how she had first read it, years before in her girlhood, in days shadowed by ill treatment from an intemperate father, for the curse had come
to her in more than one—yes, more than two relations of life, she saw from
the low window Alfred Nelson pass along the road. She lost no time calling
him in.

"Alfred," she remarked, energetically, "I thought you told me you were
coming back soon for me to write for you? Have you not waited long
enough? How is your wife?"

"She is dead," was the answer.

Mrs. Marshall started. "And how are your children doing?"

"Oh, they are all going to live with different neighbors. One is to take one
and one another; my wife knew that before she died." How quietly the man
spoke for a change that would darken every young life!

"That is a sad prospect for them," was the reply. "More than ever should
you try to find your mother or some of your family. I shall not wait for you
longer, but write myself. Did you not say you had written once and got no
answer?"

"Yes," said Alfred, "I wrote twice."

"To whom?"

"To my old master."

"You did not, surely," was the amazed answer. "Could you suppose that
any man who would be vile enough to sell a child from his mother, would
answer you and let you know anything that would be of comfort to you?"

"Yes, I thought he would," said Alfred.

"Then I think you are simple," was Lucy's answer, as she wrote down the
names of master, Alfred's mother, brother and family, giving the circumstances of his going away. She directed this letter to the ministers of the
Methodist and Baptist churches for colored people in the place he had once
lived, and begged them to read it out for a number of Sabbaths in succession morning and night, and ask the people to inquire. A stamped envelope
was also inclosed.

Alfred went away hardly seeming as much interested as Mrs. Marshall.

Henry was more outrageous than usual that week, and Mrs. Marshall
cast over every project in her agonized mind and resolved to face all and
leave him. It was no fit place to bring up children. Such language would
soon corrupt them. How her head ached that winter morning as she walked
to the village post office, receiving her own yellow envelope returned in
wonderfully quick time from the Virginia village. She could hardly credit
the contents. Alfred's mother was in church when the letter was read, and

his brother wrote that when in the union army as a soldier he had inquired for him every place he went, but could hear nothing. He was to come on at once and bring the children; they would take care of them.

"My way indeed has been dark," said Lucy, "but perhaps for this God brought me here. At any rate before I leave I will try and lighten other hearts." Out of a number of efforts, one other succeeded.

Alfred did not leave for some time, and was at first influenced by some persons for whom he worked for very low wages, who were unwilling to lose him. But at last he went with the orphans, writing back that his mother was almost wild with joy. Lucy did not say that her inefficient son was a little afraid he might have to help her, and it turned out that all were ready and willing to help Nelson.

Dear friend, my story is true, all save names, and I doubt not that it is possible for some of you to meet long-parted friends, or at least hear of them by using the same means. Is it not worth any cost or repeated effort?

1883

MARY AGNES TINCKER

From the Garden of a Friend

ARL PETERSEN was one of the innumerable company of
artists who paint pretty pictures for a living, and Mimi was
his wife. They were Danes by parentage, but had lived so
long in Rome that there was very little Dane left in them, except
the honor and simplicity of character one so frequently finds in
that people.

They were about as poor as they could comfortably be, this young couple. Carl painted from morning till night, and sold his pictures to Spilorchia, the dealer, who paid for them ten per cent. of the price they ultimately
brought. Carl knew that he got only ten per cent.; but it was better to be
sure of so much than to wait for more from purchasers who might never
come. What can a poor artist do when people *will* go to the dealers instead
of the studios to buy? But Carl had a plan of escape from this servitude.
He meant to lay by a little money, bit by bit, till he should be able to keep
back one picture from Spilorchia, and place it instead in the window of a
friendly bookseller. He might have to wait a good while; but then he would
have ten times as much. And one step made in advance, the second must
follow.

The Petersens lived in one of those Roman paradises which you reach
by passing through a Roman purgatory, if that can be called a purgatory
which soils instead of cleansing. You cross to Trastevere, pass through several dingy streets, enter a dingier one, that is narrow and dark as well, pass
a gloomy *portone* into a green and dripping court, go up a wide stair that
smells of garlic and is sometimes infested by dirty children,—up and up to
the top. There is an anteroom which has possibilities. Disgust gives place
to doubt. There is an ineffably dingy kitchen, which nevertheless calls forth
an exclamation of delight from an artist; for, going to the window, you see
through wide coincident rifts of many a succeeding line of roofs an exquisite airy vista of mountain, villa, and grove.

Carl had advertised for a studio with two or three rooms attached, and on their first visit to the locality the young couple began as we have, leaving the studio for the last. They were anxious, for they had been house-hunting for a whole month, and were nearly worn out. Besides, time was money to them.

The last door opened. They caught their breath, stepped in, and gave one glance; then turned and rushed into each other's arms. Eureka!

The chamber was palatial in size, and beautifully proportioned; but the glory of it was what came in from outside. Three windows looking toward the northeast gave them the whole of Rome, the Alban and Sabine mountains, and a flood of light. They would have a full view of the sunrise, too; and up to ten o'clock three oblique lines of sunshine moved across their floor.

This room was both studio and salon. Mimi had her work-table at one window, the dining-table stood before another, and Carl's easel was set by the third. They did everything there but cook and sleep, and the place was charming, if bare. Little by little they were covering the rough walls with pictures of all sorts, cut from illustrated papers and magazines, and at intervals Carl painted a slender panel of deep blue, or dull gold, or soft green. His few artistic properties were scattered about. There was a screen or two, a carved chair, and a beautiful oaken chest, very old and carved in palm-leaves. A graceful wicker basket hung over this chest, against one of Carl's blue panels. Mimi cherished this basket, for it had been sent to her on her wedding-day, full of white camellias and blue violets.

Besides the apartment, they had also a garden, only one story below, against the hillside. A little flight of stairs led to it from the studio. In this garden they had found a treasure,—a young mandarin orange-tree in the first year of its blooming. It was so white with blossoms that it seemed to be fainting under the weight of them. Mimi carefully pinched them all off but one.

"The tree isn't strong enough to bear," she said, "and these blossoms will perfume the studio." She carried them up in her apron, and poured the sweet white drift into her wicker basket on the wall.

The one blossom she had spared faded off in time, and left a green bullet. The bullet grew, and became a ball two inches in diameter. How they watched that little one, having no child of their own! How they guarded it from every possible harm! It was shielded from the wind, covered from hail and heavy rain; and wo to the spider which should spin its web there, or the lizard led by curiosity to whisk up the large brown vase that held their treasure!

The tree grew in the light of their eyes as well as in the sunshine, and seemed to take pride in its own achievements, holding out the laden twig as who should say, "Do you see this child of mine? I also have produced an orange, O my sisters multitudinous of Sorrento and Seville!"

The mandarin turned yellow gradually. At Christmas there were only a tiny cloud and a thread of green. But Mimi was impatient. When Carl sat down to his Christmas dinner, there lay upon his napkin a fragrant golden ball, with a pointed green leaf standing out at either side, wing-like, as if the thing had flown there.

"If it turns out to be dry or sour, I shall feel betrayed," Mimi said. "I couldn't wait any longer to know. Let's try it before we eat."

Carl gave the fruit a scientific pinch, as a cat takes her kittens up by the neck. "It will at least be juicy," he said. "The skin doesn't come off too easily."

The orange was carefully divided, as an orange ought to be, according to the manner of its putting together, and Carl leaned across the table and put one section between the two rows of pearly teeth his wife opened to receive it. Then, while she waited with immovable jaws and lips drawn back, a second section disappeared under his blonde mustache. Looking anxiously into each other's faces, they closed their teeth at the same instant, like two small wine-presses; and at the same instant a sparkling satisfaction foamed up into the eyes of both. The mandarin was a success!

"U-u-m-m-m!" growled Mimi, inarticulately and low, like a cat over a mouse. "It is the king of mandarins!" she cried, when her tongue was free. "It is the Emperor of China himself. How can we wait a whole year for another crop!"

They had to wait, however; and when blossom-time came round again, they left thirty of the finest flowers, the tree having grown stout and matronly. At Christmas thirty globes of pure gold hung amid the dark green foliage.

"I have exchanged fifteen of them for a chicken," Mimi said to her husband on the morning of December 24th. "You know, Carl, we can afford neither to eat nor to give them away, after the extra expenses we have had."

These extra expenses were for a dress coat and a silk dress with a train, or as Mimi called them for short, a *rondine* and a *strascico*. The young people had some fine friends, who did not choose that they should remain in obscurity, and they were invited out occasionally. Aside from the pleasure they found in society, they knew that it might help Carl in his art to meet such people; and therefore, with tremulous hearts, they had ventured not only to spend their little savings, but to incur a small debt, in order to make themselves presentable. Nor was this all. They had still further diminished their present means by keeping back one of Carl's pictures from the dealer, and setting it in the bookseller's window instead.

This adventurous picture was nothing less than a portrait of their mandarin orange-tree as it had been the year before. It was the same, yet not the same. It was the tree as love saw it.

There was the high, dark gray wall, with an undulating line of green Janiculum above it, and above that a band of pure azure. Below, on a jagged table of ancient masonry that had once been a wall, stood the large brown vase. The slender, supple tree leaned all one way toward the single orange that hung heavily at the tip of its foremost twig, and all the leaves seemed to be twisting their stems about in order to see it. There were still a few faint green lines upon its yellow ripeness; and, studying, one might see that they hinted forth the picture's name,—Il Primogenito. In the wall above was set a torn umbrella, with bunches of long grass carefully stopping the holes. A blue cup full of water stood beside the vase, and a painter's brush, still tinged with blue, was stuck, handle down, where it had loosened the earth about the tree. Around the vase, making a half circle from the wall, was a rough protective barrier, composed of fragments of antique sculpture, heads, arms, hands, half-seen faces, a shoulder pushing out, a strip of egg-molding as white as milk, a bit of stone-fluting, the curling tip of an acanthus leaf. Lastly, the picture was flooded with sunshine.

If Carl was ever to be famous, it would be for painting sunshine.

They had hopes of this picture, and of their new friends. Only the week before, at a musicale given by the Signora Cremona, they had made the acquaintance of the famous English poetess, Madama Landon, and the great lady had praised one of Carl's pictures which she had seen at the house of a friend. Who knew but she might wish to see others, to buy one, or at least to praise them to those who might buy!

The Primogenito unsold, then, Mimi had exchanged half of her oranges for their Christmas roast. "And I have been thinking, Carl," she said, "that we might send the other half to the Cremonas as an acknowledgment of their kindness to us. We have dined there twice, and there was the musicale. We could send them in my basket, and they will make a very pretty show."

They went to work at once. The basket was lined with moss, and over that Mimi laid a little open-wrought napkin, laboriously made by her own fingers by drawing threads out of linen. Each mandarin was cut with a stem and a leaf or two, and artistically placed.

"How beautiful!" sighed Mimi. "And there are just enough. One more would be a bump, and one less a dent."

A note was written on their last sheet of fine paper; the basket was covered with white tissue-paper, and tied with blue ribbons preserved from their wedding presents.

When Carl went out with the basket, Mimi followed him to the stairs, and looked after him with tears in her eyes.

"It's like sending one's own children out into the world," she thought. "Dear little creatures! They have never had anything but love and praising here."

And so the basket of mandarins began its travels; its grand tour, in fact.

It reached the Signora Cremona in safety.

"How pretty!" said the lady. "But we have fruit for to-day, and to-morrow we dine out. I will send the basket to Mrs. James, with our regrets for her breakfast to-morrow."

A note was written. The Signora Cremona was *so* sorry that a previous engagement would prevent their breakfasting with Mrs. James the next day, and begged her to accept a basket of mandarin oranges, which she thought would be fine, as they were from a friend's garden.

Mrs. James and her sister were just having their after-breakfast coffee and cigarettes when the present was brought in.

"The Cremonas cannot come," Mrs. James said, reading the note. "And see what a lovely basket of mandarins! If we had not bought and settled everything for to-morrow, I would set this in the middle of the table, just as it is. Oh! I'll tell you what we can do,—send it with a note to Monsignore Appetitoso. He might hear of our breakfast, you know, and feel slighted. Poor soul! I shouldn't want to offend him. He is very useful."

The note was written, the blue ribbons were tied for the third time, and the young tourists set out anew on their travels.

Monsignore Appetitoso was a *jubilato a mezza paga*; that is, having passed a certain age, he was dispensed from the duties of his office with a pension of half its salary. Besides this, the pay being small, the Pope had assigned him a free apartment in the canonicate of Santa Veronica del Fazzoletto, a palace that was nearly vacant, the canons preferring to reside outside. Here the old gentleman lived very comfortably, though without luxury; going out to dinner when he was invited, getting an afternoon cup of tea and slice of cake in some lady's drawing-room now and then, and dreaming over the happy days, long past, when he was *delegato*, and rounded his dinner off with ices, candies, and *vin santo*, instead of roasted chestnuts and a biscuit.

Monsignore dined at one o'clock, and was just eating a *biscottino* with his glass of Marsala, after the soup, boiled beef and greens, stewed pigeons and roasted chestnuts, which had formed the repast, when Mrs. James's present arrived.

(We make haste to add, lest scrupulous souls should be scandalized at a priest's eating meat on a vigil, that Monsignore was dispensed from both fasting and abstinence on account of his sixty-eight years and a disease of the stomach.)

The basket was uncovered with eagerness, and, settling himself more comfortably in his chair, Monsignore prepared to devour its whole contents then and there. But as he smilingly lifted off the topmost orange, a thought arrested him.

He had just heard—the news came in with the roasted chestnuts—that the rector of the College of Converted Zulus had been taken seriously ill that morning, and therefore could not have the honor of dining with Cardinal Inghilterra the next evening.

Now Monsignore had felt hurt at not receiving an invitation to this dinner. He loved the cardinal as only a poor gourmet can love a rich one, and had served him to the extent of his power. Who knows, he thought, but I may be asked to fill the rector's place? There was every probability of it, if only that pushing Monsignore Barili did not thrust himself in. Would not the cardinal be touched by the amiable piety of a man who should send him a basket of fruit after having been excluded from his dinner-table? He, Monsignore, was not expected to know anything about the rector of the Zulus' opportune seizure, or at least not so quickly.

He put the orange carefully back into its place, and, after ringing his bell, tied the blue ribbons again,—their fourth tying, as the creases in them began to hint.

"Giacomo," he said, when his man appeared, "run as fast as you can with this to Cardinal Inghilterra, and ask permission to see him. Make the proper compliments, and try and find out if Monsignore Barili has been there to-day."

Cardinal Inghilterra lunched when Monsignore dined, and he was still at table when Giacomo was graciously permitted to present himself. Poor Monsignore was useful to others beside Mrs. James, and the cardinal used him a good deal, and treated him with good-natured, condescending familiarity.

He sat in a room like a green tent, with a window full of sunshine and a garden behind him. Before him on the table was a cup of coffee, into which he was just dropping a lump of sugar from the tips of his white dimpled fingers. At his right hand was a liquor stand, and a gilded glass rosily full of "Perfetto Amore," one of the new Turin liquors that are trying to oust French ones from the market. An open note, the agonized regrets of the rector of the Zulus, lay at his left hand.

As Giacomo entered, and received a nod of recognition and a sign to wait, the cardinal was listening to his major-domo, who, full of reverential anxiety, was communicating to his Eminence the possibility that fish might not be forthcoming for to-morrow's dinner. A storm had driven back the fishers of the west coast the night before, and the wind there was still contrary. There was not even a minnow in the market to-day; and the dealers had promised more than they expected to receive. The cook had prayed, bribed, and threatened; but the event still remained doubtful.

The cardinal listened with tranquillity, sipping his coffee. He did not believe in impossibilities—for himself.

"There is a telegraph in Rome," he remarked, as if communicating an item of news. "And there is"—he sipped his coffee—"a telegraph at Civita Vecchia"—another sip—"and at Porto d'Anzio"—sip—"and at Ancona"—sip—"and at various other sea, and therefore fish, ports around the coast of Italy"; and he finished his coffee, and set the cup aside.

"Certainly, Eminenza!" the man struck in. "But I could not incur the expense without a special permission. If I send three telegrams to make sure of one, I may have to pay for three baskets of fishes; and besides, the price"—

"You can discuss that with the cook," interrupted his master, and, waving him away, beckoned Giacomo to advance.

"Monsignore is very good," he said, after listening to the man's errand. "Tell him that I am infinitely obliged. And"—he hesitated, and glanced at the letter beside him. He saw through Monsignore's little pious ruse perfectly; but, as we have said, he was good-natured. "Wait in the anteroom a moment," he added. "See if Antonio is there, and send him to me."

Giacomo bowed himself out backward, and Antonio bowed himself in forward. He was a man of such a villainous solemnity of aspect that, had one encountered him in heaven even, one would have recognized him as the confidential servant of a priest. Face cleanly shaven, eyes downcast, mouth firmly closed, neck advanced as if to lay its head on the block (for virtue's sake, *s'intende*), and what mocking young Italy calls an expression of *Gesu mio* made Antonio one of the cream of his kind.

"Cover these mandarins with the best roses that you can find in the garden," the cardinal said, "and take them with my compliments to the Signora Landon. Throw away the wraps; they are soiled. And you need not let Giacomo see you."

Exit Antonio in funereal silence.

About the same time two ladies were examining a picture set up frameless on a table in a little salon in Hotel Bristol.

"Isn't it charming?" said one of them. "I bought it this morning, and I am going to send it home to Tom. I can't keep it for myself, because the sunshine of it freckles me. Tom will be delighted with it, it is so Italian. I know the artist. He and his wife were at La Cremona's musicale last week. Such a nice little couple!—like two birds."

Enter Antonio.

"Oh! was it you, Antonio?" said the lady, turning. "I thought it was my shoemaker. How is his Eminence?"

Antonio, with the air of taking his last leave of his dearest friend, delivered his message.

"How perfectly lovely!" was the response. "Will you come and look at these mandarins, Lady Mary? See how well they are arranged! *Mandarini* smothered in roses! They need not blush before strawberries and cream. It is a poem. Eminenza's fruit is worthy to have grown on my painted orange-tree. Stay a moment, Antonio, while I write my thanks."

The quill went scrawling over a sheet of cream-colored paper, that had initials and a crest occupying all the left side; a prompt white hand slapped the blotting-book over those large characters, folded, inclosed, and directed the note, and sealed it with a ring worn on the writer's thumb.

Antonio received this missive as though it were his death-warrant, but with a sudden convulsion of face as he felt the generous breadth of a five-franc piece under it. He had nearly smiled.

"The cardinal has such good taste!" the poetess said, smilingly contemplating his gift, when Antonio had faded away. "But unfortunately, I never eat oranges. They make me bilious. Oh! I know what I will do. I can send them to the artist who painted that picture. It will be a pleasant way of announcing to him that his picture is sold. The bookseller told me that he had already been in this morning to see if any one had looked at it, and seemed very sad. Jeannette can carry the basket over with a note to-morrow morn-ing. There is no time this afternoon. Will you please touch the bell-knob at your elbow, Mary?"

A servant appeared.

"Bring me a vase with water for these roses," Mrs. Landon said. "And send my maid to me."

The next day Mimi and Carl had their dinner at noon. It was a poorer dinner than they had ever before eaten on a *festa* day, for there was nothing to follow their chicken but four *soldi* worth of cheese and their coffee. To be sure, there isn't much sense in eating cheese when you have no fruit; but, as Mimi said, their hearts had been so full of the mandarins that maybe their stomachs might have felt the influence. Besides, cheese gives a certain air.

Their cheerfulness was a little forced to-day. Carl had been painting since daybreak, and was tired, and his wife was not feeling well.

"Did you say that this was a chicken!" he asked, probing the fowl before him.

"Why, yes, dear, and a nice plump one, too," replied Mimi, trying to make the best of everything. "Didn't I pay fifteen golden mandarins fresh from the mint for it? Did you think that it was a goose?"

"No," said Carl, laboriously cutting, "I didn't think that it was a goose; but—err—seems to me that it has—err—a good deal of—err—character for a chicken."

"You don't mean to say that it's tough!" Mimi faltered, trying to keep back the tears that made a sudden rush for her eyes.

Carl's reply was checked by the sound of their door-bell, sharply rung.

"A beggar!" said Mimi, and started up hastily, glad to hide her face, and snatching a piece of bread as she went.

"I oughtn't to have let her know that it is tough, poor Mimi!" thought Carl.

In two minutes she came back radiant.

"See! a present and a note from Madama Landon!" she cried, holding out a basket swathed in tissue-paper, and elaborately tied with a silken cord. "Her maid brought it. It is fruit, as sure as you live. God is good! How nice it is to be remembered, and have something come in,—just in the nick of time, too! That dear lady! I knew she had a good heart, she is so bright-eyed and has so much color. She blushes if she stirs. I always notice—Why, Carl, the handle of this basket is just like ours!"

"Of course there are plenty in the world like it," remarked Carl, watching with great interest the careful undoing of the blue, softly twisted cords.

"It is heavenly to get just such a one back," said Mimi, picking carefully, with an impatient tremor, at the knots. "It makes this seem a sort of second wedding-day, doesn't it, dear?"

The last cover off, the two stared for one moment in silence at their gift, then at each other, then at their gift again. Their faces had grown very blank. Then Mimi, with a finger and thumb, lifted out by the stem one mandarin after another, setting them in a row on the table. There were fifteen.

"I didn't need this to prove it," she said in a hushed voice, picking the napkin out of the basket. "I know the looks of those mandarins as well as I know yours. I could go out now and set each one on its own twig on the tree."

Another blank silence; then Mimi burst into a laugh. "Don't you see, Carl? La Cremona must have sent them to her, they were so pretty; and she has sent them to us, without ever suspecting. Isn't it comical, and delightful? Oh, little prodigals, welcome home again!"

They bethought themselves to read the note. The lady had written:—

DEAR SIGNOR PETERSEN,—Allow me to offer you some mandarins which are worthy to have grown on your own tree, which, by the way, is now my tree. I have bought your Primogenito, and am *so* much pleased with it that I would like to have a companion picture, when you have time to favor me with one. With compliments to your charming wife, and a *buona festa* to both.

Yours sincerely, CLARE LANDON.

P. S.—I send you the basket just as it was sent to me by a cardinal. C. L.

"A cardinal!"

No matter! Let the mystery go, since it had brought a miracle of joy. Mimi was weeping with delight.

"Give me the two very largest," she said, "and I will carry them down to those two children on the ground floor. How wicked I have been to hate them, even if they do dirty the stairs and throw stones at me! I will kiss them, Carl, since I cannot kiss God!"

"We mustn't utter the word mandarins to La Cremona," Carl said.

But the very next time he met the Signora Cremona she thanked him with graceful cordiality for his present. "They were delicious," she said.

Carl bowed with perfect gravity.

And then he saw her blush slightly, as she hastened away from him to meet her friend, Mrs. James, who was coming across from the Spanish steps to speak to her.

"I want to thank you for that lovely fruit," Mrs. James said, with effusion. "It was the finest I have had this year; so fresh, and honey-sweet!"

The lady had excellent authority for her praises; for Monsignore Appetitoso had called on her that very morning to make his compliments on her gift. "Your mandarins arrived just in time for my dinner," he said, smacking his lips, as if he still had the taste of them in his mouth.

Mrs. James professed herself honored in having been allowed to contribute to Monsignore's Christmas dinner. "I thought the mandarins would be fine," she said. "They were sent me from the garden of a friend."

"Oh! it was the day before. I dined with his Eminence Cardinal Inghilterra, last evening," Monsignore replied complacently, "and I thought that you might like to see the *menu*," drawing a carefully folded paper from his pocket, and a white satin ribbon from the paper.

With a simultaneous "Oh!" Mrs. James and her sister seized the dainty gold-lettered trifle, and bumped their heads together in the eagerness with which they bent over it to see what a cardinal would give his friends for dinner.

"I hope that your Eminence enjoyed the little basket of fruit I took the liberty to send yesterday," Monsignore had said the evening before, in a momentary pause in the talk about the table. "It was from a friend's garden, and I thought it choice."

"It was excellent!" was the gracious answer. "I have never eaten better."

And here the odor of truffles stole into Monsignore's nostrils from a dish waiting at his left elbow. Oh, how he loved that man sitting opposite him, glorious in scarlet and diamonds, and still more glorious as the dispenser of such bounties! His Eminence would have been proclaimed Pope on the instant, if Monsignore Appetitoso had had the power.

"Eminence," said Mrs. Landon, the first time he visited her after Christmas, "I knew, of course, that you are intimate with the saints; but I was not aware that the pagan divinities also serve you. You must be on the best of terms with the Hesperides. Nowhere but in their orchards could have been mingled the fire and honey of your delicious mandarins."

His Eminence bowed smilingly.

"I am happy to know that you found them to your taste," he said, in his superb, deliberate way. "They were, in fact, from—err—the garden of a friend."

1886

Christmas Every Day

THE LITTLE GIRL came into her papa's study, as she always did Saturday morning before breakfast, and asked for a story. He tried to beg off that morning, for he was very busy, but she would not let him. So he began:

"Well, once there was a little pig—"

She put her hand over his mouth and stopped him at the word. She said she had heard little pig-stories till she was perfectly sick of them.

"Well, what kind of story *shall* I tell, then?"

"About Christmas. It's getting to be the season. It's past Thanksgiving already."

"It seems to me," her papa argued, "that I've told as often about Christmas as I have about little pigs."

"No difference! Christmas is more interesting."

"Well!" Her papa roused himself from his writing by a great effort. "Well, then, I'll tell you about the little girl that wanted it Christmas every day in the year. How would you like that?"

"First-rate!" said the little girl; and she nestled into comfortable shape in his lap, ready for listening.

"Very well, then, this little pig— Oh, what are you pounding me for?"

"Because you said little pig instead of little girl."

"I should like to know what's the difference between a little pig and a little girl that wanted it Christmas every day!"

"Papa," said the little girl, warningly, "if you don't go on, I'll *give* it to you!" And at this her papa darted off like lightning, and began to tell the story as fast as he could.

Well, once there was a little girl who liked Christmas so much that she wanted it to be Christmas every day in the year; and as soon as Thanksgiving was over she began to send postal-cards to the old Christmas Fairy to ask if she mightn't have it. But the old fairy never answered any of the post-

als; and after a while the little girl found out that the Fairy was pretty particular, and wouldn't notice anything but letters—not even correspondence
cards in envelopes; but real letters on sheets of paper, and sealed outside
with a monogram—or your initial, anyway. So, then, she began to send her
letters; and in about three weeks—or just the day before Christmas, it was—
she got a letter from the Fairy, saying she might have it Christmas every day
for a year, and then they would see about having it longer.

The little girl was a good deal excited already, preparing for the old-
fashioned, once-a-year Christmas that was coming the next day, and perhaps the Fairy's promise didn't make such an impression on her as it would
have made at some other time. She just resolved to keep it to herself, and
surprise everybody with it as it kept coming true; and then it slipped out of
her mind altogether.

She had a splendid Christmas. She went to bed early, so as to let Santa
Claus have a chance at the stockings, and in the morning she was up the
first of anybody and went and felt them, and found hers all lumpy with
packages of candy, and oranges and grapes, and pocket-books and rubber
balls, and all kinds of small presents, and her big brother's with nothing
but the tongs in them, and her young lady sister's with a new silk umbrella,
and her papa's and mamma's with potatoes and pieces of coal wrapped up
in tissue-paper, just as they always had every Christmas. Then she waited
around till the rest of the family were up, and she was the first to burst into
the library, when the doors were opened, and look at the large presents laid
out on the library-table—books, and portfolios, and boxes of stationery,
and breastpins, and dolls, and little stoves, and dozens of handkerchiefs,
and inkstands, and skates, and snow-shovels, and photograph-frames,
and little easels, and boxes of water-colors, and Turkish paste, and nou-
gat, and candied cherries, and dolls' houses, and waterproofs—and the big
Christmas-tree, lighted and standing in a waste-basket in the middle.

She had a splendid Christmas all day. She ate so much candy that she did
not want any breakfast; and the whole forenoon the presents kept pouring
in that the expressman had not had time to deliver the night before; and
she went round giving the presents she had got for other people, and came
home and ate turkey and cranberry for dinner, and plum-pudding and nuts
and raisins and oranges and more candy, and then went out and coasted,
and came in with a stomach-ache, crying; and her papa said he would see if
his house was turned into that sort of fool's paradise another year; and they
had a light supper, and pretty early everybody went to bed cross.

Here the little girl pounded her papa in the back, again.

"Well, what now? Did I say pigs?"

"You made them *act* like pigs."

"Well, didn't they?"

"No matter; you oughtn't to put it into a story."

"Very well, then, I'll take it all out."

Her father went on:

The little girl slept very heavily, and she slept very late, but she was wakened at last by the other children dancing round her bed with their stockings full of presents in their hands.

"What is it?" said the little girl, and she rubbed her eyes and tried to rise up in bed.

"Christmas! Christmas! Christmas!" they all shouted, and waved their stockings.

"Nonsense! It was Christmas yesterday."

Her brothers and sisters just laughed. "We don't know about that. It's Christmas to-day, anyway. You come into the library and see."

Then all at once it flashed on the little girl that the Fairy was keeping her promise, and her year of Christmases was beginning. She was dreadfully sleepy, but she sprang up like a lark—a lark that had overeaten itself and gone to bed cross—and darted into the library. There it was again! Books, and portfolios, and boxes of stationery, and breastpins—

"You needn't go over it all, papa; I guess I can remember just what was there," said the little girl.

Well, and there was the Christmas-tree blazing away, and the family picking out their presents, but looking pretty sleepy, and her father perfectly puzzled, and her mother ready to cry. "I'm sure I don't see how I'm to dispose of all these things," said her mother, and her father said it seemed to him they had had something just like it the day before, but he supposed he must have dreamed it. This struck the little girl as the best kind of a joke; and so she ate so much candy she didn't want any breakfast, and went round carrying presents, and had turkey and cranberry for dinner, and then went out and coasted, and came in with a—

"Papa!"

"Well, what now?"

"What did you promise, you forgetful thing?"

"Oh! oh yes!"

Well, the next day, it was just the same thing over again, but everybody getting crosser; and at the end of a week's time so many people had lost their tempers that you could pick up lost tempers anywhere; they perfectly strewed the ground. Even when people tried to recover their tempers they usually got somebody else's, and it made the most dreadful mix.

The little girl began to get frightened, keeping the secret all to herself; she wanted to tell her mother, but she didn't dare to; and she was ashamed to ask the Fairy to take back her gift, it seemed ungrateful and ill-bred, and she thought she would try to stand it, but she hardly knew how she could, for a whole year. So it went on and on, and it was Christmas on St. Valentine's Day and Washington's Birthday, just the same as any day, and it didn't skip even the First of April, though everything was counterfeit that day, and that was some *little* relief.

After a while coal and potatoes began to be awfully scarce, so many had been wrapped up in tissue-paper to fool papas and mammas with. Turkeys got to be about a thousand dollars apiece—

"Papa!"

"Well, what?"

"You 're beginning to fib."

"Well, *two* thousand, then."

And they got to passing off almost anything for turkeys—half-grown humming-birds, and even rocs out of the *Arabian Nights*—the real turkeys were so scarce. And cranberries—well, they asked a diamond apiece for cranberries. All the woods and orchards were cut down for Christmas-trees, and where the woods and orchards used to be it looked just like a stubble-field, with the stumps. After a while they had to make Christmas-trees out of rags, and stuff them with bran, like old-fashioned dolls; but there were plenty of rags, because people got so poor, buying presents for one another, that they couldn't get any new clothes, and they just wore their old ones to tatters. They got so poor that everybody had to go to the poor-house, except the confectioners, and the fancy-store keepers, and the picture-book sellers, and the expressmen; and *they* all got so rich and proud that they would hardly wait upon a person when he came to buy. It was perfectly shameful!

Well, after it had gone on about three or four months, the little girl, whenever she came into the room in the morning and saw those great ugly, lumpy stockings dangling at the fire-place, and the disgusting presents around everywhere, used to just sit down and burst out crying. In six months she was perfectly exhausted; she couldn't even cry any more; she just lay on the lounge and rolled her eyes and panted. About the beginning of October she took to sitting down on dolls wherever she found them— French dolls, or any kind—she hated the sight of them so; and by Thanksgiving she was crazy, and just slammed her presents across the room.

By that time people didn't carry presents around nicely any more. They flung them over the fence, or through the window, or anything; and, instead of running their tongues out and taking great pains to write "For dear Papa," or "Mamma," or "Brother," or "Sister," or "Susie," or "Sammie," or "Billie," or "Bobbie," or "Jimmie," or "Jennie," or whoever it was, and troubling to get the spelling right, and then signing their names, and "Xmas, 18—," they used to write in the gift-books, "Take it, you horrid old thing!" and then go and bang it against the front door. Nearly everybody had built barns to hold their presents, but pretty soon the barns overflowed, and then they used to let them lie out in the rain, or anywhere. Sometimes the police used to come and tell them to shovel their presents off the sidewalk, or they would arrest them.

"I thought you said everybody had gone to the poor-house," interrupted the little girl.

"They did go, at first," said her papa; "but after a while the poor-houses got so full that they had to send the people back to their own houses. They tried to cry, when they got back, but they couldn't make the least sound."

"Why couldn't they?"

"Because they had lost their voices, saying 'Merry Christmas' so much. Did I tell you how it was on the Fourth of July?"

"No; how was it?" And the little girl nestled closer, in expectation of something uncommon.

Well, the night before, the boys stayed up to celebrate, as they always do, and fell asleep before twelve o'clock, as usual, expecting to be wakened by the bells and cannon. But it was nearly eight o'clock before the first boy in the United States woke up, and then he found out what the trouble was. As soon as he could get his clothes on he ran out of the house and smashed a big cannon-torpedo down on the pavement; but it didn't make any more noise than a damp wad of paper; and after he tried about twenty or thirty more, he began to pick them up and look at them. Every single torpedo was a big raisin! Then he just streaked it up-stairs, and examined his fire-crackers and toy-pistol and two-dollar collection of fireworks, and found that they were nothing but sugar and candy painted up to look like fireworks! Before ten o'clock every boy in the United States found out that his Fourth of July things had turned into Christmas things; and then they just sat down and cried—they were so mad. There are about twenty million boys in the United States, and so you can imagine what a noise they made. Some men got together before night, with a little powder that hadn't turned into purple sugar yet, and they said they would fire off *one* cannon, anyway. But the cannon burst into a thousand pieces, for it was nothing but rock-candy, and some of the men nearly got killed. The Fourth of July orations all turned into Christmas carols, and when anybody tried to read the Declaration, instead of saying, "When in the course of human events it becomes necessary," he was sure to sing, "God rest you, merry gentlemen." It was perfectly awful.

The little girl drew a deep sigh of satisfaction.

"And how was it at Thanksgiving?"

Her papa hesitated. "Well, I'm almost afraid to tell you. I'm afraid you'll think it's wicked."

"Well, tell, anyway," said the little girl.

Well, before it came Thanksgiving it had leaked out who had caused all these Christmases. The little girl had suffered so much that she had talked about it in her sleep; and after that hardly anybody would play with her. People just perfectly despised her, because if it had not been for her greediness it wouldn't have happened; and now, when it came Thanksgiving, and she wanted them to go to church, and have squash-pie and turkey, and show their gratitude, they said that all the turkeys had been eaten up for her old Christmas dinners, and if she would stop the Christmases, they would see about the gratitude. Wasn't it dreadful? And the very next day the little girl began to send letters to the Christmas Fairy, and then telegrams, to stop it. But it didn't do any good; and then she got to calling at the Fairy's house, but the girl that came to the door always said, "Not at home," or "Engaged," or "At dinner," or something like that; and so it went on till it came to the old once-a-year Christmas Eve. The little girl fell asleep, and when she woke up in the morning—

"She found it was all nothing but a dream," suggested the little girl.

"No, indeed!" said her papa. "It was all every bit true!"

"Well, what *did* she find out, then?"

"Why, that it wasn't Christmas at last, and wasn't ever going to be, any more. Now it's time for breakfast."

The little girl held her papa fast around the neck.

"You sha'n't go if you're going to leave it *so*!"

"How do you want it left?"

"Christmas once a year."

"All right," said her papa; and he went on again.

Well, there was the greatest rejoicing all over the country, and it extended clear up into Canada. The people met together everywhere, and kissed and cried for joy. The city carts went around and gathered up all the candy and raisins and nuts, and dumped them into the river; and it made the fish perfectly sick; and the whole United States, as far out as Alaska, was one blaze of bonfires, where the children were burning up their gift-books and presents of all kinds. They had the greatest *time*!

The little girl went to thank the old Fairy because she had stopped its being Christmas, and she said she hoped she would keep her promise and see that Christmas never, never came again. Then the Fairy frowned, and asked her if she was sure she knew what she meant; and the little girl asked her, Why not? and the old Fairy said that now she was behaving just as greedily as ever, and she'd better look out. This made the little girl think it all over carefully again, and she said she would be willing to have it Christmas about once in a thousand years; and then she said a hundred, and then she said ten, and at last she got down to one. Then the Fairy said that was the good old way that had pleased people ever since Christmas began, and she was agreed. Then the little girl said, "What 're your shoes made of?" And the Fairy said, "Leather." And the little girl said, "Bargain 's done forever," and skipped off, and hippity-hopped the whole way home, she was so glad.

"How will that do?" asked the papa.

"First-rate!" said the little girl; but she hated to have the story stop, and was rather sober. However, her mamma put her head in at the door, and asked her papa:

"Are you never coming to breakfast? What have you been telling that child?"

"Oh, just a moral tale."

The little girl caught him around the neck again.

"*We* know! Don't you tell *what*, papa! Don't you tell *what*!"

1892

JOHN KENDRICK BANGS

Thurlow's Christmas Story

I

(*Being the Statement of Henry Thurlow, Author,
to George Currier, Editor of the "Idler,"
a Weekly Journal of Human Interest.*)

I HAVE ALWAYS maintained, my dear Currier, that if a man wishes to be considered sane, and has any particular regard for his reputation as a truth-teller, he would better keep silent as to the singular experiences that enter into his life. I have had many such experiences myself; but I have rarely confided them in detail, or otherwise, to those about me, because I know that even the most trustful of my friends would regard them merely as the outcome of an imagination unrestrained by conscience, or of a gradually weakening mind subject to hallucinations. I know them to be true, but until Mr. Edison or some other modern wizard has invented a search-light strong enough to lay bare the secrets of the mind and conscience of man, I cannot prove to others that they are not pure fabrications, or at least the conjurings of a diseased fancy. For instance, no man would believe me if I were to state to him the plain and indisputable fact that one night last month, on my way up to bed shortly after midnight, having been neither smoking nor drinking, I saw confronting me upon the stairs, with the moonlight streaming through the windows back of me, lighting up its face, a figure in which I recognized my very self in every form and feature. I might describe the chill of terror that struck to the very marrow of my bones, and wellnigh forced me to stagger backward down the stairs, as I noticed in the face of this confronting figure every indication of all the bad qualities which I know myself to possess, of every evil instinct which by no easy effort I have repressed heretofore, and realized that that *thing* was, as far as I knew, entirely independent of my true self, in which I hope at least the moral has made an honest fight against the immoral always. I might describe this chill, I say, as vividly as I felt it at that moment, but it would be of no use to do so, because, however realistic it might prove as a bit of description, no man would believe that the incident really happened; and yet it did happen as truly as I write, and it has happened a dozen times since, and I am certain that it will happen many times again, though I would give all that I possess to be assured that never again should that disquieting creation of mind or matter, whichever it may be, cross my path. The experience has made me afraid almost to be alone, and I have found myself unconsciously and uneasily glancing at my face in mirrors, in the plate-glass of show-windows on the shopping streets of the city, fearful lest I should find some of those evil traits which I have struggled to keep under, and have kept under so far, cropping out there where all the world, all *my* world, can see and wonder at, having known me always as a man of right doing and right feeling. Many a time in the night the thought has come to me with prostrating force, what if that thing were to be seen and recognized by others, myself and yet not my whole self, my unworthy self unrestrained and yet recognizable as Henry Thurlow.

I have also kept silent as to that strange condition of affairs which has tortured me in my sleep for the past year and a half; no one but myself has until this writing known that for that period of time I have had a continuous, logical dream-life; a life so vivid and so dreadfully real to me that I have found myself at times wondering which of the two lives I was living and which I was dreaming; a life in which that other wicked self has dominated, and forced me to a career of shame and horror; a life which, being taken up every time I sleep where it ceased with the awakening from a previous sleep, has made me fear to close my eyes in forgetfulness when others are near at hand, lest, sleeping, I shall let fall some speech that, striking on their ears, shall lead them to believe that in secret there is some wicked mystery connected with my life. It would be of no use for me to tell these things. It would merely serve to make my family and my friends uneasy about me if they were told in their awful detail, and so I have kept silent about them. To you alone, and now for the first time, have I hinted as to the troubles which have oppressed me for many days, and to you they are confided only because of the demand you have made that I explain to you the extraordinary complication in which the Christmas story sent you last week has involved me. You know that I am a man of dignity; that I am not a school-boy and a lover of childish tricks; and knowing that, your friendship, at least, should have restrained your tongue and pen when, through the former, on Wednesday, you accused me of perpetrating a trifling, and to you excessively embarrassing, practical joke—a charge which, at the moment, I was too overcome to refute; and through the latter, on Thursday, you reiterated the accusation, coupled with a demand for an explanation of my conduct satisfactory to yourself, or my immediate resignation from the staff of the *Idler*. To explain is difficult, for I am certain that you will find the explanation too improbable for credence, but explain I must. The alternative, that of resigning from your staff, affects not only my own welfare, but that of my children, who must be provided for; and if my post with you is taken from me, then are all resources gone. I have not the courage to face dismissal, for I have not sufficient confidence in my powers to please elsewhere to make me easy in my mind, or, if I could please elsewhere, the certainty of finding the immediate employment of my talents which is necessary to me, in view of the at present overcrowded condition of the literary field.

To explain, then, my seeming jest at your expense, hopeless as it appears to be, is my task; and to do so as completely as I can, let me go back to the very beginning.

In August you informed me that you would expect me to provide, as I have heretofore been in the habit of doing, a story for the Christmas issue of the *Idler*; that a certain position in the make-up was reserved for me, and that you had already taken steps to advertise the fact that the story would appear. I undertook the commission, and upon seven different occasions set about putting the narrative into shape. I found great difficulty, however, in doing so. For some reason or other I could not concentrate my mind upon the work. No sooner would I start in on one story than a better one, in my estimation, would suggest itself to me; and all the labor expended on the story already begun would be cast aside, and the new story set in motion. Ideas were plenty enough, but to put them properly upon paper seemed beyond my powers. One story, however, I did finish; but after it had come back to me from my typewriter I read it, and was filled with consternation to discover that it was nothing more nor less than a mass of jumbled sentences, conveying no idea to the mind—a story which had seemed to me in the writing to be coherent had returned to me as a mere bit of incoherence—formless, without ideas—a bit of raving. It was then that I went to you and told you, as you remember, that I was worn out, and needed a month of absolute rest, which you granted. I left my work wholly, and went into the wilderness, where I could be entirely free from everything suggesting labor, and where no summons back to town could reach me. I fished and hunted. I slept; and although, as I have already said, in my sleep I found myself leading a life that was not only not to my taste, but horrible to me in many particulars, I was able at the end of my vacation to come back to town greatly refreshed, and, as far as my feelings went, ready to undertake any amount of work. For two or three days after my return I was busy with other things. On the fourth day after my arrival you came to me, and said that the story must be finished at the very latest by October 15th, and I assured you that you should have it by that time. That night I set about it. I mapped it out, incident by incident, and before starting up to bed had actually written some twelve or fifteen hundred words of the opening chapter—it was to be told in four chapters. When I had gone thus far I experienced a slight return of one of my nervous chills, and, on consulting my watch, discovered that it was after midnight, which was a sufficient explanation of my nervousness: I was merely tired. I arranged my manuscripts on my table so that I might easily take up the work the following morning. I locked up the windows and doors, turned out the lights, and proceeded up-stairs to my room.

It was then that I first came face to face with myself—that other self, in which I recognized, developed to the full, every bit of my capacity for an evil life.

Conceive of the situation if you can. Imagine the horror of it, and then ask yourself if it was likely that when next morning came I could by any possibility bring myself to my work-table in fit condition to prepare for you anything at all worthy of publication in the *Idler*. I tried. I implore you to believe that I did not hold lightly the responsibilities of the commission you had intrusted to my hands. You must know that if any of your writers has a full appreciation of the difficulties which are strewn along the path of an editor, I, who have myself had an editorial experience, have it, and so would not, in the nature of things, do anything to add to your troubles. You cannot but believe that I have made an honest effort to fulfil my promise to you. But it was useless, and for a week after that visitation was it useless for me to attempt the work. At the end of the week I felt better, and again I started in, and the story developed satisfactorily until—*it* came again. That figure which was my own figure, that face which was the evil counterpart of my own countenance, again rose up before me, and once more was I plunged into hopelessness.

Thus matters went on until the 14th day of October, when I received your peremptory message that the story must be forthcoming the following day. Needless to tell you that it was not forthcoming; but what I must tell you, since you do not know it, is that on the evening of the 15th day of October a strange thing happened to me, and in the narration of that incident, which

I almost despair of your believing, lies my explanation of the discovery of October 16th, which has placed my position with you in peril.

At half-past seven o'clock on the evening of October 15th I was sitting in my library trying to write. I was alone. My wife and children had gone away on a visit to Massachusetts for a week. I had just finished my cigar, and had taken my pen in hand, when my front-door bell rang. Our maid, who is usually prompt in answering summonses of this nature, apparently did not hear the bell, for she did not respond to its clanging. Again the bell rang, and still did it remain unanswered, until finally, at the third ringing, I went to the door myself. On opening it I saw standing before me a man of, I should say, fifty odd years of age, tall, slender, pale-faced, and clad in sombre black. He was entirely unknown to me. I had never seen him before, but he had about him such an air of pleasantness and wholesomeness that I instinctively felt glad to see him, without knowing why or whence he had come.

"Does Mr. Thurlow live here?" he asked.

You must excuse me for going into what may seem to you to be petty details, but by a perfectly circumstantial account of all that happened that evening alone can I hope to give a semblance of truth to my story, and that it must be truthful I realize as painfully as you do.

"I am Mr. Thurlow," I replied.

"Henry Thurlow, the author?" he said, with a surprised look upon his face.

"Yes," said I; and then, impelled by the strange appearance of surprise on the man's countenance, I added, "don't I look like an author?"

He laughed, and candidly admitted that I was not the kind of looking man he had expected to find from reading my books, and then he entered the house in response to my invitation that he do so. I ushered him into my library, and, after asking him to be seated, inquired as to his business with me.

His answer was gratifying at least. He replied that he had been a reader of my writings for a number of years, and that for some time past he had had a great desire, not to say curiosity, to meet me and tell me how much he had enjoyed certain of my stories.

"I'm a great devourer of books, Mr. Thurlow," he said, "and I have taken the keenest delight in reading your verses and humorous sketches. I may go further, and say to you that you have helped me over many a hard place in my life by your work. At times when I have felt myself worn out with my business, or face to face with some knotty problem in my career, I have found much relief in picking up and reading your books at random. They have helped me to forget my weariness or my knotty problems for the time being; and to-day, finding myself in this town, I resolved to call upon you this evening and thank you for all that you have done for me."

Thereupon we became involved in a general discussion of literary men and their works, and I found that my visitor certainly did have a pretty thorough knowledge of what has been produced by the writers of to-day. I was quite won over to him by his simplicity, as well as attracted to him by his kindly opinion of my own efforts, and I did my best to entertain him, showing him a few of my little literary treasures in the way of autograph letters, photographs, and presentation copies of well-known books from the authors themselves. From this we drifted naturally and easily into a talk on the methods of work adopted by literary men. He asked me many questions as to my own methods; and when I had in a measure outlined to him the manner of life which I had adopted, telling him of my days at home, how little detail office-work I had, he seemed much interested with the picture—indeed, I painted the picture of my daily routine in almost too perfect colors, for, when I had finished, he observed quietly that I appeared to him to lead the ideal life, and added that he supposed I knew very little unhappiness.

The remark recalled to me the dreadful reality, that through some perversity of fate I was doomed to visitations of an uncanny order which were practically destroying my usefulness in my profession and my sole financial resource.

"Well," I replied, as my mind reverted to the unpleasant predicament in which I found myself, "I can't say that I know little unhappiness. As a matter of fact, I know a great deal of that undesirable thing. At the present moment I am very much embarrassed through my absolute inability to fulfil a contract into which I have entered, and which should have been filled this morning. I was due to-day with a Christmas story. The presses are waiting for it, and I am utterly unable to write it."

He appeared deeply concerned at the confession. I had hoped, indeed, that he might be sufficiently concerned to take his departure, that I might make one more effort to write the promised story. His solicitude, however, showed itself in another way. Instead of leaving me, he ventured the hope that he might aid me.

"What kind of a story is it to be?" he asked.

"Oh, the usual ghostly tale," I said, "with a dash of the Christmas flavor thrown in here and there to make it suitable to the season."

"Ah," he observed. "And you find your vein worked out?"

It was a direct and perhaps an impertinent question; but I thought it best to answer it, and to answer it as well without giving him any clew as to the real facts. I could not very well take an entire stranger into my confidence, and describe to him the extraordinary encounters I was having with an uncanny other self. He would not have believed the truth, hence I told him an untruth, and assented to his proposition.

"Yes," I replied, "the vein is worked out. I have written ghost stories for years now, serious and comic, and I am to-day at the end of my tether—compelled to move forward and yet held back."

"That accounts for it," he said, simply. "When I first saw you to-night at the door I could not believe that the author who had provided me with so much merriment could be so pale and worn and seemingly mirthless. Pardon me, Mr. Thurlow, for my lack of consideration when I told you that you did not appear as I had expected to find you."

I smiled my forgiveness, and he continued:

"It may be," he said, with a show of hesitation—"it may be that I have come not altogether inopportunely. Perhaps I can help you."

I smiled again. "I should be most grateful if you could," I said.

"But you doubt my ability to do so?" he put in. "Oh—well—yes—of course you do; and why shouldn't you? Nevertheless, I have noticed this: At times when I have been baffled in my work a mere hint from another, from one who knew nothing of my work, has carried me on to a solution of my problem. I have read most of your writings, and I have thought over some of them many a time, and I have even had ideas for stories, which, in my own conceit, I have imagined were good enough for you, and I have wished that I possessed your facility with the pen that I might make of them myself what I thought you would make of them had they been ideas of your own."

The old gentleman's pallid face reddened as he said this, and while I was hopeless as to anything of value resulting from his ideas, I could not resist the temptation to hear what he had to say further, his manner was so deliciously simple, and his desire to aid me so manifest. He rattled on with suggestions for a half-hour. Some of them were good, but none were new. Some were irresistibly funny, and did me good because they made me laugh, and I hadn't laughed naturally for a period so long that it made me shudder to think of it, fearing lest I should forget how to be mirthful. Finally I grew tired of his persistence, and, with a very ill-concealed impatience, told him plainly that I could do nothing with his suggestions, thanking him, however, for the spirit of kindliness which had prompted him to offer them. He appeared somewhat hurt, but immediately desisted, and when nine o'clock came he rose up to go. As he walked to the door he seemed to be undergoing some mental struggle, to which, with a sudden resolve, he finally succumbed, for, after having picked up his hat and stick and donned his overcoat, he turned to me and said:

"Mr. Thurlow, I don't want to offend you. On the contrary, it is my dearest wish to assist you. You have helped me, as I have told you. Why may I not help you?"

"I assure you, sir—" I began, when he interrupted me.

"One moment, please," he said, putting his hand into the inside pocket of his black coat and extracting from it an envelope addressed to me. "Let me finish: it is the whim of one who has an affection for you. For ten years I have secretly been at work myself on a story. It is a short one, but it has seemed good to me. I had a double object in seeking you out to-night. I wanted not only to see you, but to read my story to you. No one knows that I have written it; I had intended it as a surprise to my—to my friends. I had hoped to have it published somewhere, and I had come here to seek your advice in the matter. It is a story which I have written and rewritten and rewritten time and time again in my leisure moments during the ten years past, as I have told you. It is not likely that I shall ever write another. I am proud of having done it, but I should be prouder yet if it—if it could in some way help you. I leave it with you, sir, to print or to destroy; and if you print it, to see it in type will be enough for me; to see your name signed to it will be a matter of pride to me. No one will ever be the wiser, for, as I say, no one knows I have written it, and I promise you that no one shall know of it if you decide to do as I not only suggest but ask you to do. No one would believe me after it has appeared as *yours*, even if I should forget my promise and claim it as my own. Take it. It is yours. You are entitled to it as a slight measure of repayment for the debt of gratitude I owe you."

He pressed the manuscript into my hands, and before I could reply had opened the door and disappeared into the darkness of the street. I rushed to the sidewalk and shouted out to him to return, but I might as well have saved my breath and spared the neighborhood, for there was no answer. Holding his story in my hand, I re-entered the house and walked back into my library, where, sitting and reflecting upon the curious interview, I realized for the first time that I was in entire ignorance as to my visitor's name and address.

I opened the envelope hoping to find them, but they were not there. The envelope contained merely a finely written manuscript of thirty odd pages, unsigned.

And then I read the story. When I began it was with a half-smile upon my lips, and with a feeling that I was wasting my time. The smile soon faded, however; after reading the first paragraph there was no question of wasted time. The story was a masterpiece. It is needless to say to you that I am not a man of enthusiasms. It is difficult to arouse that emotion in my breast, but upon this occasion I yielded to a force too great for me to resist. I have read the tales of Hoffmann and of Poe, the wondrous romances of De La Motte Fouque, the unfortunately little-known tales of the lamented Fitz-James O'Brien, the weird tales of writers of all tongues have been thoroughly sifted by me in the course of my reading, and I say to you now that in the whole of my life I never read one story, one paragraph, one line, that could approach in vivid delineation, in weirdness of conception, in anything, in any quality which goes to make up the truly great story, that story which came into my hands as I have told you. I read it once and was amazed. I read it a second time and was—tempted. It was mine. The writer himself had authorized me to treat it as if it were my own; had voluntarily sacrificed his own claim to its authorship that he might relieve me of my very pressing embarrassment. Not only this; he had almost intimated that in putting my name to his work I should be doing him a favor. Why not do so, then, I asked myself; and immediately my better self rejected the idea as impossible. How could I put out as my own another man's work and retain my self-respect? I resolved on another and better course—to send you the story in lieu of my own with a full statement of the circumstances under which it had come into my possession, when that demon rose up out of the floor at my side, this time more evil of aspect than before, more commanding in its manner. With a groan I shrank back into the cushions of my chair, and by passing my hands over my eyes tried to obliterate forever the offending sight; but it was useless. The uncanny thing approached me, and as truly as I write sat upon the edge of my couch, where for the first time it addressed me.

"Fool!" it said, "how can you hesitate? Here is your position: you have made a contract which must be filled; you are already behind, and in a hopeless mental state. Even granting that between this and to-morrow morning you could put together the necessary number of words to fill the space allotted to you, what kind of a thing do you think that story would make? It would be a mere raving like that other precious effort of August.

The public, if by some odd chance it ever reached them, would think your mind was utterly gone; your reputation would go with that verdict. On the other hand, if you do not have the story ready by to-morrow, your hold on the *Idler* will be destroyed. They have their announcements printed, and your name and portrait appear among those of the prominent contributors. Do you suppose the editor and publisher will look leniently upon your failure?"

"Considering my past record, yes," I replied. "I have never yet broken a promise to them."

"Which is precisely the reason why they will be severe with you. You, who have been regarded as one of the few men who can do almost any kind of literary work at will—you, of whom it is said that your 'brains are on tap'—will they be lenient with *you*? Bah! Can't you see that the very fact of your invariable readiness heretofore is going to make your present unreadiness a thing incomprehensible?"

"Then what shall I do?" I asked. "If I can't, I can't, that is all."

"You can. There is the story in your hands. Think what it will do for you. It is one of the immortal stories—"

"You have read it, then?" I asked.

"Haven't you?"

"Yes—but—"

"It is the same," it said, with a leer and a contemptuous shrug. "You and I are inseparable. Aren't you glad?" it added, with a laugh that grated on every fibre of my being. I was too overwhelmed to reply, and it resumed: "It is one of the immortal stories. We agree to that. Published over your name, your name will live. The stuff you write yourself will give you present glory; but when you have been dead ten years people won't remember your name even—unless I get control of you, and in that case there is a very pretty though hardly a literary record in store for you."

Again it laughed harshly, and I buried my face in the pillows of my couch, hoping to find relief there from this dreadful vision.

"Curious," it said. "What you call your decent self doesn't dare look me in the eye! What a mistake people make who say that the man who won't look you in the eye is not to be trusted! As if mere brazenness were a sign of honesty; really, the theory of decency is the most amusing thing in the world. But come, time is growing short. Take that story. The writer gave it to you. Begged you to use it as your own. It is yours. It will make your reputation, and save you with your publishers. How can you hesitate?"

"I shall not use it!" I cried, desperately.

"You must—consider your children. Suppose you lose your connection with these publishers of yours?"

"But it would be a crime."

"Not a bit of it. Whom do you rob? A man who voluntarily came to you, and gave you that of which you rob him. Think of it as it is—and act, only act quickly. It is now midnight."

The tempter rose up and walked to the other end of the room, whence, while he pretended to be looking over a few of my books and pictures, I was aware he was eying me closely, and gradually compelling me by sheer force of will to do a thing which I abhorred. And I—I struggled weakly against the temptation, but gradually, little by little, I yielded, and finally succumbed altogether. Springing to my feet, I rushed to the table, seized my pen, and signed my name to the story.

"There!" I said. "It is done. I have saved my position and made my reputation, and am now a thief!"

"As well as a fool," said the other, calmly. "You don't mean to say you are going to send that manuscript in as it is?"

"Good Lord!" I cried. "What under heaven have you been trying to make me do for the last half hour?"

"Act like a sane being," said the demon. "If you send that manuscript to Currier he'll know in a minute it isn't yours. He knows you haven't an amanuensis, and that handwriting isn't yours. Copy it."

"True!" I answered. "I haven't much of a mind for details to-night. I will do as you say."

I did so. I got out my pad and pen and ink, and for three hours diligently applied myself to the task of copying the story. When it was finished I went over it carefully, made a few minor corrections, signed it, put it in an envelope, addressed it to you, stamped it, and went out to the mail-box on the corner, where I dropped it into the slot, and returned home. When I had returned to my library my visitor was still there.

"Well," it said, "I wish you'd hurry and complete this affair. I am tired, and wish to go."

"You can't go too soon to please me," said I, gathering up the original manuscripts of the story and preparing to put them away in my desk.

"Probably not," it sneered. "I'll be glad to go too, but I can't go until that manuscript is destroyed. As long as it exists there is evidence of your having appropriated the work of another. Why, can't you see that? Burn it!"

"I can't see my way clear in crime!" I retorted. "It is not in my line."

Nevertheless, realizing the value of his advice, I thrust the pages one by one into the blazing log fire, and watched them as they flared and flamed and grew to ashes. As the last page disappeared in the embers the demon vanished. I was alone, and throwing myself down for a moment's reflection upon my couch, was soon lost in sleep.

It was noon when I again opened my eyes, and, ten minutes after I awakened, your telegraphic summons reached me.

"Come down at once," was what you said, and I went; and then came the terrible *dénouement*, and yet a *dénouement* which was pleasing to me since it relieved my conscience. You handed me the envelope containing the story.

"Did you send that?" was your question.

"I did—last night, or rather early this morning. I mailed it about three o'clock," I replied.

"I demand an explanation of your conduct," said you.

"Of what?" I asked.

"Look at your so-called story and see. If this is a practical joke, Thurlow, it's a damned poor one."

I opened the envelope and took from it the sheets I had sent you—twenty-four of them.

They were every one of them as blank as when they left the paper-mill!

You know the rest. You know that I tried to speak; that my utterance failed me; and that, finding myself unable at the time to control my emotions, I turned and rushed madly from the office, leaving the mystery unexplained. You know that you wrote demanding a satisfactory explanation of the situation or my resignation from your staff.

This, Currier, is my explanation. It is all I have. It is absolute truth. I beg you to believe it, for if you do not, then is my condition a hopeless one. You will ask me perhaps for a *résumé* of the story which I thought I had sent you.

It is my crowning misfortune that upon that point my mind is an absolute blank. I cannot remember it in form or in substance. I have racked my brains for some recollection of some small portion of it to help to make my explanation more credible, but, alas! it will not come back to me. If I were dishonest I might fake up a story to suit the purpose, but I am not dishonest. I came near to doing an unworthy act; I did do an unworthy thing, but by some mysterious provision of fate my conscience is cleared of that.

Be sympathetic, Currier, or, if you cannot, be lenient with me this time. *Believe, believe, believe*, I implore you. Pray let me hear from you at once.

(Signed)   HENRY THURLOW.

II

(Being a Note from George Currier,
Editor of the "Idler," to Henry Thurlow, Author.)

Your explanation has come to hand. As an explanation it isn't worth the paper it is written on, but we are all agreed here that it is probably the best bit of fiction you ever wrote. It is accepted for the Christmas issue. Enclosed please find check for one hundred dollars.

Dawson suggests that you take another month up in the Adirondacks. You might put in your time writing up some account of that dream-life you are leading while you are there. It seems to me there are possibilities in the idea. The concern will pay all expenses. What do you say?

(Signed)   Yours ever,   G. C.

1894

JACK LONDON

Klondike Christmas

Mouth of the Stuart River,
North West Territory,
December 25, 1897

*M*Y DEAREST MOTHER:
Here we are, all safe and sound, and snugly settled down in winter quarters. Have received no letters yet, so you can imagine how we long to hear from home. We are in the shortest days of the year, and the sun no longer rises, even at 12 o'clock.

Uncle Hiram and Mr. Carter have gone to Dawson to record some placer claims and to get the mail. They took the dogs and sled with them, as they had to travel on the ice. We did expect them home for Christmas dinner, but I guess George and I will have to eat it alone.

I am to be cook, so you can be sure that we'll have a jolly dinner. We will begin with the staples first. There will be fried bacon, baked beans, bread raised from sourdough, and——

He seemed perplexed, and after dubiously scratching his head a couple of times, laid down the pen. Once or twice, he tried to go on, but eventually gave it up, his face assuming a very disgusted expression. He was a robust young fellow of 18 or 19, and the merry twinkle which lurked in his eyes gave the lie to his counterfeited displeasure.

It was a snug little cabin in which he sat. Built of unbarked logs, measuring not more than 10 by 12 feet on the inside, and heated by a roaring Yukon-stove, it seemed more homelike to him than any house he had ever lived in, except—of course, always the one, real home.

The two bunks, table, and stove, occupied two-thirds of the room, but every inch of space was utilized. Revolvers, rifles, hunting-knives, belts, and clothes, hung from three of the walls in picturesque confusion; the remaining one being hidden by a set of shelves, which held all their cooking utensils. Though already 11 o'clock in the morning, a sort of twilight prevailed outside, while it would have been quite dark within, if it had not been for the slush-lamp. This was merely a shallow, tin cup, filled with bacon grease. A piece of cotton caulking served for a wick; the heat of the flame melting the grease.

He leaned his elbows on the table and became absorbed in a deep scrutiny of the lamp. He was really not interested in it, and did not even know he was looking at it, so intent was he in trying to discover what else there could possibly be for the dinner.

The door was thrown open at this moment, and a stalwart young fellow entered with a rush of cold air, kicking off his snowshoes at the threshold.

"'Bout time for dinner, isn't it?" he asked gruffly, as he took off his mittens. But his brother Clarence had just discovered that "bacon," "beans," and "bread" all began with "b," and did not reply. George's face was covered with ice, so he contented himself with holding it over the stove to thaw. The rattle of the icy chunks on the sheet-iron was getting monotonous, when Clarence deigned to reply by asking a question.

"What's 'b' stand for?"

"Bad, of course," was the prompt answer.

"Just what I thought," and he sighed with great solemnity.

"But how about the dinner? You're cook. It's time to begin. What have you been doing? Oh. Writing! Let's see."

His jaw fell when he got to "bacon, beans, and bread," and he said: "It won't do to write home that that's all we've got for Christmas dinner. It would make them worry, you know. Say, haven't we some dried apples?"

"Half a cup. Not enough for a pie."

"They'll swell, you ninny. Sit down and add apple pie to that list of yours. And say dumplings, too, while you're at it. We can make a stagger at them—put two pieces of apple in two lumps of dough and boil them. Never say die. We'll make them think we're living like princes when they read that."

Clarence did as directed, and then sat with such a look of query on his face as to make George nervous and doubtful.

"Pretty slim, after all," he mused. "Let's see if we can't find something else—bread, flapjacks, and—and—why, flour-gravy, of course."

"We can bake and boil and fry the beans," Clarence suggested; "but what's to be done with the bacon except to fry it, I can't see."

"Why, parboil it; that makes another course, nine altogether. How much more do you want, anyway?" And then to change the subject, "How cold do you think it is?"

Clarence critically studied the ice which had crept far up the cracks in the door, and then gave his judgment; "Past 50."

"The spirit thermometer gives 65, and it's still falling." George could not prevent an exultant ring in his voice, though if he had been asked why, he would not have known.

"And water freezes at 32 degrees above zero," Clarence began to calculate. "That makes 97 degrees of frost. Phew! Wouldn't that open the eyes of the folks at home!"

George went into the *cache* for bacon, and began to rummage about in odd places to see what he could find. Now the *cache*, or place where their food was stored to keep it away from the perpetually-hungry native dogs, was built onto the back of the cabin. Clarence heard the racket he was making, and when George began to cheer and cry out, "Eureka! Eureka!" Clarence ran out to see what had happened.

"Manna, brother mine! Manna dropped from the clouds!" he cried, waving a large can above his head. "Mock-turtle soup. Found it in the toolbox," he went on, as they carried it into the cabin.

True enough; it was a quart-can of specially prepared and very rich mock-turtle soup. They sang and danced and were as jubilant as though they had found a gold mine. Clarence added the item to the bill of fare in his letter, while George strove to divide it up into two items, or even more. He showed a special aptitude for this kind of work; but how many tempting dishes he would have finally succeeded in evolving out of it shall never be known, for at that moment they heard a dog team pull up the river bank before the cabin.

The next instant the door opened, and two strangers came in. They were grotesque sights. Their heads were huge balls of ice, with little holes where their mouths should have been, through which they breathed. Unable to open their mouths or speak, they shook hands with the boys and headed for the stove. Clarence and George exchanged glances and watched their strange visitors curiously.

"Wal, it's jes' this way," one of them began, as he shook the remaining chunks of ice from his whiskers; "me an' my pard ha' ben nigh on two months, now, over on the Mazy May, with nothin' to eat but straight meat. Nary flour, nary beans, nary bacon. So me an' him sorto' talked it over, an' figgered it out. At last I sez, 'Wot yeh say, Jim? Let's cross the divide an' strike some camp on the Yukon, an' git some civilized grub again? Git a reg'lar Christmas dinner?' An' he sez, 'I'll go with yeh, by gum.' An' here we be. How air yeh off fer meat? Got a hunderd pound or so, on the sled outside."

Just as Clarence and George were assuring him that he was heartily welcome, the other man tore away the last hindrance to his speech, and broke in: "Say, lads; yeh haint got a leetle bit o' bread yeh might spare? I'm that hungry fer jes' a leetle bit——"

"Yeh jes' shet up, Jim!" cried his partner indignantly. "Ye'd make these kids think yeh might be starvin'. Haint yeh had all yeh wanted to eat?"

"Yes," was the gloomy reply; "but nothin' but straight meat."

However, Clarence put an end to the discussion by setting the table with sourdough bread and cold bacon, having first made them promise not to spoil their appetites for the dinner. The poor fellows handled the heavy bread reverently, and went into ecstasies of delight over it. Then they went out, unharnessed the dogs, and brought some magnificent pieces of moose meat in with them. The boys' mouths watered at the sight, for they were longing for it just as much as the others longed for the bread.

"Porterhouse moose-steak," whispered George; "tenderloin, sirloin, and round; liver and bacon; rib-roast of moose, moose stew, and fried sweetbreads. Hurry, Clarence, and add them to the bill of fare."

"Now don't bother me. I'm cook, and I'm going to boss this dinner, so you obey orders. Take a piece of that meat and go down to the cabin on the next island. They'd give most anything for it, so see that you make a good trade."

The hungry strangers sat on the bunk and watched proceedings with satisfied countenances, while Clarence mixed and kneaded the dough for a baking of bread. In a short time George returned, with one cup of dried apples and five of prunes. Yet they were all disappointed at his failure to get sugar. But the dinner already promised to be such a grand affair that they could readily forego such a trifling matter as sweets.

Just as Clarence was shortening the pie-dough with bacon grease, a second sled pulled up at the door, and another stranger entered. A vivid picture he made, as he stood for an instant in the doorway. Though his eyebrows and lashes were matted with ice, his face was clean-shaven, and hence, free from it. From his beaded moccasins to his great gauntleted mittens and wolf-skin cap from Siberia, every article of wearing apparel proclaimed him to be one of the "Eldorado Kings," or millionaire mineowners of Dawson.

He was a pleasant man to look at, though his heavy jaw and steel-blue eyes gave notice of a firm, indomitable will. About his waist was clasped a leather belt, in which reposed two large Colt's revolvers and a hunting-knife, while in his hand, besides the usual dog whip, he carried a smokeless rifle of the largest bore and latest pattern. They wondered at this, for men in the Klondike rarely go armed, and then only because of necessity.

His story was soon told. His own team of seven dogs, the finest in the country and for which he had recently refused $5,000, had been stolen five days before. He had found the clue, and discovered that the thieves had started out of the country on the ice. He had borrowed a team of dogs from a friend and taken their trail.

They marvelled at his speed, for he had left Dawson at midnight, having traveled the 75 miles in 12 hours. He wished to rest the animals and take a few hours sleep, before going on with the chase. He was sure of overtaking them, he said, for they had foolishly started with an 18-inch sled, while the regular, trail Yukon-sleds were only 16 inches wide. Thus, they had to break trail constantly for one of the runners, while his was already broken.

They recognized the party he was after, and assured him that he was certain to catch them in another 12 hours' run. Then he was made welcome and invited to dinner. To their surprise, when he returned from unhitching and feeding his dogs he brought several pounds of sugar and two cans of condensed milk.

"Thought you fellows, up river here, would be out of luxuries," he said, as he threw them upon the table; "and as I wanted to travel light, I brought them along, intending to trade for beans and flour whenever I got a chance. No, never mind thanks. I'm going to eat dinner with you. Call me when it's ready." And he climbed into one of the bunks, falling asleep a moment later.

"I say, Jim. Thet's travelin', aint it?" said the Man from Mazy May, with as much pride as though he had done it himself. "Seventy-five miles in 12 hours, an' thet cold he wa'nt able to ride more'n half the time. Bet ye'd be petered clean out if yeh done the like o' thet."

"Maybe yeh think I can't travel," his partner replied. But before he could tell what a wonderful traveler he was, their dogs and the dogs of the new arrival started a fight, and had to be separated.

At last the dinner was ready, and just as they were calling the "Eldorado King," Uncle Hiram and Mr. Carter arrived.

"Not an ounce of sugar or can of milk to be bought in Dawson," Uncle Hiram said. But his jaw dropped as he caught sight of the sugar and milk on the table, and he sheepishly held up a quart-can of strained honey as his contribution.

This addition necessitated a change in the bill of fare; so when they finally sat down, the first course of mock-turtle soup was followed by hot cakes and honey. While one after another, the delicacies of "civilized grub," as they called it, appeared, the eyes of the Men from Mazy May opened wider and wider, and speech seemed to fail them.

But one more surprise was in store for them. They heard a jingle of bells, and another ice-covered traveler entered and claimed their hospitality. The new-comer was an Associated Press reporter, on his way to Dawson from the United States. His first question was concerning the where-abouts of a Mr. Hiram Donaldson, "said to be camped on the Yukon near the mouth of the Stuart River." On Uncle Hiram being pointed out to him, the reporter handed him a letter of introduction from the Mining Syndicate which he, Mr. Donaldson, was representing. Nor was this all. A fat package of letters was also passed over—the long-looked-for letters from home.

"By gum! This do beat all," said the Man from Mazy May, after a place had been made for the last arrival. But his partner had his mouth so full of apple dumpling that he could only roll his eyes in approval.

"I know what 'b' stands for," whispered George across the table to Clarence.

"So do I. It stands for "Bully" with a big "B."

1897

STEPHEN CRANE

A Little Pilgrim

ONE NOVEMBER it became clear to childish minds in certain parts of Whilomville that the Sunday-School of the Presbyterian Church would not have for the children the usual Tree on Christmas Eve. The funds free for that ancient festival would be used for the relief of suffering among the victims of the Charleston earth-quake.

The plan had been born in the generous head of the superintendent of the Sunday-School and during one session he had made a strong plea that the children should forego the vain pleasures of a Tree and, in a glorious application of the Golden Rule, refuse a local use of the fund and will that it be sent where dire distress might be alleviated. At the end of a tearfully eloquent speech the question was put fairly to a vote and the children in a burst of virtuous abandon carried the question for Charleston. Many of the teachers had been careful to preserve a finely neutral attitude but even if they had cautioned the children against being too impetuous they could not have checked the wild impulses.

But this was a long time before Christmas.

Very early, boys held important speech together. "Huh; you ain't goin' to have no Christmas tree at the Presperterian Sunday-School."

Sullenly the victims answered, "No, we ain't."

"Huh," scoffed the other denominations, "we are goin' to have the all-firedest biggest tree that ever you saw in the world."

The little Presbyterians were greatly down-cast.

It happened that Jimmie Trescott had regularly attended the Presbyterian Sunday-School. The Trescotts were consistently undenominational but they had sent their lad on Sundays to one of the places where they thought he would receive benefits. However, on one day in December, Jimmie appeared before his father and made a strong spiritual appeal to be forthwith attached to the Sunday-School of the Big Progressive Church. Doctor Trescott mused this question considerably. "Well, Jim," he said, "why do you conclude that the Big Progressive Sunday-School is better for you than the Presbyterian Sunday-School?"

"Now—it's nicer," answered Jimmie, looking at his father with an anxious eye.

"How do you mean?"

"Why—now—some of the boys what go to the Presperterian place, they ain't very nice," explained the flagrant Jimmie.

Trescott mused the question considerably once more. In the end he said: "Well, you may change if you wish, this one time, but you must not be changing to and fro. You decide now, and then you must abide by your decision."

"Yessir," said Jimmie, brightly. "Big Progressive."

"All right," said the father. "But remember what I've told you."

On the following Sunday morning, Jimmie presented himself at the door of the basement of the Big Progressive Church. He was conspicuously washed, notably raimented, prominently polished. And, incidentally, he was very uncomfortable because of all these virtues.

A number of acquaintances greeted him contemptuously. "Hello, Jimmie! What you doin' here? Thought you was a Presperterian?"

Jimmie cast down his eyes and made no reply. He was too cowed by the change. However, Homer Phelps, who was a regular patron of the Big Progressive Sunday-School, suddenly appeared and said: "Hello, Jim." Jimmie seized upon him. Homer Phelps was amenable to Trescott laws, tribal if you like, but iron-bound, almost compulsory.

"Hello, Homer," said Jimmie and his manner was so good that Homer felt a great thrill in being able to show his superior a new condition of life.

"You ain't never come here afore, have you?" he demanded, with a new arrogance.

"No; I ain't," said Jimmie. Then they stared at each other and manoeuvred.

"You don't know *my* teacher," said Homer.

"No; I don't know *her*," admitted Jimmie but in a way which contended, modestly, that he knew countless other Sunday-School teachers.

"Better join our class," said Homer sagely. "She wears spectacles; don't see very well; sometimes we do almost what we like."

"All right," said Jimmie, glad to place himself in the hands of his friend. In due time, they entered the Sunday-School room where a man with benevolent whiskers stood on a platform and said: "We will now sing Number 33—'Pull for the Shore, Sailor, Pull for the Shore.'" And as the obedient throng burst into melody the man on the platform indicated the time with a white and graceful hand. He was an ideal Sunday-School superintendent—one who had never felt hunger or thirst or the wound of the challenge of dishonor.

Jimmie, walking carefully on his toes, followed Homer Phelps. He felt that the kingly superintendent might cry out and blast him to ashes before he could reach a chair. It was a desperate journey. But at last he heard Homer muttering to a young lady who looked at him through glasses which greatly magnified her eyes. "A new boy," she said in a deeply religious voice.

"Yes'm," said Jimmie trembling. The five other boys of the class scanned him keenly and derided his condition.

"We will proceed to the lesson," said the young lady. Then she cried sternly like a serjeant, "The Seventh Chapter of Jeremiah!"

There was a swift fluttering of leaflets. Then the name of Jeremiah, a wise man, towered over the feelings of these boys. Homer Phelps was doomed to read the fourth verse. He took a deep breath, he puffed out his lips, he gathered his strength for a great effort. His beginning was childishly explosive. He hurriedly said:

"*Trust ye not in lying words, saying The temple of the Lord, The temple of the Lord, The temple of the Lord, are these.*"

"Now," said the teacher, "Johnnie Scanlan, tell us what these words mean." The Scanlan boy shame-facedly muttered that he did not know. The teacher's countenance saddened. Her heart was in the work; she wanted to make a success of this Sunday-School class. "Perhaps Homer Phelps can tell us," she remarked.

Homer gulped; he looked at Jimmie. Through the great room hummed a steady hum. A little circle, very near, was being told about Daniel in the lion's den. They were deeply moved at the story. At the moment they liked Sunday-School.

"Why—now—it means," said Homer with a grand pomposity born of a sense of hopeless ignorance—"it means—why it means that they were in the wrong place."

"No," said the teacher, profoundly, "it means that we should be good, very good indeed. That is what it means. It means that we should love the Lord and be good. Love the Lord and be good. That is what it means."

The little boys suddenly had a sense of black wickedness as their teacher looked austerely upon them. They gazed at her with the wide-open eyes of simplicity. They were stirred again. This thing of being good—this great business of life—apparently it was always successful. They knew from the Fairy-Tales. But it was difficult, wasn't it? It was said to be the most heart-breaking task to be generous, wasn't it? One had to pay the price of one's eyes in order to be pacific, didn't one? As for patience, it was tortured martyrdom to be patient, wasn't it? Sin was simple, wasn't it? But virtue was so difficult that it could only be practised by heavenly beings, wasn't it?

And the angels, the Sunday-School superintendent, and the teacher swam in the high visions of the little boys as beings so good that if a boy scratched his shin in the same room, he was a profane and sentenced devil.

"And," said the teacher, "'The temple of the Lord'—what does that mean? I'll ask the new boy. What does that mean?"

"I dunno," said Jimmie blankly.

But here the professional bright boy of the class suddenly awoke to his obligations. "Teacher," he cried, "it means church, same as this."

"Exactly," said the teacher, deeply satisfied with this reply. "You know your lesson well, Clarence. I am much pleased."

The other boys, instead of being envious, looked with admiration upon Clarence while he adopted an air of being habituated to perform such feats every day of his life. Still, he was not much of a boy. He had the virtue of being able to walk on very high stilts but when the season of stilts had passed, he possessed no rank save this Sunday-School rank, this clever-little-Clarence business of knowing the Bible, and the lesson, better than the other boys. The other boys, sometimes looking at him meditatively, did not actually decide to thrash him as soon as he cleared the portals of the church but they certainly decided to molest him in such ways as would re-establish their self-respect. Back of the superintendent's chair hung a lithograph of the Martyrdom of St. Stephen.

Jimmie, feeling stiff and encased in his best clothes, waited for the ordeal to end. A bell pealed; the superintendent had tapped a bell. Slowly the rustling and murmuring dwindled to silence. The benevolent man faced the school. "I have to announce," he began, waving his body from side to side in the conventional bows of his kind, "that—" Bang went the bell. "Give me your attention, please, children. I have to announce that the Board has decided that this year there will be no Christmas tree, but the—"

Instantly the room buzzed with the subdued clamor of the children. Jimmie was speechless. He stood morosely during the singing of the closing hymn. He passed out into the street with the others, pushing no more than was required.

Speedily the whole idea left him. If he remembered Sunday-School at all, it was to remember that he did not like it.

1900

PAUL LAURENCE DUNBAR

An Old-Time Christmas

WHEN THE HOLIDAYS CAME round the thoughts of 'Liza Ann Lewis always turned to the good times that she used to have at home when, following the precedent of anti-bellum days, Christmas lasted all the week and good cheer held sway. She remembered with regret the gifts that were given, the songs that were sung to the tinkling of the banjo and the dances with which they beguiled the night hours. And the eating! Could she forget it? The great turkey, with the fat literally bursting from him; the yellow yam melting into deliciousness in the mouth; or in some more fortunate season, even the juicy 'possum grinning in brown and greasy death from the great platter.

In the ten years she had lived in New York, she had known no such feast-day. Food was strangely dear in the Metropolis, and then there was always the weekly rental of the poor room to be paid. But she had kept the memory of the old times green in her heart, and ever turned to it with the fondness of one for something irretrievably lost.

That is how Jimmy came to know about it. Jimmy was thirteen and small for his age, and he could not remember any such times as his mother told him about. Although he said with great pride to his partner and rival, Blinky Scott, "Chee, Blink, you ought to hear my ol' lady talk about de times dey have down we're we come from at Christmas; N'Yoick ain't in it wid dem, you kin jist bet." And Blinky, who was a New Yorker clear through with a New Yorker's contempt for anything outside of the city, had promptly replied with a downward spreading of his right hand, "Aw fu'git it!"

Jimmy felt a little crest-fallen for a minute, but he lifted himself in his own estimation by threatening to "do" Blinky and the cloud rolled by.

'Liza Ann knew that Jimmy couldn't ever understand what she meant by an old-time Christmas unless she could show him by some faint approach to its merrymaking, and it had been the dream of her life to do this. But every year she had failed, until now she was a little ahead.

Her plan was too good to keep, and when Jimmy went out that Christmas eve morning to sell his papers, she had disclosed it to him and bade him hurry home as soon as he was done, for they were to have a real old-time Christmas.

Jimmy exhibited as much pleasure as he deemed consistent with his dignity and promised to be back early to add his earnings to the fund for celebration.

When he was gone, 'Liza Ann counted over her savings lovingly and dreamed of what she would buy her boy, and what she would have for dinner on the next day. Then a voice, a colored man's voice, she knew, floated up to her. Some one in the alley below her window was singing "The Old Folks at Home."

> "All up an' down the whole creation,
>   Sadly I roam,
> Still longing for the old plantation,
>   An' for the old folks at home."

She leaned out of the window and listened and when the song had ceased and she drew her head in again, there were tears in her eyes—the tears of memory and longing. But she crushed them away, and laughed tremulously to herself as she said, "What a reg'lar ol' fool I'm a-gittin' to be." Then she went out into the cold, snow-covered streets, for she had work to do that day that would add a mite to her little Christmas store.

Down in the street, Jimmy was calling out the morning papers and racing with Blinky Scott for prospective customers; these were only transients, of course, for each had his regular buyers whose preferences were scrupulously respected by both in agreement with a strange silent compact.

The electric cars went clanging to and fro, the streets were full of shoppers with bundles and bunches of holly, and all the sights and sounds were pregnant with the message of the joyous time. People were full of the holiday spirit. The papers were going fast, and the little colored boy's pockets were filling with the desired coins. It would have been all right with Jimmy if the policeman hadn't come up on him just as he was about to toss the "bones," and when Blinky Scott had him "faded" to the amount of five hard-earned pennies.

Well, they were trying to suppress youthful gambling in New York, and the officer had to do his duty. The others scuttled away, but Jimmy was so absorbed in the game that he didn't see the "cop" until he was right on him, so he was "pinched." He blubbered a little and wiped his grimy face with his grimier sleeve until it was one long, brown smear. You know this was Jimmy's first time.

The big blue-coat looked a little bit ashamed as he marched him down the street, followed at a distance by a few hooting boys. Some of the holiday shoppers turned to look at them as they passed and murmured, "Poor little chap; I wonder what he's been up to now." Others said sarcastically, "It seems strange that 'copper' didn't call for help." A few of his brother officers grinned at him as he passed, and he blushed, but the dignity of the law must be upheld and the crime of gambling among the newsboys was a growing evil.

Yes, the dignity of the law must be upheld, and though Jimmy was only a small boy, it would be well to make an example of him. So his name and age were put down on the blotter, and over against them the offence with which he was charged. Then he was locked up to await trial the next morning.

"It's shameful," the bearded sergeant said, "how the kids are carryin' on these days. People are feelin' pretty generous, an' they'll toss 'em a nickel er a dime fur their paper an' tell 'em to keep the change fur Christmas, an' foist thing you know the little beggars are shootin' craps er pitchin' pennies. We've got to make an example of some of 'em."

'Liza Ann Lewis was tearing through her work that day to get home and do her Christmas shopping, and she was singing as she worked some such old song as she used to sing in the good old days back home. She reached her room late and tired, but happy. Visions of a "wakening up" time for her and Jimmy were in her mind. But Jimmy wasn't there.

"I wunner whah that little scamp is," she said, smiling; "I tol' him to hu'y home, but I reckon he's stayin' out latah wid de evenin' papahs so's to bring home mo' money."

Hour after hour passed and he did not come; then she grew alarmed. At two o'clock in the morning she could stand it no longer and she went over and awakened Blinky Scott, much to that young gentleman's disgust, who couldn't see why any woman need make such a fuss about a kid. He told her laconically that "Chimmie was pinched fur t'rowin' de bones."

She heard with a sinking heart and went home to her own room to walk the floor all night and sob.

In the morning, with all her Christmas savings tied up in a handkerchief, she hurried down to Jefferson Market court room. There was a full blotter that morning, and the Judge was rushing through with it. He wanted to get home to his Christmas dinner. But he paused long enough when he got to Jimmy's case to deliver a brief but stern lecture upon the evil of child-gambling in New York. He said that as it was Christmas Day he would like to release the prisoner with a reprimand, but he thought that this had been done too often and that it was high time to make an example of one of the offenders.

Well, it was fine or imprisonment. 'Liza Ann struggled up through the crowd of spectators and her Christmas treasure added to what Jimmy had, paid his fine and they went out of the court room together.

When they were in their room again she put the boy to bed, for there was no fire and no coal to make one. Then she wrapped herself in a shabby shawl and sat huddled up over the empty stove.

Down in the alley she heard the voice of the day before singing:

> "Oh, darkies, how my heart grows weary,
>   Far from the old folks at home."

And she burst into tears.

1900

PAULINE E. HOPKINS

General Washington

A CHRISTMAS STORY

I.

GENERAL WASHINGTON did any odd jobs he could find around the Washington market, but his specialty was selling chitlins.

General Washington lived in the very shady atmosphere of Murderer's Bay in the capital city. All that he could remember of father or mother in his ten years of miserable babyhood was that they were frequently absent from the little shanty where they were supposed to live, generally after a protracted spell of drunkenness and bloody quarrels when the police were forced to interfere for the peace of the community. During these absences, the child would drift from one squalid home to another wherever a woman—God save the mark!—would take pity upon the poor waif and throw him a few scraps of food for his starved stomach, or a rag of a shawl, apron or skirt, in winter, to wrap about his attenuated little body.

One night the General's daddy being on a short vacation in the city, came home to supper; and because there was no supper to eat, he occupied himself in beating his wife. After that time, when the officers took him, the General's daddy never returned to his home. The General's mammy? Oh, she died!

General Washington's resources developed rapidly after this. Said resources consisted of a pair of nimble feet for dancing the hoedown, shuffles intricate and dazzling, and the Juba; a strong pair of lungs, a wardrobe limited to a pair of pants originally made for a man, and tied about the ankles with strings, a shirt with one gallows, a vast amount of "brass," and a very, very small amount of nickel. His education was practical: "Ef a corn-dodger costs two cents, an' a fellar hain't got de two cents, how's he gwine ter git de corn-dodger?"

General Washington ranked first among the knights of the pavement. He could shout louder and hit harder than any among them; that was the reason they called him "Buster" and "the General." The General could swear, too; I am sorry to admit it, but the truth must be told.

He uttered an oath when he caught a crowd of small white aristocrats tormenting a kitten. The General landed among them in quick time and commenced knocking heads at a lively rate. Presently he was master of the situation, and marched away triumphantly with the kitten in his arms, followed by stones and other missiles which whirled about him through space from behind the safe shelter of back yards and street corners.

The General took the kitten home. Home was a dry-goods box turned on end and filled with straw for winter. The General was as happy as a lord in summer, but the winter was a trial. The last winter had been a hard one, and Buster called a meeting of the leading members of the gang to consider the advisability of moving farther south for the hard weather.

"'Pears lak to me, fellers, Wash'nton's heap colder'n it uster be, an' I'se mighty onscruplus 'bout stoppin' hyar."

"Bisness am mighty peart," said Teenie, the smallest member of the gang, "s'pose we put off menderin' tell after Chris'mas; Jeemes Henry, fellers, it hain't no Chris'mas fer me outside ob Wash'nton."

"Dat's so, Teenie," came from various members as they sat on the curbing playing an interesting game of craps.

"Den hyar we is tell after Chris'mas, fellers; then dis sonny's gwine ter move, sho, hyar me?"

"De gang's wid yer, Buster; move it is."

It was about a week before Chris'mas, and the weather had been unusually severe.

Probably because misery loves company—nothing could be more miserable than his cat—Buster grew very fond of Tommy. He would cuddle him in his arms every night and listen to his soft purring while he confided all his own hopes and fears to the willing ears of his four-footed companion, occasionally poking his ribs if he showed any signs of sleepiness.

But one night poor Tommy froze to death. Buster didn't—more's the wonder—only his ears and his two big toes. Poor Tommy was thrown off the dock into the Potomac the next morning, while a stream of salt water trickled down his master's dirty face, making visible, for the first time in a year, the yellow hue of his complexion. After that the General hated all flesh and grew morose and cynical.

Just about a week before Tommy's death, Buster met the fairy. Once, before his mammy died, in a spasm of reform she had forced him to go to school, against his better judgment, promising the teacher to go up and "wallop" the General every day if he thought Buster needed it. This gracious offer was declined with thanks. At the end of the week the General left school for his own good and the good of the school. But in that week he learned something about fairies; and so, after she threw him the pinks that she carried in her hand, he called her to himself "the fairy."

Being Christmas week, the General was pretty busy. It was a great sight to see the crowds of people coming and going all day long about the busy market; wagon loads of men, women and children, some carts drawn by horses, but more by mules. Some of the people well-dressed, some scantily clad, but all intent on getting enjoyment out of this their leisure season. This was the season for selling crops and settling the year's account. The store-keepers, too, had prepared their most tempting wares, and the thoroughfares were crowded.

"I 'clare to de Lord, I'se done busted my ol' man, shure," said one woman to another as they paused to exchange greetings outside a store door.

"N'em min'," returned the other, "he'll wurk fer mo'. Dis is Chris'mas, honey."

"To be sure," answered the first speaker, with a flounce of her ample skirts.

Meanwhile her husband pondered the advisability of purchasing a mule, feeling in his pockets for the price demanded, but finding them nearly empty. The money had been spent on the annual festival.

"Ole mule, I want yer mighty bad, but you'll have to slide dis time; it's Chris'mas, mule."

The wise old mule actually seemed to laugh as he whisked his tail against his bony sides and steadied himself on his three sound legs.

The venders were very busy, and their cries were wonderful for ingenuity of invention to attract trade:

"Hellow, dar, in de cellar, I'se got fresh aggs fer de 'casion; now's yer time fer agg-nogg wid new aggs in it."

There were the stalls, too, kept by venerable aunties and filled with specimens of old-time southern cheer: Coon, corn-pone, possum fat and hominy; there was piles of gingerbread and boiled chestnuts, heaps of walnuts and roasting apples. There were great barrels of cider, not to speak of something stronger. There were terrapin and the persimmon and the chinquapin in close proximity to the succulent viands—chine and spare-rib, sausage and crackling, savory souvenirs of the fine art of hog-killing. And everywhere were faces of dusky hue; Washington's great negro population bubbled over in every direction.

The General was peddling chitlins. He had a tub upon his head and was singing in his strong childish tones:

> "Here's yer chitlins, fresh an' sweet,
> Young hog's chitlins hard to beat,
> Methodis chitlins, jes' been biled,
> Right fresh chitlins, dey ain't spiled,
> Baptis' chitlins by de pound,
> As nice chitlins as ever was foun'."

"Hyar, boy, duz yer mean ter say dey is real Baptis' chitlins, sho nuff?"

"Yas, mum."

"How duz you make dat out?"

"De hog raised by Mr. Robberson, a hard-shell Baptis', mum."

"Well, lem-me have two poun's."

"Now," said a solid-looking man as General finished waiting on a crowd of women and men, "I want some o' de Methodess chitlins you's bin hollerin' 'bout."

"Hyar dey is, ser."

"Take 'em all out o' same tub?"

"Yas, ser. Only dair leetle mo' water on de Baptis' chitlins, an' dey's whiter."

"How you tell 'em?"

"Well, ser, two hog's chitlins in dis tub an one ob de hogs raised by Unc. Bemis, an' he's a Methodes,' ef dat don't make him a Methodes hog nuthin' will."

"Weigh me out four pounds, ser."

In an hour's time the General had sold out. Suddenly at his elbow he heard a voice:

"Boy, I want to talk to you."

The fairy stood beside him. She was a little girl about his own age, well wrapped in costly velvet and furs; her long, fair hair fell about her like an aureole of glory; a pair of gentle blue eyes set in a sweet, serious face glanced at him from beneath a jaunty hat with a long curling white feather that rested light as thistle-down upon the beautiful curly locks. The General could not move for gazing, and as his wonderment grew his mouth was extended in a grin that revealed the pearly whiteness of two rows of ivory.

"Boy, shake hands."

The General did not move; how could he?

"Don't you hear me?" asked the fairy, imperiously:

"Yas'm," replied the General meekly. "'Deed, missy. I'se 'tirely too dirty to tech dem clos o' yourn."

Nevertheless he put forth timidly and slowly a small paw begrimed with the dirt of the street. He looked at the hand and then at her; she looked at the hand and then at him. Then their eyes meeting, they laughed the sweet laugh of the free-masonry of childhood.

"I'll excuse you this time, boy," said the fairy, graciously, "but you must remember that I wish you to wash your face and hands when you are to talk with me; and," she added, as though inspired by an afterthought, "it would be well for you to keep them clean at other times, too."

"Yas'm," replied the General.

"What's your name, boy?"

"Gen'r'l Wash'nton," answered Buster, standing at attention as he had seen the police do in the courtroom.

"Well, General, don't you know you've told a story about the chitlins you've just sold?"

"Tol' er story?" queried the General with a knowing look. "Course I got to sell my chitlins ahead ob de oder fellars, or lose my trade."

"Don't you know it's wicked to tell stories?"

"How come so?" asked the General, twisting his bare toes about in his rubbers, and feeling very uncomfortable.

"Because, God says we musn't."

"Who's he?"

The fairy gasped in astonishment. "Don't you know who God is?"

"No'pe; never seed him. Do he live in Wash'nton?"

"Why, God is your Heavenly Father, and Christ was His son. He was born on Christmas Day a long time ago. When He grew a man, wicked men nailed Him to the cross and killed Him. Then He went to heaven, and we'll all live with Him some day if we are good before we die. O I love Him; and you must love Him, too, General."

"Now look hyar, missy, you kayn't make this chile b'lieve nufin lak dat."

The fairy went a step nearer the boy in her eagerness:

"It's true; just as true as you live."

"Whar'd you say He lived?"

"In heaven," replied the child, softly.

"What kin' o' place is heaven?"

"Oh, beautiful!"

The General stared at the fairy. He worked his toes faster and faster.

"Say, kin yer hab plenty to eat up dar?"

"O, yes; you'll never be hungry there."

"An' a fire, an' clos?" he queried in suppressed, excited tones.

"Yes; it's all love and plenty when we get to heaven, if we are good here."

"Well, missy, dat's a pow'ful good story, but I'm blamed ef I b'lieve it." The General forgot his politeness in his excitement.

"An' ef it's true, tain't only fer white fo'ks; you won't fin' nary nigger dar."

"But you will; and all I've told you is true. Promise me to come to my house on Christmas morning and see my mother. She'll help you, and she will teach you more about God. Will you come?" she asked eagerly, naming a street and number in the most aristocratic quarter of Washington. "Ask for Fairy, that's me. Say quick; here is my nurse."

The General promised.

"Law, Miss Fairy, honey; come right hyar. I'll tell yer mawmaw how you's done run 'way from me to talk to dis dirty little monkey. Pickin' up sech trash fer ter talk to."

The General stood in a trance of happiness. He did not mind the slurring remarks of the nurse, and refrained from throwing a brick at the buxom lady, which was a sacrifice on his part. All he saw was the glint of golden curls in the winter sunshine, and the tiny hand waving him good-bye.

"An' her name is Fairy! Jes' ter think how I hit it all by my lonesome."

Many times that week the General thought and puzzled over Fairy's words. Then he would sigh:

"Heaven's where God lives. Plenty to eat, warm fire all de time in winter; plenty o' clos', too, but I'se got to be good. 'Spose dat means keepin' my face an' han's clean an' stop swearin' an' lyin'. It kayn't be did."

The gang wondered what had come over Buster.

II.

The day before Christmas dawned clear and cold. There was snow on the ground. Trade was good, and the General, mindful of the visit next day, had bought a pair of second-hand shoes and a new calico shirt.

"Git onter de dude!" sang one of the gang as he emerged from the privacy of the dry-goods box early Christmas Eve.

The General was a dancer and no mistake. Down at Dutch Dan's place they kept the old-time Southern Christmas moving along in hot time until the dawn of Christmas Day stole softly through the murky atmosphere. Dutch Dan's was the meeting place of the worst characters, white and black, in the capital city. From that vile den issued the twin spirits murder and rapine as the early winter shadows fell; there the criminal entered in the early dawn and was lost to the accusing eye of justice. There was a dance at Dutch Dan's Christmas Eve, and the General was sent for to help amuse the company.

The shed-like room was lighted by oil lamps and flaring pine torches. The center of the apartment was reserved for dancing. At one end the inevitable bar stretched its yawning mouth like a monster awaiting his victims. A long wooden table was built against one side of the room, where the game could be played to suit the taste of the most expert devotee of the fickle goddess.

The room was well filled, early as it was, and the General's entrance was the signal for a shout of welcome. Old Unc' Jasper was tuning his fiddle and blind Remus was drawing sweet chords from an old banjo. They glided softly into the music of the Mobile shuffle. The General began to dance. He was master of the accomplishment. The pigeon-wing, the old buck, the hoe-down and the Juba followed each other in rapid succession. The crowd shouted and cheered and joined in the sport. There was hand-clapping and a rhythmic accompaniment of patting the knees and stamping the feet. The General danced faster and faster:

> "Juba up and juba down,
> Juba all aroun' de town;
> Can't you hyar de juba pat?
> Juba!"

sang the crowd. The General gave fresh graces and new embellishments. Occasionally he added to the interest by yelling, "Ain't dis fine!" "Oh, my!" "Now I'm gittin' loose!" "Hol' me, hol' me!"

The crowd went wild with delight.

The child danced until he fell exhausted to the floor. Someone in the crowd "passed the hat." When all had been waited upon the bar-keeper counted up the receipts and divided fair—half to the house and half to the dancer. The fun went on, and the room grew more crowded. General Wash'nton crept under the table and curled himself up like a ball. He was lucky, he told himself sleepily, to have so warm a berth that cold night; and then his heart glowed as he thought of the morrow and Fairy, and wondered if what she had said were true. Heaven must be a fine place if it could beat the floor under the table for comfort and warmth. He slept. The fiddle creaked, the dancers shuffled. Rum went down their throats and wits were befogged. Suddenly the General was wide awake with a start. What was that?

"The family are all away to-night at a dance, and the servants gone home. There's no one there but an old man and a kid. We can be well out of the way before the alarm is given. 'Leven sharp, Doc. And, look here, what's the number agin?"

Buster knew in a moment that mischief was brewing, and he turned over softly on his side, listening mechanically to catch the reply. It came. Buster sat up. He was wide awake then. They had given the street and number where Fairy's home was situated.

III.

Senator Tallman was from Maryland. He had owned slaves, fought in the Civil War on the Confederate side, and at its end had been returned to a seat in Congress after reconstruction, with feelings of deeply rooted hatred for the Negro. He openly declared his purpose to oppose their progress in every possible way. His favorite argument was disbelief in God's handiwork as shown in the Negro.

"You argue, suh, that God made 'em. I have my doubts, suh. God made man in His own image, suh, and that being the case, suh, it is clear that he had no hand in creating niggers. A nigger, suh, is the image of nothing but the devil." He also declared in his imperious, haughty, Southern way: "The South is in the saddle, suh, and she will never submit to the degradation of Negro domination; never, suh."

The Senator was a picture of honored age and solid comfort seated in his velvet armchair before the fire of blazing logs in his warm, well-lighted study. His lounging coat was thrown open, revealing its soft silken lining, his feet were thrust into gayly embroidered fur-lined slippers. Upon the baize covered table beside him a silver salver sat holding a decanter, glasses and fragrant mint, for the Senator loved the beguiling sweetness of a mint julep at bedtime. He was writing a speech which in his opinion would bury the blacks too deep for resurrection and settle the Negro question forever. Just now he was idle; the evening paper was folded across his knees; a smile was on his face. He was alone in the grand mansion, for the festivities of the season had begun and the family were gone to enjoy a merry-making at the house of a friend. There was a picture in his mind of Christmas in his old Maryland home in the good old days "befo' de wah," the great ball-room where giggling girls and matrons fair glided in the stately minuet. It was in such a gathering he had met his wife, the beautiful Kate Channing. Ah, the happy time of youth and love! The house was very still; how loud the ticking of the clock sounded. Just then a voice spoke beside his chair:

"Please, sah, I'se Gen'r'l Wash'nton."

The Senator bounded to his feet with an exclamation:

"Eh! Bless my soul, suh; where did you come from?"

"Ef yer please, boss, froo de winder."

The Senator rubbed his eyes and stared hard at the extraordinary figure before him. The Gen'r'l closed the window and then walked up to the fire, warmed himself in front, then turned around and stood with his legs wide apart and his shrewd little gray eyes fixed upon the man before him.

The Senator was speechless for a moment; then he advanced upon the intruder with a roar warranted to make a six-foot man quake in his boots:

"Through the window, you black rascal! Well, I reckon you'll go out through the door, and that in quick time, you little thief."

"Please, boss, it hain't me; it's Jim the crook and de gang from Dutch Dan's."

"Eh!" said the Senator again.

"What's yer cronumter say now, boss? 'Leven is de time fer de perfahmance ter begin. I reckon'd I'd git hyar time nuff fer yer ter call de perlice."

"Boy, do you mean for me to understand that burglars are about to raid my house?" demanded the Senator, a light beginning to dawn upon him.

The General nodded his head: "Dat's it, boss, ef by 'buglers' you means Jim de crook and Dutch Dan."

It was ten minutes of the hour by the Senator's watch. He went to the telephone, rang up the captain of the nearest station, and told him the situation. He took a revolver from a drawer of his desk and advanced toward the waiting figure before the fire.

"Come with me. Keep right straight ahead through that door; if you attempt to run I'll shoot you."

They walked through the silent house to the great entrance doors and there awaited the coming of the police. Silently the officers surrounded the house. Silently they crept up the stairs into the now darkened study. "Eleven" chimed the little silver clock on the mantel. There was the stealthy tread of feet a moment after, whispers, the flash of a dark lantern,—a rush by the officers and a stream of electricity flooded the room.

"It's the nigger did it!" shouted Jim the crook, followed instantly by the sharp crack of a revolver. General Washington felt a burning pain shoot through his breast as he fell unconscious to the floor. It was all over in a moment. The officers congratulated themselves on the capture they had made—a brace of daring criminals badly wanted by the courts.

When the General regained consciousness, he lay upon a soft, white bed in Senator Tallman's house. Christmas morning had dawned, clear, cold and sparkling; upon the air the joy-bells sounded sweet and strong: "Rejoice, your Lord is born." Faintly from the streets came the sound of merry voices: "Chris'mas gift, Chris'mas gift."

The child's eyes wandered aimlessly about the unfamiliar room as if seeking and questioning. They passed the Senator and Fairy, who sat beside him and rested on a copy of Titian's matchless Christ which hung over the mantel. A glorious stream of yellow sunshine fell upon the thorn-crowned Christ.

> "God of Nazareth, see!
> Before a trembling soul
> Unfoldeth like a scroll
> Thy wondrous destiny!"

The General struggled to a sitting position with arms outstretched, then fell back with a joyous, awesome cry:

"It's Him! It's Him!"

"O General," sobbed Fairy, "don't you die, you're going to be happy all the rest of your life. Grandpa says so."

"I was in time, little Missy; I tried mighty hard after I knowed whar' dem debbils was a-comin' to."

Fairy sobbed; the Senator wiped his eyeglasses and coughed. The General lay quite still a moment, then turned himself again on his pillow to gaze at the pictured Christ.

"I'm a-gittin' sleepy, missy, it's so warm an' comfurtable here. 'Pears lak I feel right happy sence Ise seed Him." The morning light grew brighter. The face of the Messiah looked down as it must have looked when He was transfigured on Tabor's heights. The ugly face of the child wore a strange, sweet beauty. The Senator bent over the quiet figure with a gesture of surprise.

The General had obeyed the call of One whom the winds and waves of stormy human life obey. Buster's Christmas Day was spent in heaven.

For some reason, Senator Tallman never made his great speech against the Negro.

1900

JACOB RIIS

The Kid Hangs Up His Stocking

THE CLOCK in the West Side Boys' Lodging-house ticked out the seconds of Christmas eve as slowly and methodically as if six fat turkeys were not sizzling in the basement kitchen against the morrow's spread, and as if two-score boys were not racking their brains to guess what kind of pies would go with them. Out on the avenue the shopkeepers were barring doors and windows, and shouting "Merry Christmas!" to one another across the street as they hurried to get home. The drays ran over the pavement with muffled sounds; winter had set in with a heavy snow-storm. In the big hall the monotonous click of checkers on the board kept step with the clock. The smothered exclamations of the boys at some unexpected, bold stroke, and the scratching of a little fellow's pencil on a slate, trying to figure out how long it was yet till the big dinner, were the only sounds that broke the quiet of the room. The superintendent dozed behind his desk.

A door at the end of the hall creaked, and a head with a shock of weather-beaten hair was stuck cautiously through the opening.

"Tom!" it said in a stage-whisper. "Hi, Tom! Come up an' git on ter de lay of de Kid."

A bigger boy in a jumper, who had been lounging on two chairs by the group of checker players, sat up and looked toward the door. Something in the energetic toss of the head there aroused his instant curiosity, and he started across the room. After a brief whispered conference the door closed upon the two, and silence fell once more on the hall.

They had been gone but a little while when they came back in haste. The big boy shut the door softly behind him and set his back against it.

"Fellers," he said, "what d'ye t'ink? I'm blamed if de Kid ain't gone an' hung up his sock fer Chris'mas!"

The checkers dropped, and the pencil ceased scratching on the slate, in breathless suspense.

"Come up an' see," said Tom, briefly, and led the way.

The whole band followed on tiptoe. At the foot of the stairs their leader halted.

"Yer don't make no noise," he said, with a menacing gesture. "You, Savoy!"—to one in a patched shirt and with a mischievous twinkle,—"you don't come none o' yer monkey-shines. If you scare de Kid you'll get it in de neck, see!"

With this admonition they stole upstairs. In the last cot of the double tier of bunks a boy much smaller than the rest slept, snugly tucked in the blankets. A tangled curl of yellow hair strayed over his baby face. Hitched to the bedpost was a poor, worn little stocking, arranged with much care so that Santa Claus should have as little trouble in filling it as possible. The edge of a hole in the knee had been drawn together and tied with a string to prevent anything falling out. The boys looked on in amazed silence. Even Savoy was dumb.

Little Willie, or, as he was affectionately dubbed by the boys, "the Kid," was a waif who had drifted in among them some months before. Except that his mother was in the hospital, nothing was known about him, which was regular and according to the rule of the house. Not as much was known about most of its patrons; few of them knew more themselves, or cared to remember. Santa Claus had never been anything to them but a fake to make the colored supplements sell. The revelation of the Kid's simple faith struck them with a kind of awe. They sneaked quietly downstairs.

"Fellers," said Tom, when they were all together again in the big room,— by virtue of his length, which had given him the nickname of "Stretch," he was the speaker on all important occasions,—"ye seen it yerself. Santy Claus is a-comin' to this here joint to-night. I wouldn't 'a' believed it. I ain't never had no dealin's wid de ole guy. He kinder forgot I was around, I guess. But de Kid says he is a-comin' to-night, an' what de Kid says goes."

Then he looked round expectantly. Two of the boys, "Gimpy" and Lem, were conferring aside in an undertone. Presently Gimpy, who limped, as his name indicated, spoke up.

"Lem says, says he—"

"Gimpy, you chump! you'll address de chairman," interrupted Tom, with severe dignity, "or you'll get yer jaw broke, if yer leg *is* short, see!"

"Cut it out, Stretch," was Gimpy's irreverent answer. "This here ain't no regular meetin', an' we ain't goin' to have none o' yer rot. Lem he says, says he, let's break de bank an' fill de Kid's sock. He won't know but it wuz ole Santy done it."

A yell of approval greeted the suggestion. The chairman, bound to exercise the functions of office in season and out of season, while they lasted, thumped the table.

"It is regular motioned an' carried," he announced, "that we break de bank fer de Kid's Chris'mas. Come on, boys!"

The bank was run by the house, with the superintendent as paying teller. He had to be consulted, particularly as it was past banking hours; but the affair having been succinctly put before him by a committee, of which Lem and Gimpy and Stretch were the talking members, he readily consented to a reopening of business for a scrutiny of the various accounts which represented the boys' earnings at selling papers and blacking boots, minus the cost of their keep and of sundry surreptitious flings at "craps" in secret corners. The inquiry developed an available surplus of three dollars and fifty cents. Savoy alone had no account; the run of craps had recently gone heavily against him. But in consideration of the season, the house voted a credit of twenty-five cents to him. The announcement was received with cheers. There was an immediate rush for the store, which was delayed only a few minutes by the necessity of Gimpy and Lem stopping on the stairs to "thump" one another as the expression of their entire satisfaction.

The procession that returned to the lodging-house later on, after wearing out the patience of several belated storekeepers, might have been the very Santa's supply-train itself. It signalized its advent by a variety of discordant noises, which were smothered on the stairs by Stretch, with much personal violence, lest they wake the Kid out of season. With boots in hand and bated breath, the midnight band stole up to the dormitory and looked in. All was safe. The Kid was dreaming, and smiled in his sleep. The report roused a passing suspicion that he was faking, and Savarese was for pinching his toe to find out. As this would inevitably result in disclosure, Savarese and his proposal were scornfully sat upon. Gimpy supplied the popular explanation.

"He's a-dreamin' that Santy Claus has come," he said, carefully working a base-ball bat past the tender spot in the stocking.

"Hully Gee!" commented Shorty, balancing a drum with care on the end of it, "I'm thinkin' he ain't far out. Looks's ef de hull shop'd come along."

It did when it was all in place. A trumpet and a gun that had made vain and perilous efforts to join the bat in the stocking leaned against the bed in expectant attitudes. A picture-book with a pink Bengal tiger and a green bear on the cover peeped over the pillow, and the bedposts and rail were festooned with candy and marbles in bags. An express-wagon with a high seat was stabled in the gangway. It carried a load of fir branches that left no doubt from whose livery it hailed. The last touch was supplied by Savoy in the shape of a monkey on a yellow stick, that was not in the official bill of lading.

"I swiped it fer de Kid," he said briefly in explanation.

When it was all done the boys turned in, but not to sleep. It was long past midnight before the deep and regular breathing from the beds proclaimed that the last had succumbed.

The early dawn was tinging the frosty window panes with red when from the Kid's cot there came a shriek that roused the house with a start of very genuine surprise.

"Hello!" shouted Stretch, sitting up with a jerk and rubbing his eyes. "Yes, sir! in a minute. Hello, Kid, what to—"

The Kid was standing barefooted in the passageway, with a base-ball bat in one hand and a trumpet and a pair of drumsticks in the other, viewing with shining eyes the wagon and its cargo, the gun and all the rest. From every cot necks were stretched, and grinning faces watched the show. In the excess of his joy the Kid let out a blast on the trumpet that fairly shook the building. As if it were a signal, the boys jumped out of bed and danced a breakdown about him in their shirt-tails, even Gimpy joining in.

"Holy Moses!" said Stretch, looking down, "if Santy Claus ain't been here an' forgot his hull kit, I'm blamed!"

1901

The Set of Poe

Mr. Waterby remarked to his wife: "I'm still tempted by that set of Poe. I saw it in the window to-day, marked down to fifteen dollars."

"Yes?" said Mrs. Waterby, with a sudden gasp of emotion, it seemed to him.

"Yes—I believe I'll have to get it."

"I wouldn't if I were you, Alfred," she said. "You have so many books now."

"I know I have, my dear, but I haven't any set of Poe, and that's what I've been wanting for a long time. This edition I was telling you about is beautifully gotten up."

"Oh, I wouldn't buy it, Alfred," she repeated, and there was a note of pleading earnestness in her voice. "It's so much money to spend for a few books."

"Well, I know, but—" and then he paused, for the lack of words to express his mortified surprise.

Mr. Waterby had tried to be an indulgent husband. He took a selfish pleasure in giving, and found it more blessed than receiving. Every salary day he turned over to Mrs. Waterby a fixed sum for household expenses. He added to this an allowance for her spending money. He set aside a small amount for his personal expenses and deposited the remainder in the bank.

He flattered himself that he approximated the model husband.

Mr. Waterby had no costly habits and no prevailing appetite for anything expensive. Like every other man, he had one or two hobbies, and one of his particular hobbies was Edgar Allan Poe. He believed that Poe, of all American writers, was the one unmistakable "genius."

The word "genius" has been bandied around the country until it has come to be applied to a long-haired man out of work or a stout lady who writes poetry for the rural press. In the case of Poe, Mr. Waterby maintained that

"genius" meant one who was not governed by the common mental pro-
cesses, but "who spoke from inspiration, his mind involuntarily taking su-
perhuman flight into the realm of pure imagination," or something of that
sort. At any rate, Mr. Waterby liked Poe and he wanted a set of Poe. He
allowed himself not more than one luxury a year, and he determined that
this year the luxury should be a set of Poe.

Therefore, imagine the hurt to his feelings when his wife objected to his
expending fifteen dollars for that which he coveted above anything else in
the world.

As he went to his work that day he reflected on Mrs. Waterby's conduct.
Did she not have her allowance of spending money? Did he ever find fault
with her extravagance? Was he an unreasonable husband in asking that he
be allowed to spend this small sum for that which would give him many
hours of pleasure, and which would belong to Mrs. Waterby as much as to
him?

He told himself that many a husband would have bought the books without consulting his wife. But he (Waterby) had deferred to his wife in all
matters touching family finances, and he said to himself, with a tincture of
bitterness in his thoughts, that probably he had put himself into the attitude
of a mere dependent.

For had she not forbidden him to buy a few books for himself? Well, no,
she had not forbidden him, but it amounted to the same thing. She had
declared that she was firmly opposed to the purchase of Poe.

Mr. Waterby wondered if it were possible that he was just beginning to
know his wife. Was she a selfish woman at heart? Was she complacent and
good-natured and kind only while she was having her own way? Wouldn't
she prove to be an entirely different sort of woman if he should do as many
husbands do—spend his income on clubs and cigars and private amusement, and gave her the pickings of small change?

Nothing in Mr. Waterby's whole experience as a married man had so
wrenched his sensibilities and disturbed his faith as Mrs. Waterby's objec-
tion to the purchase of the set of Poe. There was but one way to account
for it. She wanted all the money for herself, or else she wanted him to put
it into the bank so that she could come into it after he—but this was too
monstrous.

However, Mrs. Waterby's conduct helped to give strength to Mr. Waterby's meanest suspicions.

Two or three days after the first conversation she asked: "You didn't buy
that set of Poe, did you, Alfred?"

"No, I didn't buy it," he answered, as coldly and with as much hauteur as possible.

He hoped to hear her say: "Well, why don't you go and get it? I'm sure that you want it, and I'd like to see you buy something for yourself once in a while."

That would have shown the spirit of a loving and unselfish wife.

But she merely said, "That's right; don't buy it," and he was utterly unhappy, for he realised that he had married a woman who did not love him and who simply desired to use him as a pack-horse for all household burdens.

As soon as Mr. Waterby had learned the horrible truth about his wife he began to recall little episodes dating back years, and now he pieced them together to convince himself that he was a deeply wronged person.

Small at the time and almost unnoticed, they now accumulated to prove that Mrs. Waterby had no real anxiety for her husband's happiness. Also, Mr. Waterby began to observe her more closely, and he believed that he found new evidences of her unworthiness. For one thing, while he was in gloom over his discovery and harassed by doubts of what the future might reveal to him, she was content and even-tempered.

The holiday season approached and Mr. Waterby made a resolution. He decided that if she would not permit him to spend a little money on himself he would not buy the customary Christmas present for her.

"Selfishness is a game at which two can play," he said.

Furthermore, he determined that if she asked him for any extra money for Christmas he would say: "I'm sorry, my dear, but I can't spare any. I am so hard up that I can't even afford to buy a few books I've been wanting a long time. Don't you remember that you told me that I couldn't afford to buy that set of Poe?"

Could anything be more biting as to sarcasm or more crushing as to logic?

He rehearsed this speech and had it all ready for her, and he pictured to himself her humiliation and surprise at discovering that he had some spirit after all and a considerable say-so whenever money was involved.

Unfortunately for his plan, she did not ask for any extra spending money, and so he had to rely on the other mode of punishment. He would withhold the expected Christmas present. In order that she might fully understand his purpose, he would give presents to both of the children.

It was a harsh measure, he admitted, but perhaps it would teach her to have some consideration for the wishes of others.

It must be said that Mr. Waterby was not wholly proud of his revenge when he arose on Christmas morning. He felt that he had accomplished his purpose, and he told himself that his motives had been good and pure, but still he was not satisfied with himself.

He went to the dining-room, and there on the table in front of his plate was a long paper box, containing ten books, each marked "Poe." It was the edition he had coveted.

"What's this?" he asked, winking slowly, for his mind could not grasp in one moment the fact of his awful shame.

"I should think you ought to know, Alfred," said Mrs. Waterby, flushed, and giggling like a schoolgirl.

"Oh, it was you——"

"My goodness, you've had me *so* frightened! That first day, when you spoke of buying them and I told you not to, I was just sure that you suspected something. I bought them a week before that."

"Yes—yes," said Mr. Waterby, feeling the saltwater in his eyes. At that moment he had the soul of a wretch being whipped at the stake.

"I was determined not to ask you for any money to pay for your own presents," Mrs. Waterby continued. "Do you know I had to save for you and the children out of my regular allowance. Why, last week I nearly starved you, and you never noticed it at all. I was afraid you would."

"No, I—didn't notice it," said Mr. Waterby, brokenly, for he was confused and giddy.

This self-sacrificing angel—and he had bought no Christmas present for her!

It was a fearful situation, and he lied his way out of it.

"How did you like *your* present?" he asked.

"Why, I haven't seen it yet," she said, looking across at him in surprise.

"You haven't? I told them to send it up yesterday."

The children were shouting and laughing over their gifts in the next room, and he felt it his duty to lie for their sake.

"Well, don't tell me what it is," interrupted Mrs. Waterby. "Wait until it comes."

"I'll go after it."

He did go after it, although he had to drag a jeweller away from his home on Christmas-day and have him open his great safe. The ring which he selected was beyond his means, it is true, but when a man has to buy back his self-respect, the price is never too high.

1903

O. HENRY

A Chaparral Christmas Gift

THE ORIGINAL CAUSE of the trouble was about twenty years in growing.

At the end of that time it was worth it.

Had you lived anywhere within fifty miles of Sundown Ranch you would have heard of it. It possessed a quantity of jet-black hair, a pair of extremely frank, deep-brown eyes and a laugh that rippled across the prairie like the sound of a hidden brook. The name of it was Rosita McMullen; and she was the daughter of old man McMullen of the Sundown Sheep Ranch.

There came riding on red roan steeds—or, to be more explicit, on a paint and a flea-bitten sorrel—two wooers. One was Madison Lane, and the other was the Frio Kid. But at that time they did not call him the Frio Kid, for he had not earned the honours of special nomenclature. His name was simply Johnny McRoy.

It must not be supposed that these two were the sum of the agreeable Rosita's admirers. The bronchos of a dozen others champed their bits at the long hitching rack of the Sundown Ranch. Many were the sheeps'-eyes that were cast in those savannas that did not belong to the flocks of Dan McMullen. But of all the cavaliers, Madison Lane and Johnny McRoy galloped far ahead, wherefore they are to be chronicled.

Madison Lane, a young cattleman from the Nueces country, won the race. He and Rosita were married one Christmas day. Armed, hilarious, vociferous, magnanimous, the cowmen and the sheepmen, laying aside their hereditary hatred, joined forces to celebrate the occasion.

Sundown Ranch was sonorous with the cracking of jokes and sixshooters, the shine of buckles and bright eyes, the outspoken congratulations of the herders of kine.

But while the wedding feast was at its liveliest there descended upon it Johnny McRoy, bitten by jealousy, like one possessed.

"I'll give you a Christmas present," he yelled, shrilly, at the door, with his .45 in his hand. Even then he had some reputation as an offhand shot.

His first bullet cut a neat underbit in Madison Lane's right ear. The barrel of his gun moved an inch. The next shot would have been the bride's had not Carson, a sheepman, possessed a mind with triggers somewhat well oiled and in repair. The guns of the wedding party had been hung, in their belts, upon nails in the wall when they sat at table, as a concession to good taste. But Carson, with great promptness, hurled his plate of roast venison and frijoles at McRoy, spoiling his aim. The second bullet, then, only shattered the white petals of a Spanish dagger flower suspended two feet above Rosita's head.

The guests spurned their chairs and jumped for their weapons. It was considered an improper act to shoot the bride and groom at a wedding. In about six seconds there were twenty or so bullets due to be whizzing in the direction of Mr. McRoy.

"I'll shoot better next time," yelled Johnny; "and there'll be a next time." He backed rapidly out the door.

Carson, the sheepman, spurred on to attempt further exploits by the success of his plate-throwing, was first to reach the door. McRoy's bullet from the darkness laid him low.

The cattlemen then swept out upon him, calling for vengeance, for, while the slaughter of a sheepman has not always lacked condonement, it was a decided misdemeanour in this instance. Carson was innocent; he was no accomplice at the matrimonial proceedings; nor had any one heard him quote the line "Christmas comes but once a year" to the guests.

But the sortie failed in its vengeance. McRoy was on his horse and away, shouting back curses and threats as he galloped into the concealing chaparral.

That night was the birthnight of the Frio Kid. He became the "bad man" of that portion of the State. The rejection of his suit by Miss McMullen turned him to a dangerous man. When officers went after him for the shooting of Carson, he killed two of them, and entered upon the life of an outlaw. He became a marvellous shot with either hand. He would turn up in towns and settlements, raise a quarrel at the slightest opportunity, pick off his man and laugh at the officers of the law. He was so cool, so deadly, so rapid, so inhumanly bloodthirsty that none but faint attempts were ever made to capture him. When he was at last shot and killed by a little one-armed Mexican who was nearly dead himself from fright, the Frio Kid had the deaths of eighteen men on his head. About half of these were killed in fair duels depending upon the quickness of the draw. The other half were men whom he assassinated from absolute wantonness and cruelty.

Many tales are told along the border of his impudent courage and daring. But he was not one of the breed of desperadoes who have seasons of generosity and even of softness. They say he never had mercy on the object of his anger. Yet at this and every Christmastide it is well to give each one credit, if it can be done, for whatever speck of good he may have possessed. If the Frio Kid ever did a kindly act or felt a throb of generosity in his heart it was once at such a time and season, and this is the way it happened.

One who has been crossed in love should never breathe the odour from the blossoms of the ratama tree. It stirs the memory to a dangerous degree.

One December in the Frio country there was a ratama tree in full bloom, for the winter had been as warm as springtime. That way rode the Frio Kid and his satellite and co-murderer, Mexican Frank. The kid reined in his mustang, and sat in his saddle, thoughtful and grim, with dangerously narrowing eyes. The rich, sweet scent touched him somewhere beneath his ice and iron.

"I don't know what I've been thinking about, Mex," he remarked in his usual mild drawl, "to have forgot all about a Christmas present I got to give. I'm going to ride over to-morrow night and shoot Madison Lane in his own house. He got my girl—Rosita would have had me if he hadn't cut into the game. I wonder why I happened to overlook it up to now?"

"Ah, shucks, Kid," said Mexican, "don't talk foolishness. You know you can't get within a mile of Mad Lane's house to-morrow night. I see old man Allen day before yesterday, and he says Mad is going to have Christmas doings at his house. You remember how you shot up the festivities when Mad was married, and about the threats you made? Don't you suppose Mad Lane'll kind of keep his eye open for a certain Mr. Kid? You plumb make me tired, Kid, with such remarks."

"I'm going," repeated the Frio Kid, without heat, "to go to Madison Lane's Christmas doings, and kill him. I ought to have done it a long time ago. Why, Mex, just two weeks ago I dreamed me and Rosita was married instead of her and him; and we was living in a house, and I could see her smiling at me, and—oh! h——l, Mex, he got her; and I'll get him—yes, sir, on Christmas Eve he got her, and then's when I'll get him."

"There's other ways of committing suicide," advised Mexican. "Why don't you go and surrender to the sheriff?"

"I'll get him," said the Kid.

Christmas Eve fell as balmy as April. Perhaps there was a hint of far-away frostiness in the air, but it tingled like seltzer, perfumed faintly with late prairie blossoms and the mesquite grass.

When night came the five or six rooms of the ranch-house were brightly lit. In one room was a Christmas tree, for the Lanes had a boy of three, and a dozen or more guests were expected from the nearer ranches.

At nightfall Madison Lane called aside Jim Belcher and three other cow-boys employed on his ranch.

"Now, boys," said Lane, "keep your eyes open. Walk around the house and watch the road well. All of you know the 'Frio Kid,' as they call him now, and if you see him, open fire on him without asking any questions. I'm not afraid of his coming around, but Rosita is. She's been afraid he'd come in on us every Christmas since we were married."

The guests had arrived in buckboards and on horseback, and were making themselves comfortable inside.

The evening went along pleasantly. The guests enjoyed and praised Rosita's excellent supper, and afterward the men scattered in groups about the rooms or on the broad "gallery," smoking and chatting.

The Christmas tree, of course, delighted the youngsters, and above all were they pleased when Santa Claus himself in magnificent white beard and furs appeared and began to distribute the toys.

"It's my papa," announced Billy Sampson, aged six. "I've seen him wear 'em before."

Berkly, a sheepman, an old friend of Lane, stopped Rosita as she was passing by him on the gallery, where he was sitting smoking.

"Well, Mrs. Lane," said he, "I suppose by this Christmas you've gotten over being afraid of that fellow McRoy, haven't you? Madison and I have talked about it, you know."

"Very nearly," said Rosita, smiling, "but I am still nervous sometimes. I shall never forget that awful time when he came so near to killing us."

"He's the most cold-hearted villain in the world," said Berkly. "The citizens all along the border ought to turn out and hunt him down like a wolf."

"He has committed awful crimes," said Rosita, "but—I—don't—know. I think there is a spot of good somewhere in everybody. He was not always bad—that I know."

Rosita turned into the hallway between the rooms. Santa Claus, in muffling whiskers and furs, was just coming through.

"I heard what you said through the window, Mrs. Lane," he said. "I was just going down in my pocket for a Christmas present for your husband. But I've left one for you, instead. It's in the room to your right."

"Oh, thank you, kind Santa Claus," said Rosita, brightly.

Rosita went into the room, while Santa Claus stepped into the cooler air of the yard.

She found no one in the room but Madison.

"Where is my present that Santa said he left for me in here?" she asked.

"Haven't seen anything in the way of a present," said her husband, laughing, "unless he could have meant me."

The next day Gabriel Radd, the foreman of the X O Ranch, dropped into the post-office at Loma Alta.

"Well, the Frio Kid's got his dose of lead at last," he remarked to the postmaster.

"That so? How'd it happen?"

"One of old Sanchez's Mexican sheep herders did it!—think of it! the Frio Kid killed by a sheep herder! The Greaser saw him riding along past his camp about twelve o'clock last night, and was so skeered that he up with a Winchester and let him have it. Funniest part of it was that the Kid was dressed all up with white Angora-skin whiskers and a regular Santy Claus rig-out from head to foot. Think of the Frio Kid playing Santy!"

1903

Charlotte Perkins Gilman

According to Solomon

"He that rebuketh a man afterwards shall find more favor than he that flattereth with his tongue," said Mr. Solomon Bankside to his wife Mary.

"It's the other way with a woman, I think;" she answered him, "you might put that in."

"Tut, tut, Molly," said he; "'Add not unto his words,'—do not speak lightly of the wisdom of the great king."

"I don't mean to, dear, but—when you hear it all the time"—

"'He that turneth away his ear from the law, even his prayer shall be an abomination,'" answered Mr. Bankside.

"I believe you know every one of those old Proverbs by heart," said his wife with some heat. "Now that's *not* disrespectful!—they *are* old!—and I do wish you'd forget some of them!"

He smiled at her quizzically, tossing back his heavy silver-gray hair with the gesture she had always loved. His eyes were deep blue and bright under their bushy brows; and the mouth was kind—in its iron way. "I can think of at least three to squelch you with, Molly," said he, "but I won't."

"O I know the one you want! 'A continual dropping in a very rainy day and a contentious woman are alike!' I'm *not* contentious, Solomon!"

"No, you are not," he frankly admitted. "What I really had in mind was this—'A prudent wife is from the Lord,' and 'He that findeth a wife findeth a good thing; and obtaineth favor of the Lord.'"

She ran around the table in the impulsive way years did not alter, and kissed him warmly.

"I'm not scolding you, my dear," he continued; "but if you had all the money you'd like to give away—there wouldn't be much left!"

"But look at what you spend on me!" she urged.

"That's a wise investment—as well as a deserved reward," her husband answered calmly. "'There is that scattereth and yet increaseth,' you know, my dear; 'And there is that withholdeth more than is meet—and it tendeth to poverty!' Take all you get my dear—it's none too good for you."

He gave her his goodby kiss with special fondness, put on his heavy satin-lined overcoat and went to the office.

Mr. Solomon Bankside was not a Jew; though his last name suggested and his first seemed to prove it; also his proficiency in the Old Testament gave color to the idea. No, he came from Vermont; of generations of unbroken New England and old English Puritan ancestry, where the Solomons and Isaacs and Zedekiahs were only mitigated by the Standfasts and Praise-the-Lords. Pious, persistent pig-headed folk were they, down all the line.

His wife had no such simple pedigree. A streak of Huguenot blood she had (some of the best in France, though neither of them knew that), a grandmother from Albany with a Van to her name; a great grandmother with a Mac; and another with an O'; even a German cross came in somewhere. Mr. Bankside was devoted to genealogy, and had been at some pains to dig up these facts—the more he found the worse he felt, and the lower ran his opinion of Mrs. Bankside's ancestry.

She had been a fascinating girl; pretty, with the dash and piquancy of an oriole in a May apple-tree; clever and efficient in everything her swift hands touched; quite a spectacular housekeeper; and the sober, long-faced young downeasterner had married her with a sudden decision that he often wondered about in later years. So did she.

What he had not sufficiently weighed at the time, was her spirit of incorrigible independence, and a light-mindedness which, on maturer judgment, he could almost term irreligious. His conduct was based on principle, all of it; built firmly into habit and buttressed by scriptural quotations. Hers seemed to him as inconsequent as the flight of a moth. Studying it, in his solemn conscientious way, in the light of his genealogical researches, he felt that all her uncertainties were accounted for, and that the error was his—in having married too many kinds of people at once.

They had been, and were, very happy together none the less: though sometimes their happiness was a little tottery. This was one of the times. It was the day after Christmas, and Mrs. Bankside entered the big drawing room, redolent of popcorn and evergreen, and walked slowly to the corner where the fruits of yesterday were lovingly arranged; so few that she had been able to give—so many that she had received.

There were the numerous pretty interchangeable things given her by her many friends; "presents," suitable to any lady. There were the few perfectly selected ones given by the few who knew her best. There was the rather perplexing gift of Mrs. MacAvelly. There was her brother's stiff white envelope enclosing a check. There were the loving gifts of children and grand-children.

Finally there was Solomon's.

It was his custom to bestow upon her one solemn and expensive object, a boon as it were, carefully selected, after much thought and balancing of merits; but the consideration was spent on the nature of the gift—not on the desires of the recipient. There was the piano she could not play, the statue she did not admire, the set of Dante she never read, the heavy gold bracelet, the stiff diamond brooch—and all the others. This time it was a set of sables, costing even more than she imagined.

Christmas after Christmas had these things come to her; and she stood there now, thinking of that procession of unvalued valuables, with an expression so mixed and changeful it resembled a kaleidoscope. Love for Solomon, pride in Solomon, respect for Solomon's judgment and power to pay, gratitude for his unfailing kindness and generosity, impatience with his always giving her this one big valuable permanent thing, when he knew so well that she much preferred small renewable cheap ones; her personal dislike of furs, the painful conviction that brown was not becoming to her—all these and more filled the little woman with what used to be called "conflicting emotions."

She smoothed out her brother's check, wishing as she always did that it had come before Christmas, so that she might buy more presents for her beloved people. Solomon liked to spend money on her—in his own way; but he did not like to have her spend money on him—or on anyone for that matter. She had asked her brother once, if he would mind sending her his Christmas present beforehand.

"Not on your life, Polly!" he said. "You'd never see a cent of it! You can't buy 'em many things right on top of Christmas, and it'll be gone long before the next one."

She put the check away and turned to examine her queerest gift. Upon which scrutiny presently entered the donor.

"I'm ever so much obliged, Benigna," said Mrs. Bankside. "You know how I love to do things. It's a loom, isn't it? Can you show me how it works?"

"Of course I can, my dear; that's just what I ran in for—I was afraid you wouldn't know. But you are so clever with your hands that I'm sure you'll enjoy it. I do."

Whereat Mrs. MacAvelly taught Mrs. Bankside the time-honored art of weaving. And Mrs. Bankside enjoyed it more than any previous handicraft she had essayed.

She did it well, beginning with rather coarse and simple weaves; and gradually learning the finer grades of work. Despising as she did the more modern woolens, she bought real wool yarn of a lovely red—and made some light warm flannelly stuff in which she proceeded to rapturously enclose her little grandchildren.

Mr. Bankside warmly approved, murmuring affectionately, "'She seeketh wool and flax—she worketh willingly with her hands.'"

He watched little Bob and Polly strenuously "helping" the furnace man to clear the sidewalk, hopping about like red-birds in their new caps and coats; and his face beamed with the appositeness of his quotation, as he remarked, "'She is not afraid of the snow for her household, for all her household are clothed with scarlet!'" and he proffered an extra, wholly spontaneous kiss, which pleased her mightily.

"You dear man!" she said with a hug; "I believe you'd rather find a proverb to fit than a gold mine!"

To which he triumphantly responded: "'Wisdom is better than rubies; and all the things that may be desired are not to be compared to it.'"

She laughed sweetly at him. "And do you think wisdom stopped with that string of proverbs?"

"You can't get much beyond it," he answered calmly. "If we lived up to all there is in that list we shouldn't be far out, my dear!"

Whereat she laughed again, smoothed his gray mane, and kissed him in the back of his neck. "You *dear* thing!" said Mrs. Bankside.

She kept herself busy with the new plaything as he called it. Hands that had been rather empty were now smoothly full. Her health was better, and any hint of occasional querulousness disappeared entirely; so that her husband was moved to fresh admiration of her sunny temper, and quoted for the hundredth time, "'She openeth her mouth with wisdom, and in her tongue is the law of kindness.'"

Mrs. MacAvelly taught her to make towels. But Mrs. Bankside's skill outstripped hers; she showed inventive genius and designed patterns of her own. The fineness and quality of the work increased; and she joyfully replenished her linen chest with her own handiwork.

"I tell you, my dear," said Mrs. MacAvelly, "if you'd be willing to sell them you could get almost *any* price for those towels. With the initials woven in. I know I could get you orders—through the Woman's Exchange, you know!"

Mrs. Bankside was delighted. "What fun!" she said. "And I needn't appear at all?"

"No, you needn't appear at all—do let me try."

So Mrs. Bankside made towels of price, soft, fine, and splendid, till she was weary of them; and in the opulence of constructive genius fell to devising woven belts of elaborate design.

These were admired excessively. All her women friends wanted one, or more; the Exchange got hold of it, there was a distinct demand; and finally Mrs. MacAvelly came in one day with a very important air and a special order.

"I don't know what you'll think, my dear," she said, "but I happen to know the Percys very well—the big store people, you know; and Mr. Percy was talking about those belts of yours to me;—of course he didn't know they are yours; but he said (the Exchange people told him I knew, you see) he said, 'If you can place an order with that woman, I can take all she'll make and pay her full price for them. Is she poor?' he asked. 'Is she dependent on her work?' And I told him, 'Not altogether.' And I think he thinks it an interesting case! Anyhow, there's the order. Will you do it?"

Mrs. Bankside was much excited. She wanted to very much, but dreaded offending her husband. So far she had not told him of her quiet trade in towels; but hid and saved this precious money—the first she had ever earned.

The two friends discussed the pros and cons at considerable length; and finally with some perturbation, she decided to accept the order.

"You'll never tell, Benigna!" she urged. "Solomon would never forgive me, I'm afraid."

"Why of course I won't—you needn't have a moment's fear of it. You give them to me—I'll stop with the carriage you see; and I take them to the Exchange—and he gets them from there."

"It seems like smuggling!" said Mrs. Bankside delightedly. "I always did love to smuggle!"

"They say women have no conscience about laws, don't they?" Mrs. MacAvelly suggested.

"Why should we?" answered her friend. "We don't make 'em—nor God—nor nature. Why on earth should we respect a set of silly rules made by some men one day and changed by some more the next?"

"Bless us, Polly! Do you talk to Mr. Bankside like that?"

"Indeed I don't!" answered her hostess, holding out a particularly beautiful star-patterned belt to show to advantage. "There are lots of things I don't say to Mr. Bankside—'A man of understanding holdeth his peace' you know—or a woman."

She was a pretty creature, her hair like that of a powdered marchioness, her rosy cheeks and firm slight figure suggesting a charmer in Dresden china.

Mrs. MacAvelly regarded her admiringly. "'Where there is no wood the fire goeth out; so where there is no tale bearer the strife ceaseth,'" she proudly offered, "I can quote that much myself."

But Mrs. Bankside had many misgivings as she pursued her audacious way; the busy hours flying away from her, and the always astonishing checks flying toward her in gratifying accumulation. She came down to her well-planned dinners gracious and sweet; always effectively dressed; spent the cosy quiet evenings with her husband, or went out with him, with a manner of such increased tenderness and charm that his heart warmed anew to the wife of his youth; and he even relented a little toward her miscellaneous ancestors.

As the days shortened and darkened she sparkled more and more; with little snatches of song now and then; gay ineffectual strumming on the big piano; sudden affectionate darts at him, with quaintly distributed caresses.

"Molly!" said he, "I don't believe you're a day over twenty! What makes you act so?"

"Don't you like it, So?" she asked him. That was the nearest she ever would approximate to his name.

He did like it, naturally, and even gave her an extra ten dollars to buy Christmas presents with; while he meditated giving her an electric runabout;—to her!—who was afraid of a wheelbarrow!

When the day arrived and the family were gathered together, Mrs. Bankside, wearing the diamond brooch, the gold bracelet, the point lace handkerchief—everything she could carry of his accumulated generosity— and such an air of triumphant mystery that the tree itself was dim beside her; handed out to her astonished relatives such an assortment of desirable articles that they found no words to express their gratitude.

"Why, *Mother!*" said Jessie, whose husband was a minister and salaried as such, "Why, *Mother*—how did you know we wanted just that kind of a rug!—and a sewing-machine *too*! And this lovely suit—and—and—why *Mother!*"

But her son-in-law took her aside and kissed her solemnly. He had wanted that particular set of sociological books for years—and never hoped to get them; or that bunch of magazines either.

Nellie had "married rich"; she was less ostentatiously favored; but she had shown her thankfulness a week ago—when her mother had handed her a check.

"Sh, sh! my dear!" her mother had said, "Not one word. I know! What pleasant weather we're having."

This son-in-law was agreeably surprised, too; and the other relatives, married and single; while the children rioted among their tools and toys, taking this Christmas like any other, as a season of unmitigated joy.

Mr. Solomon Bankside looked on with growing amazement, making computations in his practiced mind; saying nothing whatever. Should he criticize his wife before others?

But when his turn came—when gifts upon gifts were offered to him— sets of silken handkerchiefs (he couldn't bear the touch of a silk handker-chief!), a cabinet of cards and chips and counters of all sorts (he never played cards), an inlaid chess-table and ivory men (the game was unknown to him), a gorgeous scarf-pin (he abominated jewelery), a five pound box of candy (he never ate it), his feelings so mounted within him, that since he would not express and could not repress them, he summarily went up stairs to his room.

She found him there later, coming in blushing, smiling, crying a little too—like a naughty but charming child.

He swallowed hard as he looked at her; and his voice was a little strained.

"I can take a joke as well as any man, Molly. I guess we're square on that. But—my dear!—where did you get it?"

"Earned it," said she, looking down, and fingering her lace handkerchief.

"Earned it! My wife, earning money! How—if I may ask?"

"By my weaving, dear—the towels and the belts—I sold 'em. Don't be angry—nobody knows—my name didn't appear at all! Please don't be angry!—It isn't wicked, and it was such fun!"

"No—it's not wicked, I suppose," said he rather grimly. "But it is certainly a most mortifying and painful thing to me—most unprecedented."

"Not so unprecedented, Dear," she urged, "Even the woman you think most of did it! Don't you remember 'She maketh fine linen and selleth it— and delivereth girdles unto the merchants!'"

Mr. Bankside came down handsomely.

He got used to it after a while, and then he became proud of it. If a friend ventured to suggest a criticism, or to sympathize, he would calmly respond,

"'The heart of her husband doth safely trust in her, so that he shall have no need of spoil. Give her of the fruit of her hands, and let her own works praise her in the gates.'"

1909

The Picture Puzzle

I

O F COURSE the instinct of the police and detectives was to run down their game. That was natural. They seemed astonished and contemptuous when I urged that all I wanted was my baby; whether the kidnappers were ever caught or not made no difference to me. They kept arguing that unless precautions were taken the criminals would escape and I kept arguing that if they became suspicious of a trap they would keep away and my only chance to recover our little girl would be gone forever. They finally agreed and I believe they kept their promise to me. Helen always felt the other way and maintained that their watchers frightened off whoever was to meet me. Anyhow I waited in vain, waited for hours, waited again the next day and the next and the next. We put advertisements in countless papers, offering rewards and immunity, but never heard anything more.

I pulled myself together in a sort of a way and tried to do my work. My partner and clerks were very kind. I don't believe I ever did anything properly in those days, but no one ever brought any blunder to my attention. If they came across any they set it right for me. And at the office it was not so bad. Trying to work was good for me. It was worse at home and worse at night. I slept hardly at all.

Helen, if possible, slept less than I. And she had terrible spasms of sobs that shook the bed. She would try to choke them down, thinking I was asleep and she might wake me. But she never went through a night without at least one frightful paroxysm of tears.

In the daylight she controlled herself better, made a heart-breaking and yet heart-warming effort at her normal cheeriness over the breakfast things, and greeted me beautifully when I came home. But the moment we were alone for the evening she would break down.

I don't know how many days that sort of thing kept up. I sympathized in silence. It was Helen herself who suggested that we must force ourselves to be diverted, somehow. The theater was out of the question. Not merely the sight of a four-year-old girl with yellow locks threw Helen into a passion of uncontrollable sobbing, but all sorts of unexpected trifles reminded her of Amy and affected her almost as much. Confined to our home we tried cards, chess and everything else we could think of. They helped her as little as they helped me.

Then one afternoon Helen did not come to greet me. Instead as I came in I heard her call, quite in her natural voice.

"Oh, I'm so glad that is you. Come and help me."

I found her seated at the library table, her back to the door. She had on a pink wrapper and her shoulders had no despondent droop, but a girlish alertness. She barely turned her head as I entered, but her profile showed no signs of recent weeping. Her face was its natural color.

"Come and help me," she repeated. "I can't find the other piece of the boat."

She was absorbed, positively absorbed in a picture puzzle.

In forty seconds I was absorbed too. It must have been six minutes before we identified the last piece of the boat. And then we went on with the sky and were still at it when the butler announced dinner.

"Where did you get it?" I asked, over the soup, which Helen really ate.

"Mrs. Allstone brought it," Helen replied, "just before lunch."

I blessed Mrs. Allstone.

Really it seems absurd, but those idiotic jig-saw puzzles were our salvation. They actually took our minds off everything else. At first I dreaded finishing one. No sooner was the last piece in place than I felt a sudden revulsion, a booming of blood in my ears, and the sense of loss and misery rushed over me like a wave of scalding water. And I knew it was worse for Helen.

But after some days each seemed not merely a respite from pain, but a sedative as well. After a two hours' struggle with a fascinating tangle of shapes and colors, we seemed numb to our bereavement and the bitterness of the smart seemed blunted.

We grew fastidious as to manufacture and finish; learned to avoid crude and clumsy products as bores; developed a pronounced taste for pictures neither too soft nor too plain in color-masses; and became connoisseurs as to cutting, utterly above the obvious and entirely disenchanted with the painfully difficult. We evolved into adepts, quick to recoil from fragments barren of any clue of shape or markings and equally prompt to reject those whose meaning was too definite and insistent. We trod delicately the middle way among segments not one of which was without some clue of outline or tint, and not one of which imparted its message without interrogation, inference and reflection.

Helen used to time herself and try the same puzzle over and over on successive days until she could do it in less than half an hour. She declared that a really good puzzle was interesting the fourth or fifth time and that an especially fine puzzle was diverting if turned face down and put together from the shapes merely, after it had been well learned the other way. I did not enter into the craze to that extent, but sometimes tried her methods for variety.

We really slept, and Helen, though worn and thin, was not abject, not agonized. Her nights passed, if not wholly without tears, yet with only those soft and silent tears, which are more a relief than suffering. With me she was nearly her old self and very brave and patient. She greeted me naturally and we seemed able to go on living.

Then one day she was not at the door to welcome me. I had hardly shut it before I heard her sobbing. I found her again at the library table and over a puzzle. But this time she had just finished it and was bowed over it on the table, shaken all over by her grief.

She lifted her head from her crossed arms, pointed and buried her face in her hands. I understood. The picture I remembered from a magazine of the year before: a Christmas tree with a bevy of children about it and one (we had remarked it at the time) a perfect likeness of our Amy.

As she rocked back and forth, her hands over her eyes, I swept the pieces into their box and put on the lid.

Presently Helen dried her eyes and looked at the table.

"Oh! why did you touch it," she wailed. "It was such a comfort to me."

"You did not seem comforted," I retorted. "I thought the contrast: . . ." I stopped.

"You mean the contrast between the Christmas we expected and the Christmas we are going to have?" she queried. "You mean you thought that was too much for me?"

I nodded.

"It wasn't that at all," she averred. "I was crying for joy. That picture was a sign."

"A sign?" I repeated.

"Yes," she declared, "a sign that we shall get her back in time for Christmas. I'm going to start and get ready right away."

At first I was glad of the diversion. Helen had the nursery put in order as if she expected Amy the next day, hauled over all the child's clothes and was in a bustling state of happy expectancy. She went vigorously about her preparation for a Christmas celebration, planned a Christmas Eve dinner for our brothers and sisters and their husbands and wives, and a children's party afterwards with a big tree and a profusion of goodies and gifts.

"You see," she explained, "everyone will want their own Christmas at home. So shall we, for we'll just want to gloat over Amy all day. We won't want them on Christmas any more than they'll want us. But this way we can all be together and celebrate and rejoice over our good luck."

She was as elated and convinced as if it was a certainty. For a while her occupation with preparations was good for her, but she was so forehanded that she was ready a week ahead of time and had not a detail left to arrange. I dreaded a reaction, but her artificial exaltation continued unabated. All the more I feared the inevitable disappointment and was genuinely concerned for her reason. The fixed idea that that accidental coincidence was a prophecy and a guarantee dominated her totally. I was really afraid that the shock of the reality might kill her. I did not want to dissipate her happy delusion, but I could not but try to prepare her for the certain blow. I talked cautiously in wide circles around what I wanted and I did not want to say.

II

On December 22nd, I came home early, just after lunch, in fact. Helen met me, at the door, with such a demeanor of suppressed high spirits, happy secrecy and tingling anticipation that for one moment I was certain Amy had been found and was then in the house.

"I've something wonderful to show you," Helen declared, and led me to the library.

There on the table was a picture-puzzle fitted together.

She stood and pointed to it with the air of exhibiting a marvel.

I looked at it but could not conjecture the cause of her excitement. The pieces seemed too large, too clumsy and too uniform in outline. It looked a crude and clumsy puzzle, beneath her notice.

"Why did you buy it?" I asked.

"I met a peddler on the street," she answered, "and he was so wretched-looking, I was sorry for him. He was young and thin and looked haggard and consumptive. I looked at him and I suppose I showed my feelings. He said:

"Lady, buy a puzzle. It will help you to your heart's desire."

"His words were so odd I bought it, and now just look at what it is."

I was groping for some foothold upon which to rally my thoughts.

"Let me see the box in which it came," I asked.

She produced it and I read on the top:

"GUGGENHEIM'S DOUBLE PICTURE PUZZLE.

TWO IN ONE.

MOST FOR THE MONEY.

ASK FOR GUGGENHEIM'S"

And on the end—

"ASTRAY.

A BREATH OF AIR.

50 CENTS."

"It's queer," Helen remarked. "But it is not a double puzzle at all, though the pieces have the same paper on both sides. One side is blank. I suppose this is ASTRAY. Don't you think so?"

"Astray?" I queried, puzzled.

"Oh," she cried, in a disappointed, disheartened, almost querulous tone. "I thought you would be so much struck with the resemblance. You don't seem to notice it at all. Why even the dress is identical!"

"The dress?" I repeated. "How many times have you done this?"

"Only this once," she said. "I had just finished it when I heard your key in the lock."

"I should have thought," I commented, "that it would have been more interesting to do it face up first."

"Face up!" She cried. "It is face up."

Her air of scornful superiority completely shook me out of my sedulous consideration of a moment before.

"Nonsense," I said, "that's the back of the puzzle. There are no colors there. It's all pink."

"Pink!" she exclaimed pointing. "Do you call that pink!"

"Certainly it's pink," I asserted.

"Don't you see there the white of the old man's beard," she queried, pointing again. "And there the black of his boots? And there the red of the little girl's dress?"

"No," I declared. "I don't see anything of the kind. It's all pink. There isn't any picture there at all."

"No picture!" she cried. "Don't you see the old man leading the child by the hand?"

"No," I said harshly, "I don't see any picture and you know I don't. There isn't any picture there. I can't make out what you are driving at. It seems a senseless joke."

"Joke! I joke!" Helen half whispered. The tears came into her eyes.

"You are cruel," she said, "and I thought you would be struck by the resemblance."

I was overwhelmed by a pang of self-reproach, solicitude and terror.

"Resemblance to what?" I asked gently.

"Can't you see it?" she insisted.

"Tell me," I pleaded. "Show me just what you want me to notice most."

"The child," she said pointing, "is just exactly Amy and the dress is the very red suit she had on when——"

"Dear," I said, "try to collect yourself. Indeed you only imagine what you tell me. There is no picture on this side of the sections. The whole thing is pink. That is the back of the puzzle."

"I don't see how you can say such a thing," she raged at me. "I can't make out why you should. What sort of a test are you putting me through? What does it all mean?"

"Will you let me prove to you that this is the back of the puzzle?" I asked.

"If you can," she said shortly.

I turned the pieces of the puzzle over, keeping them together as much as possible. I succeeded pretty well with the outer pieces and soon had the rectangle in place. The inner pieces were a good deal mixed up, but even before I had fitted them I exclaimed:

"There look at that!"

"Well," she asked. "What do you expect me to see?"

"What do you see?" I asked in turn.

"I see the back of a puzzle," she answered.

"Don't you see those front steps?" I demanded, pointing.

"I don't see anything," she asserted, "except green."

"Do you call that green?" I queried pointing.

"I do," she declared.

"Don't you see the brickwork front of the house?" I insisted, "and the lower part of a window and part of a door. Yes and those front-steps in the corner?"

"I don't see anything of the kind," she asseverated. "Any more than you do. What I see is just what you see. It's the back of the puzzle, all pale green."

I had been feverishly putting together the last pieces as she spoke. I could not believe my eyes and, as the last piece fitted in, was struck with amazement.

The picture showed an old red-brick house, with brown blinds, all open. The top of the front steps was included in the lower right hand corner, most of the front door above them, all of one window on its level, and the side of another. Above appeared all of one of the second floor windows, and parts of those to right and left of it. The other windows were closed, but the sash of the middle one was raised and from it leaned a little girl, a child with frowzy hair, a dirty face and wearing a blue and white check frock. The child was a perfect likeness of our lost Amy, supposing she had been starved and neglected. I was so affected that I was afraid I should faint. I was positively husky when I asked:

"Don't you see that?"

"I see Nile green," she maintained. "The same as you see."

I swept the pieces into the box.

"We are neither of us well," I said.

"I should think you must be deranged to behave so," she snapped, "and it is no wonder I am not well the way you treat me."

"How could I know what you wanted me to see?" I began.

"Wanted you to see!" she cried. "You keep it up? You pretend you didn't see it, after all? Oh! I have no patience with you."

She burst into tears, fled upstairs and I heard her slam and lock our bedroom door.

I put that puzzle together again and the likeness of that hungry, filthy child in the picture to our Amy made my heart ache.

I found a stout box, cut two pieces of straw-board just the shape of the puzzle and a trifle larger, laid one on top of it and slid the other under it. Then I tied it together with string and wrapped it in paper and tied the whole.

I put the box in my overcoat pocket and went out carrying the flat parcel.

I walked round to MacIntyre's.

I told him the whole story and showed him the puzzle.

"Do you want the truth?" he asked.

"Just that," I said.

"Well," he reported. "You are as overstrung as she is and the same way. There is absolutely no picture on either side of this. One side is solid green and the other solid pink."

"How about the coincidence of the names on the box?" I interjected. "One suited what I saw, one what she said she saw."

"Let's look at the box," he suggested.

He looked at it on all sides.

"There's not a letter on it," he announced. "Except 'picture puzzle' on top and '50 cents' on the end."

"I don't feel insane," I declared.

"You aren't," he reassured me. "Nor in any danger of being insane. Let me look you over."

He felt my pulse, looked at my tongue, examined both eyes with his oph-thalmoscope, and took a drop of my blood.

"I'll report further," he said, "in confirmation to-morrow. You're all right, or nearly so, and you'll soon be really all right. All you need is a little rest. Don't worry about this idea of your wife's, humor her. There won't be any terrible consequences. After Christmas go to Florida or somewhere for a week or so. And don't exert yourself from now till after that change."

When I reached home, I went down into the cellar, threw that puzzle and its box into the furnace and stood and watched it burn to ashes.

III

When I came upstairs from the furnace Helen met me as if nothing had happened. By one of her sudden revulsions of mood she was even more gracious than usual, and was at dinner altogether charming. She did not refer to our quarrel or to the puzzle.

The next morning over our breakfast we were both opening our mail. I had told her that I should not go to the office until after Christmas and that I wanted her to arrange for a little tour that would please her. I had phoned to the office not to expect me until after New Year's.

My mail contained nothing of moment.

Helen looked up from hers with an expression curiously mingled of dis-appointment, concern and a pleased smile.

"It is so fortunate you have nothing to do," she said. "I spent four whole days choosing toys and favors and found most of those I selected at Bleich's. They were to have been delivered day before yesterday but they did not come. I telephoned yesterday and they said they would try to trace them. Here is a letter saying that the whole lot was missent out to Roundwood. You noticed that Roundwood station burned Monday night. They were all burnt up. Now I'll have to go and find more like them. You can go with me."

I went.

The two days were a strange mixture of sensations and emotions.

Helen had picked over Bleich's stock pretty carefully and could duplicate from it few of the burned articles, could find acceptable substitutes for fewer. There followed an exhausting pursuit of the unattainable through a bewildering series of toy-shops and department-stores. We spent most of our time at counters and much of the remainder in a taxicab.

In a way it was very trying. I did not mind the smells and bad air and other mere physical discomforts. But the mental strain continually intensified. Helen's confidence that Amy would be restored to us was steadily waning and her outward exhibition of it was becoming more and more artificial, and consciously sustained, and more and more of an effort. She was coming to foresee, in spite of herself, that our Christmas celebration would be a most terrible mockery of our bereavement. She was forcing herself not to confess it to herself and not to show it to me. The strain told on her. It told on me to watch it, to see the inevitable crash coming nearer and nearer and to try to put away from myself the pictures of her collapse, of her probable loss of reason, of her possible death, which my imagination kept thrusting before me.

On the other hand Helen was to all appearance, if one had no prevision by which to read her, her most charming self. Her manner to shop-girls and other sales-people was a delight to watch. Her little speeches to me were full of her girlish whimsicality and unexpectedness. Her good will towards all the world, her resolution that everything must come right and would come right haloed her in a sort of aureole of romance. Our lunches were ideal hours, full of the atmosphere of courtship, of lovemaking, of exquisite companionship. In spite of my forebodings, I caught the contagion of the Christmas shopping crowds; in spite of her self-deception Helen revelled in it. The purpose to make as many people as possible as happy as might be irradiated Helen with the light of fairyland; her resolve to be happy herself in spite of everything made her a sort of fairy queen. I found myself less and less anxious and more and more almost expectant. I knew Helen was looking for Amy every instant. I found myself in the same state of mind.

Our lunch on Christmas Eve was a strange blend of artificiality and genuine exhilaration. After it we had but one purchase to make.

"We are in no hurry," Helen said. "Let's take a horse-hansom for old sake's sake."

In it we were like boy and girl together until the jeweler's was reached.

There gloom, in spite of us, settled down over our hopes and feelings. Helen walked to the hansom like a gray ghost. Like the whisper of some far-off stranger I heard myself order the driver to take us home.

In the hansom we sat silent, looking straight in front of us at nothing. I stole a glance at Helen and saw a tear in the corner of her eye. I sat choking.

All at once she seized my hand.

"Look!" she exclaimed, "Look!"

I looked where she pointed, but discerned nothing to account for her excitement.

"What is it?" I queried.

"The old man!" she exclaimed.

"What old man?" I asked bewildered.

"The old man on the puzzle," she told me. "The old man who was leading Amy."

Then I was sure she was demented. To humor her I asked:

"The old man with the brown coat?"

"Yes," she said eagerly. "The old man with the long gray hair over his collar."

"With the walking stick?" I inquired.

"Yes," she answered. "With the crooked walking stick."

I saw him too! This was no figment of Helen's imagination.

It was absurd of course, but my eagerness caught fire from hers. I credited the absurdity. In what sort of vision it mattered not she had seen an old man like this leading our lost Amy.

I spoke to the driver, pointed out to him the old man, told him to follow him without attracting his attention and offered him anything he asked to keep him in sight.

Helen became possessed with the idea that we should lose sight of the old man in the crowds. Nothing would do but we must get out and follow him on foot. I remonstrated that we were much more likely to lose sight of him that way, and still more likely to attract his notice, which would be worse than losing him. She insisted and I told the man to keep us in view.

A weary walk we had, though most of it was mere strolling after a tottering figure or loitering about shops he entered.

It was near dusk and full time for us to be at home when he began to walk fast. So fast he drew away from us in spite of us. He turned a corner a half a square ahead of us. When we turned into that street he was nowhere to be seen.

Helen was ready to faint with disappointment. With no hope of helping her, but some instinctive idea of postponing the evil moment I urged her to walk on, saying that perhaps we might see him. About the middle of the square I suddenly stood still.

"What is the matter?" Helen asked.

"The house!" I said.

"What house?" she queried.

"The house in the puzzle picture," I explained. "The house where I saw Amy at the window."

Of course she had not seen any house on the puzzle, but she caught at the last straw of hope.

It was a poor neighborhood of crowded tenements, not quite a slum, yet dirty and unkempt and full of poor folks.

The house door was shut, I could find no sign of any bell. I knocked. No one answered. I tried the door. It was not fastened and we entered a dirty hallway, cold and damp and smelling repulsively. A fat woman stuck her head out of a door and jabbered at us in an unknown tongue. A man with a fez on his greasy black hair came from the back of the hallway and was equally unintelligible.

"Does nobody here speak English?" I asked.

The answer was as incomprehensible as before.

I made to go up the stairs.

The man, and the woman, who was now standing before her door, both chattered at once, but neither made any attempt to stop me. They waved vaguely explanatory, deprecating hands towards the blackness of the stairway. We went up.

On the second floor landing we saw just the old man we had been following.

He stared at us when I spoke to him.

"Son-in-law," he said, "son-in-law."

He called and a door opened. An oldish woman answered him in apparently the same jargon. Behind was a young woman holding a baby.

"What is it?" she asked with a great deal of accent but intelligibly.

Three or four children held on by her skirts.

Behind her I saw a little girl in a blue-check dress.

Helen screamed.

IV

The people turned out to be refugees from the settlement about the sacked German Mission at Dehkhargan near Tabriz, Christianized Persians, such stupid villagers that they had never thought or had been incapable of reporting their find to the police, so ignorant that they knew nothing of rewards or advertisements, such simple-hearted folk that they had shared their narrow quarters and scanty fare with the unknown waif their grandfather had found wandering alone, after dark, months before.

Amy, when we had leisure to ask questions and hear her experiences, declared they had treated her as they treated their own children. She could give no description of her kidnappers except that the woman had on a hat with roses in it and the man had a little yellow mustache. She could not tell how long they had kept her nor why they had left her to wander in the streets at night.

It needed no common language, far less any legal proof, to convince Amy's hosts that she belonged to us. I had a pocket full of Christmas money, new five and ten dollar gold pieces and bright silver quarters for the servants and children. I filled the old grandfather's hands and plainly overwhelmed him. They all jabbered at us, blessings, if I judged the tone right. I tried to tell the young woman we should see them again in a day or two and I gave her a card to make sure.

I told the cabman to stop the first taxicab he should see empty. In the hansom we hugged Amy alternately and hugged each other.

Once in the taxicab we were home in half an hour; more, much more than half an hour late. Helen whisked Amy in by the servants' door and flew upstairs with her by the back way. I faced a perturbed and anxious parlorful of interrogative relatives and in-laws.

"You'll know before many minutes," I said, "why we were both out and are in late. Helen will want to surprise you and I'll say nothing to spoil the effect."

Nothing I could have said would have spoiled the effect because they would not have believed me. As it was Helen came in sooner than I could have thought possible, looking her best and accurately playing the formal hostess with a feeble attempt at a surprise in store.

The dinner was a great success, with much laughter and high spirits, everybody carried away by Helen's sallies and everybody amazed that she could be so gay.

"I cannot understand," Paul's wife whispered to me, "how she can ever get through the party. It would kill me in her place."

"It won't kill her," I said confidently. "You may be sure of that."

The children had arrived to the number of more than thirty and only the inevitably late Amstelhuysens had not come. Helen announced that she would not wait for them.

"The tree is lighted," she said. "We'll have the doors thrown open and go in."

We were all gathered in the front parlor. The twins panted in at the last instant. The grown-ups were pulling motto-crackers and the children were throwing confetti. The doors opened, the tree filled all the back of the room. The candles blazed and twinkled. And in front of it, in a simple little white dress, with a fairy's wand in her hand, tipped with a silver star, clean, healthy-looking and full of spirits was Amy, the fairy of the hour.

1909

A Christmas Party

THAT PREVENTED A SPLIT IN THE CHURCH

PART I

"GOODNESS," EXCLAIMED MILLY BROWN. "All these things to move and dust, they're a sight and if I had my way, I'd get rid of some of them. No single man needs all this trash around, especially a minister."

"Always getting rid of something," said Sara Simpson, "I declare you are the limit; perhaps you'll want to be getting rid of your daughter Alice—now we are having a new minister and he a single man."

"I guess you are the one who'll be wanting the minister to marry them," laughed Milly. But Sara Simpson did not see the joke, you see Sara was past thirty—and did not like it mentioned—had a lovely home in town and everybody knew she was sore at Mrs. Jake Todd because Jake preferred her when she was Margaret Clayton instead of Sara Simpson—whose father was the leading lawyer in town and who gave his wife and daughter anything they wanted.

Sara was a pretty girl but Margery was much prettier and had such a sweet disposition that everybody loved her, even if she did have to wear cheap cotton dresses—and her hats and coats two winters and couldn't afford furs. But Sara snubbed poor Margery every chance she got and poor Milly Brown also—because she was Margery's friend.

Mrs. Milly Brown was a widow with only one daughter who lived beyond the town a lonely way and made her living by doing plain sewing.

You see there was only one church in this very small town—you or I would call it a village—which would surely have insulted the small population of St. Michaels because they felt themselves very important people and more especially now—as they were able to support a minister by themselves.

No more circuit riding minister for them. Since attaining the dignity of supporting a minister and having a parsonage rent free—they had organized a Mite Society for the grown people and a Helping Hand Society for the young folks and a Sunday afternoon Literary Society, hence the self-satisfied feeling among them.

Their last pastor had been a married man with a large family, a wife and six children, and the poor man had had so much trouble and such poor charges (which is the fate of a good many Methodist ministers) that he felt after he got to St. Michaels that he should take a rest, and he rested so well, and so long, that the people sent the Bishop word they did not want him back. So the good Bishop had now sent them not only a young man, but a single one, and St. Michaels folks were going out of their way to make things pleasant for the new minister.

He was very young and considered a genius, and as St. Michaels always gave the parsonage ready furnished and found the good parson coal and wood—it felt as this was a young man they could go a step farther and stock his pantry with all things needful and have him a good housekeeper, so they had installed old Aunt Eliza West as his housekeeper.

There had been a meeting of the Ladies' Aid Society, and a Committee appointed to get things in readiness for the pastor's arrival.

The Board of Trustees and Board of Stewards had also held meetings, but the Ladies' Aid had taken things in their hands and the men were well content to step aside and let them do the work—as most of their wives belonged to the Aid Society and those whose wives did not, thought it good policy to not object.

So there was just lots of help—because as Mrs. Orion Tucker remarked, "Wherever they had a married minister all the women stayed at home except a few old stand-bys—who could always be depended on, but if he was a single man, every spinster and young girl and married woman in the town was in evidence to help, they had all they needed and more."

So they scrubbed floors—cleaned paints and windows—and swept and dusted and polished dishes and silver until it seemed as tho the things would surely come to life and cry out—enough! oh, enough! or melt into nothing.

At last everything was in readiness and St. Michaels was in a state of expectancy.

Only Brother Tucker and Sister Marion Ford had attended the conference at Greenville and neither of them could give a very clear account of what he looked like.

Brother Tucker said "He was pretty pert and spry looking youngster," and

Sister Marion Ford said "He was a handsome young chap—straight and tall as a young poplar and with the snappiest black eyes she'd ever seen—altogether quite 'stinguished looking."

"But" as Marie Phillips sarcastically remarked, "you can't depend on either one of these old folks, because everybody is 'pert and spry' to Brother Tucker, who walks and talks pretty slick and as for Sister Marion Ford—Oh pshaw! she can't see good anyway."

But "all's well that ends well"—and Rev. Jonathan Steele had arrived and was quite all both Brother Tucker and Sister Ford had described and more some of them thought. In plain words—"he came, he saw, he conquered" and after several months with the town folks—he was still "The new preacher"—at least he was as new as seven months steady wear in a small town could leave him. You see new silver does not tarnish very quickly and Rev. Steele was still untarnished. Of course he made mistakes—and this Thursday night at the meeting of the Ladies' Aid they were discussing the fact that the Rev. Mr. Steele did not or could not seem to grasp the fact that Mrs. John Taylor was the leader of the Ladies' Aid and a shining light in the church, and that Mrs. Orion Tucker was to be church treasurer for life and that the Trustees and Stewards' Boards were composed of lifetime members and also that Mrs. St. Anthony was the head deaconness of the church and as her husband had donated the ground on which the church stood and donated five thousand dollars towards the building fund she must be consulted on all matters pertaining to the welfare of the church.

How was the Rev. Jonathan Steele, not a day over twenty-five and a young snipe just out of college, as Mrs. Tucker emphatically declared, to realize the importance of each separate man's and woman's work in his ever increasing congregation.

Altho after seven months—if he really had failed to grasp these many cited facts—it was no fault of the members of St. Michaels Church.

"Things seem to be moving along rather smoothly," remarked Mrs. Phillips—"I think the Reverend has commenced to appreciate his charge"—which remark was due to the fact that the Rev. Steele had lately congratulated Mrs. Phillips on her executive ability.

The ladies were lingering over the task of sorting out table linen and dishes after the yearly oyster supper for the benefit of the Stewards' Board.

"Yes," said Mrs. Phillips, "how our girls did work; they are coming into the church and working like soldiers, and are not near so thoughtless and silly as they used to be."

"Oh yes!" said Mrs. Tucker sarcastically. "It is really remarkable how they work. An unmarried minister can inspire so much enthusiasm among spinsters—and women with marriageable daughters."

"Well, I'm not making any unkind remarks," said Mrs. Phillips virtuously.

"Well," replied Mrs. Tucker—"Neither am I, but I can't help noticing things when they happen right under your nose. I have eyes to see with and altho we might not care to spread it broad cast, we can all see the difference between the treatment accorded Rev. Butler and that given Rev. Steele. You see Rev. Butler was an antiquated, married man, while Rev. Steele is a very live young man. With Rev. Butler we crawled along and the community hardly knew we existed, while now we are increasing by leaps and bounds—fairly flying."

"Well," said Mrs. Phillips, "it's natural isn't it. The young——"

"Of course it's natural," broke in Mrs. Tucker. "Life is just a succession of thrills anyway, and we all run after that we don't have. Didn't I run a little after my old man Orion, and didn't you run after Nathan?"

"No, I didn't," snapped Mrs. Phillips, "I never took one step out of my way for Nathan Phillips."

"Oh, well, you grabbed him mighty quick when he asked you—and that's what I'm thinking about these girls and old maids—any one of them would grab Rev. Steele mighty quick if he asks them."

A light laugh startled them and made them turn rather quickly—they had forgotten they were in church.

"I'm glad my girl lives such a distance from the church—that she can't take part in everything. Until she does her school work and helps me a little she has no time to join church clubs and Ladies' Aid Societies, and talk scandal," said the irrepressible Milly Brown. "But I guess you'll soon have a new member any way for your society—because Hannah Burke Starks has come home and is occupying the Powell place adjoining us. You remember her don't you Mrs. Phillips."

"Well, I should say," replied Mrs. Phillips, "she married young Dr. Stark of Cleveland. So she's home. Is her husband with her?"

"Oh no, she is a widow" said Milly "and I'm thinking a pretty wealthy one at that."

"You don't say," said Mrs. Tucker. "How do you know."

"Well by the style of her and the way she lives and the improvements she is making in the place. She has house servants, a gardener, and chauffeur and a man to tend the farm and she has had the house all done over, you won't know the place when it is finished. And she has an immense touring car, and the dearest coupe she runs herself. Then she rides and has a beautiful thoroughbred horse and has just the finest of clothes."

"Well" said Mrs. Phillips "that don't sound like she'll be much of a church worker—but we'll wait and see. You never can tell."

"Alice says she's lovely"—replied Milly. "She's been very good to Alice."

"We must call," said Mrs. Tucker, "it is so lonely out there."

"Yes, it's lonely with only Milly and her Alice for neighbors" retorted Mrs. Phillips. "But I'll have to study over it first. You see I knew Hannah before she was married, and she was always a mighty independent little piece and held her head very high."

"Oh, that's nothing," said Mrs. Tucker, "birds fly high too, but they always come down for water. So perhaps your Hannah was lonesome and home-sick for the sight of home and old faces, the reason she returned to St. Michaels."

"Well—we'll soon see," said Mrs. Phillips. And see they did in a way that didn't suit St. Michaels folks at all.

The following Thursday the Ladies' Aid met at Mrs. St. Anthony's. They always met at Mrs. St. Anthony's whenever they could—and that was nine times out of ten—because her home was just a few steps below the parsonage and they could see Rev. Steele whenever he came out or in or had visitors, and then being close—he sometimes dropped in and took tea with the ladies, only when he came they served cocoa and tea cakes because it was more fashionable.

But this Thursday they were doomed to disappointment because Rev. Steele came out his gate—and every girl and old maid's heart beat a little faster, and each one either took her little chamois and touched up her nose a little for fear it might be shiny or patted her hair a little smoother or tucked a hair pin a little tighter—but with a gasp of astonishment—instead of turning in at Mrs. St. Anthony's and sauntering slowly up the walk as usual—he walked briskly by without so much as a glance at the house.

The Ladies' Aiders sat as tho paralyzed—and little Marie Phillips, who thought he was on the eve of proposing to her, said "Well the nerve of him, I wonder where he can be going?"

"Well if you say so," said Lillian Tucker. "I'll run and ask him."

"Now girls," said Miss Sara Simpson "don't get excited, you know a pastor of a church like ours has so many important duties to attend to that he can't always attend our meetings."

"Don't make excuses Sara," retorted Mrs. Phillips—"there isn't anything more important than our meetings."

"Stung" laughed Lillian Tucker—"perhaps he has gone to see the great and beautiful widow Stark"—and as tho she had been a prophetess—the widow and the pastor came into view quietly talking and seemingly interested only in each other.

Everybody looked and if only the pastor could have known each one's thought of him—who watched him so closely.

The young girls were mostly amused but the spinsters and married women were not so charitably inclined.

Mrs. Stark was dressed in a fashionable tailor made suit with hat, gloves and shoes to match and carried an armful of beautiful hot-house tea roses.

At his gate they stopped and she put out her hand and took his and put all the roses in them—and then stooped and buried her face in them as tho loath to part with them and when she raised her face he said something to her and buried his face in them as she had done.

"Look," said Miss Sara Simpson with a look of disgust on her face—"he is kissing and caressing them because she did so—right out in the street isn't it disgusting, and he seems to like her too and here last Sunday he took us to task about expensive cloths, and street walking and flirting and love-making in public and——"

"Do hush Sara" said Mrs. St. Anthony. "Look at the bunch of roses, it hasn't cost a cent less than $5. I imagine I can smell them here. I wonder if he really likes roses?"

Mrs. Tucker seemed genuinely amused at some unspoken thought and her quick light laugh—fell jarringly upon the members.

"Oh dear!" said one "do keep quiet."

"I don't see anything to laugh about," said another.

"Well he likes roses well enough to keep those" said some one else.

"It seems so" said another.

The gate clicked shut and Mrs. Stark walked along up the street, unconscious of the storm she had stirred up.

"If she is so intimate with him, it's a wonder she wouldn't come to church and help with the church work or join the society and help to do something, and she wouldn't have time to flirt with the minister" said Mrs. St. Anthony.

"Has anyone"—asked Mrs. Phillips—"asked Hannah Stark to join our society or one of our church clubs?"

No one had——

"I'll do it now" said Mrs. Phillips.

"Hurry or she'll be out of sight——" they urged. They followed Mrs. Phillips to the door.

Mrs. Stark had gone by—but she came back with a smile on her face, and not a little amused at being accosted thus. Mrs. Phillips stood on the top step and resolved to do what she thought was her duty.

"I am Mrs. Phillips—Mrs. Stark and remember you as Hannah Burke—we saw you talking to Rev. Steele"—she said by way of introduction—"We thought you might like to join our society or our young people's Helping Hand Club."

Mrs. Phillips was unaware how she spoke—her voice cut the air like a whip saw—and said plainly—we do not want you, but you should think it your duty—and an honor, that I, Mrs. Lawyer Phillips, should ask you to join.

Mrs. Stark's eyes snapped—and her head went up a little higher—"Thank you"—she said—"I feel honored. Does your pastor belong to these clubs and is he a member of the Church Aid Society?"

"No," exclaimed indignant Mrs. Phillips. —"Then I'm sorry to decline the honor, but I can't possibly belong to anything of which he is not a member, and not under his direct supervision."

She was gone—Mrs. Phillips had to be helped in the house to the couch—and Mrs. St. Anthony was so angry she was blue in the face. I thought she would explode, and poor Miss Sara Simpson fainted in fact everybody was out of commission but Mrs. Tucker, who got on everybody's nerves by laughing and saying——

"I like that woman. She's got spunk and brains enough to give you a dose of nicely sugar-coated pills that helps immensely."

Before night all St. Michaels had heard the story of the roses and the invitation to join the club and it did not lose anything in the telling.

Unconsciously all St. Michaels formed a detective bureau to watch the pastor.

They played detective and they watched poor Rev. Steele's every move and at last it had come to the conclusion that he was hopelessly in love with the widow.

Poor Mrs. Stark, did she know how St. Michaels regarded her, or what they thought of her? If she did—no one in St. Michaels was any the wiser.

Then one Sunday morning just a few weeks before Xmas, Mrs. Stark appeared at church, and the Ladies' Aid members that were present, I'm afraid paid more attention to Mrs. Stark than they did to the sermon—in fact I'm afraid they could not have given the text if asked—but I'm sure they could have told you all about Mrs. Stark's costume.

At the Thursday afternoon meeting following—Mrs. Stark was the topic as usual.

"What's wrong with her now," said Mrs. Tucker. "At first she was just a butterfly and a flirt, then she was haughty and proud, then she did not attend church, she was a heathen, now she attends church, you are still faultfinding and she is a hypocrite—what is wrong with her now?" she challenged.

"Well she is not a member," said Mrs. Phillips, "and she just came to have the pastor walk her home."

"Well whose business is it if she does. Don't you think Rev. Steele is old enough to look after himself?" said Mrs. Tucker.

"Well what do you expect of us? You'd be suspicious yourself—after those roses—if you were not so in love with both her and the pastor, that it takes all your time to champion their cause and snub your neighbors, all on account of a city woman, who is supposed to have plenty of money and fine clothes. I think she's bewitched you" remarked Mrs. Phillips, "as you have gone clean daft about her."

"Well I'm satisfied"—retorted Mrs. Tucker. "My opinion of the matter is that we will lose all the ground we've gained—and waste our profits—if we don't stop this unseasonable unreasonable squabbling—come to our senses and adjust the differences which have suddenly sprung up between the pastor and this society all on account of his attention to a woman, and we are not sure that he is paying special attention to her. Because a man calls on a woman or walks home with her is no sign he wants to marry her."

"Quite a sermon Mrs. Tucker, have you taken the Rev. Steele's place? Who elected you his champion?"—sarcastically asked Mrs. St. Anthony. "Perhaps the members here are not to your liking and you wish to resign."

"I am not trying to take anyone's place," retorted Mrs. Tucker—"but three weeks from now is Xmas, and this is hold together time—not hold-up or split-up time. A similar opportunity to have a big Xmas fete in the church and to get and keep all the younger folks working may never occur again and I move we take time by the forelock and get busy."

"The pastor gave those roses to old Mother Carey," explained Mrs.

Tucker triumphantly—and I bet Mrs. Stark knew all about it—perhaps she sent them by him."

"Humph!" said Miss Sara Simpson, "Jonathan Steele is a sly one—probably his pricking conscience told him the Ladies' Aid was watching."

PART II

"The marriageable women of our church are nice and would be a plus for any man. They are as pretty and dutiful as he'll find elsewhere, but he won't marry one of them. He can't see the pot over the sill of the window for the rain," said Mrs. Phillips. "If there was another church here we would leave, my husband says."

"And I would follow you," said Mrs. St. Anthony and Mrs. Ford in chorus—and then the trouble started.

Rev. Steele called a meeting of the Mite Society—and Ladies' Aid Society—and organized a Young People's Get-together for Wednesday evening at 7 o'clock. Although the three organizations consisted of seventy-five or more members among them, only five young folks and three older ones turned out—Milly Brown, Mrs. Tucker and Mrs. Ford. Rev. Steele made no comment on the presence or the absence of the members.

"Well," said he, "this will be my first meeting with you, and as you have all been faithful the past seven months, I thought with your help—we will have a Xmas this year that will leave a sweet memory to every person at St. Michaels as long as life itself. Are you willing to help?"

"We certainly are," exclaimed Mrs. Tucker, and the rest acquiesced.

Several committees were appointed and those that were absent were notified of their appointments and the jobs they were expected to do.

Some agreed half-heartedly and some refused point blank to not only serve on the committees, but to attend church—and a split in the church of St. Michaels loomed large on the horizon.

Sunday morning two weeks before Xmas, Rev. Steele preached his second formal sermon in St. Michaels Church on "Gossip" and truly St. Michaels was in an up-heaval.

No one knew if he was aware of the feelings of his congregation or not. He had chosen "Gossip" for his subject, but in the middle of his sermon he told his congregation that no matter what happened—even if he was to render his resignation within the next twelve hours—he would have the satisfaction of knowing that he had been a p-a-s-t-o-r and not a figure head.

He got everyone to thinking and Mrs. St. Anthony wondered if "he could rightly know what had been said about him by the Ladies' Aid."

"It makes no difference if he does" said Mrs. Phillips. "It would do him not to know what I think of him."

"Humph"—said Mrs. Tucker, "much he cares for your opinion or any one of the rest of us, I'm thinking. He believed Rev. Butler to be led by the nose wheresoever a set of crazy men and women chose to lead him."

When Frank Coombs resigned as superintendent of the Sunday School they thought he'd be coaxed to remain, but when no one coaxed, only a few old heads—and Harry Young was asked to fill his place—it was like stirring up a hornet's nest. "Mrs. Coombs and her sister, Mrs. Cook, do come to church—but I declare they would be better at home," said Mrs. Ford.

"Mrs. Cook told me" said Mrs. Phillips, "she'd looked at the pipes of the organ so long and so hard that she could tell every move on them and where, with her eyes shut, and it was no wonder they had not fallen down on her before this.

"Old Mrs. Lake sits with the book up-side down—and pretends to read, when we all know she can't tell A from B if they were a yard high. Even the members of the Trustees' and Stewards' Boards are at logger heads, because he appointed some young men, who have lately joined church, on the boards and asked for the resignation of some of the old men on the board—they had been on the board so long they were moss-covered."

"Well I can't see"—said Mrs. St. Anthony, "why he wanted to change things around."

"I can tell you" said Mrs. Tucker "he thinks if you want to keep young people in the church after they join—you should put them to work and make them feel they are wanted. You see it's useless to try to hold young folks anywhere now-a-days unless they have something to do. There is too much of this wanting to be boss all the time and a few old fogies wanting the church to stay in a rut and keeping things like they were fifty years ago. Times are changing and you've simply got to change with them or get out of the running. A piece of antique china is admired for its age—but it is put upon the shelf for safekeeping and admired for what it was and is not for its present use. So it is with us—we must either help the younger folks along or stand to be put on the shelf. I say live and let live.

"The whole thing in a nut-shell is he hasn't paid the attention to our marriageable daughters we thought he should" said Mrs. Tucker. "He goes among us—loves us—and thinks for our interest—which should make him loved by all—but it seems there must always be a few discontented ones among the flock."

"What's the use of jangling" said Mrs. Todd. "Let us get busy. What will you give towards the Xmas fete, Mrs. Hunter?"

"I—oh, I don't know" said Mrs. Hunter—"I guess 2 quarts of cream and a chocolate cake."

"What will you give Mrs. Phillips?"

"Not one single thing"—she replied "count me out of it. Mr. Phillips says we'll not take any part in the affair."

"What will you give Mrs. Tucker?"

"A cake, a chicken, 2 lbs of coffee and help to do whatever I can."

"And you Mrs. Ford?"

"Oh—Mr. Ford says we'll not take any part in it."

"Look here ladies, before I go any further" said Mrs. Todd "let me ask you that won't help—please do not hinder."

"Goodness gracious—Margery Todd put that list up—and don't use the Ladies' Aid's time for such foolishness," said Mrs. Phillips.

"Alright," said Mrs. Todd—"but I'll call on every one of you tomorrow."

"I can't get over that sermon" said Mrs. St. Anthony—hopping back to the old subject.

"Neither can I" said Mrs. Phillips.

"There goes the Reverend and the widow now!" said Marie Phillips.

"Well that caps the climax," said old Mrs. Ford bitterly, as the Reverend and the widow passed out of sight.

But she was mistaken. Something happened a few days later that threw the community into a tizzy. The whole community began to talk to each other through back doors, across to their neighbors, or talked across fences—back and front by the hour. They even called special meetings to discuss it, in fact everybody you met was talking about it and everybody held a square white envelope which contained a beautifully printed square white card which was drawn out and compared with other cards just like it, and soon St. Michaels awoke to the fact that every member and non-member of St. Michaels—men—women and young people—was invited to an elaborate Xmas party.

In the words of Mrs. Tucker—"Mrs. Stark was giving a big Xmas blow out."

After the first surprise was over, everybody was wondering why he or she had been invited and one and all came to the conclusion, to get in with St.

Michaels folks—except the Ladies' Aid—who said she was taking this way to show she was sorry for the way she had acted.

Tho—Mrs. Tucker says—"What she had to be sorry for was beyond her."

Then came the getting ready for the party. The boy that blowed the organ thought his checkered pants and blue coat with his new tan shoes was just the thing. The sexton's wife bought a pretty white dimity dress—much too tight and which seemed to make her look twice as broad. But the leaders of the church—the Ladies' Aid—such a flurry—such a bustling.

Of course Mrs. St. Anthony, Mrs. Phillips—the lawyer's wife, and the doctor's wife, Mrs. Jameson—and Miss Simpson and Mrs. White, and their daughters could and did go to the city to get their outfit, and as Marie Phillips told Mrs. Tucker the dresses will be real creations of art.

But the rest of St. Michaels had to be content to buy in St. Michaels, and to trust to Milly Brown, Violet Cunningham and old Mrs. Thomas to make them.

Said Mrs. Tucker—"I'm mighty glad I'm invited—and I'm satisfied with any old plum-colored silk, because it's no use to go to that party trying to outdress Mrs. Stark, because she knows how to dress, and as Mr. Tucker says, she could put on my old plum-colored silk and look like an angel in it, with that mop of hair as black as a raven's wing and eyes as black as a coal and a complexion like a rose leaf—she looks like a big doll anyway. I'll dress to suit Mrs. Tucker who is short and inclined to stoutness and past forty-five and not like Hannah"—with which common sense remarks——"

Mrs. Tucker took her ancient plum-colored silk and sewed some real lace in the sleeves and fixed a dainty white fichu around the neck which would tend to make her look decidedly sweet and motherly and altogether lovely.

The wonderful night rolled around all too quickly, they went in conveyances of all kinds—wagons, ancient carriages, buggies, daytons, and autos, all carried their quota of guests.

But Mrs. Tucker and Mrs. Todd said the street cars were good enough for them so accompanied by Mr. Tucker and Mr. Todd, they wended their way there.

Everybody went—not one invitation was refused or ignored—they were there to eat, to listen, to enjoy, and above all to see how Rev. Steele and Mrs. Stark would act before the people of St. Michaels.

When they arrived, they were more than surprised at the display that met their gaze, and they were awed into silence—and as they gazed, they, one and all thought how beautiful.

Even Mrs. St. Anthony and Mrs. Phillips and Miss Simpson who were used to such things—had never seen anything quite as elaborate as this. Whatever else they may think, there was only one thing that could be said of her in regards to this Xmas party—it was gotten together on an elaborate scale and it was well done.

When they entered they were turned over to the maid who took them upstairs and ushered them into a room, where wraps were removed and checked and a chance to pin back a stray strand of hair or adjust a ribbon if they so wished, then when returning down stairs were announced by the butler—who was none other than young Bill Winston, hired and dressed up for the occasion, and who walked so straight and held his head so high that they wondered he could see the folks he announced.——They entered timidly and in nervous little groups—following each other sheep-fashion, to the place where the hostess stood to receive them—not knowing, the most of them, whether to shake hands or simply bow, nor what to do with themselves afterwards.

But once the hostess greeted them they forgot their self-consciousness and their nervousness in looking at the vision of loveliness that had greeted them. She wore a lovely dress—"a most wonderful gown" Mrs. Tucker said—"of some sort of white stuff—that looked soft, billowy clouds of fleece—dotted here and there with stones that shone like hundreds of stars and sparkled like thousands of diamonds under the blazing electric light;" and as old Mrs. Ford said "she made everybody feel so homey and comfortable."

"Well I declare" said Mrs. Phillips, "a bridal costume as I live"—as she gazed at the little spray of orange blossoms that nestled so lovingly in Mrs. Stark's abundant dark hair.

"Do you know," said Sara Simpson, "I believe she has invited us all to her wedding."

Some one whispered "Isn't she glorious?" And it floated from one to the other around the room, there was a gentle hum as of bees in the distance, everybody seemed happy.

"I wonder where the Reverend is?" said old Mrs. St. Anthony.

Time passed and the older folks commenced to get restless—the younger ones were in dream-land and as the orchestral music was wafted so softly and temptingly on the air the younger folks looked longingly at the waxed floor glistening in the distance and wished the pastor would not show up so they could dance.

"Oh!" said Marie Phillips, "just for one turn on that floor"—and the rest echoed her wish.

People commenced to move nervously about, and to stand and talk in excited little groups. There was a hint of something in the air that no one could tell what it was—where was Rev. Steele? Why didn't the wedding take place? Who was going to marry them?

Even Mrs. Stark was getting restless, her cheeks were flushed, and her eyes fairly glistened and kept roaming toward the side entrance. Her hands played nervously with her fan, [   ] the young folks were almost tempted to ask could they dance.

The time seemed to pass so slowly and a wave of restlessness hard to control was fast gaining possession of the guests.

Everybody took to cautiously watching Mrs. Stark, who was walking aimlessly here and there around the rooms and talking nervously to first one guest and then another, but it was noticed that her glance wandered continually toward the side entrance, the music itself seemed to accelerate the restlessness of the crowd.

Suddenly the music changed—as the strains of Lohengrin's Wedding March pealed joyously forth—the side door was thrown wide and the foot-man announced in a stentorian voice—"Mr. and Mrs. Jonathan Steele."

Everybody turned to look, and there standing framed in the doorway, smilingly stood the Rev. Jonathan Steele—and standing by his side—cling-ing to his arm stood his bride—timid little Alice Brown—in a simple white dress—looking for all the world like a happy Brown Thrush.

Of course everybody in the room could have told you, that they knew it was Alice Brown the pastor had been coming out into the lonely end of town to see.

And all the girls and spinsters who had held high hopes of becoming the pastor's wife, will tell you that Rev. Steele is a passably good-looking man, but he is a long way from being a handsome one.

"Sour grapes"—says Mrs. Tucker. But the Ladies' Aid and the Helping Hand ladies just looked at Milly Brown and wondered to themselves how she ever kept it to herself.

But it did not matter, only to a few like Miss Sara Simpson—whose chances of a husband were getting fewer each year and to Mrs. Phillips—who was anxious to see Marie safely settled, and to Mrs. St. Anthony, who could not now meddle so easily in the pastor's household affairs. To the majority—he had married a St. Michaels girl and that was the main thing, so the church was decorated, good things donated and the Xmas fete was a royal reception to the pastor and his bride. And to this day St. Michaels folks love to tell of the Xmas party and how it prevented a split in the church.

1916

Dorothy Parker

The Christmas Magazines

AND THE INEVITABLE STORY OF THE SNOWBOUND TRAIN

EVERY YEAR I buy them,—the Christmas magazines. Every year I say, hopefully, "Perhaps this time." And every year I say, wearily, "Never again."

But I'll go on buying them, and I know it. Hope does die so hard within me. Somewhere, some time, possibly here, perhaps in Heaven, I shall find a Christmas magazine without the story of the snowbound train.

You know it, don't you? The lonely old millionaire who snorts at the mere mention of Christmas, and, on the same train, the little golden-haired child who is going to spend Christmas out at Grandma's in the country? You know how the snow piles up, and the wires are blown down, and the anxious train-hand says that there is no chance of going on? And then, don't you remember how the lonely old millionaire always sees the pathetic little stocking dangling out the berth occupied by the golden-haired child? So the l. o. m. (who has perhaps made his millions as a conjuror) immediately produces an elaborately decorated Christmas tree and a seething mass of toys. Maybe it isn't conjury, though. Perhaps all millionaires can do it. I don't know any regular millionaires, you see. I knew a man once who was supposed to be a millionaire, and he couldn't even do card tricks, but, then, the reports of his income were probably exaggerated. According to the writers of snowbound train stories, this feat of producing Christmas trees from thin air is a very common one among millionaires.

It seems to be a trait they share with actresses. For the snowbound train story sometimes has an actress in it instead of a lonely old millionaire,—though he is first choice, I suppose on account of the child's future. If it's an actress, she is always a self-made blonde, a member of a traveling burlesque troupe, and she unfailingly has a little golden-haired child of her own, hidden away in the West. Sometimes, to make it harder, she has *two* little golden-haired children, but the story goes just the same,—stocking, tree, toys, etc., etc.

That's the story. If they have ever published a Christmas number of any magazine without it, it must have been before I was born. Words are powerless to convey the loathing which I have for that story. It ruins the holidays for me. I buy hordes of magazines in the hope of finding one—just one—without it. But there it always is. Even "Snappy Stories" has it,—the actress version of it, of course. And the horrible part of it is that when I see the title "Christmas on the Train," or "A Snow-Bound Santa Claus," or "A Little Child Shall Lead Them," or any of the hideous titles under which it masquerades, I cannot drop the book and run. No, a morbid fascination makes me read every word of it. Perhaps I shall have my reward, some day. Perhaps it will be my lot to discover the radical spirit who will give that child dark hair.

And the rest of the average Christmas number is no better than that terrible story. Look at any one of the magazines. They are just the same this year as last. The verses may be a bit freer, but that's all.

The first page is always given up to a highly decorated poem. You know the kind, one of those poems with mediæval spelling. It is one of those hearty, good-cheer things, and it usually contains frequent requests to "let the welkin ring." Just what *is* a welkin, anyway? I wrote one of that kind of Christmas poems a week or so ago, just to see if I could do it. I sent it to a poor little magazine that hadn't many friends, and I had such a nice note from the editor, saying that he would be most glad to accept it. That was all. I shook the envelope, but nothing fell out. Do you know what I am going to do? I shall give him one more week, and then I shall write to him and tell him that he is under a misapprehension,—my contribution was not meant to be free verse.

Then come the stories. The one about the burglar whom the child thinks is Santa Claus,—you know that one, don't you? Then the strong, red-corpuscled one about the half-breed's Christmas. And the misery story that starts, "She counted them again. Seven cents,—seven worn, thin, sweat-stained pennies, and to-morrow would be Christmas!" And the sweet, sweet, sweet little tale of Christmas in the old South. And the one about the erring wife who comes back to her husband, or the erring husband who comes back to his wife,—it depends on whether a man or a woman writes it—just as the Christmas chimes ring out on the old village clock. Then there are the "Christmas in the Trenches" articles, and the masterpiece in Harper's which is always called "Christmas in Many Lands."

Then there is the double-page spread about how certain actresses spend their Christmas at home. There they all are—the vampire lady, the heroine of the glad play, the musical comedy star, and all the rest of them, photographed at home, exclusively for every magazine on the news-stands. One gathers from the photographs that these ladies carry their art into their home and holiday life. The vampire lady, for instance, wears one of those home-wrecking gowns, drapes herself over an evil-looking divan, and spends a merry Christmas leaning on her elbows and looking at a skull. The heroine of the "glad" play is perched girlishly in the middle of her dining-room table, hugging a Teddy bear and smiling sunnily—for it is Christmas, and a blizzard is raging, and all the trains are tied up, and thousands of people are freezing and starving to death, and she is glad, glad, glad. And the musical comedy star is photographed in pink silk pajamas (the picture isn't colored, of course, but you just *know* they're pink). She is on her way to enter her holly-wreathed bath-tub, but she has paused for a moment to gloat over the brimming stocking which hangs by the fireplace,—though goodness only knows why a filled stocking should be any treat to her.

Then the pages and pages of What to Give. Oh, how I skip those pages! That awful page headed "Gifts for *Her*," with its scentless sachets, and its timeless wristwatches, and its Harrison Fisher calendar with the lady and gentleman executing a different kiss for every month in the year.

And always there is that page of jokes. "Christmas Jests," they are called, instead of the usual "Sense and Nonsense" or "Verse and Worse." They are the customary little parlor anecdotes that you cannot remember even while you're reading them, made timely by the use of such phrases as "said Willie, passing his plate for more plum-pudding," and "Mother asked, as she trimmed the tree." There is nothing on earth so serviceable as a joke. Later on, these same jests may be successfully used for the July number by the simple method of changing the Christmas phrases to "said Willie, as he stooped over the lighted firecracker," and "Mother asked, as she bandaged Baby's eye." I read the jokes through quickly, dread in my soul. I always expect to find the snowbound train tale among them, considerably condensed, and with the fun lying in the train-hand's remark to the Lonely Old Millionaire.

I bought all the Christmas numbers this year. Just at present I am deep in the "never again" stage. But I shall probably buy them again next year,—I feel it hanging over me. Oh, is there no great public-spirited soul, no intrepid reformer working for the future of the race, who will found a Society for the Suppression of Christmas Issues?

1916

ROBERT BENCHLEY

Christmas Afternoon
DONE IN THE MANNER, IF NOT THE SPIRIT, OF DICKENS

WHAT AN AFTERNOON! Mr. Gummidge said that, in his estimation, there never had *been* such an afternoon since the world began, a sentiment which was heartily endorsed by Mrs. Gummidge and all the little Gummidges, not to mention the relatives who had come over from Jersey for the day.

In the first place, there was the *ennui*. And such *ennui* as it was! A heavy, overpowering *ennui*, such as results from a participation in eight courses of steaming, gravied food, topping off with salted nuts which the little old spinster Gummidge from Oak Hill said she never knew when to stop eating—and true enough she didn't—a dragging, devitalizing *ennui*, which left its victims strewn about the living-room in various attitudes of prostration suggestive of those of the petrified occupants in a newly unearthed Pompeiian dwelling; an *ennui* which carried with it a retinue of yawns, snarls and thinly veiled insults, and which ended in ruptures in the clan spirit serious enough to last throughout the glad new year.

Then there were the toys! Three and a quarter dozen toys to be divided among seven children. Surely enough, you or I might say, to satisfy the little tots. But that would be because we didn't know the tots. In came Baby Lester Gummidge, Lillian's boy, dragging an electric grain-elevator which happened to be the only toy in the entire collection which appealed to little Norman, five-year-old son of Luther, who lived in Rahway. In came curly-headed Effie in frantic and throaty disputation with Arthur, Jr., over the possession of an articulated zebra. In came Everett, bearing a mechanical negro which would no longer dance, owing to a previous forcible feeding by the baby of a marshmallow into its only available aperture. In came Fonlansbee, teeth buried in the hand of little Ormond, which bore a popular but battered remnant of what had once been the proud false-bosom of a hussar's uniform. In they all came, one after another, some crying, some snapping, some pulling, some pushing—all appealing to their respective parents for aid in their intra-mural warfare.

And the cigar smoke! Mrs. Gummidge said that she didn't mind the smoke from a good cigarette, but would they mind if she opened the windows for just a minute in order to clear the room of the heavy aroma of used cigars? Mr. Gummidge stoutly maintained that they were good cigars. His brother, George Gummidge, said that he, likewise, would say that they were. At which colloquial sally both the Gummidge brothers laughed testily, thereby breaking the laughter record for the afternoon.

Aunt Libbie, who lived with George, remarked from the dark corner of the room that it seemed just like Sunday to her. An amendment was offered to this statement by the cousin, who was in the insurance business, stating that it was worse than Sunday. Murmurings indicative of as hearty agreement with this sentiment as their lethargy would allow came from the other members of the family circle, causing Mr. Gummidge to suggest a walk in the air to settle their dinner.

And then arose such a chorus of protestations as has seldom been heard. It was too cloudy to walk. It was too raw. It looked like snow. It looked like rain. Luther Gummidge said that he must be starting along home soon, anyway, bringing forth the acid query from Mrs. Gummidge as to whether or not he was bored. Lillian said that she felt a cold coming on, and added that something they had had for dinner must have been undercooked. And so it went, back and forth, forth and back, up and down, and in and out, until Mr. Gummidge's suggestion of a walk in the air was reduced to a tattered impossibility and the entire company glowed with ill-feeling.

In the meantime, we must not forget the children. No one else could. Aunt Libbie said that she didn't think there was anything like children to make a Christmas; to which Uncle Ray, the one with the Masonic fob, said, "No, thank God!" Although Christmas is supposed to be the season of good cheer, you (or I, for that matter) couldn't have told, from listening to the little ones, but what it was the children's Armageddon season, when Nature had decreed that only the fittest should survive, in order that the race might be carried on by the strongest, the most predatory and those possessing the best protective coloring. Although there were constant admonitions to Fonlansbee to "Let Ormond have that whistle now; it's his," and to Arthur, Jr., not to be selfish, but to "give the kiddie-car to Effie; she's smaller than you are," the net result was always that Fonlansbee kept the whistle and Arthur, Jr., rode in permanent, albeit disputed, possession of the kiddie-car.

Oh, that we mortals should set ourselves up against the inscrutable work-ings of Nature!

Hallo! A great deal of commotion! That was Uncle George stumbling over the electric train, which had early in the afternoon ceased to function and which had been left directly across the threshold. A great deal of cry-ing! That was Arthur, Jr., bewailing the destruction of his already useless train, about which he had forgotten until the present moment. A great deal of recrimination! That was Arthur, Sr., and George fixing it up. And finally a great crashing! That was Baby Lester pulling over the tree on top of him-self, necessitating the bringing to bear of all of Uncle Ray's knowledge of forestry to extricate him from the wreckage.

And finally Mrs. Gummidge passed the Christmas candy around. Mr. Gummidge afterward admitted that this was a tactical error on the part of his spouse. I no more believe that Mrs. Gummidge thought they wanted that Chrismas candy than I believe that she thought they wanted the cold turkey which she later suggested. My opinion is that she wanted to drive them home. At any rate, that is what she succeeded in doing. Such cries as there were of "Ugh! Don't let me see another thing to eat!" and "Take it away!" Then came hurried scramblings in the coat-closet for overshoes. There were the rasping sounds made by cross parents when putting wraps on children. There were insincere exhortations to "come and see us soon" and to "get together for lunch some time." And, finally, there were slam-mings of doors and the silence of utter exhaustion, while Mrs. Gummidge went about picking up stray sheets of wrapping paper.

And, as Tiny Tim might say in speaking of Christmas afternoon as an institution, "God help us, every one."

1920

W.E.B. DU BOIS

The Sermon in the Cradle

NOW WHEN JESUS was born in Benin of Nigeria in the days of English rule, behold, there came wise men from the East to London.

Saying, Where is he that is born King of the Blacks? For we have seen his star in the east, and are come to worship him.

When the Prime Minister had heard these things, he was troubled, and all England with him.

And when he had gathered all the chief priests and scholars of the land together, he demanded of them where this new Christ should be born.

And they said unto him, in Benin of Nigeria: for thus it was written by the prophet:

And thou Benin, in the land of Nigeria, art not the least among the princes of Africa: for out of thee shall come a Governor, that shall rule my Negro people.

Then the Prime Minister, when he had privily called the wise men, inquired of them diligently what time the star appeared.

And he sent them to Benin, and said, "Go and search diligently for the young child; and when ye have found him, bring me word again, that I may come and worship him also."

When they had heard the Premier, they departed; and lo, the star, which they saw in the east, went before them, till it came and stood over where the young child was.

When they saw the star, they rejoiced with exceeding great joy.

And when they were come into the house, they saw the young child with Mary his mother, and fell down, and worshipped him: and when they had opened their treasures, they presented unto him gifts: gold and medicine and perfume.

And being warned of God in a dream that they should not return to England, they departed into their own country another way.

Save one, and he was black. And his own country was the country where he was; so the black Wise Man lingered by the cradle and the new-born babe.

The perfume of his gift rose and filled the house until through it and afar came the dim form of years and multitudes. And the child, seeing the multitudes, opened his mouth and taught them, saying:

Blessed are poor folks for they shall go to heaven.

Blessed are sad folks for someone will bring them joy.

Blessed are they that submit to hurts for they shall sometime own the world.

Blessed are they that truly want to do right for they shall get their wish.

Blessed are those who do not seek revenge for vengeance will not seek them.

Blessed are the pure for they shall see God.

Blessed are those who will not fight for they are God's children.

Blessed are those whom people like to injure for they shall sometime be happy.

Blessed are you, Black Folk, when men make fun of you and mob you and lie about you. Never mind and be glad for your day will surely come.

Always the world has ridiculed its better souls.

1921

Ben Hecht

Holiday Thoughts

TRADITIONS ARE THINGS which take the place of initiative. And so people lean on them. Traditions make it seemingly necessary for them to do things that they would not ordinarily do because they were too tired, too empty or too lacking in interest. The observing of great holidays is a matter of tradition. There are many noble-hearted people who might experience a dawn of love for their fellow man toward the end of the year if there had never been a Christmas. But they are in the minority.

The loop is a bit more congested than usual. I have been very busy elsewhere. Thus, walking or pushing my way down State street, I wonder what great general is visiting the city to-day and where the parade was. Then I remember that it is the holiday season and that these are shoppers. Then the stores must be crowded once more. Holly wreaths are hanging from the columns. Cotton batting is doing service for snow decorations. Tinsel and glittering artifices gleam from the shelves. Allons—we will investigate.

A hullabaloo. The heavy shuffle and a dim roar. The crowd sucks you in like a vacuum. Counters of smart gloves, perfumes, laces, jewelry, waists, stockings. They drift by. People like the business of buying gifts. Aside from the bartering aspects of the thing—of hoping to get presents as nice as they sent—there is the glow of altruism. People like to do good to others. It gives them a feeling of strength, an emotion of intimacy. Also to buy something that appeals to you and to send it to a friend is like winning an argument hands down. In so doing you impose your own tastes graciously upon him.

The shuffle of the huge store crowds is so determined it seems as if the thing had direction and plan. As if every one were going somewhere instead of drifting aimlessly like myself up and down aimless aisles.

The elevator is jammed. It takes fifteen minutes to get inside of one.

The toy department! Here's a piquant chance to expand sentimentally. A vaguely familiar air of glamour rests on the scene. Vaguely familiar noises, music, shouts. Vaguely familiar counters. I pause and stare for two long minutes at a crokinole table. I can remember. Yes. And across the aisle toy trains. They wind up. And one that runs by electricity. Hm! Indian suits and drums. Wooden clowns, great cardboard games in which you spin a needle and advance markers according to—according to something.

The toy department is like an almost familiar memory. It brings a faint sadness. One stands repeating to one's self: "I remember. Yes, of course. I remember this. And that."

It seems suddenly preposterous that one was ever a child. Impossible. One says without words: "It couldn't have been me. Some one else. Not me." And then the things on the counters begin to gesture hauntingly. The names of games wink intimately from gaudy cardboard boxes. The electric train whirs teasingly round and round the white tin track.

Noises blur. The scene becomes a blur also. And one drifts along staring with amazed eyes at a toy clown, at a toy Noah's ark. There is a poignancy in the moment—the poignancy of revisiting old scenes after a long absence. The old scenes contain magically a part of one's youth. Yesterdays are embalmed in them.

And here each toy is like an old scene. Each toy seems crowded with yesterdays.

I look around. A crowd of people. Chiefly people older than myself. And a minority of children. Middle-aged, tired-faced people handling toys. Staring with almost idiotic enthusiasm at dolls and drums and mechanical contrivances that dance or jiggle or crawl.

The eyes of these people tell a haunting story. They say: "Look, we have grown old. We once played with toys. Now we are old and tired." And their fingers stay caressingly on pieces of tin and cardboard.

Then there is a psychology of toys. Of course. Children like them. They take the place of ideas and institutions in the minds of children. But men and women use them more determinedly. Men and women play with them during the furtive moments of purchase and the half-sad, half-elated consciousness of having once been children and of having once reveled in such things comes to them.

Somehow this connects my thought with the notion of tradition. Around Christmas tradition addresses people in a peremptory voice. This is because the tradition in this case is based upon innumerable other traditions and has been canonized and made powerful by long and enthusiastic worship. The peremptory voice of the Christmas tradition makes it socially as well as spiritually necessary to "observe Christmas." Pity the absurd iconoclast maintaining an absurder rationality in the face of the colorful sentimentalism of the holidays. An outcast. Worse.

The memory of the toy department comes with me into the street. Middle aged, tired faces. Riding home in the crowded street car I look at faces. I notice that people seldom hold their necks stiff, that they permit their heads to loll to a side and downward and that their features droop. They sit in an open-eyed conscious sleep. Their attitudes remind one of people who have been pommeled and manhandled and tossed into the discard.

Along the evening residential streets the homecomers appear to become a little more alive. I pass the grocery store, butcher shop, drug store, corset shop. These are store fronts familiar on the way to my home. Usually their lighted interiors animate me, and make me think of labyrinths.

Now, these interiors and the dark streets that seem interiors also appear for the moment simplified. They are for tired people, worn people. Very sad people whose single great fortune is that they were once children. Now they go around wearing absurdly long faces and devoting themselves to the absurd business of earning money and spending it again.

And once a year these tired, aging ones come to the confessional of the toy department and with poignant grimacings coo and gurgle once more over dolls and drums.

"We once lived in a world of toys. In a world of adventure. In a world of strange thoughts and weird imaginings. Adventure, thoughts and imaginings were toys like these. Yes, these toys have souls because we remember that they meant something, were something. What is it they meant or were? But we've forgotten that—almost."

And the crowd of men and women shuffle up and down the aisles, up and down the streets outside. The holidays bring them all an identical gift. The holidays bring them the gift of memory.

1921

HEYWOOD BROUN

Bethlehem, Dec. 25

WHEN WE FIRST came into the office it looked like a dreary Christmas afternoon. To us there is something mournful in the sight of a scantily staffed city room. Just two men were at work typing away at stories of small moment. The telegraph instruments appeared to be meditating. One continued to chatter along, but there was nobody to set down what it said.

Its shrill, staccato insistence seemed momentous. But telegraph instruments are always like that. Their tone is just as excited whether the message tells of mighty tremors in the earth or baby parades at Asbury Park. Probably a job in a newspaper office is rather unhealthy for a telegraph instrument. The contrivance is too emotional and excitable to live calmly under the strain. Even an old instrument seldom learns enough about news values to pick and choose suitable moments in which to grow panicky. As soon as a story begins to move along a wire the little key screams and dances. It is devoid of reticence. Every distant whisper which comes to it must be rattled out at top voice and at once. Words are its very blood stream and for all the telegraph instrument knows one word is just as good and just as important as another.

And so the one restless key in the telegraph room shrieked, and whined, and implored listeners. We tried to help by coming close and paying strict attention, but we could not get even the gist of the message. It seemed to us as if the key were trying to say, with clicking tumult, that some great one, a King perhaps, was dead or dying. Or, maybe, it was a war and each dash and dot stood for some contending soldier moving forward under heavy fire. And again, it might be that a volcano had stirred and spit. Or great waves had swept a coast. And we thought of sinking steamers and trains upended.

Certainly it was an affair of great moment. Even though we discounted the passion and vehemence of the machine there was something almost awe inspiring in its sincerity and insistence. After a time it seemed to us as if this was in fact no long running narrative, but one announcement repeated over and over again. And suddenly we wondered why we had assumed from the beginning that only catastrophes were important and epoch making. By now we realized that though the tongue was alien we did recognize the color of its clamor. These dots and dashes were seeking to convey something of triumph. That was not to be doubted.

And in a flash we knew what the machine said. It was nothing more than, "A child is born." And of course nobody paid any attention to that. It is an old story.

1923

CHRISTOPHER MORLEY

The Tree That Didn't Get Trimmed

I F YOU WALK through a grove of balsam trees you will notice that the young trees are silent; they are listening. But the old tall ones—especially the firs—are whispering. They are telling the story of The Tree That Didn't Get Trimmed. It sounds like a painful story, and the murmur of the old trees as they tell it is rather solemn; but it is an encouraging story for young saplings to hear. On warm autumn days when your trunk is tickled by ants and insects climbing, and the resin is hot and gummy in your knots, and the whole glade smells sweet, drowsy, and sad, and the hardwood trees are boasting of the gay colours they are beginning to show, many a young evergreen has been cheered by it.

All young fir trees, as you know by that story of Hans Andersen's—if you've forgotten it, why not read it again?—dream of being a Christmas Tree some day. They dream about it as young girls dream of being a bride, or young poets of having a volume of verse published. With the vision of that brightness and gayety before them they patiently endure the sharp sting of the ax, the long hours pressed together on a freight car. But every December there are more trees cut down than are needed for Christmas. And that is the story that no one—not even Hans Andersen—has thought to put down.

The tree in this story should never have been cut. He wouldn't have been, but it was getting dark in the Vermont woods, and the man with the ax said to himself, "Just one more." Cutting young trees with a sharp, beautifully balanced ax is fascinating; you go on and on; there's a sort of cruel pleasure in it. The blade goes through the soft wood with one whistling stroke and the boughs sink down with a soft swish.

He was a fine, well-grown youngster, but too tall for his age; his branches were rather scraggly. If he'd been left there he would have been an unusually big tree some day; but now he was in the awkward age and didn't have the tapering shape and the thick, even foliage that people like on Christmas trees. Worse still, instead of running up to a straight, clean spire, his top was a bit lopsided, with a fork in it.

But he didn't know this as he stood with many others, leaning against the side wall of the greengrocer's shop. In those cold December days he was very happy, thinking of the pleasures to come. He had heard of the delights of Christmas Eve: the stealthy setting-up of the tree, the tinsel balls and coloured toys and stars, the peppermint canes and birds with spun-glass tails. Even that old anxiety of Christmas trees—burning candles—did not worry him, for he had been told that nowadays people use strings of tiny electric bulbs which cannot set one on fire. So he looked forward to the festival with a confident heart.

"I shall be very grand," he said. "I hope there will be children to admire me. It must be a great moment when the children hang their stockings on you!" He even felt sorry for the first trees that were chosen and taken away. It would be best, he considered, not to be bought until Christmas Eve. Then, in the shining darkness someone would pick him out, put him carefully along the running board of a car, and away they would go. The tire-chains would clack and jingle merrily on the snowy road. He imagined a big house with fire glowing on a hearth; the hushed rustle of wrapping paper and parcels being unpacked. Someone would say, "Oh, what a beautiful tree!" How erect and stiff he would brace himself in his iron tripod stand.

But day after day went by, one by one the other trees were taken, and he began to grow troubled. For everyone who looked at him seemed to have an unkind word. "Too tall," said one lady. "No, this one wouldn't do, the branches are too skimpy," said another. "If I chop off the top," said the greengrocer, "it wouldn't be so bad?" The tree shuddered, but the customer had already passed on to look at others. Some of his branches ached where the grocer had bent them upward to make his shape more attractive.

Across the street was a Ten Cent Store. Its bright windows were full of scarlet odds and ends; when the doors opened he could see people crowded along the aisles, cheerfully jostling one another with bumpy packages. A buzz of talk, a shuffle of feet, a constant ringing of cash drawers came noisily out of that doorway. He could see flashes of marvellous colour, ornaments for luckier trees. Every evening, as the time drew nearer, the pavements were more thronged. The handsomer trees, not so tall as he but more bushy and shapely, were ranked in front of him; as they were taken away he could see the gayety only too well. Then he was shown to a lady who wanted a tree very cheap. "You can have this one for a dollar," said the grocer. This was only one third of what the grocer had asked for him at first, but even so the lady refused him and went across the street to buy a little artificial tree at the toy store. The man pushed him back carelessly, and he toppled over and fell alongside the wall. No one bothered to pick him up. He was almost glad, for now his pride would be spared.

Now it was Christmas Eve. It was a foggy evening with a drizzling rain; the alley alongside the store was thick with trampled slush. As he lay there among broken boxes and fallen scraps of holly strange thoughts came to him. In the still northern forest already his wounded stump was buried in forgetful snow. He remembered the wintry sparkle of the woods, the big trees with crusts and clumps of silver on their broad boughs, the keen singing of the lonely wind. He remembered the strong, warm feeling of his roots reaching down into the safe earth. That is a good feeling; it means to a tree just what it means to you to stretch your toes down toward the bottom of a well-tucked bed. And he had given up all this to lie here, disdained and forgotten, in a littered alley. The splash of feet, the chime of bells, the cry of cars went past him. He trembled a little with self-pity and vexation. "No toys and stockings for me," he thought sadly, and shed some of his needles.

Late that night, after all the shopping was over, the grocer came out to clear away what was left. The boxes, the broken wreaths, the empty barrels, and our tree with one or two others that hadn't been sold, all were thrown through the side door into the cellar. The door was locked and he lay there in the dark. One of his branches, doubled under him in the fall, ached so he thought it must be broken. "So this is Christmas," he said to himself.

All that day it was very still in the cellar. There was an occasional creak as one of the bruised trees tried to stretch itself. Feet went along the pavement overhead, and there was a booming of church bells, but everything had a slow, disappointed sound. Christmas is always a little sad, after such busy preparations. The unwanted trees lay on the stone floor, watching the furnace light flicker on a hatchet that had been left there.

The day after Christmas a man came in who wanted some green boughs to decorate a cemetery. The grocer took the hatchet, and seized the trees without ceremony. They were too disheartened to care. Chop, chop, chop, went the blade, and the sweet-smelling branches were carried away. The naked trunks were thrown into a corner.

And now our tree, what was left of him, had plenty of time to think. He no longer could feel anything, for trees feel with their branches, but they think with their trunks. What did he think about as he grew dry and stiff? He thought that it had been silly of him to imagine such a fine, gay career for himself, and he was sorry for other young trees, still growing in the fresh hilly country, who were enjoying the same fantastic dreams.

Now perhaps you don't know what happens to the trunks of leftover Christmas trees. You could never guess. Farmers come in from the suburbs and buy them at five cents each for bean-poles and grape arbours. So perhaps (here begins the encouraging part of this story) they are really happier, in the end, than the trees that get trimmed for Santa Claus. They go back into the fresh, moist earth of spring, and when the sun grows hot the quick tendrils of the vines climb up them and presently they are decorated with the red blossoms of the bean or the little blue globes of the grape, just as pretty as any Christmas trinkets.

So one day the naked, dusty fir-poles were taken out of the cellar, and thrown into a truck with many others, and made a rattling journey out into the land. The farmer unloaded them in his yard and was stacking them up by the barn when his wife came out to watch him.

"There!" she said. "That's just what I want, a nice long pole with a fork in it. Jim, put that one over there to hold up the clothesline." It was the first time that anyone had praised our tree, and his dried-up heart swelled with a tingle of forgotten sap. They put him near one end of the clothesline, with his stump close to a flower bed. The fork that had been despised for a Christmas star was just the thing to hold up a clothesline. It was wash-day, and soon the farmer's wife began bringing out wet garments to swing and freshen in the clean, bright air. And the very first thing that hung near the top of the Christmas pole was a cluster of children's stockings.

That isn't quite the end of the story, as the old fir trees whisper it in the breeze. The Tree That Didn't Get Trimmed was so cheerful watching the stockings, and other gay little clothes that plumped out in the wind just as though waiting to be spanked, that he didn't notice what was going on—or going up—below him. A vine had caught hold of his trunk and was steadily twisting upward. And one morning, when the farmer's wife came out intending to shift him, she stopped and exclaimed. "Why, I mustn't move this pole," she said. "The morning glory has run right up it." So it had, and our bare pole was blue and crimson with colour.

Something nice, the old firs believe, always happens to the trees that don't get trimmed. They even believe that some day one of the Christmas-tree bean-poles will be the starting-point for another Magic Beanstalk, as in the fairy tale of the boy who climbed up the bean-tree and killed the giant. When that happens, fairy tales will begin all over again.

1925

SHERWOOD ANDERSON

A Criminal's Christmas

THE CONFESSIONS OF A YOUTHFUL OFFENDER
WHO, IN LATER LIFE, BECAME AN AUTHOR

EVERY MAN'S HAND against me. There I was in the darkness of the empty house. It was cold outside and snow was falling. I crept to a window and raising a curtain peered out. A man walked in the street. Now he had stopped at a corner and was looking about. He was looking toward the house I was in. I drew back into the darkness.

Two o'clock, four o'clock. The night before Christmas.

Yesterday I had walked freely in the streets. Then temptation came. I committed a crime. The man hunt was on.

Always men creeping in darkness in cities, in towns, in alley-ways in cities, on dark country roads.

Man wanted. The man hunt. Who was my friend? Whom could I trust? Where should I go?

It was my own fault. I had brought it on myself. We were hard up that year and I had got a job in Willmott's grocery and general store. I was twelve years old and was to have fifty cents a day.

During the afternoon of the day before Christmas there was a runaway on Main Street. Everyone rushed out. I was tying a package and there—right at my hand—was an open cash drawer.

I did not think. I grabbed. There was so much silver. Would anyone know? Afterward I found I had got six dollars, all in quarters, nickels and dimes. It made a handful. How heavy it felt. When I put it in my pocket what a noise it made.

No one knew. Yes, they did. Now wait. Don't be nervous.

You know what such a boy—twelve years of age—would tell himself. I wanted presents for the other kids of our family,—wanted something for mother. Mother had been ill. She was just able to sit up.

When I got out of the store that evening it was for a time all right. I spent a dollar seventy five. Fifty cents of it was for mother—a lacy looking kind of thing to put around her neck. There were five other children. I spent a quarter on each.

Then I spent a quarter on myself. That left four dollars. I bought a kite. That was silly. You don't fly kites in the winter. When I got home and before I went into the house I hid it in a shed. There were some old boxes in a corner. I put it in behind the boxes.

It was grand going in with the presents in my arms. Toys, candy, the lace for mother.

Mother never said a word. She never asked me where I got the money to buy so many things.

I got away as soon as I could. There was a boy named Bob Mann giving a party. I went there.

I had come too early. I looked through a window and saw I had come long before the party was to start so I went for a walk.

It had begun to snow. I had told mother I might stay at Bob Mann's all night.

That was what raised the devil—just walking about. When I had grabbed the money out of the cash drawer I did not think there was a soul in the store. There wasn't. But just as I was slipping it into my pocket a man came in.

The man was a stranger. What a noise the silver made. Even when I was walking in the street that night, thinking about the man, it made a noise. Every step I took it jingled in my pockets.

A fine thing to go to a party making a noise like that. Suppose they played some game. In lots of games you chase each other.

I was frightened now. I might have thrown the money away, buried it in the snow, but I thought . . .

I was full of remorse. If they did not find me out I could go back to the store next day and slip the four dollars back into the drawer.

"They won't send me to jail for two dollars," I thought, but there was that man.

I mean the one who came into the store just when I had got the money all safe and was putting it into my pocket.

He was such a strange acting man. He just came into the store and then went right out. I was confused of course. I must have acted rather strange. No doubt I looked scared.

He may have been just a man who had got into a wrong place. Perhaps he was a man looking for his wife.

When he had gone all the others came back. There had been a rush before the runaway happened and there was a rush again. No one paid any attention to me. I never even asked whose horse ran away.

The man might however have been a detective. That thought did not come until I went to Bob Mann's party and got there too early. It came when I was walking in the street waiting for the party to begin.

I never did go to the party. Like any other boy I had read a lot of dime novels. There was a boy in our town named Roxie Williams who had been in a reform school. What I did not know about crime and detectives he had told me.

I was walking in the street thinking of that man who came into the store just as I stole the money and then, when I began to think of detectives, I began to be afraid of every man I met.

In a snow like that, in a small town where there aren't many lights, you can't tell who anyone is.

There was a man started to go into a house. He went right up to the front door and seemed about to knock and then he didn't. He stood by the front door a minute and then started away.

It was the Musgraves' house. I could see Lucy Musgrave inside through a window. She was putting coal in a stove. All the houses I saw that evening, while I was walking around, getting more and more afraid all the time, seemed the most cheerful and comfortable places.

There was Lucy Musgrave inside a house and that man outside by the front door, only a few feet away and she never knowing. It might have been the detective and he might have thought the Musgrave house was our house.

After that thought came I did not dare go home and did not know where I could go. Fortunately the man at the Musgraves' front door hadn't seen me. I had crouched behind a fence. When he went away along the street I started to run but had to stop.

The loose silver in my pocket made too much racket. I did not dare go and hide it anywhere because I thought, "If they find and arrest me and I have four dollars to give back maybe they'll let me go."

Then I thought of a house where a boy named Jim Moore lived. It was right near Buckeye Street—a good place. Mrs. Moore was a widow and only had Jim and one daughter and they had gone away for Christmas.

I made it there all right, creeping along the streets. I knew the Moores hid their key in a woodshed, under a brick near the door. I had seen Jim Moore get it dozens of times.

It was there all right and I got in. Such a night! I got some clothes out of a closet to put on and keep me warm. They belonged to Mrs. Moore and her grown up daughter. Afterward they found them all scattered around the house and it was a town wonder. I would get a coat and skirt and wrap them around me. Then I'd put them down somewhere and as I did not dare light a match would have to get some more. I took some spreads off beds.

It was all like being crazy or dead or something. Whenever anyone went along the street outside I was so scared I trembled all over. Pretty soon I had got the notion the whole town was on the hunt.

Then I began thinking of mother. Perhaps by this time they had been to our house. I could not make up my mind what to do.

Sometimes I thought,—well, in stories I was always at that time reading—boys about my own age were always beginning life as bootblacks and rising to affluence and power. I thought I would slide out of town before daylight and get me a bootblack's outfit somehow. Then I'd be all right.

I remember that I thought I'd start my career at a place called Cairo, Illinois. Why Cairo I do not know.

I thought that all out, crouching by a window in the Moores' house that Christmas eve, and then, when no one came along the street for a half hour and I began to be brave again, I thought that if I had a pistol I would let myself out of the house and go boldly home. If, as I supposed, detectives were hid in front of the house, I'd shoot my way through.

I would get desperately wounded of course. I was pretty sure I would get a mortal wound but before I died I would stagger in at the door and fall at my mother's feet.

There I would lie dying, covered with blood. I made up some dandy speeches. "I stole the money, mother, to bring a moment of happiness into your life. It was because it was Christmas eve." That was one of the speeches. When I thought of it—of my getting it off and then dying, I cried.

Well, I was cold and frightened enough to cry anyway.

What really happened was that I stayed in the Moores' house until daylight came. After midnight it got so quiet in the street outside that I risked a fire in the kitchen stove but I went to sleep for a moment in a chair beside the stove and falling forward made a terrible burned place on my forehead.

The mark of Cain. I am only telling this story to show that I know just how a criminal feels.

I got out of the Moore house at daylight and went home and got into our house without anyone knowing. I had to crawl into bed with a brother but he was asleep. Next morning, in the excitement of getting all the presents they did not expect, no one asked me where I had been. When mother asked me where I had got the burn I said, "at the party," and she put some soda on it and did not say anything more.

And on the day after Christmas I went back to the store and sure enough got the four dollars back into the drawer. Mr. Willmott gave me a dollar. He said I had hurried away so fast on Christmas eve that he hadn't got a chance to give me a present.

They did not need me any more after that week and I was all right and knew the man that came in such an odd way into the store, wasn't a detective at all.

As for the kite, in the spring I traded it off. I got me a pup but the pup got distemper and died.

1926

James Thurber

A Visit from Saint Nicholas
(in the Ernest Hemingway manner)

 IT WAS THE NIGHT before Christmas. The house was very quiet. No creatures were stirring in the house. There weren't even any mice stirring. The stockings had been hung carefully by the chimney. The children hoped that Saint Nicholas would come and fill them.

The children were in their beds. Their beds were in the room next to ours. Mamma and I were in our beds. Mamma wore a kerchief. I had my cap on. I could hear the children moving. We didn't move. We wanted the children to think we were asleep.

"Father," the children said.

There was no answer. He's there, all right, they thought.

"Father," they said, and banged on their beds.

"What do you want?" I asked.

"We have visions of sugarplums," the children said.

"Go to sleep," said mamma.

"We can't sleep," said the children. They stopped talking, but I could hear them moving. They made sounds.

"Can you sleep?" asked the children.

"No," I said.

"You ought to sleep."

"I know. I ought to sleep."

"Can we have some sugarplums?"

"You can't have any sugarplums," said mamma.

"We just asked you."

There was a long silence. I could hear the children moving again.

"Is Saint Nicholas asleep?" asked the children.

"No," mamma said. "Be quiet."

"What the hell would he be asleep tonight for?" I asked.

"He might be," the children said.

"He isn't," I said.

"Let's try to sleep," said mamma.

The house became quiet once more. I could hear the rustling noises the children made when they moved in their beds.

Out on the lawn a clatter arose. I got out of bed and went to the window. I opened the shutters; then I threw up the sash. The moon shone on the snow. The moon gave the lustre of mid-day to objects in the snow. There was a miniature sleigh in the snow, and eight tiny reindeer. A little man was driving them. He was lively and quick. He whistled and shouted at the reindeer and called them by their names. Their names were Dasher, Dancer, Prancer, Vixen, Comet, Cupid, Donder, and Blitzen.

He told them to dash away to the top of the porch, and then he told them to dash away to the top of the wall. They did. The sleigh was full of toys.

"Who is it?" mamma asked.

"Some guy," I said. "A little guy."

I pulled my head in out of the window and listened. I heard the reindeer on the roof. I could hear their hoofs pawing and prancing on the roof. "Shut the window," said mamma. I stood still and listened.

"What do you hear?"

"Reindeer," I said. I shut the window and walked about. It was cold. Mamma sat up in the bed and looked at me.

"How would they get on the roof?" mamma asked.

"They fly."

"Get into bed. You'll catch cold."

Mamma lay down in bed. I didn't get into bed. I kept walking around.

"What do you mean, they fly?" asked mamma.

"Just fly is all."

Mamma turned away toward the wall. She didn't say anything.

I went out into the room where the chimney was. The little man came down the chimney and stepped into the room. He was dressed all in fur. His clothes were covered with ashes and soot from the chimney. On his back was a pack like a peddler's pack. There were toys in it. His cheeks and nose were red and he had dimples. His eyes twinkled. His mouth was little, like a bow, and his beard was very white. Between his teeth was a stumpy pipe. The smoke from the pipe encircled his head in a wreath. He laughed and his belly shook. It shook like a bowl of red jelly. I laughed. He winked his eye, then he gave a twist to his head. He didn't say anything.

He turned to the chimney and filled the stockings and turned away from the chimney. Laying his finger aside his nose, he gave a nod. Then he went up the chimney. I went to the chimney and looked up. I saw him get into his sleigh. He whistled at his team and the team flew away. The team flew as lightly as thistledown. The driver called out, "Merry Christmas and good night." I went back to bed.

"What was it?" asked mamma. "Saint Nicholas?" She smiled.

"Yeah," I said.

She sighed and turned in the bed.

"I saw him," I said.

"Sure."

"I did see him."

"Sure you saw him." She turned farther toward the wall.

"Father," said the children.

"There you go," mamma said. "You and your flying reindeer."

"Go to sleep," I said.

"Can we see Saint Nicholas when he comes?" the children asked.

"You got to be asleep," I said. "You got to be asleep when he comes. You can't see him unless you're unconscious."

"Father knows," mamma said.

I pulled the covers over my mouth. It was warm under the covers. As I went to sleep I wondered if mamma was right.

1927

LANGSTON HUGHES

One Christmas Eve

STANDING OVER the hot stove cooking supper, the colored maid, Arcie, was very tired. Between meals today, she had cleaned the whole house for the white family she worked for, getting ready for Christmas tomorrow. Now her back ached and her head felt faint from sheer fatigue. Well, she would be off in a little while, if only the Missus and her children would come on home to dinner. They were out shopping for more things for the tree which stood all ready, tinsel-hung and lovely in the living-room, waiting for its candles to be lighted.

Arcie wished she could afford a tree for Joe. He'd never had one yet, and it's nice to have such things when you're little. Joe was five, going on six. Arcie, looking at the roast in the white folks' oven, wondered how much she could afford to spend tonight on toys. She only got seven dollars a week, and four of that went for her room and the landlady's daily looking after Joe while Arcie was at work.

"Lord, it's more'n a notion raisin' a child," she thought.

She looked at the clock on the kitchen table. After seven. What made white folks so darned inconsiderate? Why didn't they come on home here to supper? They knew she wanted to get off before all the stores closed. She wouldn't have time to buy Joe nothin' if they didn't hurry. And her landlady probably wanting to go out and shop, too, and not be bothered with little Joe.

"Dog gone it!" Arcie said to herself. "If I just had my money, I might leave the supper on the stove for 'em. I just got to get to the stores fo' they close." But she hadn't been paid for the week yet. The Missus had promised to pay her Christmas Eve, a day or so ahead of time.

Arcie heard a door slam and talking and laughter in the front of the house. She went in and saw the Missus and her kids shaking snow off their coats.

"Umm-mm! It's swell for Christmas Eve," one of the kids said to Arcie.

"It's snowin' like the deuce, and mother came near driving through a stop light. Can't hardly see for the snow. It's swell!"

"Supper's ready," Arcie said. She was thinking how her shoes weren't very good for walking in snow.

It seemed like the white folks took as long as they could to eat that evening. While Arcie was washing dishes, the Missus came out with her money.

"Arcie," the Missus said, "I'm so sorry, but would you mind if I just gave you five dollars tonight? The children have made me run short of change, buying presents and all."

"I'd like to have seven," Arcie said. "I needs it."

"Well, I just haven't got seven," the Missus said. "I didn't know you'd want all your money before the end of the week, anyhow. I just haven't got it to spare."

Arcie took five. Coming out of the hot kitchen, she wrapped up as well as she could and hurried by the house where she roomed to get little Joe. At least he could look at the Christmas trees in the windows downtown.

The landlady, a big light yellow woman, was in a bad humor. She said to Arcie, "I thought you was comin' home early and get this child. I guess you know I want to go out, too, once in awhile."

Arcie didn't say anything for, if she had, she knew the landlady would probably throw it up to her that she wasn't getting paid to look after a child both night and day.

"Come on, Joe," Arcie said to her son, "Let's us go in the street."

"I hears they got a Santa Claus down town," Joe said, wriggling into his worn little coat. "I wants to see him."

"Don't know 'bout that," his mother said, "but hurry up and get your rubbers on. Stores'll all be closed directly."

It was six or eight blocks downtown. They trudged along through the falling snow, both of them a little cold. But the snow was pretty!

The main street was hung with bright red and blue lights. In front of the City Hall there was a Christmas tree—but it didn't have no presents on it, only lights. In the store windows there were lots of toys—for sale.

Joe kept on saying, "Mama, I want . . ."

But mama kept walking ahead. It was nearly ten, when the stores were due to close, and Arcie wanted to get Joe some cheap gloves and something to keep him warm, as well as a toy or two. She thought she might come across a rummage sale where they had children's clothes. And in the ten-cent store, she could get some toys.

"O-oo! Lookee . . . ," little Joe kept saying, and pointing at things in the windows. How warm and pretty the lights were, and the shops, and the electric signs through the snow.

It took Arcie more than a dollar to get Joe's mittens and things he needed. In the A. & P. Arcie bought a big box of hard candies for 49¢. And then she guided Joe through the crowd on the street until they came to the dime store. Near the ten-cent store they passed a moving picture theatre. Joe said he wanted to go in and see the movies.

Arcie said, "Ump-un! No, child! This ain't Baltimore where they have shows for colored, too. In these here small towns, they don't let colored folks in. We can't go in there."

"Oh," said little Joe.

In the ten-cent store, there was an awful crowd. Arcie told Joe to stand outside and wait for her. Keeping hold of him in the crowded store would be a job. Besides she didn't want him to see what toys she was buying. They were to be a surprise from Santa Claus tomorrow.

Little Joe stood outside the ten-cent store in the light, and the snow, and people passing. Gee, Christmas was pretty. All tinsel and stars and cotton. And Santa Claus a-coming from somewhere, dropping things in stockings. And all the people in the streets were carrying things, and the kids looked happy.

But Joe soon got tired of just standing and thinking and waiting in front of the ten-cent store. There were so many things to look at in the other windows. He moved along up the block a little, and then a little more, walking and looking. In fact, he moved until he came to the white folks' picture show.

In the lobby of the moving picture show, behind the plate glass doors, it was all warm and glowing and awful pretty. Joe stood looking in, and as he looked his eyes began to make out, in there blazing beneath holly and colored streamers and the electric stars of the lobby, a marvellous Christmas tree. A group of children and grown-ups, white, of course, were standing around a big jovial man in red beside the tree. Or was it a man? Little Joe's eyes opened wide. No, it was not a man at all. It was Santa Claus!

Little Joe pushed open one of the glass doors and ran into the lobby of the white moving picture show. Little Joe went right through the crowd and up to where he could get a good look at Santa Claus. And Santa Claus was giving away gifts, little presents for children, little boxes of animal crackers and stick-candy canes. And behind him on the tree was a big sign (which little Joe didn't know how to read). It said, to those who understood, MERRY XMAS FROM SANTA CLAUS TO OUR YOUNG PATRONS.

Around the lobby, other signs said, WHEN YOU COME OUT OF THE SHOW STOP WITH YOUR CHILDREN AND SEE OUR SANTA CLAUS. And another announced, GEM THEATRE MAKES ITS CUS-TOMERS HAPPY—SEE OUR SANTA.

And there was Santa Claus in a red suit and a white beard all sprinkled with tinsel snow. Around him were rattles and drums and rocking horses which he was not giving away. But the signs on them said (could little Joe have read) that they would be presented from the stage on Christmas Day to the holders of the lucky numbers. Tonight, Santa Claus was only giving away candy, and stick-candy canes, and animal crackers to the kids.

Joe would have liked terribly to have a stick-candy cane. He came a little closer to Santa Claus, until he was right in the front of the crowd. And then Santa Claus saw Joe.

Why is it that lots of white people always grin when they see a Negro child? Santa Claus grinned. Everybody else grinned, too, looking at little black Joe—who had no business in the lobby of a white theatre. Then Santa Claus stooped down and slyly picked up one of his lucky number rattles, a great big loud tin-pan rattle such as they use in cabarets. And he shook it fiercely right at Joe. That was funny. The white people laughed, kids and all. But little Joe didn't laugh. He was scared. To the shaking of the big rattle, he turned and fled out of the warm lobby of the theatre, out into the street where the snow was and the people. Frightened by laughter, he had begun to cry. He went looking for his mama. In his heart he never thought Santa Claus shook great rattles at children like that—and then laughed.

In the crowd on the street he went the wrong way. He couldn't find the ten-cent store or his mother. There were too many people, all white people, moving like white shadows in the snow, a world of white people.

It seemed to Joe an awfully long time till he suddenly saw Arcie, dark and worried-looking, cut across the side-walk through the passing crowd and grab him. Although her arms were full of packages, she still managed with one free hand to shake him until his teeth rattled.

"Why didn't you stand where I left you?" Arcie demanded loudly. "Tired as I am, I got to run all over the streets in the night lookin' for you. I'm a great mind to wear you out."

When little Joe got his breath back, on the way home, he told his mama he had been in the moving picture show.

"But Santa Claus didn't give me nothin'," Joe said tearfully. "He made a big noise at me and I runned out."

"Serves you right," said Arcie, trudging through the snow. "You had no business in there. I told you to stay where I left you."

"But I seed Santa Claus in there," little Joe said, "so I went in."

"Huh! That wasn't no Santa Claus," Arcie explained. "If it was, he wouldn't a-treated you like that. That's a theatre for white folks—I told you once— and he's just a old white man."

"Oh . . . ," said little Joe.

1933

Damon Runyon

The Three Wise Guys

ONE COLD WINTER afternoon I am standing at the bar in Good Time Charley's little drum in West 49th Street, partaking of a mixture of rock candy and rye whisky, and this is a most surprising thing for me to be doing, as I am by no means a rumpot, and very seldom indulge in alcoholic beverages in any way, shape, manner, or form.

But when I step into Good Time Charley's on the afternoon in question, I am feeling as if maybe I have a touch of grippe coming on, and Good Time Charley tells me that there is nothing in this world as good for a touch of grippe as rock candy and rye whisky, as it assassinates the germs at once.

It seems that Good Time Charley always keeps a stock of rock candy and rye whisky on hand for touches of the grippe, and he gives me a few doses immediately, and in fact Charley takes a few doses with me, as he says there is no telling but what I am scattering germs of my touch of the grippe all around the joint, and he must safeguard his health. We are both commencing to feel much better when the door opens, and who comes in but a guy by the name of Blondy Swanson.

This Blondy Swanson is a big, six-foot-two guy, with straw-colored hair, and pink cheeks, and he is originally out of Harlem, and it is well known to one and all that in his day he is the largest puller on the Atlantic seaboard. In fact, for upwards of ten years, Blondy is bringing wet goods into New York from Canada, and one place and another, and in all this time he never gets a fall, which is considered a phenomenal record for an operator as extensive as Blondy.

Well, Blondy steps up alongside me at the bar, and I ask him if he cares to have a few doses of rock candy and rye whisky with me and Good Time Charley, and Blondy says he will consider it a privilege and a pleasure, because, he says, he always has something of a sweet tooth. So we have these few doses, and I say to Blondy Swanson that I hope and trust that business is thriving with him.

"I have no business," Blondy Swanson says. "I retire from business."

Well, if J. Pierpont Morgan, or John D. Rockefeller, or Henry Ford step up and tell me they retire from business, I will not be more astonished than I am by this statement from Blondy Swanson, and in fact not as much. I consider Blondy's statement the most important commercial announcement I hear in many years, and naturally I ask him why he makes such a decision, and what is to become of thousands of citizens who are dependent on him for merchandise.

"Well," Blondy says, "I retire from business because I am one hundred per cent American citizen. In fact," he says, "I am a patriot. I serve my country in the late war. I am cited at Château-Thierry. I always vote the straight Democratic ticket, except," he says, "when we figure it better to elect some Republican. I always stand up when the band plays the Star Spangled Banner. One year I even pay an income tax," Blondy says.

And of course I know that many of these things are true, although I remember hearing rumors that if the draft officer is along half an hour later than he is, he will not see Blondy for heel dust, and that what Blondy is cited for at Château-Thierry is for not robbing the dead.

But of course I do not speak of these matters to Blondy Swanson, because Blondy is not such a guy as will care to listen to rumors, and may become indignant, and when Blondy is indignant he is very difficult to get along with.

"Now," Blondy says, "I am a bootie for a long time, and supply very fine merchandise to my trade, as everybody knows, and it is a respectable business, because one and all in this country are in favor of it, except the prohibitionists. But," he says, "I can see into the future, and I can see that one of these days they are going to repeal the prohibition law, and then it will be most unpatriotic to be bringing in wet goods from foreign parts in competition with home industry. So I retire," Blondy says.

"Well, Blondy," I say, "your sentiments certainly do you credit, and if we have more citizens as high minded as you are, this will be a better country."

"Furthermore," Blondy says, "there is no money in booting any more. All the booties in this country are broke. I am broke myself," he says. "I just lose the last piece of property I own in the world, which is the twenty-five-G home I build in Atlantic City, figuring to spend the rest of my days there with Miss Clarabelle Cobb, before she takes a runout powder on me. Well," Blondy says, "if I only listen to Miss Clarabelle Cobb, I will now be an honest clerk in a gents' furnishing store, with maybe a cute little apartment up around 110th Street, and children running all around and about."

And with this, Blondy sighs heavily, and I sigh with him, because the romance of Blondy Swanson and Miss Clarabelle Cobb is well known to one and all on Broadway.

It goes back a matter of anyway six years when Blondy Swanson is making money so fast he can scarcely stop to count it, and at this time Miss Clarabelle Cobb is the most beautiful doll in this town, and many citizens almost lose their minds just gazing at her when she is a member of Mr. Georgie White's Scandals, including Blondy Swanson.

In fact, after Blondy Swanson sees Miss Clarabelle Cobb in just one performance of Mr. Georgie White's Scandals, he is never quite the same guy again. He goes to a lot of bother meeting up with Miss Clarabelle Cobb, and then he takes to hanging out around Mr. Georgie White's stage door, and sending Miss Clarabelle Cobb ten-pound boxes of candy, and floral horseshoes, and wreaths, and also packages of trinkets, including such articles as diamond bracelets, and brooches, and vanity cases, for there is no denying that Blondy is a fast guy with a dollar.

But it seems that Miss Clarabelle Cobb will not accept any of these offerings, except the candy and the flowers, and she goes so far as to return a sable coat that Blondy sends her one very cold day, and she is openly criticized for this action by some of the other dolls in Mr. Georgie White's Scandals, for they say that after all there is a limit even to eccentricity.

But Miss Clarabelle Cobb states that she is not accepting valuable offerings from any guy, and especially a guy who is engaged in trafficking in the demon rum, because she says that his money is nothing but blood money that comes from breaking the law of the land, although, as a matter of fact, this is a dead wrong rap against Blondy Swanson, as he never handles a drop of rum in his life, but only Scotch, and furthermore he keeps himself pretty well straightened out with the law.

The idea is, Miss Clarabelle Cobb comes of very religious people back in Akron, Ohio, and she is taught from childhood that rum is a terrible thing, and personally I think it is myself, except in cocktails, and furthermore, the last thing her mamma tells her when she leaves for New York is to beware of any guys who come around offering her diamond bracelets and fur coats, because her mamma says such guys are undoubtedly snakes in the grass, and probably on the make.

But while she will not accept his offerings, Miss Clarabelle Cobb does not object to going out with Blondy Swanson now and then, and putting on the chicken Mexicaine, and the lobster Newburg, and other items of this nature, and any time you put a good-looking young guy and a beautiful doll together over the chicken Mexicaine and the lobster Newburg often enough, you are apt to have a case of love on your hands.

And this is what happens to Blondy Swanson and Miss Clarabelle Cobb, and in fact they become in love more than somewhat, and Blondy Swanson is wishing to marry Miss Clarabelle Cobb, but one night over a batch of lobster Newburg, she says to him like this:

"Blondy," she says, "I love you, and," she says, "I will marry you in a minute if you get out of trafficking in rum. I will marry you if you are out of the rum business, and do not have a dime, but I will never marry you as long as you are dealing in rum, no matter if you have a hundred million."

Well, Blondy says he will get out of the racket at once, and he keeps saying this every now and then for a year or so, and the chances are that several times he means it, but when a guy is in this business in those days as strong as Blondy Swanson it is not so easy for him to get out, even if he wishes to do so. And then one day Miss Clarabelle Cobb has a talk with Blondy, and says to him as follows:

"Blondy," she says, "I still love you, but you care more for your business than you do for me. So I am going back to Ohio," she says. "I am sick and tired of Broadway, anyhow. Some day when you are really through with the terrible traffic you are now engaged in, come to me."

And with this, Miss Clarabelle Cobb takes plenty of outdoors on Blondy Swanson, and is seen no more in these parts. At first Blondy thinks she is only trying to put a little pressure on him, and will be back, but as the weeks become months, and the months finally count up into years, Blondy can see that she is by no means clowning with him. Furthermore, he never hears from her, and all he knows is she is back in Akron, Ohio.

Well, Blondy is always promising himself that he will soon pack in on hauling wet goods, and go look up Miss Clarabelle Cobb and marry her, but he keeps putting it off, and putting it off, until finally one day he hears that Miss Clarabelle Cobb marries some legitimate guy in Akron, and this is a terrible blow to Blondy, indeed, and from this day he never looks at another doll again, or anyway not much.

Naturally, I express my deep sympathy to Blondy about being broke, and I also mention that my heart bleeds for him in his loss of Miss Clarabelle Cobb, and we have a few doses of rock candy and rye whisky on both propositions, and by this time Good Time Charley runs out of rock candy, and anyway it is a lot of bother for him to be mixing it up with the rye whisky, so we have the rye whisky without the rock candy, and personally I do not notice much difference.

Well, while we are standing there at the bar having our rye whisky without the rock candy, who comes in but an old guy by the name of The Dutchman, who is known to one and all as a most illegal character in every respect. In fact, The Dutchman has no standing whatever in the community, and I am somewhat surprised to see him appear in Good Time Charley's, because The Dutchman is generally a lammie from some place, and the gendarmes everywhere are always anxious to have a chat with him. The last I hear of The Dutchman he is in college somewhere out West for highway robbery, although afterwards he tells me it is a case of mistaken identity. It seems he mistakes a copper in plain clothes for a groceryman.

The Dutchman is an old-fashioned looking guy of maybe fifty-odd, and he has gray hair, and a stubby gray beard, and he is short, and thickset, and always good-natured, even when there is no call for it, and to look at him you will think there is no more harm in him than there is in a preacher, and maybe not as much.

As The Dutchman comes in, he takes a peek all around and about as if he is looking for somebody in particular, and when he sees Blondy Swanson he moves up alongside Blondy and begins whispering to Blondy until Blondy pulls away and tells him to speak freely.

Now The Dutchman has a very interesting story, and it goes like this:

It seems that about eight or nine months back The Dutchman is mobbed up with a party of three very classy heavy guys who make quite a good thing of going around knocking off safes in small-town jugs, and post offices, and stores in small towns, and taking the money, or whatever else is valuable in these safes. This is once quite a popular custom in this country, although it dies out to some extent of late years because they improve the brand of safes so much it is a lot of bother knocking them off, but it comes back during the depression when there is no other way of making money, until it is a very prosperous business again. And of course this is very nice for old-time heavy guys, such as The Dutchman, because it gives them something to do in their old age.

Anyway, it seems that this party The Dutchman is with goes over into Pennsylvania one night on a tip from a friend and knocks off a safe in a factory office, and gets a pay roll amounting to maybe fifty G's. But it seems that while they are making their getaway in an automobile, the gendarmes take out after them, and there is a chase, during which there is considerable blasting back and forth.

Well, finally in this blasting, the three guys with The Dutchman get cooled off, and The Dutchman also gets shot up quite some, and he abandons the automobile out on an open road, taking the money, which is in a gripsack, with him, and he somehow manages to escape the gendarmes by going across country, and hiding here and there.

But The Dutchman gets pretty well petered out, what with his wounds, and trying to lug the gripsack, and one night he comes to an old deserted barn, and he decides to stash the gripsack in this barn, because there is no chance he can keep lugging it around much longer. So he takes up a few boards in the floor of the barn, and digs a nice hole in the ground underneath and plants the gripsack there, figuring to come back some day and pick it up.

Well, The Dutchman gets over into New Jersey one way and another, and lays up in a town by the name of New Brunswick until his wounds are healed, which requires considerable time as The Dutchman cannot take it nowadays as good as he can when he is younger.

Furthermore, even after The Dutchman recovers and gets to thinking of going after the stashed gripsack, he finds he is about half out of confidence, which is what happens to all guys when they commence getting old, and he figures that it may be a good idea to declare somebody else in to help him, and the first guy he thinks of is Blondy Swanson, because he knows Blondy Swanson is a very able citizen in every respect.

"Now, Blondy," The Dutchman says, "if you like my proposition, I am willing to cut you in for fifty per cent, and fifty per cent of fifty G's is by no means pretzels in these times."

"Well, Dutchman," Blondy says, "I will gladly assist you in this enterprise on the terms you state. It appeals to me as a legitimate proposition, because there is no doubt this dough is coming to you, and from now on I am strictly legit. But in the meantime, let us have some more rock candy and rye whisky, without the rock candy, while we discuss the matter further."

But it seems The Dutchman does not care for rock candy and rye whisky even without the rock candy, so Blondy Swanson and me and Good Time Charley continue taking our doses, and Blondy keeps getting more enthusiastic about The Dutchman's proposition until finally I become enthusiastic myself, and I say I think I will go along as it is an opportunity to see new sections of the country, while Good Time Charley states that it will always be the great regret of his life that his business keeps him from going, but that he will provide us with an ample store of rock candy and rye whisky, without the rock candy, in case we run into any touches of the grippe.

Well, anyway, this is how I come to be riding around in an old can belonging to The Dutchman on a very cold Christmas Eve with The Dutchman and Blondy Swanson, although none of us happen to think of it being Christmas Eve until we notice that there seems to be holly wreaths in windows here and there as we go bouncing along the roads, and finally we pass a little church that is all lit up, and somebody opens the door as we are passing, and we see a big Christmas tree inside the church, and it is a very pleasant sight, indeed, and in fact it makes me a little homesick, although of course the chances are I will not be seeing any Christmas trees even if I am home.

We leave Good Time Charley's along in mid-afternoon, with The Dutchman driving this old can of his, and all I seem to remember about the trip is going through a lot of little towns so fast they seem strung together, because most of the time I am dozing in the back seat.

Blondy Swanson is riding in the front seat with The Dutchman and Blondy also cops a little snooze now and then as we are going along, but whenever he happens to wake up he pokes me awake, too, so we can take a dose of rock candy and rye whisky, without the rock candy. So in many respects it is quite an enjoyable journey.

I recollect the little church because we pass it right after we go busting through a pretty fair-sized town, and I hear The Dutchman say the old barn is now only a short distance away, and by this time it is dark, and colder than a deputy sheriff's heart, and there is snow on the ground, although it is clear overhead, and I am wishing I am back in Mindy's restaurant wrapping myself around a nice T-bone steak, when I hear Blondy Swanson ask The Dutchman if he is sure he knows where he is going, as this seems to be an untraveled road, and The Dutchman states as follows:

"Why," he says, "I know I am on the right road. I am following the big star you see up ahead of us, because I remember seeing this star always in front of me when I am going along this road before."

So we kept following the star, but it turns out that it is not a star at all, but a light shining from the window of a ramshackle old frame building pretty well off to one side of the road and on a rise of ground, and when The Dutchman sees this light, he is greatly nonplussed, indeed, and speaks as follows:

"Well," he says, "this looks very much like my barn, but my barn does not call for a light in it. Let us investigate this matter before we go any farther."

So The Dutchman gets out of the old can, and slips up to one side of the building and peeks through the window, and then he comes back and motions for Blondy and me to also take a peek through this window, which is nothing but a square hole cut in the side of the building with wooden bars across it, but no window panes, and what we behold inside by the dim light of a lantern hung on a nail on a post is really most surprising.

There is no doubt whatever that we are looking at the inside of a very old barn, for there are several stalls for horses, or maybe cows, here and there, but somebody seems to be living in the barn, as we can see a table, and a couple of chairs, and a tin stove, in which there is a little fire, and on the floor in one corner what seems to be a sort of a bed.

Furthermore, there seems to be somebody lying on the bed and making quite a fuss in the way of groaning and crying and carrying on generally in a loud tone of voice, and there is no doubt that it is the voice of a doll, and anybody can tell that this doll is in some distress.

Well, here is a situation, indeed, and we move away from the barn to talk it over.

The Dutchman is greatly discouraged, because he gets to thinking that if this doll is living in the barn for any length of time, his plant may be discovered. He is willing to go away and wait awhile, but Blondy Swanson seems to be doing quite some thinking, and finally Blondy says like this:

"Why," Blondy says, "the doll in this barn seems to be sick, and only a bounder and a cad will walk away from a sick doll, especially," Blondy says, "a sick doll who is a total stranger to him. In fact, it will take a very large heel to do such a thing. The idea is for us to go inside and see if we can do anything for this sick doll," Blondy says.

Well, I say to Blondy Swanson that the chances are the doll's ever-loving husband, or somebody, is in town, or maybe over to the nearest neighbors digging up assistance, and will be back in a jiffy, and that this is no place for us to be found.

"No," Blondy says, "it cannot be as you state. The snow on the ground is anyway a day old. There are no tracks around the door of this old joint, going or coming, and it is a cinch if anybody knows there is a sick doll here, they will have plenty of time to get help before this. I am going inside and look things over," Blondy says.

Naturally, The Dutchman and I go too, because we do not wish to be left alone outside, and it is no trouble whatever to get into the barn, as the door is unlocked, and all we have to do is walk in. And when we walk in with Blondy Swanson leading the way, the doll on the bed on the floor half raises up to look at us, and although the light of the lantern is none too good, anybody can see that this doll is nobody but Miss Clarabelle Cobb, although personally I see some change in her since she is in Mr. Georgie White's Scandals.

She stays half raised up on the bed looking at Blondy Swanson for as long as you can count ten, if you count fast, then she falls back and starts crying and carrying on again, and at this The Dutchman kneels down on the floor beside her to find out what is eating her.

All of a sudden The Dutchman jumps up and speaks to us as follows:

"Why," he says, "this is quite a delicate situation, to be sure. In fact," he says, "I must request you guys to step outside. What we really need for this case is a doctor, but it is too late to send for one. However, I will endeavor to do the best I can under the circumstances."

Then The Dutchman starts taking off his overcoat, and Blondy Swanson stands looking at him with such a strange expression on his kisser that The Dutchman laughs out loud, and says like this:

"Do not worry about anything, Blondy," The Dutchman says. "I am maybe a little out of practice since my old lady put her checks back in the rack, but she leaves eight kids alive and kicking, and I bring them all in except one, because we are seldom able to afford a croaker."

So Blondy Swanson and I step out of the barn and after a while The Dutchman calls us and we go back into the barn to find he has a big fire going in the stove, and the place nice and warm.

Miss Clarabelle Cobb is now all quieted down, and is covered with The Dutchman's overcoat, and as we come in The Dutchman tiptoes over to her and pulls back the coat and what do we see but a baby with a noggin no bigger than a crab apple and a face as wrinkled as some old pappy guy's, and The Dutchman states that it is a boy, and a very healthy one, at that.

"Furthermore," The Dutchman says, "the mamma is doing as well as can be expected. She is as strong a doll as ever I see," he says, "and all we have to do now is send out a croaker when we go through town just to make sure there are no complications. But," The Dutchman says, "I guarantee the croaker will not have much to do."

Well, the old Dutchman is as proud of this baby as if it is his own, and I do not wish to hurt his feelings, so I say the baby is a darberoo, and a great credit to him in every respect, and also to Miss Clarabelle Cobb, while Blondy Swanson just stands there looking at it as if he never sees a baby before in his life, and is greatly astonished.

It seems that Miss Clarabelle Cobb is a very strong doll, just as The Dutchman states, and in about an hour she shows signs of being wide awake, and Blondy Swanson sits down on the floor beside her, and she talks to him quite a while in a low voice, and while they are talking The Dutchman pulls up the floor in another corner of the barn, and digs around underneath a few minutes, and finally comes up with a gripsack covered with dirt, and he opens this gripsack and shows me it is filled with lovely, large coarse banknotes.

Later Blondy Swanson tells The Dutchman and me the story of Miss Clarabelle Cobb, and parts of this story are rather sad. It seems that after Miss Clarabelle Cobb goes back to her old home in Akron, Ohio, she winds up marrying a young guy by the name of Joseph Hatcher, who is a book-keeper by trade, and has a pretty good job in Akron, so Miss Clarabelle Cobb and this Joseph Hatcher are as happy as anything together for quite a spell.

Then about a year before the night I am telling about, Joseph Hatcher is sent by his firm to these parts where we find Miss Clarabelle Cobb, to do the bookkeeping in a factory there, and one night a few months afterwards, when Joseph Hatcher is staying after hours in the factory office working on his books, a mob of wrong gees breaks into the joint, and sticks him up, and blows open the safe, taking away a large sum of money and leaving Joseph Hatcher tied up like a turkey.

When Joseph Hatcher is discovered in this predicament the next morning, what happens but the gendarmes put the sleeve on him, and place him in the pokey, saying the chances are Joseph Hatcher is in and in with the safe blowers, and that he tips them off the dough is in the safe, and it seems that the guy who is especially fond of this idea is a guy by the name of Ambersham, who is manager of the factory, and a very hard-hearted guy, at that.

And now, although this is eight or nine months back, there is Joseph Hatcher still in the pokey awaiting trial, and it is 7 to 5 anywhere in town that the judge throws the book at him when he finally goes to bat, because it seems from what Miss Clarabelle Cobb tells Blondy Swanson that nearly everybody figures Joseph Hatcher is guilty.

But of course Miss Clarabelle Cobb does not put in with popular opinion about her ever-loving Joe, and she spends the next few months trying to spring him from the pokey, but she has no potatoes, and no way of getting any potatoes, so things go from bad to worse with Miss Clarabelle Cobb.

Finally, she finds herself with no place to live in town, and she happens to run into this old barn, which is on an abandoned property owned by a doctor in town by the name of Kelton, and it seems that he is a kind-hearted guy, and he gives her permission to use it any way she wishes. So Miss Clarabelle moves into the barn, and the chances are there is many a time when she wishes she is back in Mr. Georgie White's Scandals.

Now The Dutchman listens to this story with great interest, especially the part about Joseph Hatcher being left tied up in the factory office, and finally The Dutchman states as follows:

"Why, my goodness," The Dutchman says, "there is no doubt but what this is the very same young guy we are compelled to truss up the night we get this gripsack. As I recollect it, he wishes to battle for his employers' dough, and I personally tap him over the coco with a blackjack.

"But," he says, "he is by no means the guy who tips us off about the dough being there. As I remember it now, it is nobody but the guy whose name you mention in Miss Clarabelle Cobb's story. It is this guy Ambersham, the manager of the joint, and come to think of it, he is supposed to get his bit of this dough for his trouble, and it is only fair that I carry out this agreement as the executor of the estate of my late comrades, although," The Dutchman says, "I do not approve of his conduct toward this Joseph Hatcher. But," he says, "the first thing for us to do is to get a doctor out here to Miss Clarabelle Cobb, and I judge the doctor for us to get is this Doc Kelton she speaks of."

So The Dutchman takes the gripsack and we get into the old can and head back the way we come, although before we go I see Blondy Swanson bend down over Miss Clarabelle Cobb, and while I do not wish this to go any farther, I will take a paralyzed oath I see him plant a small kiss on the baby's noggin, and I hear Miss Clarabelle Cobb speak as follows:

"I will name him for you, Blondy," she says. "By the way, Blondy, what is your right name?"

"Olaf," Blondy says.

It is now along in the early morning and not many citizens are stirring as we go through town again, with Blondy in the front seat again holding the gripsack on his lap so The Dutchman can drive, but finally we find a guy in an all-night lunch counter who knows where Doc Kelton lives, and this guy stands on the running board of the old can and guides us to a house in a side street, and after pounding on the door quite a spell, we roust the Doc out and Blondy goes inside to talk with him.

He is in there quite a spell, but when he comes out he says everything is okay, and that Doc Kelton will go at once to look after Miss Clarabelle Cobb, and take her to a hospital, and Blondy states that he leaves a couple of C's with the Doc to make sure Miss Clarabelle Cobb gets the best of care.

"Well," The Dutchman says, "we can afford a couple of C's out of what we have in this gripsack, but," he says, "I am still wondering if it is not my duty to look up this Ambersham, and give him his bit."

"Dutchman," Blondy says, "I fear I have some bad news for you. The gripsack is gone. This Doc Kelton strikes me as a right guy in every respect, especially," Blondy says, "as he states to me that he always half suspects there is a wrong rap in on Miss Clarabelle Cobb's ever-loving Joe, and that if it is not for this guy Ambersham agitating all the time other citizens may suspect the same thing, and it will not be so tough for Joe.

"So," Blondy says, "I tell Doc Kelton the whole story, about Ambersham and all, and I take the liberty of leaving the gripsack with him to be re-turned to the rightful owners, and Doc Kelton says if he does not have Miss Clarabelle Cobb's Joe out of the sneezer, and this Ambersham on the run out of town in twenty-four hours, I can call him a liar. But," Blondy says, "let us now proceed on our way, because I only have Doc Kelton's word that he will give us twelve hours' leeway before he does anything except attend to Miss Clarabelle Cobb, as I figure you need this much time to get out of sight, Dutchman."

Well, The Dutchman does not say anything about all this news for a while, and seems to be thinking the situation over, and while he is think-ing he is giving his old can a little more gas than he intends, and she is fairly popping along what seems to be the main drag of the town when a

gendarme on a motorcycle comes up alongside us, and motions The Dutchman to pull over to the curb.

He is a nice-looking young gendarme, but he seems somewhat hostile as
he gets off his motorcycle, and walks up to us very slow, and asks us where
the fire is.

Naturally, we do not say anything in reply, which is the only thing to say
to a gendarme under these circumstances; so he speaks as follows:

"What are you guys carrying in this old skillet, anyway?" he says. "Stand
up, and let me look you guys over."

And then as we stand up, he peeks into the front and back of the car, and
under our feet, and all he finds is a bottle which once holds some of Good
Time Charley's rock candy and rye whisky without the rye whisky, but
which is now very empty, and he holds this bottle up, and sniffs at the noz-
zle, and asks what is formerly in this bottle, and I tell him the truth when I
tell him it is once full of medicine, and The Dutchman and Blondy Swanson nod their heads in support of my statement. But the gendarme takes
another sniff, and then he says like this:

"Oh," he says, very sarcastic, "wise guys, eh? Three wise guys, eh? Trying
to kid somebody, eh? Medicine, eh?" he says. "Well, if it is not Christmas
Day I will take you in and hold you just on suspicion. But I will be Santa
Claus to you, and let you go ahead, wise guys."

And then after we get a few blocks away, The Dutchman speaks as
follows:

"Yes," he says, "that is what we are, to be sure. We are wise guys. If we are
not wise guys, we will still have the gripsack in this car for the copper to
find. And if the copper finds the gripsack, he will wish to take us to the jail
house for investigation, and if he wishes to take us there I fear he will not
be alive at this time, and we will be in plenty of heat around and about, and
personally," The Dutchman says, "I am sick and tired of heat."

And with this The Dutchman puts a large Betsy back in a holster under
his left arm, and turns on the gas, and as the old can begins leaving the
lights of the town behind, I ask Blondy if he happens to notice the name of
this town.

"Yes," Blondy says, "I notice it on a signboard we just passed. It is Bethlehem, Pa."

1933

Leo Rosten

Mr. K*A*P*L*A*N and the Magi

WHEN MR. PARKHILL saw that Miss Mitnick, Mr. Bloom, and Mr. Hyman Kaplan were absent, and that a strange excitement pervaded the beginners' grade, he realized that it was indeed the last night before the holidays and that Christmas was only a few days off. Each Christmas the classes in the American Night Preparatory School for Adults gave presents to their respective teachers. Mr. Parkhill, a veteran of many sentimental Yuletides, had come to know the procedure. That night, before the class session had begun, there must have been a hurried collection; a Gift Committee of three had been chosen; at this moment the Committee was probably in Mickey Goldstein's Arcade, bargaining feverishly, arguing about the appropriateness of a pair of pajamas or the color of a dozen linen handkerchiefs, debating whether Mr. Parkhill would prefer a pair of fleece-lined slippers to a set of mother-of-pearl cuff links.

"We shall concentrate on—er—spelling drill tonight," Mr. Parkhill announced.

The students smiled wisely, glanced at the three empty seats, exchanged knowing nods, and prepared for spelling drill. Miss Rochelle Goldberg giggled, then looked ashamed as Mrs. Rodriguez shot her a glare of reproval.

Mr. Parkhill always chose a spelling drill for the night before the Christmas vacation: it kept all the students busy simultaneously; it dampened the excitement of the occasion; above all, it kept him from the necessity of resorting to elaborate pedagogical efforts in order to hide his own embarrassment.

Mr. Parkhill called off the first words. Pens and pencils scratched, smiles died away, eyes grew serious, preoccupied, as the beginners' grade assaulted the spelling of "Banana . . . Romance . . . Groaning." Mr. Parkhill sighed. The class seemed incomplete without its star student, Miss Mitnick, and barren without its most remarkable one, Mr. Hyman Kaplan. Mr. Kaplan's most recent linguistic triumph had been a fervent speech extolling the

D'Oyly Carte Company's performance of an operetta by two English gentlemen referred to as "Goldberg and Solomon."

"Charming . . . Horses . . . Float," Mr. Parkhill called off.

Mr. Parkhill's mind was not really on "Charming . . . Horses . . . Float." He could not help thinking of the momentous event which would take place that night. After the recess the students would come in with flushed faces and shining eyes. The Committee would be with them, and one member of the Committee, carrying an elaborately bound Christmas package, would be surrounded by several of the largest students in the class, who would try to hide the parcel from Mr. Parkhill's eyes. The class would come to order with uncommon rapidity. Then, just as Mr. Parkhill resumed the lesson, one member of the Committee would rise, apologize nervously for interrupting, place the package on Mr. Parkhill's desk, utter a few half-swallowed words, and rush back to his or her seat. Mr. Parkhill would say a few halting phrases of gratitude and surprise, everyone would smile and fidget uneasily, and the lesson would drag on, somehow, to the final and distant bell.

"*Accept* . . . *Except* . . . Cucumber."

And as the students filed out after the final bell, they would cry "Merry Christmas, Happy New Year!" in joyous voices. The Committee would crowd around Mr. Parkhill with tremendous smiles to say that if the present wasn't *just right* in size or color (if it was something to wear) or in design (if it was something to use), Mr. Parkhill could exchange it. He didn't *have* to abide by the Committee's choice. He could exchange the present for *any*thing. They would have arranged all that carefully with Mr. Mickey Goldstein himself.

That was the ritual, fixed and unchanging, of the last night of school before Christmas.

"Nervous . . . Goose . . . Violets."

The hand on the clock crawled around to eight. Mr. Parkhill could not keep his eyes off the three seats, so eloquent in their vacancy, which Miss Mitnick, Mr. Bloom, and Mr. Kaplan ordinarily graced with their presences. He could almost see these three in the last throes of decision in Mickey Goldstein's Arcade, harassed by the competitive attractions of gloves, neckties, an electric clock, a cane, spats, a "lifetime" fountain pen. Mr. Parkhill grew cold as he thought of a fountain pen. Three times already he had been presented with "lifetime" fountain pens, twice with "lifetime" pencils to match. Mr. Parkhill had exchanged these gifts: he had a fountain pen. Once he had chosen a woollen vest instead; once a pair of mittens and a watch chain. Mr. Parkhill hoped it wouldn't be a fountain pen. Or a smoking jacket. He had never been able to understand how the Committee in '32 had decided upon a smoking jacket. Mr. Parkhill did not smoke. He had exchanged it for fur-lined gloves.

Just as Mr. Parkhill called off "Sardine . . . *Exquisite* . . . Palace" the recess bell rang. The heads of the students bobbed up as if propelled by a single spring. There was a rush to the door, Mr. Sam Pinsky well in the lead. Then, from the corridor, their voices rose. Mr. Parkhill began to print "Banana" on the blackboard, so that the students could correct their own papers after recess. He tried not to listen, but the voices in the corridor were like the chatter of a flock of sparrows.

"Hollo, Mitnick!"

"Bloom, Bloom, vat is it?"

"So vat did you gat, Keplen? Tell!"

Mr. Parkhill could hear Miss Mitnick's shy "We bought—" interrupted by Mr. Kaplan's stern cry, "Mitnick! Don' say! Plizz, faller-students! Come *don* mit de voices! Titcher vill awreddy hearink, you hollerink so lod! Still! Order! Plizz!" There was no question about it: Mr. Kaplan was born to command.

"Did you bought a Tsheaffer's Fontain Pan Sat, guarantee for de whole life, like *I* said?" one voice came through the door. A Sheaffer Fountain Pen Set, Guaranteed. That was Mrs. Moskowitz. Poor Mrs. Moskowitz, she showed so little imagination, even in her homework. "Moskovitz! Mein Gott!" the stentorian whisper of Mr. Kaplan soared through the air. "Vy you don' open op de door Titcher should *positivel* hear? Ha! Let's goink to odder and fromm de hall!"

The voices of the beginners' grade died away as they moved to the "odder and" of the corridor, like the chorus of "Aïda" vanishing into Egyptian wings.

Mr. Parkhill printed "Charming" and "Horses" on the board. For a moment he thought he heard Mrs. Moskowitz's voice repeating stubbornly, "Did—you—bought—a—Tsheaffer—Fontain—Pan—Sat—*Guarantee?*"

Mr. Parkhill began to say to himself, "Thank you, all of you. It's *just* what I wanted," again and again. One Christmas he hadn't said "It's just what I wanted" and poor Mrs. Oppenheimer, chairman of the Committee that year, had been hounded by the students' recriminations for a month.

It seemed an eternity before the recess bell rang again. The class came in *en masse*, and hastened to the seats from which they would view the impending spectacle. The air hummed with silence.

Mr. Parkhill was printing "Cucumber." He did not turn his face from the board as he said, "Er—please begin correcting your own spelling. I have printed most of the words on the board."

There was a low and heated whispering. "Stend op, Mitnick!" he heard Mr. Kaplan hiss. "You should stend op *too!*"

"The *whole* Committee," Mr. Bloom whispered. "Stand op!"

Apparently Miss Mitnick, a gazelle choked with embarrassment, did not have the fortitude to "stend op" with her colleagues.

"A fine raprezantitif *you'll* gonna make!" Mr. Kaplan hissed scornfully. "Isn't for *mine* sek I'm eskink, Mitnick. Plizz *stend op!*"

There was a confused, half-muted murmur, and the anguished voice of Miss Mitnick saying, "I *can't.*" Mr. Parkhill printed "Violets" on the board. Then there was a tense silence. And then the voice of Mr. Kaplan rose, firmly, clearly, with a decision and dignity which left no doubt as to its purpose.

"Podden me, Mr. Pockheel!"

It had come.

"Er—yes?" Mr. Parkhill turned to face the class.

Messrs. Bloom and Kaplan were standing side by side in front of Miss Mitnick's chair, holding between them a large, long package, wrapped in cellophane and tied with huge red ribbons. A pair of small hands touched the bottom of the box, listlessly. The owner of the hands, seated in the front row, was hidden by the box.

"De hends is Mitnick," Mr. Kaplan said apologetically.

Mr. Parkhill gazed at the tableau. It was touching.

"Er—yes?" he said again feebly, as if he had forgotten his lines and was repeating his cue.

"Hau Kay!" Mr. Kaplan whispered to his confreres. The hands disappeared behind the package. Mr. Kaplan and Mr. Bloom strode to the platform with the box. Mr. Kaplan was beaming, his smile rapturous, exalted. They placed the package on Mr. Parkhill's desk, Mr. Bloom dropped back a few paces, and Mr. Kaplan said, "Mr. Pockheel! Is mine beeg honor, becawss I'm Chairman fromm de Buyink an' Deliverink to You a Prazent Committee, to givink to you dis fine peckitch."

Mr. Parkhill was about to stammer, "Oh, thank you," when Mr. Kaplan added hastily, "Also I'll sayink a few voids."

Mr. Kaplan took an envelope out of his pocket. He whispered loudly, "Mitnick, *you still got time to comm op mit de Committee,*" but Miss Mitnick only blushed furiously and lowered her eyes. Mr. Kaplan sighed, straightened the envelope, smiled proudly at Mr. Parkhill, and read.

"Dear Titcher—dat's de beginnink. Ve stendink on de adge fromm a beeg holiday." He cleared his throat. "Ufcawss is all kinds holidays in U. S. A. Holidays for politic, for religious, an' *plain* holidays. In Fabrary, ve got Judge Vashington's boitday, a *fine* holiday. Also Abram Lincohen's. In May ve got Memorable Day, for dad soldiers. In July comms, netcheral, Fort July. Also ve have Labor Day, Denksgivink, for de Peelgrims, an' for de feenish fromm de Voild Var, *Armistress* Day."

Mr. Parkhill played with a piece of chalk nervously.

"But arond dis time year ve have a *difference* kind holiday, a spacial, movvellous time. Dat's called—Chrissmas."

Mr. Parkhill put the chalk down.

"All hover de voild," Mr. Kaplan mused, "is pipple celebraking dis vunderful time. Becawss for som pipple is Chrissmas like for *odder* pipple is Passover. Or Chanukah, batter. De most fine, de most beauriful, de most *secret* holiday fromm de whole bunch!"

("'Sacred,' Mr. Kaplan, 'sacred,'" Mr. Parkhill thought, ever the pedagogue.)

"Ven ve valkink don de stritt an' is snow on de floor an' all kinds tarrible cold!" Mr. Kaplan's hand leaped up dramatically, like a flame. "Ven ye see in de vindows trees mit rad an' grin laktric lights boinink! Ven is de time for tellink de fancy-tales abot Sandy Claws commink fromm Naut Pole on rain-enimals, an' climbink don de jiminies mit *stockings* for all de leetle kits! Ven ve hearink abot de beauriful toughts of de Tree Vise Guys who vere follerink a star fromm de dasert! Ven pipple sayink, 'Oh, Mary Chrissmas! Oh, Heppy Noo Yiss! Oh, bast regotts!' Den ve *all* got a varm fillink in de heart for all humanity vhich should be brodders!"

Mr. Feigenbaum nodded philosophically at this profound thought; Mr. Kaplan, pleased, nodded back.

"*You* got de fillink, Mr. Pockheel. *I* got de fillink, dat's no qvastion abot! Bloom, Pinsky, Caravello, Schneiderman, even Mitnick"—Mr. Kaplan was punishing Miss Mitnick tenfold for her perfidy—"got de fillink! An' vat is it?" There was a momentous pause. "De Chrissmas Spirits!"

("'Spir*it*,' Mr. Kaplan, 'spir*it*,'" the voice of Mr. Parkhill's conscience said.)

"Now I'll givink de prazent," Mr. Kaplan announced subtly. Mr. Bloom shifted his weight. "Becawss you a foist-cless titcher, Mr. Pockheel, an' learn abot gremmer an' spallink an' de hoddest pots pernonciation—ve know is a planty hod jop mit soch students—so ve fill you should havink a sample fromm our—fromm our—" Mr. Kaplan turned the envelope over hastily—"aha! Fromm our santimental!"

Mr. Parkhill stared at the long package and the huge red ribbons.

"Fromm de cless, to our lovely Mr. Pockheel!"

Mr. Parkhill started. "Er—?" he asked involuntarily.

"Fromm de cless, to our lovely Mr. Pockheel!" Mr. Kaplan repeated with pride.

(*"Beloved,"* Mr. Kaplan, *'beloved.'"*)

A hush had fallen over the room. Mr. Kaplan, his eyes bright with joy, waited for Mr. Parkhill to take up the ritual. Mr. Parkhill tried to say, "Thank you, Mr. Kaplan," but the phrase seemed meaningless, so big, so ungainly, that it could not get through his throat. Without a word Mr. Parkhill began to open the package. He slid the big red ribbons off. He broke the tissue paper inside. For some reason his vision was blurred and it took him a moment to identify the present. It was a smoking jacket. It was black and gold, and a dragon with a green tongue was embroidered on the breast pocket.

"Horyantal style," Mr. Kaplan whispered delicately.

Mr. Parkhill nodded. The air trembled with the tension. Miss Mitnick looked as if she were ready to cry. Mr. Bloom peered intently over Mr. Kaplan's shoulder. Mrs. Moskowitz sat entranced, sighing with behemothian gasps. She looked as if she were at her daughter's wedding.

"Thank you," Mr. Parkhill stammered at last. "Thank you, all of you."

Mr. Bloom said, "Hold it op everyone should see."

Mr. Kaplan turned on Mr. Bloom with an icy look. "*I'm* de chairman!" he hissed.

"I—er—I can't tell you how much I appreciate your kindness," Mr. Parkhill said without lifting his eyes.

Mr. Kaplan smiled. "So now you'll plizz hold op de prazent. Plizz."

Mr. Parkhill took the smoking jacket out of the box and held it up for all to see. There were gasps—"Oh!"'s and "Ah!"'s and Mr. Kaplan's own ecstatic "My! Is beauriful!" The green tongue on the dragon seemed alive.

"Maybe ve made a mistake," Mr. Kaplan said hastily. "Maybe you don' smoke—dat's how *Mitnick* tought." The scorn dripped. "But I said, 'Ufcawss is Titcher smokink! Not in de cless, netcheral. At home! At least a *pipe!*'"

"No, no, you didn't make a mistake. It's—it's *just* what I wanted!"

The great smile on Mr. Kaplan's face became dazzling. "Hooray! Vear in de bast fromm helt!" he cried impetuously. "Mary Chrissmas! Heppy Noo Yiss! You should have a *hondert* more!"

This was the signal for a chorus of acclaim. "Mary Chrissmas!" "Wear in best of health!" "Happy New Year!" Miss Schneiderman burst into applause, followed by Mr. Scymzak and Mr. Weinstein. Miss Caravello, carried away by all the excitement, uttered some felicitations in rapid Italian. Mrs. Moskowitz sighed once more and said, "Soch a *sveet* ceremonia." Miss Mitnick smiled feebly, blushing, and twisted her handkerchief.

The ceremony was over. Mr. Parkhill began to put the smoking jacket back into the box with fumbling hands. Mr. Bloom marched back to his seat. But Mr. Kaplan stepped a little closer to the desk. The smile had congealed on Mr. Kaplan's face. It was poignant and profoundly earnest.

"Er—thank you, Mr. Kaplan," Mr. Parkhill said gently.

Mr. Kaplan shuffled his feet, looking at the floor. For the first time since Mr. Parkhill had known him, Mr. Kaplan seemed to be embarrassed. Then, just as he turned to rush back to his seat, Mr. Kaplan whispered, so softly that no ears but Mr. Parkhill's heard it, "Maybe de spitch I rad vas too *form-mal*. But avery void I said—it came fromm *below mine heart!*"

Mr. Parkhill felt that, for all his weird, unorthodox English, Mr. Kaplan had spoken with the tongues of the Magi.

1937

John Henrik Clarke

Santa Claus is a White Man

A STORY OF THE COLOR LINE

WHEN HE LEFT the large house where his Negro mother was a servant, he was happy. She had embraced him lovingly and had given him—for the first time in his life!—a quarter. "Now you go do your Christ'mus shopping," she had said. "Get somethin' for Daddy and something for Baby and something for Aunt Lil. And something for Mummy too, if it's any money left."

He had already decided how he would divide his fortune. A nickel for something for Daddy, another nickel for Baby, another for Aunt Lil. And ten whole cents for Mummy's present. Something beautiful and gorgeous, like a string of pearls, out of the ten-cent store.

His stubby legs moved fast as he headed toward the business district. Although it was mid-December, the warm southern sun brought perspiration flooding to his little, dark-skinned face. He was so happy . . . exceedingly happy! Effortlessly he moved along, feeling light and free, as if the wind was going to sweep him up to the heavens, up where everybody could see him—Randolph Johnson, the happiest little colored boy in all Louisiana!

When he reached the outskirts of the business district, where the bulk of the city's poor-whites lived, he slowed his pace. He felt instinctively that if he ran, one of them would accuse him of having stolen something; and if he moved too slow, he might be charged with looking for something to steal. He walked along with quick, cautious strides, glancing about fearfully now and then. Temporarily the happiness which the prospect of going Christmas shopping had brought him was subdued.

He passed a bedraggled Santa Claus, waving a tinny bell beside a cardboard chimney. He did not hesitate even when the tall fat man smiled at him through whiskers that were obviously cotton. He had seen the one real Santa weeks ago, in a big department store downtown, and had asked for all the things he wanted. This forlorn figure was merely one of Santa's helpers, and he had no time to waste on him just at the moment.

Further down the street he could see a gang of white boys, urchins of the street, clustered about an outdoor fruit stand. They were stealing apples, he was sure. He saw the white-aproned proprietor rush out; saw them disperse in all directions like a startled flock of birds, then gather together again only a few hundred feet ahead of him.

Apprehension surged through his body as the eyes of the gang leader fell upon him. Fear gripped his heart, and his brisk pace slowed to a cautious walk. He decided to cross the street to avoid the possibility of an encounter with this group of dirty, ragged white boys.

As he stepped from the curb the voice of the gang leader barked a sharp command. "Hey you, come here!"

The strange, uncomfortable fear within him grew. His eyes widened and every muscle in his body trembled with sudden uneasiness. He started to run, but before he could do so a wall of human flesh had been pushed around him. He was forced back onto the sidewalk, and each time he tried to slip through the crowd of laughing white boys he was shoved back abruptly by the red-headed youngster who led the others.

He gazed dumbfoundedly over the milling throng which was surrounding him, and was surprised to see that older persons, passersby, had joined to watch the fun. He looked back up the street, hopefully, toward the bell-ringing Santa Claus, and was surprised to find him calmly looking on from a safe distance, apparently enjoying the excitement.

He could see now that there was no chance to escape the gang until they let him go, so he just stood struggling desperately to steady his trembling form. His lips twitched nervously and the perspiration on his round black face reflected a dull glow. He could not think; his mind was heavy with confusion.

The red-headed boy was evidently the leader. He possessed a robustness that set him off from the others. They stared impatiently at him, waiting for his next move. He shifted his position awkwardly and spoke with all the scorn that he could muster:

"Whereya goin', nigger? An' don't you know we don't allow niggers in this neighborhood?"

His tone wasn't as harsh as he had meant it to be. It sounded a bit like poor play-acting.

"I'm jes' goin' to the ten-cent store," the little black boy said meekly. "Do my Chris'mus shopping."

He scanned the crowd hurriedly, hoping there might be a chance to escape. But he was completely engulfed. The wall of people about him was rapidly thickening; restless, curious people, laughing at him because he was frightened. Laughing and sneering at a little colored boy who had done nothing wrong, had harmed no one.

He began to cry. "Please, lemme go. I ain' done nothin'."

One of the boys said, "Aw, let 'im go." His suggestion was abruptly laughed down. The red-headed boy held up his hand. "Wait a minute, fellers," he said. "This nigger's goin' shoppin', he must have money, huh? Maybe we oughta see how much he's got."

The little black boy pushed his hand deeper into his pocket and clutched his quarter frantically. He looked about the outskirts of the crowd for a sympathetic adult face. He saw only the fat, sloppy-looking white man in the bedraggled Santa Claus suit that he had passed a moment earlier. This strange, cotton-bearded apparition was shoving his way now through the cluster of people, shifting his huge body along in gawky, poorly-timed strides like a person cursed with a sub-normal mentality.

When he reached the center of the circle within which the frightened boy was trapped, he waved the red-haired youth aside and, yanking off his flowing whiskers, took command of the situation.

"What's yo name, niggah?" he demanded.

The colored boy swallowed hard. He was more stunned than frightened; never in his life had he imagined Santa—or even one of Santa's helpers—in a role like this.

"My name's Randolph," he got out finally.

A smile wrinkled the leathery face of the man in the tattered red suit.

"Randolph!" he exclaimed, and there was a note of mockery in his tone. "Dat's no name fer er niggah! No niggah's got no business wit er nice name like dat!" Then, bringing his broad hand down forcefully on the boy's shoulder, he added, "Heah after yo' name's Jem!"

His words boomed over the crowd in a loud, brusque tone, defying all other sound. A series of submerged giggles sprang up among the boys as they crowded closer to get a better glimpse of the unmasked Santa Claus and the little colored boy. . . .

The latter seemed to have been decreasing in size under the heavy intensity of their gaze. Tears mingled with the perspiration flooding his round black face. Numbness gripped his body.

"Kin I go on now?" he pleaded. His pitifully weak tone was barely audible. "My momma told me to go straight to the ten-cent store. I ain't been botherin' nobody."

"If you don't stop dat damn cryin', we'll send you t'see Saint Peter." The fat white man spoke with anger and disgust. The cords in his neck quivered and new color came to his rough face, lessening its haggardness. He paused as if reconsidering what he had just said, then added: "Second thought, don't think we will. . . . Don't think Saint Peter would have anything t' do with a nigger."

The boys laughed long and heartily. When their laughter diminished, the red-coated man shifted his gawky figure closer to the little Negro and scanned the crowd, impatient and undecided.

"Let's lynch 'im," one of the youths cried.

"Yeah, let's lynch 'im!" another shouted, much louder and with more enthusiasm.

As if these words had some magic attached to them, they swept through the crowd. Laughter, sneers, and queer, indistinguishable mutterings mingled together.

Anguish was written on the boy's dark face. Desperately he looked about for a sympathetic countenance.

The words, "Let's lynch him," were a song now, and the song was floating through the December air, mingling with the sounds of tangled traffic.

"I'll get a rope!" the red-haired boy exclaimed. Wedging his way through the crowd, he shouted gleefully, "Just wait'll I get back!"

Gradually an ominous hush fell over the crowd. They stared questioningly, first at the frightened boy, then at the fat man dressed like Santa Claus who towered over him.

"What's that you got in yo' pocket?" the fat man demanded suddenly.

Frightened, the boy quickly withdrew his hands from his pockets and put them behind his back. The white man seized the right one and forced it open. On seeing its content, his eyes glittered with delight.

"Ah, a quarter!" he exclaimed. "Now tell me, niggah, where in th' hell did you steal this?"

"Didn't steal hit," the boy tried to explain. "My momma gave it to me."

"Momma gave it to you, heh?" The erstwhile Santa Claus snorted. He took the quarter and put it in a pocket of his red suit. "Niggahs ain't got no business wit' money whilst white folks is starving," he said. "I'll jes keep this quarter fer myself."

Worry spread deep lines across the black boy's forehead. His lips parted, letting out a short, muted sob. The crowd around him seemed to blur.

As far as his eyes could see, there were only white people all about him. One and all they sided with the curiously out-of-place Santa Claus. Ill-nourished children, their dirty, freckled faces lighted up in laughter. Men clad in dirty overalls, showing their tobacco-stained teeth. Women whose rutted faces had never known cosmetics, moving their bodies restlessly in their soiled housedresses. . . .

Suddenly the red-coated figure held up his hand for silence. He looked down at the little black boy and a new expression was on his face. It was not pity; it was more akin to a deep irksomeness. When the crowd quieted slightly, he spoke.

"Folks," he began hesitantly, "ah think this niggah's too li'l t' lynch. Besides, it's Christmas time. . . ."

"What's that got to do with it?" someone yelled.

"Well," the fat man answered slowly, "it jus' ain't late 'nuf in the season. 'Taint got cold yet round these parts. In this weather a lynched niggah would make the whole neighborhood smell bad."

A series of disappointed grunts belched up from the crowd. Some laughed; others stared protestingly at the red-coated white man. They were hardly pleased with his decision.

However, when the red-haired boy returned with a length of rope, the "let's lynch 'im" song had died down. He handed the rope to the white man, who took it and turned it over slowly in his gnarled hands.

"Sorry, sonny," he said. His tone was dry, with a slight tremor. He was not firmly convinced that the decision he had reached was the best one. "We 'sided not to lynch him; he's too li'l and it's too warm yet. And besides, what's one li'l niggah who ain't ripe enough to be lynched? Let's let 'im live a while . . . maybe we'll get 'im later."

The boy frowned angrily. "Aw, you guys!" he groaned. "T'think of all th' trouble I went to gettin' that rope. . . ."

In a swift, frenzied gesture his hand was raised to strike the little black boy, who curled up, more terrified than ever. But the bedraggled Santa stepped between them.

"Wait a minute, sonny," he said. "Look a here." He put his hand in the pocket of his suit and brought forth the quarter, which he handed to the red-haired boy.

A smile came to the white youth's face and flourished into jubilant laughter. He turned the quarter from one side to the other in the palm of his hand, marveling at it. Then he held it up so the crowd could see it, and shouted gleefully, "Sure there's a Santa Claus!"

The crowd laughed heartily.

Still engulfed by the huge throng, still bewildered beyond words, the crestfallen little colored boy stood whimpering. They had taken his fortune from him and there was nothing he could do about it. He didn't know what to think about Santa Claus now. About anything, in fact.

He saw that the crowd was falling back, that in a moment there would be a path through which he could run. He waited until it opened, then sped through it as fast as his stubby legs could carry him. With every step a feeling of thankfulness swelled within him.

The red-haired boy who had started the spectacle threw a rock after him. It fell short. The other boys shouted jovially, "Run, nigger, run!" The erstwhile Santa Claus began to readjust his mask.

The mingled chorus of jeers and laughter was behind the little colored boy, pushing him on like a great invisible force. Most of the crowd stood on the sidewalk watching him until his form became vague and finally disappeared around a corner. . . .

After a while he felt his legs weakening. He slowed down to a brisk walk, and soon found himself on the street that pointed toward his home.

Crestfallen, he looked down at his empty hands and thought of the shiny quarter that his mother had given him. He closed his right hand tightly, trying to pretend that it was still there. But that only hurt the more.

Gradually the fear and worry disappeared from his face. He was now among his neighbors, people that he knew. He felt bold and relieved. People smiled at him, said, "Hello." The sun had dried his tears.

He decided he would tell no one, except his mother, of his ordeal. She, perhaps, would understand, and either give him a new quarter or do his shopping for him. But what would she say about that awful figure of a Santa Claus? He decided not to ask her. There were some things no one, not even mothers, could explain.

1939

John Collier

Back for Christmas

"**D**octor," said Major Sinclair, "we certainly must have you with us for Christmas." Tea was being poured, and the Carpenters' living-room was filled with friends who had come to say last-minute farewells to the Doctor and his wife.

"He shall be back," said Mrs. Carpenter. "I promise you."

"It's hardly certain," said Dr. Carpenter. "I'd like nothing better, of course."

"After all," said Mr. Hewitt, "you've contracted to lecture only for three months."

"Anything may happen," said Dr. Carpenter.

"Whatever happens," said Mrs. Carpenter, beaming at them, "he shall be back in England for Christmas. You may all believe me."

They all believed her. The Doctor himself almost believed her. For ten years she had been promising him for dinner parties, garden parties, committees, heaven knows what, and the promises had always been kept.

The farewells began. There was a fluting of compliments on dear Hermione's marvellous arrangements. She and her husband would drive to Southampton that evening. They would embark the following day. No trains, no bustle, no last-minute worries. Certain the Doctor was marvellously looked after. He would be a great success in America. Especially with Hermione to see to everything. She would have a wonderful time, too. She would see the skyscrapers. Nothing like that in Little Godwearing. But she must be very sure to bring him back. "Yes, I will bring him back. You may rely upon it." He mustn't be persuaded. No extensions. No wonderful post at some super-American hospital. Our infirmary needs him. And he must be back by Christmas. "Yes," Mrs. Carpenter called to the last departing guest, "I shall see to it. He shall be back by Christmas."

The final arrangements for closing the house were very well managed. The maids soon had the tea things washed up; they came in, said goodbye, and were in time to catch the afternoon bus to Devizes.

Nothing remained but odds and ends, locking doors, seeing that everything was tidy. "Go upstairs," said Hermione, "and change into your brown tweeds. Empty the pockets of that suit before you put it in your bag. I'll see to everything else. All you have to do is not to get in the way."

The Doctor went upstairs and took off the suit he was wearing, but instead of the brown tweeds, he put on an old, dirty bath gown, which he took from the back of his wardrobe. Then, after making one or two little arrangements, he leaned over the head of the stairs and called to his wife, "Hermione! Have you a moment to spare?"

"Of course, dear. I'm just finished."

"Just come up here for a moment. There's something rather extraordinary up here."

Hermione immediately came up. "Good heavens, my dear man!" she said when she saw her husband. "What are you lounging about in that filthy old thing for? I told you to have it burned long ago."

"Who in the world," said the Doctor, "has dropped a gold chain down the bathtub drain?"

"Nobody has, of course," said Hermione. "Nobody wears such a thing."

"Then what is it doing there?" said the Doctor. "Take this flashlight. If you lean right over, you can see it shining, deep down."

"Some Woolworth's bangle off one of the maids," said Hermione. "It can be nothing else." However, she took the flashlight and leaned over, squinting into the drain. The Doctor, raising a short length of lead pipe, struck two or three times with great force and precision, and tilting the body by the knees, tumbled it into the tub.

He then slipped off the bathrobe and, standing completely naked, unwrapped a towel full of implements and put them into the washbasin. He spread several sheets of newspaper on the floor and turned once more to his victim.

She was dead, of course—horribly doubled up, like a somersaulter, at one end of the tub. He stood looking at her for a very long time, thinking of absolutely nothing at all. Then he saw how much blood there was and his mind began to move again.

First he pushed and pulled until she lay straight in the bath, then he removed her clothing. In a narrow bathtub this was an extremely clumsy business, but he managed it at last and then turned on the taps. The water rushed into the tub, then dwindled, then died away, and the last of it gurgled down the drain.

"Good God!" he said. "She turned it off at the main."

There was only one thing to do: the Doctor hastily wiped his hands on a towel, opened the bathroom door with a clean corner of the towel, threw it back onto the bath stool, and ran downstairs, barefoot, light as a cat. The cellar door was in a corner of the entrance hall, under the stairs. He knew just where the cut-off was. He had reason to: he had been pottering about down there for some time past—trying to scrape out a bin for wine, he had told Hermione. He pushed open the cellar door, went down the steep steps, and just before the closing door plunged the cellar into pitch darkness, he put his hand on the tap and turned it on. Then he felt his way back along the grimy wall till he came to the steps. He was about to ascend them when the bell rang.

The Doctor was scarcely aware of the ringing as a sound. It was like a spike of iron pushed slowly up through his stomach. It went on until it reached his brain. Then something broke. He threw himself down in the coal dust on the floor and said, "I'm through. I'm through!"

"They've got no *right* to come," he said. Then he heard himself panting. "None of this," he said to himself. "None of this."

He began to revive. He got to his feet, and when the bell rang again the sound passed through him almost painlessly. "Let them go away," he said. Then he heard the front door open. He said, "I don't care." His shoulder came up, like that of a boxer, to shield his face. "I give up," he said.

He heard people calling. "Herbert!" "Hermione!" It was the Wallingfords. "Damn them! They come butting in. People anxious to get off. All naked! And blood and coal dust! I'm done! I'm through! I can't do it."

"Herbert!"

"Hermione!"

"Where the dickens can they be?"

"The car's there."

"Maybe they've popped round to Mrs. Liddell's."

"We must see them."

"Or to the shops, maybe. Something at the last minute."

"Not Hermione. I say, listen! Isn't that someone having a bath? Shall I shout? What about whanging on the door?"

"Sh-h-h! Don't. It might not be tactful."

"No harm in a shout."

"Look, dear. Let's come in on our way back. Hermione said they wouldn't be leaving before seven. They're dining on the way, in Salisbury."

"Think so? All right. Only I want a last drink with old Herbert. He'd be hurt."

"Let's hurry. We can be back by half-past six."

The Doctor heard them walk out and the front door close quietly behind them. He thought, "Half-past six. I can do it."

He crossed the hall, sprang the latch of the front door, went upstairs, and taking his instruments from the washbasin, finished what he had to do. He came down again, clad in his bath gown, carrying parcel after parcel of towelling or newspaper neatly secured with safety pins. These he packed carefully into the narrow, deep hole he had made in the corner of the cellar, shovelled in the soil, spread coal dust over all, satisfied himself that everything was in order, and went upstairs again. He then thoroughly cleansed the bath, and himself, and the bath again, dressed, and took his wife's clothing and his bath gown to the incinerator.

One or two more little touches and everything was in order. It was only quarter past six. The Wallingfords were always late; he had only to get into the car and drive off. It was a pity he couldn't wait till after dusk, but he could make a detour to avoid passing through the main street, and even if he was seen driving alone, people would only think Hermione had gone on ahead for some reason and they would forget about it.

Still, he was glad when he had finally got away, entirely unobserved, on the open road, driving into the gathering dusk. He had to drive very carefully; he found himself unable to judge distances, his reactions were abnormally delayed, but that was a detail. When it was quite dark he allowed himself to stop the car on the top of the downs, in order to think.

The stars were superb. He could see the lights of one or two little towns far away on the plain below him. He was exultant. Everything that was to follow was perfectly simple. Marion was waiting in Chicago. She already believed him to be a widower. The lecture people could be put off with a word. He had nothing to do but establish himself in some thriving out-of-the-way town in America and he was safe for ever. There were Hermione's clothes, of course, in the suitcases; they could be disposed of through the porthole. Thank heaven she wrote her letters on the typewriter—a little thing like handwriting might have prevented everything. "But there you are," he said. "She was up-to-date, efficient all along the line. Managed everything. Managed herself to death, damn her!"

"There's no reason to get excited," he thought. "I'll write a few letters for her, then fewer and fewer. Write myself—always expecting to get back, never quite able to. Keep the house one year, then another, then another; they'll get used to it. Might even come back alone in a year or two and clear it up properly. Nothing easier. But not for Christmas!" He started up the engine and was off.

In New York he felt free at last, really free. He was safe. He could look back with pleasure—at least after a meal, lighting his cigarette, he could look back with a sort of pleasure—to the minute he had passed in the cellar listening to the bell, the door, and the voices. He could look forward to Marion.

As he strolled through the lobby of his hotel, the clerk, smiling, held up letters for him. It was the first batch from England. Well, what did that matter? It would be fun dashing off the typewritten sheets in Hermione's downright style, signing them with her squiggle, telling everyone what a success his first lecture had been, how thrilled he was with America but how certainly she'd bring him back for Christmas. Doubts could creep in later.

He glanced over the letters. Most were for Hermione. From the Sinclairs, the Wallingfords, the vicar, and a business letter from Holt & Sons, Builders and Decorators.

He stood in the lounge, people brushing by him. He opened the letters with his thumb, reading here and there, smiling. They all seemed very confident he would be back for Christmas. They relied on Hermione. "That's where they make their big mistake," said the Doctor, who had taken to American phrases. The builders' letter he kept to the last. Some bill, probably. It was:

Dear Madam,

We are in receipt of your kind acceptance of estimate as below and also of key.

We beg to repeat you may have every confidence in same being ready in ample time for Christmas present as stated. We are setting men to work this week.

We are, Madam,

Yours faithfully,
PAUL HOLT & SONS

To excavating, building up, suitably lining one sunken wine bin in cellar as indicated, using best materials, making good, etc.

. . . . £ 18/0/0

1939

EDNA FERBER

No Room at the Inn

"NOBODY" IS BORN IN NO MAN'S LAND

*Prague, Oct. 25 (U.P.)—A baby born in the no man's land south of
Brno, where 200 Jewish refugees have been living in a ditch between
Germany and Czechoslovakia for two weeks, was named Niemand
(Nobody) today.*

SHE HAD MADE every stitch herself, literally, every stitch, and
the sewing was so fairylike that the eye scarcely could see it.
Everything was new, too. She had been almost unreasonable
about that, considering Joe's meager and uncertain wage and the
frightening time that had come upon the world. Cousin Elisabeth
had offered to give her some of the clothing that her baby had outgrown,
but Mary had refused, politely, to accept these.

"That is dear and good of you, 'Lisbeth," Mary had said. "I know it seems
ungrateful, maybe, and even silly not to take them. It's hard to tell you how
I feel. I want everything of his to be new. I want to make everything myself.
Every little bit myself."

Cousin Elisabeth was more than twice as old as Mary. She understood
everything. It was a great comfort to have Elisabeth so near, with her wisdom and her warm sympathy. "No, I don't think it's silly at all. I know just
how you feel. I felt the same way when my John was coming." She laughed
then, teasingly: "How does it happen you're so sure it's going to be a boy?
You keep saying 'he' all the time."

Mary had gone calmly on with her sewing, one infinitesimal stitch after
the other, her face serene. "I know. I know." She glanced up at her older
cousin, fondly. "I only hope he'll be half as smart and good as your little
John."

Elisabeth's eyes went to the crib where the infant lay asleep. "Well, if I say
so myself, John certainly is smart for his age. But then"—hastily, for fear
that she should seem too proud—"but, then, Zach and I are both kind of

middle-aged. And they say the first child of middle-aged parents is likely to be unusually smart."

The eighteen-year-old Mary beamed at this. "Joe's middle-aged!" she boasted happily. Then she blushed the deep, flaming crimson of youth and innocence; for Joe's astonishment at the first news of the child's coming had been as great as her own. It was like a miracle wrought by some outside force.

Cousin Elisabeth had really made the match between the young girl and the man well on in years. People had thought it strange; but this Mary, for all her youth, had a wisdom and sedateness beyond her years, and an unexpected humor, too, quiet and strangely dry, such as one usually finds associated with long observation and experience. Joe was husband, father, brother to the girl. It was wonderful. They were well mated. And now, when life in this strange world had become so frightening, so brutal, so terrible, it was more than ever wonderful to have his strength and goodness and judgment as a shield and staff. She knew of younger men, hotheaded, who had been taken away in the night and never again heard from. Joe went quietly about his business. But each morning as he left her he said, "Stay at home until I come back this evening. Or, if you must do your marketing, take Elisabeth with you. I'll stop by and tell her to call for you. Don't go into the streets alone."

"I'll be all right," she said. "Nobody would hurt me." For here pregnant women were given special attention. The government wanted children for future armies.

"Not our children," Joe said bitterly.

So they lived quietly, quietly they obeyed the laws; they went nowhere. Two lower-middle-class people. Dreadful, unspeakable things were happening; but such things did not happen to her and to her husband and to her unborn child. Everything would right itself. It must.

Her days were full. There were the two rooms to keep clean, the marketing, the cooking, the sewing. The marketing was a tiring task, for one had to run from shop to shop to get a bit of butter, an egg for Joe, a piece of meat however coarse and tough. Sometimes when she came back to the little flat in the narrow street and climbed the three flights of stairs, the beads of sweat stood on her lip and forehead and her breath came painfully, for all her youth. Still, it was glorious to be able at night to show Joe a pan of coffeecake or a meat ball, or even a pat of pretty good butter. On Friday she always tried her hardest to get a fowl, however skinny, or a bit of beef or lamb because Friday was the eve of the Sabbath. She rarely could manage it; but that made all the sweeter her triumph when she did come home, panting up the stairs, with her scrap of booty.

Mary kept her sewing in a wicker basket neatly covered over with a clean white cloth. The little pile grew and grew. Joe did not know that she had regularly gone without a midday meal in order to save even that penny or two for the boy's furnishings. Sometimes Joe would take the sewing from her busy hands and hold it up, an absurd fragment of cloth, a miniature garment that looked the smaller in contrast with his great, work-worn hand. He would laugh as he held it, dangling. It seemed so improbable that anything alive and sentient should be small enough to fit into this scrap of cloth. Then, in the midst of his laugh, he would grow serious. He would stare at her and she at him and they would listen, hushed, as for a dreaded and expected sound on the stairs.

Floors to scrub, pots and pans to scour, clothes to wash, food to cook, garments to sew. It was her life, it was for Joe, it was enough and brimming over. Hers was an enormous pride in keeping things in order, the pride of possession inherited from peasant ancestors. Self-respect.

The men swarmed up the stairway so swiftly that Mary and Joe had scarcely heard their heavy boots on the first landing before they were kicking at the door and banging it with their fists. Joe sprang to his feet and she stood up, one hand at her breast and in that hand a pink knitted hood, no bigger than a fist, that she was knitting. Then they were in the room; they filled the little clean room with their clamor and their oaths and their great brown-clad bodies. They hardly looked at Joe and Mary, they ransacked the cupboards, they pulled out the linen and the dishes, they trampled these. One of the men snatched the pink cap from her hand and held it up and then put it on his own big, round head, capering with a finger in his mouth.

"Stop that!" said one in charge. "We've no time for such foolishness." And snatched off the pink hood, and blew his nose into it, and threw it in a corner.

In the cupboard they came upon the little cakes. She had saved drippings, she had skimmed such bits of rare fat as came their way, she had used these to fashion shortening for four little cakes, each with a dab of dried plum on top. Joe had eaten two for his supper and there had been two left for his breakfast. She had said she did not want any. Cakes made her too fat. It was bad for the boy.

"Look!" yelled the man who had found these. "Cakes! These swine have cakes to eat, so many that they can leave them uneaten in the cakebox." He broke one between his fingers, sniffed it like a dog, then bolted it greedily.

"Enough of this!" yelled the man in authority. "Stop fooling and come on! You want to stay in this pigsty all night! There's a hundred more. Come on. Out!"

Then they saw Mary, big as she was, and they made a joke of this, and one of them poked her a little with his finger, and still Joe did nothing; he was like a man standing asleep with his eyes wide open. Then they shoved them both from the room. As they went, Mary made a gesture toward the basket in the corner—the basket that had been covered so neatly with the clean white cloth. Her hand was outstretched; her eyes were terrible. The little stitches so small that even she had scarcely been able to see them, once she had pricked them into the cloth.

The man who had stuffed the cakes into his mouth was now hurriedly wiping his soiled boots with a bit of soft white, kneeling by the overturned basket as he did so. He was very industrious and concentrated about it, as they were taught to be thorough about everything. His tongue was out a little way between his strong yellow teeth and he rubbed away industriously. Then, at an impatient oath from the leader, he threw the piece of cloth into a corner with the rest of the muddied, trampled garments and hurried after so that he was there to help load them into the truck with the others huddled close.

Out of the truck and on the train they bumped along for hours—or it may have been days. Mary had no sense of time. Joe pillowed her head on his breast and she even slept a little, like a drugged thing, her long lashes meeting the black smudges under her eyes. There was no proper space for them all; they huddled on the floor and in the passages. Soon the scene was one of indescribable filth. Children cried, sometimes women screamed hysterically, oftenest they sat, men and women, staring into space. The train puffed briskly along with the businesslike efficiency characteristic of the country.

It was interesting to see these decent middle-class people reduced to dreadful squalor, to a sordidness unthought of in their lives. From time to time the women tried to straighten their clothing, to wash their bodies, but the cup of water here and there was needed for refreshment. Amidst these stenches and sounds, amidst the horror and degradation, Joe and Mary sat, part of the scene, yet apart from it. She had wakened curiously refreshed. It was as though a dream she had dreamed again and again, only to awake in horror, had really come to pass, and so, seeing it come true, she was better able to bear it, knowing the worst of it. Awake, she now laid his head in its turn on her breast and through exhaustion he slept, his eyes closed flutteringly but his face and hands clenched even in sleep. Joe had aged before her eyes, overnight. A strong and robust man, of sturdy frame, he had withered; there were queer hollows in his temples and blue veins throbbed there in welts she had never before seen.

Big though she was with her burden, she tried to help women younger and older than she. She was, in fact, strangely full of strength and energy, as often is the case with pregnant women.

The train stopped, and they looked out, and there was nothing. It started again, and they came to the border of the next country. Men in uniform swarmed amongst them, stepping over them and even on them as if they were vermin. Then they talked together and alighted from the train, and the train backed until it came again to the open fields where there was nothing. Barren land, and no sign of habitation. It was nowhere. It was nothing. It was neither their country nor the adjoining country. It was no man's land.

They could not enter here, they could not turn back there. Out they went, shoved and pushed, between heaven and hell, into purgatory. Lost souls.

They stumbled out into the twilight. It was October, it was today. Nonsense, such things do not happen, this is a civilized world, they told themselves. Not like this, to wander until they dropped and died.

They walked forward together, the two hundred of them, dazedly but with absurd purposefulness, too, as if they were going somewhere. The children stumbled and cried and stumbled again. Shed, barn, shelter there was none. There was nothing.

And then that which Mary had expected began to take place. Her pains began, wave on wave. Her eyes grew enormous and her face grew very little and thin and old. Presently she could no longer walk with the rest. They came upon a little flock of sheep grazing in a spot left still green in the autumn, and near by were two shepherds and a tiny donkey hardly bigger than a dog.

Joe went to the shepherds, desperate. "My wife is ill. She is terribly ill. Let me take your donkey. There must be some place near by—an inn. Some place."

One of the shepherds, less oafish than the other, and older, said, "There's an inn, but they won't take her."

"Here," said Joe, and held out a few poor coins that had been in his pocket. "Let her ride just a little way."

The fellow took the coins. "All right. A little way. I'm going home. It's suppertime. She can ride a little way."

So they hoisted her to the donkey's back and she crouched there, but presently it was her time, and she slipped off and they helped her to the ditch by the side of the road.

She was a little silly by now, what with agony and horror. "Get all the nice clean things, Joe. The linen things, they're in the box in the cupboard. And call Elisabeth. Put the kettle on to boil. No, not my best nightgown, that comes later, when everything is over and I am tidy again. Men don't know."

Her earth rocked and roared and faces were blurred and distorted and she was rent and tortured and she heard someone making strange noises like an animal in pain, and then there came merciful blackness.

When she awoke there were women bending over her, and they had built a fire from bits of wood and dried grass, and in some miraculous way there was warm water and strips of cloth and she felt and then saw the child by her side in the ditch and he was swaddled in decent wrappings. She was beyond the effort of questioning, but at the look in her eyes the woman bending over here said, "It's a boy. A fine boy." And she held him up. He waved his tiny arms and his hair was bright in the reflection of the fire behind him. But they crowded too close around her, and Joseph waved them away with one arm and slipped his other under her head and she looked up at him and even managed to smile.

As the crowd parted there was the sound of an automobile that came to a grinding halt. They were officials, you could see that easily enough, with their uniforms and their boots and their proud way of walking.

"Hr-r-rmph!" they said. "Here, all of you. Now then, what's all this! We had a hell of a time finding you, we never would have got here if we hadn't seen the light in the sky from your fire. Now, then, answer to roll call; we've got the names of all of you, so speak up or you'll wish you had."

They called the roll of the two hundred and each answered, some timidly, some scornfully, some weeping, some cringing, some courageously.

"Mary!" they called. "Mary."

She opened her eyes. "Mary," she said, in little more than a whisper.

"That must be the one," they said amongst themselves, the three. "That's the one had the kid just born." They came forward then and saw the woman Mary and the newborn babe in the ditch. "Yep, that's it. Born in a ditch to one of these damned Jews."

"Well, let's put it on the roll call. Might as well get it in now, before it grows up and tries to sneak out. What d'you call it? Heh, Mary?" He prodded her a little, not too roughly, with the toe of his boot.

She opened her eyes again and smiled a little as she looked up at him and then at the boy in her arm. She smiled while her eyes were clouded with agony.

"Niemand," she whispered.

"What's that? Speak up! Can't hear you."

She concentrated all her energies, she formed her lips to make sound again, and licked them because they were quite dry, and said once more, "Niemand . . . Nobody."

One man wrote it down, but the first man stared as though he resented being joked with, a man of his position. But at the look in her eyes he decided that she had not been joking. He stared and stared at the boy, the firelight shining on his tiny face, making a sort of halo of his hair.

"Niemand, eh? That the best you can do for him! . . . Jesus! . . . Well, cheer up, he's a fine-looking boy. He might grow up to be quite a kid, at that."

1939

Two People He Never Saw

EDDIE CASAVAN and Harry Marnix were walking up Fifth Avenue, around Fiftieth Street, when Christmas suddenly closed in on them. It got a tighter hold on Casavan, but the feel of Christmas clamped down on both of them. The store windows, the sharp air, the lights coming on in the late afternoon, and the couple of drinks they had on their walk must have done it.

They were turning off the Avenue when Eddie said, "I don't seem to want anything for Christmas any more."

"It's for the kids," Harry said. "It's a time for the kids, Christmas."

"Long after I was a kid I still wanted something for Christmas," Eddie said. "I'm forty-nine and it must have been only a couple of years ago that it came to me I didn't want anything for Christmas any more. I don't this year. The stuff in the windows looks nice, but I don't want any of it."

"It's mostly kids' stuff—things for kids for Christmas," Harry said.

"I know about that, but it's not what I mean," Eddie answered. "Let's go in this place. I got an hour. You going anyplace?"

"All right," said Harry. "No, I'm not. Not right away."

They weren't high. A little talky, maybe—nothing like tight. Eddie ordered two drinks. "Two Scotch highballs," he said, the more old-fashioned way of saying what practically everybody in New York now means by saying "Scotch-and-soda."

"I don't even want to go anyplace for Christmas, that's what I mean," Eddie went on as the bartender made up the drinks and left the bottle on the bar.

"I used to like to go to the six-day bike races," said Harry.

"They didn't have them at Christmas," Eddie said.

"I know it, but I used to like to go to them in winter and I don't seem to want to any more," Harry explained. "They don't have them, anyway, come to think of it."

"For Christmas I used to plan ahead," Eddie said. "Even up to a couple of years ago. And I always figured someplace to go or something to do special for Christmas. Now there's nothing I want and nothing I want to do."

"They used to yell 'B-r-r-rocco!' at the bike races," Harry said.

That got nowhere, and Eddie and Harry fiddled with the long glass sticks in their glasses.

"There *is* something I'd like to do Christmas at that," Eddie said after a while. "But it's impossible, maybe nuts."

"Christmas is nuts, a little," Harry said.

"Only way it could happen'd be an Aladdin's lamp. You rub it, you get what you want," Eddie continued. "Or if one of those kindhearted demons or something would hop out of that Scotch bottle there and grant a wish. That's kid stuff, I guess."

"Christmas is a kids' gag," Harry said. "As childish as six-day bike races, come to think of it. It felt like Christmas walking up the Avenue, didn't it? What if the gink should hop out of the bottle? What about it?"

"I was thinking that, too," Eddie said. "He could cook it up for me."

"What?"

"I'd like to take two people to Christmas dinner, a couple a people I never saw."

"Yuh?"

"One of them would be maybe forty now, a woman," Eddie said. "Oh, I don't know how old, tell the truth. Don't know how old she was when I first met her. No, wait a minute. The point is, I never met her."

"Movie star? Some notion like that?"

"No, no. Hell, no. Do you think I'm a kid?"

"No, what I mean is, Christmas is for kids. I didn't have you in mind."

"I often thought of her since. This was when I was having it tough one time, maybe fifteen years ago. Living in a furnished room on East Thirty-ninth Street—"

"And are they something, furnished rooms!" Harry put in.

"Furnished rooms are something if you've lived through and pull out of it you never forget them," Eddie said.

"I been in 'em." Harry nodded.

"God, I was sunk then!" Eddie said. "I was drinking too much and I lost one job after another. This time I was looking for a job and coming back every afternoon to the furnished room about four o'clock. That's how I never saw this girl."

"What girl?" Harry asked.

"The one I want to take to dinner at Christmas."

"If the gink comes out of the bottle," Harry said.

"Yeh, if he does. I remember I'd have a few beers after getting half promises of jobs, and I'd plank myself down on the bed in this little bit of a room when I came home four o'clock in the afternoon. It was the smallest room I was ever in. And the lonesomest."

"They get lonesome," Harry said.

"The walls are thin, too. The wall next to my bed was thin. Must have been like cardboard. This girl lived in the next room, the one I never met."

"Oh, yeh, yeh?" Harry said.

"I could hear her moving around. Sometimes she'd be humming and I could hear that. I could hear her open the window, or shut it if it was raining."

"Never see her?" Harry asked.

"No, that's the point of it. I almost thought I knew her, the way I could hear her. I could hear her leave every afternoon, about quarter past four. She had a kind of a lively step. I figured she was a waitress somewhere. Some job like that, don't you think?"

"I don't know, maybe a waitress, but *why*, though?" Harry said, and took a drink.

"Why *was* she a waitress, or why did I figure it out she's a waitress?" Eddie asked.

"Yeh, I mean why?" Harry answered in such a way that it meant how was it figured out.

"Oh, I could have been wrong. She had some steady job like waitress. She used to come home almost on the dot, quarter past one in the morning. You could set your clock on it. I used to look at my clock when she came in. Gee, her steps sounded tired when she was coming up the hall. She must have worked hard. She'd put the key in the lock and I'd hear that. I didn't sleep very good then. Worrying about a job, one thing and another. It'd be quarter past one by my clock. I hung on to that clock. I got it yet."

"Some people hate clocks in their room while they're sleeping," Harry said.

"They haven't lived in furnished rooms," Eddie said. "A clock is a great thing in a furnished room. This was a green one, ninety-eight cents. In a furnished room a clock is somebody there with you, anyway. The ticking sounds as if you're not altogether alone, for God's sake, if it's only the clock that's there with you."

"Never saw this girl—that's what you said?"

"Never saw her. Maybe she wasn't exactly a girl. I couldn't prove she wasn't a woman, older than a girl. When she hummed, though, I figured it sounded like a girl. Funny I never bumped into her in the hallway. Just didn't happen to. But I spoke to her once."

"Spoke to her?" Harry asked.

"Yeh. It was a gag. I told you I could hear everything. Well, her bunk was right next to mine—with only this wall there. And one afternoon she was getting up and she sneezed. It sounded funny from the next room. So I said very loud, '*Gesundheit!*' I remember she laughed. Her laugh sounded twenty-five."

"But you don't know, do you?"

"No, I don't and I won't. But if she was that age then, she'd be forty, around that, now, wouldn't she?"

"When was this?"

"I said about fifteen, could be sixteen years ago."

"Twenty-five and fifteen is forty, yes. She could be forty now," Harry said. "She could have been a bum. Did you ever think of that?"

"Harry, Harry, Harry, you don't get it at all! She couldn't have been a bum. A bum wouldn't have to live in such a bad room. I wanted to know her only because we were two people both having it tough together, and still and all we weren't together except when I said '*Gesundheit.*'"

Harry finished his drink and said pleasantly, "No, I don't mean it. I don't think she could have been a bum. Anyway, she would be about forty now, all right."

Eddie finished his drink and beckoned to the barkeep, who came and poured soda into the glasses. Eddie put in the whiskey, and when he put down the bottle he looked expectantly at it for a minute or two.

"And the guy would be about my own age now, about forty-nine or so, wouldn't he?" Eddie asked.

"Excuse me, but what guy?" Harry asked. "Oh, yeh, yeh, the guy."

"The one I'd like to take to Christmas dinner with her to the best place in town. Take the two of them. I've got a few bucks these days. I pulled through the furnished rooms all right, didn't I? I was thinking that, coming up the Avenue when the lights were going on."

"You're rambling, chum. Who is this feller, or maybe who was he?" Harry asked.

"It's 'who was he?' I don't know where he is, or is he dead or alive. I never saw his face. He was the soldier who picked me up in France. He picked me up off the ground, in the pitch dark, and he didn't have to."

"In the war?"

"Sure, in the war. Not this one, the other. But I bet it's happening too in this one."

"When you got hit, you mean?" Harry asked.

"That's the time, of course. You know how I hate professional ex-soldiers, guys always talking the other war. I don't want to be one of those."

"Oh, I know that, Eddie, I know it. But I know you were in the other one and got hit."

"It wasn't getting hit. That wasn't so much. It's this feller I often thought about at odd times all these years. Just to boil it down, it certainly was dark as hell, and there was no shooting going on at all. The first sergeant, guy named Baker, was with me. He got killed, I found out later. He stopped the big pieces of this shell. I only got the little pieces. We were going back through this town, going to find a place to sleep."

"A little French town?" Harry asked.

"What else? This was in France, for God's sake, so it was a little French town. Anyway, they suddenly threw one over and it hit right where we were, because the next thing I was pawing the wall of the house we were walking alongside of. I was trying to get up and my legs felt like ropes under me. When I went to stand up, they coiled."

"You were hit, all right," Harry said. "I saw your legs in swimming many a time, the marks on them."

"Oh, I don't care about that. The point is, this feller. I come to, there in the pitch dark, and somebody was prodding me with his foot. And whoever it was, he was saying, 'What's the matter, what's the matter?' I answered him. I said, 'My goddam legs.'"

"It was this guy, you mean?"

"Yes, him," Eddie said. "And then I passed out again. Well, I never saw the guy. I never saw his face. He could be black or white. He could be an angel, for all I know to this day. Anyway, he's who carried me through that pitch dark, and he didn't have to. He could have left me there. And I must have been bleeding like hell. Next thing, I came to, and I was lying on a table. It was an aid station in a cellar someplace. A doc was pouring ether by the canful over holes in my leg. That ether turns cold as hell if you pour it on anything. The guy wasn't around. Anyway, I didn't think of him then. Who the hell was he? I don't know. If it wasn't for that feller I never saw, I wouldn't be here today."

"It's a pretty good day to be here," Harry said.

Eddie took a drink and so did Harry. "That's the two of them—the ones I'd like to take to dinner when it comes to be Christmas night. But I won't."

"No, you won't," said Harry. "There's nothing coming out of the bottle but Scotch."

1944

MARY ROBERTS RINEHART

The Butler's Christmas Eve

WILLIAM STOOD in the rain waiting for the bus. In the fading daylight he looked rather like a freshly washed eighty-year-old and beardless Santa Claus, and underneath his raincoat he clutched a parcel which contained a much-worn nightshirt, an extra pair of socks, a fresh shirt and a brand-new celluloid collar. It also contained a pint flask of the best Scotch whisky.

Not that William drank, or at least not to speak of. The whisky was a gift, and in more than one way it was definitely contraband. It was whisky which had caused his trouble.

The Christmas Eve crowd around him was wet but amiable.

"Look, mama, what have you done with the suitcase?"

"What do you think you're sitting on? A bird cage?"

The crowd laughed. The rain poured down. The excited children were restless. They darted about, were lost and found again. Women scolded.

"You stand right here, Johnny. Keep under this umbrella. That's your new suit."

When the bus came along one of them knocked William's package into the gutter, and he found himself shaking with anxiety. But the bottle was all right. He could feel it, still intact. The Old Man would have it, all right, Miss Sally or no Miss Sally; the Old Man, left sitting in a wheelchair with one side of his big body dead and nothing warm in his stomach to comfort him. Just a year ago tonight on Christmas Eve William had slipped him a small drink to help him sleep, and Miss Sally had caught him at it.

She had not said anything. She had kissed her grandfather good-night and walked out of the room. But the next morning she had come into the pantry where William was fixing the Old Man's breakfast tray and dismissed him, after fifty years.

"I'm sorry, William. But you know he is forbidden liquor."

William put down the Old Man's heated egg cup and looked at her.

"It was only because it was Christmas Eve, Miss Sally. He was kind of low, with Mr. Tony gone and everything."

She went white at that, but her voice was even.

"I am trying to be fair," she said. "But even without this— You have worked a long time, and grandfather is too heavy for you to handle. I need a younger man, now that—"

She did not finish. She did not say that her young husband had enlisted in the Navy after Pearl Harbor, and that she had fought tooth and nail against it. Or that she suspected both her grandfather and William of supporting him.

William gazed at her incredulously.

"I've handled him, one way and another, for fifty years, Miss Sally."

"I know all that. But I've talked to the doctor. He agrees with me."

He stood very still. She couldn't do this to him, this girl he had raised, and her father before her. She couldn't send him out at his age to make a life for himself, after living a vicarious one in this house for half a century. But he saw helplessly that she could and that she meant to.

"When am I to go?" he asked.

"It would be kinder not to see him again, wouldn't it?"

"You can't manage alone, Miss Sally," he said stubbornly. But she merely made a little gesture with her hands.

"I'm sorry, William. I've already arranged for someone else."

He took the breakfast tray to the Old Man's door and gave it to the nurse. Then he went upstairs to his room and standing inside looked around him. This had been his room for most of his life. On the dresser was the faded snapshot of the Old Man as a Major in the Rough Riders during the Spanish War. There was a picture of Miss Sally's father, his only son, who had not come home from France in 1918. There was a very new one of Mr. Tony, young and good-looking and slightly defiant, taken in his new Navy uniform. And of course there were pictures of Miss Sally herself, ranging from her baby days to the one of her, smiling and lovely, in her wedding dress.

William had helped to rear her. Standing there he remembered the day when she was born. The Major—he was Major Bennett then, not the Old Man—had sent for him when he heard the baby's mother was dead.

"Well," he said heavily, "it looks as though we've got a child to raise. A girl at that! Think we can do it?"

"We've done harder things, sir," said William.

"All right," said the Major. "But get this, William, I want no spoiled brat around the place. If I find you spoiling her, by the Lord Harry I'll fire you."

"I won't spoil her," William had said sturdily. "But she'll probably be as stubborn as a mule."

"Now why the hell do you say that?" the Major had roared.

But William had only smiled.

So she had grown up. She was lovable, but she was wild as a March wind and as stubborn as the Bennetts had always been. Then—it seemed almost no time to William—she met Mr. Tony, and one day she was walking down a church aisle on her grandfather's arm, looking beautiful and sedate, and when she walked out again she was a married woman.

The old house had been gay after that. It was filled with youth and laughter. Then one day Miss Sally had gone to the hospital to have her baby, and her grandfather, gray of face, had waited for the news. William had tried to comfort him.

"I understand it's a perfectly normal process, sir," he said. "They are born every day. Millions of them."

"Get your smug face out of here," roared the Major. "You and your millions! What the hell do I care about them? It's my girl who's in trouble."

He was all right then. He was even all right when the message came that it was over, and Miss Sally and Mr. Tony had a ten-minute-old son. But going out of the hospital he had staggered and fallen, and he had never walked again. That was when the household began to call him the Old Man. Behind his back, of course.

It was tragic, because Miss Sally had had no trouble at all. She wakened at the hospital to learn that she had borne a man-child, asked if he had the proper number of fingers and toes, stated flatly that she had no intention of raising him for purposes of war, and then asked for a cigarette.

That had been two years ago, and she had come home on Christmas Eve. Mr. Tony had a little tree for the baby in the Old Man's bedroom, with Miss Sally's battered wax angel on the top, and the Old Man lay in his bed and looked at it.

"I suppose this kind of thing will save us, in the end," he said to William. "Damn it, man, people will go on having babies, and the babies will have Christmas trees, long after Hitler is dead and rotted."

The baby of course had not noticed the tree, and there was nothing to indicate that a year later William would be about to be dismissed, or that Mr. Tony, feverishly shaking a rattle before his sleeping offspring, would be in his country's uniform and somewhere on the high seas.

It was a bad year, in a way. It had told on Miss Sally, William thought. Her grandfather had taken his stroke badly. He would lie for hours, willing that stubborn will of his to move an arm, a leg, even a finger, on the stricken side. Nothing happened, of course, and at last he had accepted it, wheelchair and all. William had helped to care for him, turning his big body when the nurse changed the sheets, bathing him when he roared that he would be eternally damned if he would allow any woman to wash him. And during the long hours of the night it had been William who sat with him while he could not sleep.

Yet Miss Sally had taken it bravely.

"He cared for me all my life," she said. "Now I can care for him. William and I."

She had done it, too. William had to grant her that. She had turned a wing of the ground floor over to him, with a porch where he could sit and look out at the sea. She gave him time and devotion. Until Pearl Harbor, that is, and the night when Mr. Tony had slipped into the Old Man's room while William was playing chess with him, and put his problem up to them.

"You know, Sally," he said. "I can't even talk to her about this war. But she's safe here, and the boy too. And—well, somebody's got to fight."

The Old Man had looked down at that swollen helpless hand of his, lying in his lap.

"I see," he said. "You want to go, of course?"

"It isn't a question of wanting, is it?"

"It is, damn it," said the Old Man fiercely. "I wanted to go to Cuba. Her father couldn't get to France fast enough. I wouldn't give a tinker's curse for the fellow who doesn't want to go. But"—his voice softened—"it will hurt Sally like hell, son. She's had enough of war."

It had hurt her. She had fought it tooth and nail. But Tony had enlisted in the Navy almost at once, and he had gone a few days before Christmas. She did not cry when she saw him off, but she had the bleak look in her face which had never since entirely left it.

"I hope you enjoy it," she said.

"I don't expect to enjoy it, darling."

She was smiling, a strange stiff smile.

"Then why are you going?" she asked. "There are plenty of men who don't have to leave a wife to look after a baby and a helpless old man. Two old men," she said, and looked at William, standing by with the bags.

She was still not crying when after he had gone she had walked to the Old Man's room. William was there. She stood in the doorway looking at them.

"I hope you're both satisfied," she said, her voice frozen. "You can sit here, safe and sound, and beat the drums all you like. But I warn you, don't beat them where I can hear them. I won't have it."

Her grandfather eyed her.

"I raised you," he said. "William and I raised you. I guess we went wrong somewhere. You're spoiled after all. And I'll beat the drums all I damn please. So will William."

Only William knew that she had not gone to bed at all that night. Some time toward morning he had seen her down on the beach in the cold, staring out at the sea.

He had trimmed the boy's tree for him that Christmas Eve. And when it was finished, with the same ancient wax angel on the top, the Old Man had suddenly asked for a drink.

"To hell with the doctors," he said. "I'll drink to Tony if it's the last thing I ever do."

As it happened, it was practically the last thing William had to do for him. For of course he had just got the liquor down when Miss Sally walked in.

She dismissed William the next morning. He had gone upstairs and packed, leaving his livery but taking the photographs with him in his battered old suitcase. When he came down the stairs Miss Sally was waiting for him. He thought she had been crying, but the bleak look was in her face again.

"I'm sorry it has to be like this, William," she said stiffly. "I have your check here, and of course if you ever need any help—"

"I've saved my money," he told her stiffly. "I can manage. If it's all right I'd like to see the baby before I go."

She nodded, and he left her and went outside. The baby toddled to him, and William picked him up and held him close.

"You be a good boy," he said. "Be a good boy and eat your cereal every day."

"Dood boy," said the child.

William stood for a minute, looking out at the winter ocean where perhaps even now Mr. Tony might be. Then he put the child down.

"Look after him, Miss Jones," he told the nurse huskily. "He's about all his great-grandfather has left."

He found he was shaking when he got into the station wagon. Paul, the chauffeur, had to lift his suitcase. Evidently he knew. He looked concerned.

"This'll be hard as hell on the Old Man," he said. "What happened, anyhow?"

"Miss Sally's upset," said William evenly. "Mr. Tony going, and all that. She has no reason to like war."

"Who does?" said Paul glumly. "What do you bet they'll get me next?"

As they left a taxi was turning in at the gate. There was a tall swarthy man inside, and William disliked him instantly. Paul grunted.

"If that's the new fellow the Old Man will have him on his backside in a week," he said.

But so far as William knew the man was still there, and now he himself was on his way back, after a year, on some mysterious business he did not understand.

The bus rattled and roared along. The crowd was still amiable. It called Merry Christmas to each other, and strangers talked across the aisle. It was as though for this one night in the year one common bond united them. William, clutching his parcel, felt some of its warmth infecting him.

He had been very lonely. He had taken a room in the city, but most of the people he knew had died or moved away. He took out a card to the public library, and read a good bit. And when the weather was good he sat in the park at the edge of the river, watching the ships on their way up to the Sound to join their convoys. They traveled one after the other, great grayish black monsters, like elephants in a circus holding each other's tails. Sometimes they were battleships, sometimes freighters, laden to their Plimsoll marks, their decks covered with tanks and huge crates. So close were they that once on the bridge of a destroyer he thought he saw Mr. Tony. He stood up and waved his old hat, and the young officer saluted. But it was not Tony.

When the sinkings began he watched the newspapers, his heart beating fast. Then one day he saw Tony's picture. His ship had helped to rescue a crew at sea, and Tony was smiling. He looked tired and older, however. William had cut it out and sent it to the Old Man. But the only acknowledgment had been a post card. It had been duly censored for the United States Mail, and so all it said was: "Come back, you blankety blank fool."

However, if the Old Man had his pride, so did William. He had not gone back.

Then, just a week before, he had received a telegram. It too had evidently been censored, this time for the benefit of the telegraph company. So it read: DRAT YOUR STIFF-NECKED PRIDE. COME AND SEE ME. LETTER FOLLOWS.

As the bus rattled along he got out the letter. The crowd had settled down by that time. One by one the tired children had dropped off to sleep, and even the adults looked weary, as though having worked themselves into a fine pitch of excitement they had now relapsed into patient waiting. He got out his spectacles and re-read the letter.

It was a very odd sort of letter, written as it was in the Old Man's cramped hand. It was almost as though he had expected someone else to read it. If there was anything wrong it did not say so. In fact, it alluded only to a Christmas surprise for the baby. Nevertheless the directions were puzzling. William was to arrive quietly and after dark. He was to leave his taxi at the gate, walk in, and rap on the Old Man's bedroom window. It added that the writer would get rid of the nurse if he had to drown her in the bathtub, and it closed with what sounded like an appeal. "Don't be a damn fool. I need you."

He was still thinking about it when the bus reached its destination. The rain had continued, and the crowd got out to an opening of umbrellas and another search for missing parcels. William was stiff from the long ride, and the town surprised him. It was almost completely blacked out and his taxi, when he found one, had some sort of black material over all but a narrow strip on its headlights.

"Good thing too," said the driver companionably. "We're right on the coast. Too many ships getting sunk these days. One sunk off here only a week ago. If you ask me them Germans has fellows at work right in this place. Where'd you say to go?"

"The Bennett place. Out on the beach."

The driver grinned.

"Used to drive the Major now and then," he said. "Kind of a violent talker, ain't he?"

"He's had quite a bit of trouble," said William.

"Well, his granddaughter's a fine girl," said the driver. "Know where she is tonight? Trimming a tree out at the camp. I seen her there myself."

"She always was a fine girl," said William sturdily.

The driver protested when he got out at the gate.

"Better let me take you in. It's raining cats and dogs."

But William shook his head.

"I want to surprise them. I know the way."

The cab drove off to an exchange of Christmas greetings, and William started for the house. There were no lights showing as he trudged along the driveway, but he could hear ahead of him the steady boom of the waves as the Atlantic rolled in, the soft hiss of the water as it rolled up the beach. Just so for fifty years had he heard it. Only now it meant something new and different. It meant danger, men in ships watching against death; Mr. Tony perhaps somewhere out there in the dark, and the Old Man knowing it and listening, as he was listening.

He was relieved when he saw the garage doors open and no cars inside. He made his way cautiously around the house to the Old Man's wing, and stood listening under the bedroom window. There was no sound inside, however, and he wondered what to do. If he was asleep— Suddenly he sneezed, and he almost jumped out of his skin when a familiar voice spoke, almost at his ear.

"Come in, damn it," said the voice irritably. "What the hell are you waiting for? Want to catch your death of pneumonia?"

Suddenly William felt warm and comfortable again. This was what he had needed, to be sworn at and shouted at, to see the Old Man again, to hear him roar, or to be near him in contented silence. He crawled through the window, smiling happily.

"Nothing wrong with your voice, anyhow," he said. "Well, here I am, sir."

"And about time," said the Old Man. "Turn up the light and let me look at you. Shut the window and draw those curtains. Hah! You're flabby!"

"I've gained a little weight," William admitted.

"A little! Got a tummy like a bowl of jelly."

These amenities over they grinned at each other, and the Old Man held out his good hand.

"God," he said, "I'm glad to see you. We're going straight to the devil here. Well, a Merry Christmas to you anyhow."

"The same to you, sir."

They shook hands, and William surveyed the Old Man, sitting bolt upright in his wheelchair. He looked as truculent as ever, but some of the life had gone out of his face.

"So you ran out on me!" he said. "Why the devil didn't you turn Sally over your knee and spank her? I've seen you do it."

"I'm not as strong as I used to be," said William apologetically. The Old Man chuckled.

"She's a Bennett," he said. "Always was, always will be. But she's learning. Maybe it's the hard way, but she's learning." He eyed William. "Take off that coat, man," he said. "You're dripping all over the place. What's that package? Anything in it but your nightshirt?"

"I've got a pint of Scotch," William admitted.

"Then what are we waiting for?" shouted the Old Man. "Sally's out. The nurse is out. Jarvis is out—that's the butler, if he is a butler and if that's his name. And the rest have gone to bed. Let's have it. It's Christmas Eve, man!"

"They oughtn't to leave you like that," William said reprovingly.

"Each of them thinks somebody else is looking after me." The Old Man chuckled. "Get some glasses. I guess you know your way. And take a look around when you get there."

William went back to the familiar rear of the house. His feet were wet and a small trickle of water had escaped his celluloid collar and gone down his back; but he walked almost jauntily. Until he saw his pantry, that is.

He did not like what he saw. The place even smelled unclean, and the silver was only half polished, the glasses he held to the light were smeared, and the floor felt sticky under his feet.

Resentfully he washed two glasses, dried them on a not too clean dish towel, and went back. The Old Man watched him from under his heavy eyebrows.

"Well, what do you think of it?" he inquired. "Is the fellow a butler?"

"He's not a good one, sir."

But the Old Man said nothing more. He took his glass and waited until William had poured his own drink. Then he lifted the glass.

"To Tony," he said. "A safe Christmas to him, and to all the other men with the guts to fight this war."

It was like a prayer. It probably was a prayer, and William echoed it.

"To Mr. Tony," he said, "and all the rest."

Then at last the Old Man explained his letter. He didn't trust the man Jarvis. Never had. Too smooth. Sally, of course, did not suspect him, although he was damned inefficient. Anyhow what could she do, with every able-bodied man in service or making armament?

"But there's something queer about him," he said. "And you may not know it, but we had a ship torpedoed out here last week. Some of the men landed on the beach. Some never landed anywhere, poor devils."

"I heard about it," said William. "What do you want me to do?"

"How the hell do I know?" said the Old Man. "Look around. See if there's anything suspicious. And if there isn't, get rid of him anyhow. I don't like him."

A thin flush rose to William's wrinkled face.

"You mean I'm to stay?" he inquired.

"Why the devil do you suppose I brought you back?" shouted the Old Man. "Don't stand there staring. Get busy. We haven't got all night."

William's strictly amateur activities, however, yielded him nothing. His old room—now belonging to Jarvis—surprised him by its neatness, but unless that in itself was suspicious, there was nothing more. No flashlight for signaling, no code book, which William would certainly not have recognized anyhow, not even a radio.

"Tidy, is it?" said the Old Man when he reported back. "Well, I suppose that's that. I'd hoped to hand the F. B. I. a Christmas gift, but— All right, no spy. I've got another job for you, one you'll like better." He leaned back in his chair and eyed William quizzically. "Sally's not having a tree this year for the boy. I don't blame her. For months she's worked her fool head off. Army, Navy, and what have you. She's tired. Maybe she's breaking her heart. Sometimes I think she is. But by the Lord Harry he's having a tree just the same."

William looked at his watch.

"It's pretty late to buy one," he said. "But of course I can try."

The Old Man grinned, showing a perfect set of his own teeth, only slightly yellowed.

"Think I'm getting old, don't you?" he scoffed. "Always did think you were smarter than I was, didn't you? Well, I'm not in my dotage yet. The tree's on the porch. Had it delivered tonight. Unless," he added unkindly, "you're too feeble to drag it in!"

William also grinned, showing a perfect set of teeth, certainly not his own, except by purchase.

"I suppose you wouldn't care to take a bet on it, sir?" he said happily.

Ten minutes later the tree was in place in a corner of the Old Man's sitting room. William was perspiring but triumphant. The Old Man himself was exhilarated with one small drink and an enormous pride. Indeed, both were eminently cheerful until, without warning, they heard the sound of a car outside.

It was Sally, and before she had put up her car and got back to the house, William was hidden in the darkened sitting room, and her grandfather was sedately reading in his chair beside a lamp. From where he stood William could see her plainly. She had changed, he thought. She looked older. But she looked gentler, too, as though at last she had learned some of the lessons of life. Her eyes were no longer bleak, but they were sunken in her head. Nevertheless William felt a thrill of pride. She was their girl, his and the Old Man's, and now she was a woman. A lovely woman, too. Even William, no connoisseur, could see that.

"Good gracious, why aren't you in bed?" she said, slipping off her fur coat. "And where's the nurse?"

"It's Christmas Eve, my dear. I sent her off for a while. She'll be back."

But Sally was not listening. Even William could see that. She sat down on the edge of a chair and twisted her fingers in her lap.

"There wasn't any mail, was there?"

"I'm afraid not. Of course we don't know where he is. It may be difficult for him to send any."

Suddenly she burst out.

"Why don't you say it?" she demanded. "You always say what you think. I sent Tony off wrong. I can't forgive myself for that. I was wrong about William, too. You miss him, don't you?"

"Miss him?" said the Old Man, deliberately raising his voice. "Why would I miss the old rascal? Always pottering around and doing nothing! I get along fine without him."

"I think you're lying to make me feel better," she said, and got up. "I was wrong about him, and tonight I realized I'd been wrong about the baby's tree. When I saw the men around the one we'd fixed for them— I've made a mess of everything, haven't I?"

"Most of us do, my dear," said her grandfather. "But we learn. We learn."

She went out then, closing the door quietly behind her. When William went into the bedroom he found the Old Man staring somberly at the fire.

"Damn war anyhow," he said violently. "Damn the blasted lunatics who wished it on the earth. All I need now is for some idiots to come around and sing 'Peace on earth, good will to men!'"

As though it might have been a signal, from beyond the window suddenly came a chorus of young voices, and William gingerly raised the shade. Outside, holding umbrellas in one hand and clutching their blowing cassocks around them with the other, the choir boys from the nearby church were singing, their small scrubbed faces earnest and intent. They sang about peace, and the King of peace who had been born to save the world, and the Old Man listened. When they had gone he grinned sheepishly.

"Well, maybe they're right at that," he said. "Sooner or later peace has to come. How about a small drink to the idea, anyhow?"

They drank it together and in silence, and once more they were back where they had been a year ago. No longer master and man, but two friends of long standing, content merely to be together.

"So you've been doing fine without me, sir?" said William, putting down his glass.

"Hell, did you hear that?" said the Old Man innocently.

They chuckled as at some ancient joke.

It was after eleven when William in his socks made his way to the attic where the trimmings for the tree were stored. Sally was still awake. He could hear her stirring in her room. For a moment he stood outside and listened, and it seemed no time at all since he had done the same thing when she was a child, and had been punished and sent to bed. He would stand at her door and tap, and she would open it and throw herself sobbing into his arms.

"I've been a bad girl, William."

He would hold her and pat her thin little back.

"Now, now," he would say. "Take it easy, Sally. Maybe William can fix it for you."

But of course there was nothing he could fix now. He felt rather chilly as he climbed the attic stairs.

To his relief the attic was orderly. He turned on the light and moving cautiously went to the corner where the Christmas tree trimmings, neatly boxed and covered, had always stood. They were still there. He lifted them, one by one, and placed them behind him. Then he stiffened and stood staring.

Neatly installed behind where they had been was a small radio transmitter.

He knew it at once for what it was, and a slow flush of fury suffused his face as he knelt down to examine it.

"The spy!" he muttered thickly, "the dirty devil of a spy!"

So this was how it was done. This was how ships were being sunk at sea; the convoys assembling, the ships passing along the horizon, and men like Jarvis watching, ready to unleash the waiting submarine wolves upon them.

He was trying to tear it out with his bare hands when he heard a voice behind him.

"Stay where you are, or I'll shoot."

But it was not Jarvis. It was Sally, white and terrified, in a dressing gown over her nightdress and clutching a revolver in her hand. William got up slowly and turned, and she gasped and dropped the gun.

"Why, William!" she said. "What are you doing here?"

He stood still, concealing the transmitter behind his stocky body.

"Your grandfather sent for me," he said, with dignity. "He was planning a little surprise for you and the boy, in the morning."

She looked at him, at his dependable old face, at the familiar celluloid collar gleaming in the light, at his independent sturdy figure, and suddenly her chin quivered.

"Oh, William," she said. "I've been such a dreadful person."

All at once she was in his arms, crying bitterly.

"Everything's so awful," she sobbed. "I'm so frightened, William. I can't help it."

And once more he was holding her and saying:

"It will be all right, Sally girl. Don't you worry. It will be all right."

She quieted, and at last he got her back to her room. He found that he was shaking, but he went methodically to work. He did what he could to put the transmitter out of business. Then he piled up the boxes of trimmings and carried them down the stairs. There was still no sign of Jarvis, and the Old Man was dozing in his chair. William hesitated. Then he shut himself in the sitting room and cautiously called the chief of the local police.

"This is William," he said. "The butler at Major Bennett's. I—"

"So you're back, you old buzzard, are you?" said the chief. "Well, Merry Christmas and welcome home."

But he sobered when William told him what he had discovered. He promised to round up some men, and not—at William's request—to come as if they were going to a fire.

"We'll get him all right," he said. "We'll get all these dirty polecats sooner or later. All right. No siren. We'll ring the doorbell."

William felt steadier after that. He was in the basement getting a ladder for trimming the tree when he heard Jarvis come back. But he went directly up the back stairs to his room, and William, listening below, felt that he would not visit the attic that night.

He was singularly calm now. The Old Man was sound asleep by that time, and snoring as violently as he did everything else. William placed the ladder and hung the wax angel on the top of the tree. Then he stood precariously and surveyed it.

"Well, we're back," he said. "We're kind of old and battered, but we're still here, thank God."

Which in its way was a prayer too, like the Old Man's earlier in the evening.

He got down, his legs rather stiff, and going into the other room touched the sleeper lightly on the shoulder. He jerked awake.

"What the hell did you do that for?" he roared. "Can't a man take a nap without your infernal interfering?"

"The tree's ready to trim," said William quietly.

Fifteen minutes later the nurse came back. The bedroom was empty, and in the sitting room before a half-trimmed tree the Old Man was holding a small—a very small—drink in his hand. He waved his glass at her outraged face.

"Merry Christmas," he said, a slight—a very slight—thickness in his voice. "And get me that telegram that came for Sally today."

She looked disapprovingly at William, a William on whom the full impact of the situation—plus a very small drink—had suddenly descended like the impact of a pile-driver. Her austere face softened.

"You look tired," she said. "You'd better sit down."

"Tired? Him?" scoffed the Old Man. "You don't know him. And where the hell's that telegram?"

She brought it, and he put on his spectacles to read it.

"Sally doesn't know about it," he explained. "Held it out on her. Do her good." Then he read it aloud. "Home for breakfast tomorrow. Well. Love. Merry Christmas. Tony."

He folded it and looked around, beaming.

"How's that for a surprise?" he demanded. "Merry Christmas! Hell, it will be a real Christmas for everybody."

William stood still. He wanted to say something, but his voice stuck in his throat. Then he stiffened. Back in the pantry the doorbell was ringing.

1944

KATHERINE ANNE PORTER

A Christmas Story

WHEN SHE WAS five years old, my niece asked me again why we celebrated Christmas. She had asked when she was three and when she was four, and each time had listened with a shining, believing face, learning the songs and gazing enchanted at the pictures which I displayed as proof of my stories. Nothing could have been more successful, so I began once more confidently to recite in effect the following:

The feast in the beginning was meant to celebrate with joy the birth of a Child, an event of such importance to this world that angels sang from the skies in human language to announce it and even, if we may believe the old painters, came down with garlands in their hands and danced on the broken roof of the cattle shed where He was born.

"Poor baby," she said, disregarding the angels, "didn't His papa and mama have a house?"

They weren't quite so poor as all that, I went on, slightly dashed, for last year the angels had been the center of interest. His papa and mama were able to pay taxes at least, but they had to leave home and go to Bethlehem to pay them, and they could have afforded a room at the inn, but the town was crowded because everybody came to pay taxes at the same time. They were quite lucky to find a manger full of clean straw to sleep in. When the baby was born, a goodhearted servant girl named Bertha came to help the mother. Bertha had no arms, but in that moment she unexpectedly grew a fine new pair of arms and hands, and the first thing she did with them was to wrap the baby in swaddling clothes. We then sang together the song about Bertha the armless servant. Thinking I saw a practical question dawning in a pure blue eye, I hurried on to the part about how all the animals—cows, calves, donkeys, sheep——

"And pigs?"

Pigs perhaps even had knelt in a ring around the baby and breathed upon Him to keep Him warm through His first hours in this world. A new star appeared and moved in a straight course toward Bethlehem for many nights to guide three kings who came from far countries to place important gifts in the straw beside Him: gold, frankincense and myrrh.

"What beautiful clothes," said the little girl, looking at the picture of Charles the Seventh of France kneeling before a meek blond girl and a charming baby.

It was the way some people used to dress. The Child's mother, Mary, and His father, Joseph, a carpenter, were such unworldly simple souls they never once thought of taking any honor to themselves nor of turning the gifts to their own benefit.

"What became of the gifts?" asked the little girl.

Nobody knows, nobody seems to have paid much attention to them, they were never heard of again after that night. So far as we know, those were the only presents anyone ever gave to the Child while He lived. But He was not unhappy. Once he caused a cherry tree in full fruit to bend down one of its branches so His mother could more easily pick cherries. We then sang about the cherry tree until we came to the words *Then up spake old Joseph, so rude and unkind.*

"Why was he unkind?"

I thought perhaps he was just in a cross mood.

"What was he cross about?"

Dear me, what should I say now? After all, this was not *my* daughter, whatever would her mother answer to this? I asked her in turn what she was cross about when she was cross? She couldn't remember ever having been cross but was willing to let the subject pass. We moved on to *The Withy Tree*, which tells how the Child once cast a bridge of sunbeams over a stream and crossed upon it, and played a trick on little John the Baptist, who followed Him, by removing the beams and letting John fall in the water. The Child's mother switched Him smartly for this with a branch of withy, and the Child shed loud tears and wished bad luck upon the whole race of withies for ever.

"What's a withy?" asked the little girl. I looked it up in the dictionary and discovered it meant osiers, or willows.

"Just a willow like ours?" she asked, rejecting this intrusion of the commonplace. Yes, but once, when His father was struggling with a heavy piece of timber almost beyond his strength, the Child ran and touched it with one finger and the timber rose and fell properly into place. At night His mother cradled Him and sang long slow songs about a lonely tree waiting for Him in a far place; and the Child, moved by her tears, spoke long before it was time for Him to speak and His first words were, "Don't be sad, for you shall be Queen of Heaven." And there she was in an old picture, with the airy jeweled crown being set upon her golden hair.

I thought how nearly all of these tender medieval songs and legends about this Child were concerned with trees, wood, timbers, beams, cross-pieces; and even the pagan north transformed its great druidic tree fes-tooned with human entrails into a blithe festival tree hung with gifts for the Child, and some savage old man of the woods became a rollicking saint with a big belly. But I had never talked about Santa Claus, because myself I had not liked him from the first, and did not even then approve of the boisterous way he had almost crowded out the Child from His own birth-day feast.

"I like the part about the sunbeam bridge the best," said the little girl, and then she told me she had a dollar of her own and would I take her to buy a Christmas present for her mother.

We wandered from shop to shop, and I admired the way the little girl, surrounded by tons of seductive, specially manufactured holiday merchan-dise for children, kept her attention fixed resolutely on objects appropriate to the grown-up world. She considered seriously in turn a silver tea service, one thousand dollars; an embroidered handkerchief with lace on it, five dollars; a dressing-table mirror framed in porcelain flowers, eighty-five dol-lars; a preposterously showy crystal flask of perfume, one hundred twenty dollars; a gadget for curling the eyelashes, seventy-five cents; a large plaque of colored glass jewelry, thirty dollars; a cigarette case of some fraudulent material, two dollars and fifty cents. She weakened, but only for a moment, before a mechanical monkey with real fur who did calisthenics on a cross-bar if you wound him up, one dollar and ninety-eight cents.

The prices of these objects did not influence their relative value to her and bore no connection whatever to the dollar she carried in her hand. Our shopping had also no connection with the birthday of the Child or the legends and pictures. Her air of reserve toward the long series of blear-eyed, shapeless old men wearing red flannel blouses and false, white-wool whiskers said all too plainly that they in no way fulfilled her notions of Christmas merriment. She shook hands with all of them politely, could not be persuaded to ask for anything from them and seemed not to question the obvious spectacle of thousands of persons everywhere buying presents instead of waiting for one of the army of Santa Clauses to bring them, as they all so profusely promised.

Christmas is what we make it and this is what we have so cynically made of it: not the feast of the Child in the straw-filled crib, nor even the homely winter bounty of the old pagan with the reindeer, but a great glittering commercial fair, gay enough with music and food and extravagance of feeling and behavior and expense, more and more on the order of the ancient Saturnalia. I have nothing against Saturnalia, it belongs to this season of the year: but how do we get so confused about the true meaning of even our simplest-appearing pastimes?

Meanwhile, for our money we found a present for the little girl's mother. It turned out to be a small green pottery shell with a colored bird perched on the rim which the little girl took for an ash tray, which it may as well have been.

"We'll wrap it up and hang it on the tree and *say* it came from Santa Claus," she said, trustfully making of me a fellow conspirator.

"You don't believe in Santa Claus any more?" I asked carefully, for we had taken her infant credulity for granted. I had already seen in her face that morning a skeptical view of my sentimental legends, she was plainly trying to sort out one thing from another in them; and I was turning over in my mind the notion of beginning again with her on other grounds, of making an attempt to draw, however faintly, some boundary lines between fact and fancy, which is not so difficult; but also further to show where truth and poetry were, if not the same being, at least twins who could wear each other's clothes. But that couldn't be done in a day nor with pedantic intention. I was perfectly prepared for the first half of her answer, but the second took me by surprise.

"No, I don't," she said, with the freedom of her natural candor, "but please don't tell my mother, for she still does."

For herself, then, she rejected the gigantic hoax which a whole powerful society had organized and was sustaining at the vastest pains and expense, and she was yet to find the grain of truth lying lost in the gaudy debris around her, but there remained her immediate human situation, and that she could deal with, or so she believed: her mother believed in Santa Claus, or she would not have said so. The little girl did not believe in what her mother had told her, she did not want her mother to know she did not believe, yet her mother's illusions must not be disturbed. In that moment of decision her infancy was gone forever, it had vanished there before my eyes.

Very thoughtfully I took the hand of my budding little diplomat, whom we had so lovingly, unconsciously prepared for her career, which no doubt would be quite a successful one; and we walked along in the bright sweet-smelling Christmas dusk, myself for once completely silenced.

1946

"Santa Clo" Comes to La Cuchilla

A PIECE OF RED bunting on a bamboo pole marked the location of Peyo Mercé's one-room schoolhouse. A partition down the middle divided the tiny school into two classrooms; over one of them a new teacher—Mister Johnny Rosas—now presided.

Because of a lamentable incident in which Peyo Mercé had made the superintendent appear in an unfavorable light, the latter thought it wise to appoint a second teacher to the district of La Cuchilla so he could instruct Peyo in the newest educational methods and bring the lamp of progress to illuminate that unenlightened district.

He called the young teacher to his office. Johnny Rosas, a recent graduate, had spent a short time in the United States. Solemnly the superintendent said to him:

"Listen, Johnny; I'm going to send you to the district of La Cuchilla so you can take them the most up-to-date techniques you learned in your Education courses. That Peyo doesn't know a thing about it; he's forty years behind the times in the subject. Try to change their ways, and above all you must teach a great deal of English . . . a lot of English."

One day Peyo Mercé saw the fledgling teacher coming up the hill toward the school on an old horse. He even felt a little sorry for him, and said to himself: "Life is probably cutting furrows in him already, just as a plough does in the earth." And he told some farm children to take the harness off the horse and put it out to pasture.

Peyo knew that life was going to be very hard for the young man. Out in the country living conditions are bad, and meals are poor: rice, beans, codfish, and plenty of water. The roads are almost impassable, and always full of puddles. Baths had to be taken in mountain streams, and the only drinking water was rain water. Peyo Mercé had to make his lesson plans by the flickering light of an oil lamp.

One day Johnny Rosas said to Peyo, "This district is very backward; we have to make it over. It is imperative to bring in new things, replace what is traditional. Remember what the superintendent said: 'Down with tradition.' We have to teach a great deal of English, and copy the customs of the Americans."

And Peyo, not very enthusiastic, managed to squeeze out these words:

"True, English is good, and we need it. But good Heavens! We don't even know how to speak Spanish well! And hungry children turn into dull-witted little animals. Once the fox said to the snails: 'You have to learn how to walk before you can run.'"

But Johnny didn't understand what Peyo meant.

The tobacco region took on a somewhat livelier mood: the Christmas holidays were approaching. Peyo had already observed with affection that some of his pupils were fashioning rustic guitars out of cedar wood. These fiestas always brought him happy memories of times gone by, and he seemed to hear the Christmas carol that goes

> *The door of this house is open wide;*
> *It shows a gentleman lives inside.*

Johnny Rosas ended Peyo's pleasant reverie with these words:

"This year Santa Claus will make his debut in La Cuchilla. All that business about the gifts of the Three Wise Men on January 6th is growing old-fashioned; it's no longer done to any extent in San Juan. That belongs to the past. I'll invite the superintendent, Mister Rogelio Escalera, to the party; he'll like that a lot."

Peyo scratched his head and said quietly, "I'm just a country fellow who's never left these hills, so the story of the Three Wise Men is right here in my heart. We country folk are sensitive to the things in the atmosphere around us, just as we can smell codfish cooking."

Johnny, by means of class projects, set to work preparing the atmosphere for what he called the "gala première" of Santa Claus in La Cuchilla. He showed his pupils a picture of Santa Claus riding in a sleigh pulled by reindeer. And Peyo, who had stopped for a moment at the threshold of the door between the two classrooms, saw in his mind's eye another picture: an old farmer pulled along on a palm-leaf sledge by goats.

Mister Rosas asked the farm children, "Who is this important person?"

And Benito answered, "Mister, that is the Old Year, painted red."

Johnny was amazed at the ignorance of those children, and at the same time angry at Peyo Mercé's negligence.

Christmas came, and the parents were invited. Peyo held a typical little fiesta in his room. Some farm children sang Puerto Rican songs and Christmas carols to the accompaniment of rustic guitars. And to conclude the performance the Three Wise Men appeared, while an old singer named Simón improvised verses like this:

> *They come and go from far and near;*
> *We country folk just stay right here.*

Peyo handed out traditional rice sweets and candies, and the children exchanged little presents. Then he told his children to file into the room of Mister Johnny Rosas, who had a surprise for them and had even invited the superintendent, Mister Rogelio Escalera.

In the middle of the classroom stood an artificial Christmas tree. Red streamers were stretched from one bookcase to another, and from the walls hung little wreaths with green leaves and red berries. In frosted white letters was a sign that said in English, "Merry Christmas." Artificial snow was sprinkled over the whole display.

The spectators looked in amazement at all this, which they had never seen before. Mister Rogelio Escalera was greatly pleased.

Some of the children went up on an improvised platform and arranged themselves so that they spelled out "Santa Claus." One told about the life of Father Christmas, and a children's chorus sang "Jingle Bells" in English as they shook some tiny bells. The parents looked at one another in astonishment.

Mister Rosas went outside a moment. Superintendent Escalera spoke to the parents and children. He congratulated the district upon such a lovely Christmas party, and upon having such a progressive teacher as Mister Rosas. And then Mister Escalera asked the audience to be very quiet, because soon they were going to meet a strange and mysterious person.

A tiny chorus immediately burst into song:

> *Santa's coming in his sleigh,*
> *Riding slowly all the way.*
> *Clip, clop! Clip, clop!*

Suddenly there appeared at the classroom door the figure of Santa Claus, carrying a pack over his shoulder. His deep voice boomed out in English: "Here is Santa! Merry Christmas to you all!"

A scream of terror shook the classroom. Some farmers threw themselves out the windows; the smallest children began to cry, and clung to their mothers' skirts as they fled in wild disorder. Everyone looked for a way to escape. Mister Rosas ran after them to explain that he was the one who had dressed up so strangely. But this only increased the screaming and made the panic worse. An old woman crossed herself and said:

"Heaven help us! It's the Devil himself talking American!"

The superintendent made useless efforts to calm the people and shouted:

"Don't run away! Don't act like a bunch of Puerto Rican hillbillies! Santa Claus is human, and a good man!"

In the distance the shouts of the fleeing people could be heard. Mister Escalera, observing that Peyo Mercé had been standing there unconcerned, vented all his anger upon him, and shouted at the top of his voice:

"It's your fault, Peyo Mercé, that such stupidity should exist here in the middle of the twentieth century!"

Peyo Mercé answered, without changing his expression:

"Mister Escalera, it is not my fault that Santa Claus is not listed among the Puerto Rican saints."

1947

RAY BRADBURY

The Gift

TOMORROW WOULD BE Christmas, and even while the three of them rode to the rocket port the mother and father were worried. It was the boy's first flight into space, his very first time in a rocket, and they wanted everything to be perfect. So when, at the customs table, they were forced to leave behind his gift which exceeded the weight limit by no more than a few ounces and the little tree with the lovely white candles, they felt themselves deprived of the season and their love.

The boy was waiting for them in the Terminal room. Walking toward him, after their unsuccessful clash with the Interplanetary officials, the mother and father whispered to each other.

"What shall we do?"

"Nothing, nothing. What *can* we do?"

"Silly rules!"

"And he so wanted the tree!"

The siren gave a great howl and people pressed forward into the Mars Rocket. The mother and father walked at the very last, their small pale son between them, silent.

"I'll think of something," said the father.

"What . . . ?" asked the boy.

And the rocket took off and they were flung headlong into dark space.

The rocket moved and left fire behind and left Earth behind on which the date was December 24, 2052, heading out into a place where there was no time at all, no month, no year, no hour. They slept away the rest of the first "day." Near midnight, by their Earth-time New York watches, the boy awoke and said, "I want to go look out the porthole."

There was only one port, a "window" of immensely thick glass of some size, up on the next deck.

"Not quite yet," said the father. "I'll take you up later."

"I want to see where we are and where we're going."

"I want you to wait for a reason," said the father.

He had been lying awake, turning this way and that, thinking of the abandoned gift, the problem of the season, the lost tree and the white candles. And at last, sitting up, no more than five minutes ago, he believed he had found a plan. He need only carry it out and this journey would be fine and joyous indeed.

"Son," he said, "in exactly one half hour it will be Christmas."

"Oh," said the mother, dismayed that he had mentioned it. Somehow she had rather hoped that the boy would forget.

The boy's face grew feverish and his lips trembled. "I know, I know. Will I get a present, will I? Will I have a tree? You promised—— "

"Yes, yes, all that, and more," said the father.

The mother started. "But—— "

"I mean it," said the father. "I really mean it. All and more, much more. Excuse me, now. I'll be back."

He left them for about twenty minutes. When he came back he was smiling. "Almost time."

"Can I hold your watch?" asked the boy, and the watch was handed over and he held it ticking in his fingers as the rest of the hour drifted by in fire and silence and unfelt motion.

"It's Christmas *now*! Christmas! Where's my present?"

"Here we go," said the father and took his boy by the shoulder and led him from the room, down the hall, up a rampway, his wife following.

"I don't understand," she kept saying.

"You will. Here we are," said the father.

They had stopped at the closed door of a large cabin. The father tapped three times and then twice in a code. The door opened and the light in the cabin went out and there was a whisper of voices.

"Go on in, son," said the father.

"It's dark."

"I'll hold your hand. Come on, Mama."

They stepped into the room and the door shut, and the room was very dark indeed. And before them loomed a great glass eye, the porthole, a window four feet high and six feet wide, from which they could look out into space.

The boy gasped.

Behind him, the father and the mother gasped with him, and then in the dark room some people began to sing.

"Merry Christmas, son," said the father.

And the voices in the room sang the old, the familiar carols, and the boy moved forward slowly until his face was pressed against the cool glass of the port. And he stood there for a long long time, just looking and looking out into space and the deep night at the burning and the burning of ten billion billion white and lovely candles. . . .

1952

RAYMOND E. BANKS

Christmas Trombone

 I T WAS Christmas Eve and Shorty went into the closet and dug out his old trombone. He pumped it a couple of times and made a lip on it and let out a blast. It came out as two sour bleats.

"Hold the phone," he told himself. "You've dialed yourself a wrong number."

There came the insistent cracking of Mrs. Thompson's thimble on the radiator pipes. He had a very particular landlady, the toughest old gal in Blessington, and she didn't encourage her roomers in their self-expression.

Shorty made two soft, low mocking notes on the horn. Clean stuff that rolled off the ear. Too bad he didn't dare toot out loud what he thought of her.

He shoved his horn under his coat and went downstairs. Mrs. Thompson met him in the living room.

"You playing that old horn again, Shorty?" she said.

"Figure on a few carols," he said.

"The singing cones," she said firmly, "can do it better. If you try to play carols, they'll run you out of town for peace-disturbing."

"I've lived in Blessington for 45 years," said Shorty, "man, boy and tadpole. I want to see them run me out of town."

"Chief Nelson said the next time you tried to play that horn he was going to take it from you," she said. "The singing cones do it better."

"Who's afraid of Chief Nelson?" he said.

She sniffed in reply and went to the end table and turned on her singing cone. She punched out a number—inside, the wafer-thin discs of Venusian heavy water responded with real, throbbing stuff. Quarter of a million earth musicians had played to make those discs. All dissonance matched out by the peculiar properties of the inch-wide Venusian solidified water discs. If you had a perfect recording material and knew what to expect from the organ of Corti in the human cochlear structure of the ear you could even write an equation for the cones' "perfect" music. Shorty grunted and went out into the cold night with his horn.

He listened. Moon was out; stars were out. A light, crusty snow covered the earth. He could see the lights of Blessington twinkling on the snow. He could hear the voices of far-off carolers. They were fewer every year. He could hear, most of all, the singing cones. From private homes, from the bars, from Salvation Army kettles, Christmas music hung heavy on the air.

Over on Grover Cleveland Street he could hear the dominating throb of the biggest singing cone in Blessington. It was going to be a big night at the Church of All-Comers, and the Rev. Dr. Blaine was warming them up with a candlelight service.

Straight out from Venus, that cone. Not a factory job stuffed with Venusian water discs, like Mrs. Thompson's, but a real Venusian cone. Eight feet high. Inside gallons and gallons of purest Venusian water, hungry for the sound of music. Once a clean pattern of sound was heard by that container, it solidified a portion of the water and remained in crystallized perfection, captured for the centuries-long life of the cone . . . come midnight and Dr. Blaine would give the signal to the altar boy. Altar boy would play the exciter cone and the big cone would pour forth its tones throughout the Dominic Valley like an unearthly benediction and everybody would shudder in delight at the sound of the All-Comers cone—they would sure know it was Christmas!

Shorty's nose got cold and his feet went numb as he crunched through the snow. In one pocket bulged the package that he had for Dr. Blaine, in the other the one he had for Edith. After that, a quick cup of Christmas cheer at the Dogleg; then home and he'd be in bed by 10 o'clock. With his ears stuffed with cotton. He didn't want to hear the singing cones on Christmas Eve. He had always made his own music, always would. He wouldn't play for the singing cones like the other fools of earth musicians, giving up their souls to the gadgets. He had something better inside.

Hadn't come out yet, but someday he'd show them. When he was ready. None of this stuff of having the cones change around and delete like they did, because they'd heard the tune better somewhere else.

He walked resolutely past the Dogleg. Time for that later. A few citizens were just going in for Christmas cheer and one of them asked Shorty how soon his aircar would be repaired and out of Shorty's garage. Whenever Shorty had a particularly tough repair to do, like this job, he always mumbled something about getting parts "from upstate." The citizen rolled his eyes and shrugged while his companions laughed.

"When the singing cones came, we lost a good musician and gained a poor mechanic," said one. "That right, Shorty?"

"Don't talk to me about the singing cones. They hit me in my income."

"Where you going with that trombone, Shorty?" asked another. "Chief Nelson sees you with that old slush pump, he'll run you in."

"Let him try," said Shorty, passing on.

He ran into Chief Nelson just a block before he got to the church. The Chief stopped him.

"Now, look, Shorty. Last Fourth of July I told you that you couldn't be playing that horn and disturbing the peace."

"I'm not playing it, Chief. I'm carrying it."

The Chief blew on his cold hands and stamped his feet in the snow, his face red from the gleam of the Christmas lights strung overhead on the street lamps.

"Man carries a gun, he figures to use it," he said.

"It's my own personal, private property."

"I got rights too," said the Chief. "To protect the peace. That sour old horn of yours always makes trouble when you get a couple of Dogleg Specials in you. Hand it over."

"I won't."

"You can have it back tomorrow, Shorty. I'd rather put the horn in the jail safe than put you in the jail cell."

"Go to hell."

"May I be forgiven for preventive maintenance," said the Chief. His burly arms slapped at Shorty and he jerked the trombone from Shorty's grasp. Shorty shouted something incoherent and slugged at the Chief. But in the snow he missed his footing and slid to the ground.

"Stay with your repair business," said the Chief, marching off triumphantly with the horn.

The sharp wind stung his eyes and they filled with tears as he rose again, alone on the street. He felt a cold, unpleasant place where the snow clung to his clothes. Time was when he played for all their local affairs. Time was when he played the organ for weddings (including Chief Nelson's) and funerals (it'd be a pleasure to rumble that old boy down), led the choir and provided the hot music for local dances. That was before the singing cones.

A whiff of Christmas cooking fell on his nostrils as he went up the street to the church. Everybody was busy, happy, alert with Christmas, but it was agony for him.

Dr. Blaine smiled up at him as he entered the study, sniffing because the warm air made his nose run.

"It's good to see you on Christmas Eve," said the clergyman. "Just like the old days when we had the choir and organ."

Shorty handed over his gift and got one in return. "I sure do miss that midnight service," said Shorty. "Church crowded, the special feeling of importance in the decorations and the occasion, the choir all worried and nervous about the long, extra-special program they had to get through with perfection . . ."

"I'm afraid Christmas for you was waffles at 1 A.M. in the rectory," smiled Dr. Blaine. "It's more than just a show, Shorty. It has something to do with Christ, remember?"

He felt better at the scolding. Dr. Blaine was a real soul-chaser. Felt good to have somebody worry about you.

"Sure," he said.

"Coming to the midnight service tonight, Shorty?"

Shorty frowned. "You've got your singing cone," he said.

Dr. Blaine took him by the arm and led him into the nave. Across from them rested the only true singing cone in Blessington. It was almost eight feet high, a tapering mound of pure whiteness, just as it had been on Venus. It "lived" on sound, not talking voices, not explosions or discords. It "lived" on music adding every sweet sound it heard to its repertory until all its water was solidified and it could no longer hear and remember.

Near it stood the exciter cone, an ordinary cone-shaped home recorder which gave off the first few notes of the required tune and then surrendered to the swelling grandeur of the big cone that picked up the tune and played it through in perfection—remembering all of the overtones of all the musicians or singers it had ever heard play or sing. One decibel for four, and if you turned up your little exciter cone high, the Venusian cone roared loud enough to shake the church and fling its quivering harmonies throughout the length of Dominic Valley.

"Here," said Dr. Blaine, "I've got all the great artists who ever recorded Christmas music, Shorty. The best voices, the best arrangements."

"I know."

"People need the solemn pageantry of the greatest church music to find the Christmas spirit in these commercial times."

"Yeah."

"This cone was a foot-high mound on Venus the night Christ was born in Bethlehem, Shorty. It's been on earth now for twenty years, adding only the purest and best church music to its being."

"It's only been in Blessington five years," said Shorty, "while I been here 45, man, boy and molecule."

Dr. Blaine sighed. "Nobody wants the old choir and organ any more, Shorty. When the cone plays we go back along the centuries to Bethlehem, we watch the miracles beside the Red Sea, we are in the room where the Last Supper was served and we walk with Christ up that final hill—"

"A couple of times I got 'em pretty excited with that old organ you got stashed in the basement."

"Then play for the cone, Shorty," said Dr. Blaine. "Play for the cone and make it hear and remember your notes along with the world's best musicians."

Shorty cleared his throat. "I been meaning to tell you, Reverend. I took a look at your aircar today. You need a new rotor blade."

In the silence that followed, Dr. Blaine shrugged and then went across and opened the stained glass windows behind the cone. Shorty knew why he did that. In a few hours now it would be time for that cone to fill the valley with sound. Funny, nobody ever opened the windows to let the music out in the old days. Just as well, though. You take a choir singer with a cold, he gets mean.

"You've lost a lot of friends in these last years, Shorty," said Dr. Blaine. "Even Edith's been worrying about you lately. I think you need to come to church."

"That's a thought, Reverend," said Shorty without conviction. He turned to leave. "Merry Christmas."

"Merry Christmas," said Dr. Blaine sadly, watching him go.

Edith wore bangs. Her round face was wrong for bangs, but Shorty had long ago given up worrying about her face because below the chin she was all woman. She had a bowl of Christmas punch and they had one. She looked pretty good, he thought, in her new Christmas dress.

"Thought I might go to the Church of All-Comers tonight," she said. "What're you going to do?"

"Thinking of breaking into jail."

"Why?"

"They went and arrested my trombone."

Her eyes mocked him. "Give it up, old boy. When the All-Comers cone gets rolling, nobody wants to hear your sour old horn."

"Time was—"

"Give it up, Shorty! In the old days you were something else beside the aircar repairman when you stood up before the people of this town and played your music. Now you're just Shorty from the aircar repair shop with a musician's pension."

Her face was incredibly soft in the dim, multi-colored glow of the Christmas tree lights. It was a good, factory tree with bulb-shaped projections that were part of the plant and yet gave off tender, colored lights, finer than the old-fashioned Christmas tree lights. And approved by Underwriters' Lab, of course, since the tree generated its own electricity and was shockproof.

"What're you trying to say?"

"Maybe I'm tired of waiting for you to snap out of it. Maybe I'm going to Church tonight anyway—with Del Gentry."

"I guess it's legal," he said, "as long as you save me New Year's for the jam session over in Kingsbury."

"New Year's I'm going to Del Gentry's party," she said. "I'm tired of a sour old aircar repairman for company."

He couldn't control himself. He sent the tree down with an angry flip of his hand. She sat with a set smile on her face, her Christmas cup before her face, both arms resting on the table. Like somebody who'd said something a long time coming.

"Phoney!" he shouted. "Like the singing cones. Everything phoney!"

"Sure," she said. "Everything that's been invented since you were twenty is phoney, Shorty. But the world moves on. That tree is better than the old ones. The singing cones make better music than the old music—"

He jerked the home-sized singing cone she had on the end table from its socket and smashed it at the wall. The wafer-discs raced over the floor in aimless circles.

Edith didn't move. "You can't go on being twenty and smelling the apple blossoms in the spring forever, Shorty—"

"I've got a soul!" he yelled at her. "I ain't no aircar repairman!"

"You've got an ego," she said.

Shorty wheeled and ran out, slamming the door.

"Merry C-Christmas," Edith whispered.

Chief Nelson was at the Dogleg. Shorty went to the jail instead and sat down at the desk with the extra man.

"Sure is cold out."

"Yeah." Shorty's hands had finally stopped trembling.

"Chief said you might be around," said the extra man. "I was to tell you—no playin' on trombones."

"Who wants to play on a trombone?" asked Shorty. "I got my musician's pension."

The man leaned forward. There wasn't anybody in the jail and he was bored. This was diversion. "How about that pension stuff?" he said. "How about that?"

Shorty shrugged. "When the singing cones idea was brought in from Venus, the music companies did a right noble thing. Gave everybody who held a card the amount of dough they could reasonably expect to make over a lifetime. They even subsidized schools for the kids—"

"Subsawhooed?"

"Gave dough," said Shorty shortly. "So the kids that're coming up would get a chance to play—for the singing cones. Then the cones gobble up *their* music too. Get fat offa the young talent. They still buy new tunes, even for the cones. But there ain't no real music any more."

"You ever played for the cones?"

"I been asked," said Shorty, "but I never have; I'm not ready. You stand up in front of a real one—the cones record you forever. But they only pick up your best stuff and delete the rest." He shuddered. "They suck up the soul you put in music. I still got self-respect, even if I only play for myself."

He eased open the bottom drawer of the man's desk with his toe; saw the glint of a bottle.

"I don't know," said the man. "Seems to me when my singing cone plays a sad tune I want to cry. Happy makes me laugh. I ain't much for music, but those cones sure make you wiggle better than the old music."

"Why not? They've got the souls of all the earth's best musicians." Shorty peered down into the drawer. "Looks like a bottle down there," he said.

The extra man peered down. "Say, you're right."

"Looks like whisky," said Shorty.

The extra man's face was almost angelic. "Say, it sure does," he said. "How'd a bottle of liquor get into this little, old jail?"

"It ain't too far to reach," hinted Shorty.

"By God, I bleeve I can make it," said the extra man, reaching for it.

Shorty clipped him on the neck. The man went "gawwwk!" and rolled over on the floor, unconscious. "Merry Christmas," Shorty muttered to him, digging for the keys to Chief Nelson's safe.

*

It was midnight. Shorty was pretty well away from town now. The moon was big in an amazingly clear sky. The powdery snow numbed his feet; the air stung his lungs. The horn felt cold even through his gloves. Down below he could see the lights from the windows and doors of the Church of All-Comers dancing on the snow.

Suddenly he wondered about himself. "What am I doing out here all alone?" he asked himself. "Got to get out of town to even play my horn any more." His hands were trembling as he took off his gloves.

"Man likes to play horn; man's gotta play a horn," he said, scowling at a jackrabbit that broke through the underbrush and then quickly retreated.

He looked over the silent, snow-covered empty hills and then back at the friendly lights of the All-Comers Church and then he knew that this would have to be the last time he ever played the horn. Otherwise you'd be going up the mountain for keeps, he told himself.

He blew a blast. It sounded real loud. He stirred in surprise when he heard an answering blast from the singing cone down in the Church.

Shorty pumped his chest full of the open valley air. He remembered all the years he'd been in the center and how they were gone and felt sad—so he blew happy. He ran off "Joy to the World." He made a couple of sour notes, but it was loud and bold and joyful and he felt better. "How do you like that, cone?" he asked silently.

As if in response the singing cone down below in the Church gave it back to him—"Joy to the World." He stood still in shock, because it had picked up some of his own notes. He could see some of the people still outside the church, turning to stare at the hill where he stood. By gosh, they could hear him. Even the cone. Old Blaine must've turned the big cone around to those open windows when he heard that challenging blast.

He felt hot and cold inside. He thought how it was with people with everything changing and being different and nothing was really eternal, and pretty soon it was your last chance to toot your own horn. He felt lightheaded with anger and frustration and sadness and then suddenly he needed his own music real bad. Something to say everything he'd felt in a simple, dignified way.

Here goes.

Silent Night. Not too gooey, not too sweet. Firm and clear and certain. He began to cry at his own music; he couldn't help it. The tune was somber and great and all-embracing, and the occasional catch in his throat gave the old horn a tremolo he'd never had before.

Silent night, Holy night!
All is calm, All is bright,

The cone was silent, listening. He could feel its presence in the background. A moment before it had been scouring out the valley with its sound. Now it was comparing his notes with all the wonderful music stored in its memory.

Softly, you son-of-a-bitch, he told himself. This is final. Shorty, by God, now we've *got* to do the thing!

For 45 seconds he reached the great plane of art that he'd been trying to reach all his life. For 45 seconds he made music that no human or nonhuman agency had ever made before or would ever make again. It was one of those moments. It was clear and clean, human but not gooey. It was one tiny notch more than satisfactory.

Silent night, Holy night!
All is calm, All is bright,
Round yon Virgin Mother and Child,
Holy Infant so tender and mild—

After it was over, he had just enough left to start again and use his horn as an exciter cone to the big one. Then he stood there, silent, horn to his lips, unable to move.

Now they came back to him, those golden, unforgettable 45 seconds; solo, nothing added, nothing taken away. No other sound except his own horn and his own soul. The cone had listened and compared down through its centuries of experience. The cone had found it good—all of it—nothing deleted, nothing added.

In Bethlehem, on Venus and beyond to outer space it was a thing of perfect uniqueness.

Shorty drew back his horn and hurled it as far away from him as he could. It had been inside and he knew it, but nobody else did—now they did. There was no need to play any more.

If you've got influence or friends, you can attend the world-famous Christmas Trombone services at the Church of All-Comers in Blessington. But it's pretty hard to get in on Christmas Eve. When they do that original version of "Silent Night" on the Christmas Trombone, you'll be glad you came, though. It's solo stuff with a keen, cutting edge and you'll never forget it. They've made a million discs for the home recorders but it's not the same.

And if you take a look over to your right, you'll see a short, fat man sitting in a pew, nodding and smiling. When they play the Christmas Trombone, everybody in Blessington watches him with a little awe. And his wife, Edith, grins. She's got a right to grin. That's Shorty Williams, the best doggone aircar repairman in Dominic Valley, and the man who taught the singing cones how to handle Christmas carols.

1954

MILDRED CLINGERMAN

The Wild Wood

I	T SEEMED to Margaret Abbott that her children, as they grew older, clung more and more zealously to the family Christmas traditions. Her casual suggestion that, just this once, they try something new in the way of a Christmas tree met with such teen-age scorn and genuine alarm that Margaret hastily abandoned the idea. She found it wryly amusing that the body of ritual she herself had built painstakingly through the years should now have achieved sacrosanctity. Once again, then, she would have to endure the secret malaise of shopping for the tree at Cravolini's Christmas Tree Headquarters. She tried to comfort herself with the thought that one wretchedly disquieting hour every year was not too much to pay for her children's happiness. After all, the episode always came far enough in advance of Christmas so that it never *quite* spoiled the great day for her.

Buying the tree at Cravolini's began the year Bonnie was four. Bruce had been only a toddler, fat and wriggling, and so difficult for Margaret to carry that Don had finally loaded Margaret with the packages and perched his son on his shoulder. Margaret remembered that night clearly. All day the Abbotts had promised Bonnie that when evening came, when all the shop lights blazed inside the fairy-tale windows, the four of them would stroll the crowded streets, stopping or moving on at Bonnie's command. At some point along the way, the parents privately assured each other, Bonnie would grow tired and fretful but unwilling to relinquish the dazzling street and her moment of power. That would be the time to allow her to choose the all-important tree, which must then of course, be carried to their car in triumph with Bonnie as valiant, proud helper. Once she had been lured to the car it would be simple to hurry her homeward and to bed. The fragrant green mystery of the tree, sharing their long ride home, would insure her sleepiness and contentment.

As it turned out (why hadn't they foreseen it?), the child showed no sign of fatigue that evening other than her captious rejection of every Christmas tree pointed out to her. Margaret, whose feet and back ached with Bruce's weight, swallowed her impatience and shook out yet another small tree and twirled its dark bushiness before Bonnie's cool, measuring gaze.

"No," Bonnie said. "It's too little. Daddy, let's go that way." She pointed down one of the darker streets, leading to the area of pawn-shops and narrow little cubbyholes that displayed cheap jewelry. These, in turn, verged on the ugly blocks that held credit clothiers, shoe repair shops, and empty, boarded-up buildings where refuse gathered ankle-deep in the entrance ways.

"I won't," Margaret said. "This is silly. What's the matter with this tree, Bonnie? It isn't so small. We certainly aren't going to wander off down there. I assure you, they don't *have* Christmas trees on that street, do they, Don?"

Don Abbott shook his head, but he was smiling down at his daughter, allowing her to drag him to the street crossing.

Like a damn, lumbering St. Bernard dog, Margaret thought, *towed along by a simpering chee-ild*. She stared after her husband and child as if they were strangers. They were waiting for her at the corner, Don with the uneasy, sheepish look of a man who knows his wife is angry but unlikely to make a scene. Bonnie was still tugging at his hand, flashing sweet, smug little smiles at her mother. Margaret dropped the unfurled tree with a furious, open-fingered gesture, shifted Bruce so that he rode on one hip, and joined them.

The traffic light changed and they all crossed together. Don slowed and turned a propitiating face to his wife. "You all right, hon? Here, you carry the packages and I'll take Bruce. If you want to, you could go sit in the car. Bonnie and I, we'll just check down this street a little way to make sure. . . . She says they've got some big trees someplace down here." He looked doubtfully down at his daughter then. "Are you sure, Bonnie? How do you know?"

"I saw them. Come on, Daddy."

"Probably she *did* see some," Don said. "Maybe last week when we drove through town. You know, kids see things we don't notice. Lord, with traffic the way it is, who's got time to see anything? And besides, Margaret, you said she could pick the tree. You said it was time to start building traditions, so the kids would have . . . uh . . . security and all that. Seems to me the tree won't mean much to her if we make her take the one we choose. Anyway, that's the way I figure it."

Margaret moved close to him and took his arm, squeezing it to show both her forgiveness and apology. Don smiled down at her and Margaret's whole body warmed. For a long moment she allowed her eyes to challenge his with the increased moisture and blood-heat that he called "smoky," and which denoted for both of them her frank desire. He stared back at her with alerted male tension, and then consciously relaxed.

"Well, not right here and now," he said. "See me later."

Margaret, reassured, skipped a few steps. This delighted the children. The four of them were laughing, then, when they found themselves in front of the derelict store that housed Cravolini's Christmas Tree Headquarters.

Perhaps it was their gaiety, that first year, that made Cravolini's such a pleasant memory for Don and the children. For the first few minutes Margaret, too, had found the dim, barny place charming. It held a bewildering forest of upright trees, aisles and aisles of them, and the odor of fir and spruce and pine was a tingling pleasure to the senses. The floor was covered with damp sawdust, the stained old walls hung with holly wreaths and Della Robbia creations that showed real artistry. Bonnie had gone whooping off in the direction of the taller trees, disappearing from sight so quickly that Don had hurried after her, leaving Margaret standing just inside the door.

She found herself suddenly struggling with that queer and elusive conviction that "this has happened before." Not since her own childhood had she felt so strongly that she was capable of predicting in detail the events that would follow this moment. Already her flesh prickled with foreknowledge of the touch that would come . . . *now*.

She whirled to stare into the inky eyes of the man who stood beside her, his hand poised lightly on her bare forearm. Yes, he was part of the dream she'd returned to—the long, tormenting dream in which she cried out for wholeness, for decency, and love, only to have the trees close in on her, shutting away the light. "The trees, the trees . . ." Margaret murmured. The dream began to fade. She looked down across the packages she held at the dark hand that smoothed the golden hairs on her forearm. *I got those last summer when I swam so much.*

She straightened suddenly as the dream ended, trying to shake off the languor that held her while a strange, ugly man stroked her arm. She managed to jerk away from him, spilling the packages at her feet. He knelt with her to pick them up, his head so close to hers that she smelled his dirty, oily hair. The odor of it conjured up for her (again?) the small, cramped room and the bed with the thin mattress that never kept out the cold. Onions were browning in olive oil there over the gas plate. The man standing at the window with his back turned . . . *He needed her; nobody else needed her in just that way. Besides, Mama had said to watch over Alberto. How could she leave him alone? But Mama was dead.* . . . *And how could Mama know all the bad things Alberto had taught her?*

"Margaret." Don's voice called her rather sharply out of the dream that had again enveloped her. Margaret's sigh was like a half-sob. She laughed up at her husband, and he helped her to her feet, and gathered up the packages. The strange man was introducing himself to Don. He was Mr. Cravolini, the proprietor. He had seen that the lady was very pale, ready to faint, perhaps. He'd stepped up to assist her, unfortunately frightening her, since his step had not been heard—due, doubtless, to the great depth of the sawdust on the floor. Don, she saw, was listening to the overtones of the apology. If Mr. Cravolini's voice displayed the smallest hint of insolence and pride in the lies he was telling, then Don would grab him by the shirt front and shake him till he stopped lying and begged for mercy. Don did not believe in fighting. Often while he and Margaret lay warmly and happily in bed together Don spoke regretfully of his "wild-kid" days, glad that with maturity he need not prove on every street corner that he was not afraid to fight, glad to admit to Margaret that often he'd been scared, and always he'd been sick afterwards. Don approved of social lies, the kind that permitted people to live and work together without too much friction. So Mr. Cravolini had made a mistake. Finding Margaret alone, he'd made a pass. He knew better now. OK. Forget it. Thus Margaret read her husband's face and buried very deeply the sharp, small stab of disappointment. *A fight would have ended it, for good.* She frowned a little with the effort to understand her own chaotic thoughts, her vision of a door that had almost closed on a narrow, stifling room, but was now wedged open . . . waiting.

Don led her down one of the long aisles of trees to where Bonnie and Bruce were huddled beside their choice. Margaret scarcely glanced at the tree. Don was annoyed with her—half-convinced, as he always was, that Margaret had invited the pass. Not by any overt signal on her part, but simply because she forgot to look busy and preoccupied.

"Don't go dawdling along in that wide-eyed dreamy way," he'd said so often. "I don't know what it is, but you've got that look—as if you'd say yes to a square meal or to a panhandler or to somebody's bed."

Bonnie was preening herself on the tree she'd chosen, chanting a maddening little refrain that Bruce would comprehend at any moment: "And Bru-cie did-unt he-ulp. . . ." Already Bruce recognized that the singsong words meant something scornful and destructive to his dignity. His face puckered, and he drew the three long breaths that preceded his best screaming.

Margaret hoisted him up into her arms, while Don and Bonnie hastily beat a retreat with the excuse that they must pay Mr. Cravolini for the tree. Bruce screamed his fury at a world that kept trying to confine him, limit him, or otherwise squeeze his outsize ego down to puny, civilized proportions. Margaret paced up and down the aisles with him, wondering why Don and Bonnie were taking so long.

Far back at the rear of the store building, where the lights were dimmest, Margaret caught sight of a display of handmade candles. Still joggling Bruce up and down as if she were churning butter, she paused to look them over. Four pale blue candles of varying lengths rose gracefully from a flat base moulded to resemble a sheaf of laurel leaves. Very nice, and probably very expensive. Margaret turned away to find Mr. Cravolini standing immediately in front of her.

"Do you like those candles?" he asked softly.

"Where is my husband?" Margaret kept her eyes on Bruce's fine, blonde hair. *Don't let the door open any more. . . .*

"Your husband has gone to bring his car. He and your daughter. The tree is too large to carry so far. Why are you afraid?"

"I'm not afraid. . . ." She glanced fleetingly into the man's eyes, troubled again that her knowledge of his identity wavered just beyond reality. "Have we met before?" she asked.

"I almost saw you once," Cravolini said. "I was standing at a window. You were reflected in it, but when I turned around you were gone. There was nobody in the room but my sister . . . the stupid cow . . ." Cravolini spat into the sawdust. "That day I made a candle for you. Wait." He reached swiftly behind the stacked packing boxes that held the candles on display. He had placed it in her hand before she got a clear look at it. Sickeningly pink, loathsomely slick and hand-filling. It would have been cleaner, more honest, she thought, if it had been a frank reproduction of what it was intended to suggest. She dropped it and ran awkwardly with the baby towards the lights at the entrance way. Don was just parking the car. She wrenched the door open and half fell into the front seat. Bonnie had rushed off with Don to bring out the tree. Margaret buried her face in Bruce's warm, sweet-smelling neck and nuzzled him till he laughed aloud. She never quite remembered afterwards the ride home that night. She must have been very quiet—in one of her "lost" moods, as Don called them. The next morning she was surprised to see that Bonnie had picked one of Cravolini's largest, finest trees, and to discover the tissue-wrapped pale blue candles he had given Bonnie as a special Christmas gift.

Every year after that Margaret promised herself that this year she'd stay at home on the tree-buying night. But something always forced her to go—some errand, a last bit of shopping, or Don's stern injunctions not to be silly, that he could not handle Bonnie, Bruce, *and* the biggest tree in town. Once there, she never managed to escape Cravolini's unctuous welcome. If she sat in the car, then he came out to speak to her. Much better go inside and stick close by Don and the children. But that never quite worked, either. Somehow the three of them eluded her; she might hear their delighted shouts two aisles over, but when she hastened in their direction, she found only Cravolini waiting. She never eluded him. Sometimes on New Year's Day, when she heard so much about resolutions on radio and television, she thought that surely this year she'd tell Don at least some of the things Cravolini said to her—did to her—enough, anyway, to assure the Abbotts never going back there again. But she never did. It would be difficult to explain to Don why she'd waited so long to speak out about it. Why hadn't she told him that first night?

She could only shake her head in puzzlement and distaste for motivations that were tangled in a long, bad dream. And how could a woman of almost-forty explain and deeply explore a woman in her twenties? Even if they were the same woman, it was impossible.

When Cravolini's "opening announcement" card arrived each year, Margaret was jolted out of the peacefulness that inevitably built in her between Christmases. It was as if a torn and raw portion of her brain healed in the interim. *But the door was still invitingly wedged open, and every Christmas something tried to force her inside.* Margaret's spirit fought the assailant that seemed to accompany Mr. Cravolini (hovering there beyond the lights, flitting behind the trees), but the fighting left her weak and tired and without any words to help her communicate her distress. *If only Don would see,* she thought. *If there were no need for words. It ought to be like that. . . .* At such times she accused herself of indulging in Bruce's outgrown baby fury, crying out against things as they are.

Every time she saw Cravolini the dream gained in reality and continuity. He was very friendly with the Abbotts now. They were among his "oldest customers," privileged to receive his heartiest greetings along with the beautiful candles and wreaths he gave the children. Margaret had hoped this year that she could convince Bonnie and Bruce to have a different kind of tree—something modern and a little startling, perhaps, like tumble-weeds sprayed pink and mounted on a tree-shaped form. Anything. But they laughed at her bad taste, and were as horrified as if she were trying to bypass Christmas itself.

I wonder if I'll see *her* this year, Margaret thought. Alberto's sister. She knew so much about her now—that she was dumb, but that she had acute, morbidly sensitive hearing—that once she'd heard Cravolini murmuring his lust to Margaret, because that was the time the animal-grunting, laughing sounds had come from the back of the store, there where extra trees lay stacked against the wall. Her name was Angela, and she was very gross, very fat, very ugly. Unmarriageable, Alberto said. Part of what Margaret knew of Angela came from Alberto's whispered confidences (unwanted, oh unasked for!), and the rest grew out of the dream that lived and walked with Margaret there in the crumbling building, beginning the moment she entered the door, ending only with Don's voice, calling her back to sanity and to another life.

There were self-revelatory moments in her life with Don when Margaret was able to admit to herself that the dream had power to call her back. She would like to know the ending. It was like a too-short book that left one hungry and dissatisfied. So this year she gave way to the children, to tradition, and went once again to Cravolini's.

Margaret was aware that she looked her best in the dull red velveteen suit. The double golden hoops at her ears tinkled a little when she walked and made her feel like an arrogant gypsy. She and Don had stopped at their favorite small bar for several drinks while the children finished their shopping.

Maybe it's the drinks, Margaret thought, and maybe it's the feeling that tonight, at last, I'll settle Mr. Cravolini, that makes me walk so jut-bosomed and proud. Don, already on his way with her to Cravolini's, had dropped into a department store with the mumbled excuse that always preceded his gift-buying for Margaret. He had urged her to go on alone, reminding her that the children might be there waiting. For once, Margaret went fearlessly, almost eagerly.

The children were not waiting, but the woman was. *Angela.* Margaret knew her instantly, just as she'd known Alberto. Angela stared up and down at Margaret and did not bother to hide her amusement, or her knowledge of Margaret's many hot, protesting encounters with her brother. Margaret started to speak, but the woman only jerked her head meaningfully towards the back of the store. Margaret did not move. The dream was beginning.

Alberto is waiting, there beyond the stacked-high Christmas trees. See the soft, springy nest he has built for you with pine boughs. Margaret stirred uneasily and began to move down the aisle, Angela beside her.

I must go to him. He needs me. Mama said to look after Alberto. That I would win for myself a crown in Heaven . . . Did she know how unnatural a brother Alberto is? Did she know how he learned the seven powers from the old forbidden books? And taught them to me? He shall have what he desires, and so shall I. Here, Alberto, comes the proud, silly spirit you've won . . . and listen, Don and the children are coming in the door.

Margaret found the soft, springy bed behind the stacked trees. Alberto was there, waiting. She heard Don call for her and struggled to answer, struggled desperately to rise to go to him. But she was so fat, so heavy, so ugly. . . . She heard the other woman's light, warm voice answering, heard her happy, foolish joking with the children, her mock-protestations, as always, at the enormous tree they picked. Margaret fought wildly and caught a last glimpse of the Abbotts, the four of them, and saw the dull, red suit the woman wore, heard the final, flirtatious tinkling of the golden earrings, and then they were gone.

A whole year I must wait, Margaret thought, *and maybe next year they won't come. She will see to that.*

"My sister, my love . . ." Alberto crooned at her ear.

1957

Shirley Jackson

from Raising Demons

Suddenly it was only two weeks to wait until Christmas, and the temperature was twenty-two below the night of the school Christmas pageant. Then it was only eight days to go; formally, the children and I hung a Christmas wreath on each gatepost. Then, some hours less than a week, and my husband's present, ordered from that place in Seattle, might not come in time; then it was five days and then sixty hours and fourteen minutes, and we brought the Christmas tree home and stood it on the back porch. The store in Seattle was criminally slow, perhaps even forgetful; it was only thirty-seven hours before Christmas. Then, the morning of Christmas Eve I stuffed the turkey and decided on apple pie, after all, because last year no one had touched the pumpkin. All afternoon the children and I drove around town to the houses of their friends, leaving little packages of candy, and chocolate apples, and all afternoon their friends had been stopping off at our house ("Can't stay; just want to leave this, and Merry Christmas!") and leaving little packages of Christmas cookies and fruit cake. Then at last it was five o'clock in the afternoon, and the special delivery truck pulled up outside with the package from Seattle. Laurie and his father went to bring in the tree and I signed for the package and Jannie stirred the eggnog and Sally salted the popcorn and Barry sat in a corner of the kitchen, wide-eyed and still.

"Deck the halls with boughs of holly," Jannie sang, and Sally chanted, "Christmas, Christmas."

"You'll have to get the ax," my husband told Laurie. "Unless your mother would prefer a hole cut in the ceiling."

"You say that every year," I said, going past him sideways so he would not see the package I was holding behind me. "If you would only measure the tree before you bring it in—"

"You say that every year," he said. "Why are you walking like that?"

"Because I have your Christmas present behind me and I don't want you to notice," I said with dignity, and scurried into the kitchen to put the package behind the washing machine.

It takes three enormous cartons to hold all our Christmas decorations, and all during the green spring and the hot summer months and the long sunny days and the gray rainy days the cartons sit on a shelf in the far corner of the barn. Then, at last, Laurie and Jannie lift them down and carry them together through the snow to the house, going very slowly, cautioning one another, coming indoors with snow on their boots. I never look at the cartons labeled CHRISTMAS: LIGHTS, ORNAMENTS, DECORATIONS without remembering the sadness of putting them away last year, assuring the children that Christmas would come again, it would surely come again, they would hardly notice the length of the year before Christmas came again. Then Christmas comes again and I perceive that I, at least, have certainly not felt the year slip away; it has gone before I knew it.

Sighing, I lifted the carton named LIGHTS onto one of the dining room chairs to open it. "By the way," my husband asked Laurie very casually, "what *was* in that package, the one your mother just took into the kitchen?"

"Why, I wouldn't have any idea," Laurie said innocently. He called to me, "Did you remember to cut holes in the top so it could breathe?" he asked.

"Come on, you," his father said. "Get up on that ladder."

Jannie ladled eggnog into cups, Sally sat on the couch next to Barry with her lap full of popcorn, and spoke to him softly. "In the morning," she said, "when you wake up, what do you do?"

"I wake Laurie and I wake Jannie and I wake Mommy and I wake—"

"No, no," I said. "Tomorrow I plan to sleep very late."

"Eight o'clock by the playroom clock," Sally said.

"Eight-thirty," I said.

"Nine," my husband said.

"But *last* year it was eight o'clock," Sally said indignantly, "you know perfectly *well*. Last year and the year before that and the year before that and the year before *that* it was eight o'clock."

"Yeah." Laurie turned. "And no setting back the playroom clock, either, like you did that time."

Sally murmured to Barry, "So when you wake up tomorrow morning, what do you do?"

"I wake Laurie and I wake—"

My husband and Laurie had cut the tree down to size, and Jannie took the cut branches into the dining room and wreathed them around the punch bowl. She began to sing "Joy to the World," and my husband caught the tree as it toppled forward. "Hey," Laurie said, peering down between the branches, "you trying to knock me off this ladder or something? Entertain the kids seeing me go crash on the floor?"

"We need a new tree stand," my husband said.

"Don't be silly," I said. "We've *always* used that one."

We keep a spool of fine wire with the tree stand, and Laurie and his father contrived to secure the tree upright by fastening it with wire and thumbtacks to the frames of the bay window. "Look," Laurie called down, "last year it was maybe three inches farther over left; here's one of last year's thumbtacks."

I can remember, back in the dim time when I was a little girl, my father taking the strings of Christmas tree lights out of the flowered box, standing with his hands full, saying wistfully, "These lights again? No new ones?" and my mother, turning, frowning slightly, "But you said they were good for another year; last Christmas you said they were—"

"These lights?" my husband said. "You didn't get any new ones?"

A good deal of the tire tape which holds the light strings together was put on by my father, and some by my brother—kneeling on the floor, entangled, asking madly, "Why can't we get *new* lights, will someone please tell me?"—and of course my husband has put on tape of his own. He has taken off some of the tape my father put on and replaced it where it was getting ragged, and last year there was a new spot which Laurie taped. I went out one year (as I suppose my mother must have done at least once before me) and bought three new strings of lights, but somehow their bright green cord was so gaudy among the soft old ornaments, and there was nothing for my husband to do during the half hour when the rest of us were drinking eggnog and he would usually have been taping the light cords, so I put the new lights in the box with the old ones and they are still there; every year my husband takes them out of the box, looks at them, and puts them back again. "We ought to get new tree lights," Laurie said, unwinding the tire tape, "for heaven's sake, how long do you expect these will last?"

"They'll do for another year or so," my husband said absently. "Look, here's more of Grandpa's tire tape peeling off."

"—and Donner and Blitzen and Dasher and Prancer—" Sally told Barry. Jannie tugged at my arm. "Can you come a minute?" she asked. "I got to show you something." I followed her up the back stairs to her room, which had a sign on the door threatening the most dire vengeance on any who entered for any reason whatsoever. Jannie shut the door tight behind us and

I sat down on her bed while with much pausing to listen apprehensively she took from her bottom dresser drawer a candy box. She set this down on the bed next to me and opened it carefully. Taking out one of the small packages inside, she set it on my lap. It was brightly wrapped, and the card on it read, "To Daddy from Jannie."

"It's fine," I said. "What is it?"

"Not so loud," Jannie said, whispering. "It's a potholder."

"A potholder?"

"Yes, we learned how to make potholders in Starlight 4-H Club. And this is for Sally."

"A potholder?"

"Yes, and this is for Laurie, and this is for Barry."

"A potholder for Barry?"

"Yes, because in the mornings when his cereal's too hot. Oh, golly." Hastily she snatched the bottom package from the box and put it under her pillow. "You weren't supposed to see that," she said.

"I didn't see it," I told her. "I never even noticed it."

"Good," she said, "because that's a secret, that one. I won't even tell you who it's for."

Voices called from downstairs, and I helped Jannie get the packages back into the box and the box back into her dresser drawer and her dresser drawer shut and then we closed the door of her room behind us, with its forbidding sign, and hurried downstairs. The tree burst into light as we came into the living room, turning itself suddenly from an alien, faintly disturbing presence in the house into a thing of loveliness and color. "Ooh," said Sally, and Barry nodded, smiling.

I took up the box named ORNAMENTS and opened it. On top was the stuffed Santa Claus doll which is always the responsibility of the youngest child, who must see that it is put under the Christmas tree and then put safely away again when the Christmas tree comes down. The Santa Claus doll is always on top of the last box because it must always be wrested at the last minute from the youngest child ("Christmas will come again, *really* it will") and gotten hastily into the box and hidden. Now, just as I had promised last year, I took the Santa Claus doll and handed it into Barry's waiting arms. "Santa Claus," Barry said in confirmation, and returned to his place on the couch, holding the Santa Claus doll tight. Jannie began to sing "O Little Town of Bethlehem" and Laurie said sharply, "No, Dad, please. Let *me* do it; you'll fall."

Sally sat on the floor as close to the tree as she could get and chanted musically, "When *I* was youngest child it was the year of two trees, because when Mommy came to the man he had forgotten and our tree was gone for someone else. So Mommy said to the man where will I get a Christmas tree for my little children and for my little child Sally and the man said here are two thin trees with almost no branches will they do and Mommy said yes, I will take these two thin trees for my little children and for my little child Sally and we made red chains and golden bells and frankincense and garlands of red flowers and we put them around and about the two thin trees and it was Christmas and the loveliest Christmas there ever was. . . ."

"And the Christmas when Laurie was covered with spots," Jannie said. "That was before you were born," she told Sally.

"But I know it was because they gave him a paintbox and they thought *that* was why he was spotty," Sally said.

"Remember the Christmas the furnace went off and we opened our presents all wrapped in blankets?" Laurie peered out from under the star he was fastening on top of the tree. "Boy, *that* was a real cool Yule."

"Did you notice that I put 'fur coat' on my Christmas list again this year?" I remarked to my husband. "Not that I really expect—"

"Here it is, here it is," said Jannie breathlessly. "The one I am going to give to my own dear daughter someday." She had taken out her own particular treasure, a little china lady with a wide spun-glass skirt. "My own little daughter," Jannie said.

"And you will tell her," Sally continued smoothly, "how you used to hang it on *your* Christmas tree when you were a little girl, and how your mommy used to hang it on *her* Christmas tree when *she* was a little girl—"

"Mommy?" said Barry, perplexed. He turned to look at me curiously.

"When *Mommy* was a little girl," Sally said, "they used to go in sleighs and sleigh bells and bring in a Yule log, but of course that was *very* long ago."

"Hey," I said, protesting, and Jannie started "God Rest Ye Merry, Gentlemen." Barry gave me a reassuring nod, shifted his Santa Claus to his other arm, and reached out for the popcorn.

I began to lift out the bright fragile ornaments. I handed them carefully to Jannie and Sally, who went back and forth from the tree, carrying the ornaments carefully with both hands and setting them with caution on the tips of the branches. Barry took the funny little wooden man, colored red and yellow, and hung him on a bottom branch, and then he came back for the little cardboard pictures of drums and soldiers and old-fashioned dolls which had come with my grandmother from England. He took them one by one and with great concentration, always holding the Santa Claus, tucked the little strings over the ends of the low branches and the little soldiers and dolls swung around and back, bending down the branches. Laurie came to the dining room table to select ornaments for the top of the tree. "Varnish dry yet?" I whispered.

"Shh." He turned to watch his father, who was helping Sally with an ornament. "I think so," he whispered. "You think he'll like it?"

"It's exactly what he's been wanting," I said.

"He's going to be so surprised I can't *wait*," Laurie said happily. "By the way," he added, "you just didn't happen to notice a .22 rifle tucked away in a closet somewhere?"

"I wouldn't even know what a .22 rifle looked like," I assured him. "You know perfectly well I'm afraid of guns."

"Brother," Laurie said. "When Sally sees that—"

"Shh," I said.

Laurie took up two ornaments and made for the tree. "Watch out here, you kids," he said grandly. "This is where the professionals go into action." He climbed onto his ladder again.

"—you will hear bells jingling and reindeers' feet on the roof," Sally told Barry confidentially.

I poured my husband a glass of eggnog and Jannie began to sing "The First Noel."

"And milk and crackers for Santa Claus," Sally went on busily, "and then we have breakfast, and you are all always *my* guests at breakfast and we sit on the floor in my room and eat cereal from the new cereal bowls green and red, red and green. And what do you do when you wake up?" she demanded suddenly of Barry.

"Wake Laurie and—"

I opened the last carton, labeled DECORATIONS. There on top was the cardboard candle Jannie had made in kindergarten. That always went on the dining room buffet and then there was the big Santa Claus face Sally had done in first grade and that went on the back door and the red and green paper chains Laurie had made when he was a Cub Scout went over the doorway. Not two weeks ago Barry had come home from nursery school with a greenish kind of a picture of a Christmas tree and that had somehow got itself established on the refrigerator next to the big chart Laurie always made early in December so we could all fill out our Christmas lists and keep them in plain sight. Here were the popcorn strings my mother strung when *I* was youngest child, and the paper bells Laurie and I made when he was so small it seems unbelievable now, and the jigsaw Santa my husband cut out that same year, and the painted candy canes and the red ribbons and the green paper wreaths. "Oh, my," I said, looking at all of it.

"Here, you just sit down," Jannie said. "You just don't remember, is all. You sit down and I'll do it."

She sent Sally with the paper bells for the front door and Barry with the Santa Claus face and Laurie got back on his ladder and put up the paper chains and Jannie put the candy canes on the doorknob and the paper wreaths on the kitchen cabinets and the popcorn strings went around the foot of the tree because they were so old and delicate by now that they broke if we tried to hang them. Jannie and Laurie together put up the paper bells and Sally set the jigsaw Santa in the center of the dining room table. Sally reached into the box and took out the string of bells and Jannie sang "Jingle Bells." Barry hung the bells on the nail by the front door where they hang every year. "Bells and reindeers and presents," Barry sang, and Jannie came over to drape a piece of tinsel in my hair.

"Tell me," my husband asked Jannie confidentially, "what *was* in that package?"

Jannie thought. "A lovely new tie," she said at last. "Colored red and green for Christmas and pink and yellow for Easter and red and white and blue for Fourth of July, and black."

"I been telling you and telling you and *telling* you," Sally said to Barry. "Now, do you peek?"

"No?" Barry said uncertainly.

"You get up in the morning and what do you do?"

Barry opened his mouth and said "I wake—" Sally sighed and said, "Well, then, who is coming tonight?"

Jannie began to sing "Silent Night."

The tree was growing; it was hung with tinsel now, and every possible corner of the house held some touch of Christmas. "If one more child makes one more decoration," my husband said, "we'll have to move out to the barn next year."

"You'd think some of it would fall apart from one year to the next," I said helplessly.

"Tomorrow morning," Sally said, "all under the tree will be presents."

"That reminds me," my husband said to Laurie, "you'd better get out the screwdriver and the hammer, for a couple of construction jobs we've got to do later. Last year I needed the wrench, too."

"—and an orange in your stocking," Sally said, and then at last it was time. Solemnly, reluctantly, Barry climbed down from the couch with the stuffed Santa Claus. He stood for a minute looking up at the lighted tree, his small face touched with reflected color, and then, bending low and wiggling, he crept underneath and set the Santa Claus against the trunk of the tree. "Now," he said to the Santa Claus, "make it be Christmas."

"He ought to say 'God bless us every one' or something like *that*," Jannie pointed out.

"Say," my husband said to Sally in a low voice, "how about that package hidden in the kitchen?"

"Mice," Sally said firmly. "Full of mice."

"Listen," Laurie said in my ear, "suppose he *doesn't* like it, after all? I mean, suppose he doesn't *like* it?"

"Don't worry about *that*," I said. "It's just beautiful."

Barry climbed up into his father's lap to look further at the tree and his father bent and whispered in his ear. "What package?" said Barry, turning.

"Careful," said Laurie warningly.

"Don't tell," Sally said.

Barry chuckled. "A elephant," he said.

Jannie sang "Hark the Herald Angels Sing," Laurie took out the cartons to stack them on the back porch until we took the tree down again, Sally sat cross-legged on the floor watching the tree. Suddenly Sally and Barry spoke at once.

"Last Christmas—" Sally said.

"Next Christmas—" Barry said.

1957

GRACE PALEY

The Loudest Voice

THERE IS A certain place where dumbwaiters boom, doors slam, dishes crash; every window is a mother's mouth bidding the street shut up, go skate somewhere else, come home. My voice is the loudest.

There, my own mother is still as full of breathing as me and the grocer stands up to speak to her. "Mrs. Abramowitz," he says, "people should not be afraid of their children."

"Ah, Mr. Bialik," my mother replies, "if you say to her or her father 'Ssh,' they say, 'In the grave it will be quiet.'"

"From Coney Island to the cemetery," says my papa. "It's the same subway; it's the same fare."

I am right next to the pickle barrel. My pinky is making tiny whirlpools in the brine. I stop a moment to announce: "Campbell's Tomato Soup. Campbell's Vegetable Beef Soup. Campbell's S-c-otch Broth . . ."

"Be quiet," the grocer says, "the labels are coming off."

"Please, Shirley, be a little quiet," my mother begs me.

In that place the whole street groans: Be quiet! Be quiet! but steals from the happy chorus of my inside self not a tittle or a jot.

There, too, but just around the corner, is a red brick building that has been old for many years. Every morning the children stand before it in double lines which must be straight. They are not insulted. They are waiting anyway.

I am usually among them. I am, in fact, the first, since I begin with "A."

One cold morning the monitor tapped me on the shoulder. "Go to Room 409, Shirley Abramowitz," he said. I did as I was told. I went in a hurry up a down staircase to Room 409, which contained sixth-graders. I had to wait at the desk without wiggling until Mr. Hilton, their teacher, had time to speak.

After five minutes he said, "Shirley?"

"What?" I whispered.

He said, "My! My! Shirley Abramowitz! They told me you had a particularly loud, clear voice and read with lots of expression. Could that be true?"

"Oh yes," I whispered.

"In that case, don't be silly; I might very well be your teacher someday. Speak up, speak up."

"Yes," I shouted.

"More like it," he said. "Now, Shirley, can you put a ribbon in your hair or a bobby pin? It's too messy."

"Yes!" I bawled.

"Now, now, calm down." He turned to the class. "Children, not a sound. Open at page 39. Read till 52. When you finish, start again." He looked me over once more. "Now, Shirley, you know, I suppose, that Christmas is coming. We are preparing a beautiful play. Most of the parts have been given out. But I still need a child with a strong voice, lots of stamina. Do you know what stamina is? You do? Smart kid. You know, I heard you read 'The Lord is my shepherd' in Assembly yesterday. I was very impressed. Wonderful delivery. Mrs. Jordan, your teacher, speaks highly of you. Now listen to me, Shirley Abramowitz, if you want to take the part and be in the play, repeat after me, 'I swear to work harder than I ever did before.'"

I looked to heaven and said at once, "Oh, I swear." I kissed my pinky and looked at God.

"That is an actor's life, my dear," he explained. "Like a soldier's, never tardy or disobedient to his general, the director. Everything," he said, "absolutely everything will depend on you."

That afternoon, all over the building, children scraped and scrubbed the turkeys and the sheaves of corn off the schoolroom windows. Goodbye Thanksgiving. The next morning a monitor brought red paper and green paper from the office. We made new shapes and hung them on the walls and glued them to the doors.

The teachers became happier and happier. Their heads were ringing like the bells of childhood. My best friend, Evie, was prone to evil, but she did not get a single demerit for whispering. We learned "Holy Night" without an error. "How wonderful!" said Miss Glacé, the student teacher. "To think that some of you don't even speak the language!" We learned "Deck the Halls" and "Hark! The Herald Angels" . . . They weren't ashamed and we weren't embarrassed.

Oh, but when my mother heard about it all, she said to my father: "Misha, you don't know what's going on there. Cramer is the head of the Tickets Committee."

"Who?" asked my father. "Cramer? Oh yes, an active woman."

"Active? Active has to have a reason. Listen," she said sadly, "I'm surprised to see my neighbors making tra-la-la for Christmas."

My father couldn't think of what to say to that. Then he decided: "You're
in America! Clara, you wanted to come here. In Palestine the Arabs would
be eating you alive. Europe you had pogroms. Argentina is full of Indians.
Here you got Christmas . . . Some joke, ha?"

"Very funny, Misha. What is becoming of you? If we came to a new country a long time ago to run away from tyrants, and instead we fall into a
creeping pogrom, that our children learn a lot of lies, so what's the joke?
Ach, Misha, your idealism is going away."

"So is your sense of humor."

"That I never had, but idealism you had a lot of."

"I'm the same Misha Abramovitch, I didn't change an iota. Ask anyone."

"Only ask me," says my mama, may she rest in peace. "I got the answer."

Meanwhile the neighbors had to think of what to say too.

Marty's father said: "You know, he has a very important part, my boy."

"Mine also," said Mr. Sauerfeld.

"Not my boy!" said Mrs. Klieg. "I said to him no. The answer is no. When
I say no! I mean no!"

The rabbi's wife said, "It's disgusting!" But no one listened to her. Under
the narrow sky of God's great wisdom she wore a strawberry-blond wig.

Every day was noisy and full of experience. I was Right-hand Man. Mr.
Hilton said: "How could I get along without you, Shirley?"

He said: "Your mother and father ought to get down on their knees every
night and thank God for giving them a child like you."

He also said: "You're absolutely a pleasure to work with, my dear, dear
child."

Sometimes he said: "For godsakes, what did I do with the script? Shirley!
Shirley! Find it."

Then I answered quietly: "Here it is, Mr. Hilton."

Once in a while, when he was very tired, he would cry out: "Shirley, I'm
just tired of screaming at those kids. Will you tell Ira Pushkov not to come
in till Lester points to that star the second time?"

Then I roared: "Ira Pushkov, what's the matter with you? Dope! Mr. Hilton told you five times already, don't come in till Lester points to that star
the second time."

"Ach, Clara," my father asked, "what does she do there till six o'clock she
can't even put the plates on the table?"

"Christmas," said my mother coldly.

"Ho! Ho!" my father said. "Christmas. What's the harm? After all, history teaches everyone. We learn from reading this is a holiday from pagan times also, candles, lights, even Hanukkah. So we learn it's not altogether Christian. So if they think it's a private holiday, they're only ignorant, not patriotic. What belongs to history belongs to all men. You want to go back to the Middle Ages? Is it better to shave your head with a secondhand razor? Does it hurt Shirley to learn to speak up? It does not. So maybe someday she won't live between the kitchen and the shop. She's not a fool."

I thank you, Papa, for your kindness. It is true about me to this day. I am foolish but I am not a fool.

That night my father kissed me and said with great interest in my career, "Shirley, tomorrow's your big day. Congrats."

"Save it," my mother said. Then she shut all the windows in order to prevent tonsillitis.

In the morning it snowed. On the street corner a tree had been decorated for us by a kind city administration. In order to miss its chilly shadow our neighbors walked three blocks east to buy a loaf of bread. The butcher pulled down black window shades to keep the colored lights from shining on his chickens. Oh, not me. On the way to school, with both my hands I tossed it a kiss of tolerance. Poor thing, it was a stranger in Egypt.

I walked straight into the auditorium past the staring children. "Go ahead, Shirley!" said the monitors. Four boys, big for their age, had already started work as propmen and stagehands.

Mr. Hilton was very nervous. He was not even happy. Whatever he started to say ended in a sideward look of sadness. He sat slumped in the middle of the first row and asked me to help Miss Glacé. I did this, although she thought my voice too resonant and said, "Show-off!"

Parents began to arrive long before we were ready. They wanted to make a good impression. From among the yards of drapes I peeked out at the audience. I saw my embarrassed mother.

Ira, Lester, and Meyer were pasted to their beards by Miss Glacé. She almost forgot to thread the star on its wire, but I reminded her. I coughed a few times to clear my throat. Miss Glacé looked around and saw that everyone was in costume and on line waiting to play his part. She whispered, "All right . . ." Then:

Jackie Sauerfeld, the prettiest boy in first grade, parted the curtains with his skinny elbow and in a high voice sang out:

Parents dear
We are here
To make a Christmas play in time.
It we give
In narrative
And illustrate with pantomime.

He disappeared.

My voice burst immediately from the wings to the great shock of Ira, Lester, and Meyer, who were waiting for it but were surprised all the same.

"I remember, I remember, the house where I was born . . ."

Miss Glacé yanked the curtain open and there it was, the house—an old hayloft, where Celia Kornbluh lay in the straw with Cindy Lou, her favorite doll. Ira, Lester, and Meyer moved slowly from the wings toward her, sometimes pointing to a moving star and sometimes ahead to Cindy Lou.

It was a long story and it was a sad story. I carefully pronounced all the words about my lonesome childhood, while little Eddie Braunstein wandered upstage and down with his shepherd's stick, looking for sheep. I brought up lonesomeness again, and not being understood at all except by some women everybody hated. Eddie was too small for that and Marty Groff took his place, wearing his father's prayer shawl. I announced twelve friends, and half the boys in the fourth grade gathered round Marty, who stood on an orange crate while my voice harangued. Sorrowful and loud, I declaimed about love and God and Man, but because of the terrible deceit of Abie Stock we came suddenly to a famous moment. Marty, whose remembering tongue I was, waited at the foot of the cross. He stared desperately at the audience. I groaned, "My God, my God, why hast thou forsaken me?" The soldiers who were sheiks grabbed poor Marty to pin him up to die, but he wrenched free, turned again to the audience, and spread his arms aloft to show despair and the end. I murmured at the top of my voice, "The rest is silence, but as everyone in this room, in this city—in this world—now knows, I shall have life eternal."

That night Mrs. Kornbluh visited our kitchen for a glass of tea.

"How's the virgin?" asked my father with a look of concern.

"For a man with a daughter, you got a fresh mouth, Abramovitch."

"Here," said my father kindly, "have some lemon, it'll sweeten your disposition."

They debated a little in Yiddish, then fell in a puddle of Russian and Polish. What I understood next was my father, who said, "Still and all, it was certainly a beautiful affair, you have to admit, introducing us to the beliefs of a different culture."

"Well, yes," said Mrs. Kornbluh. "The only thing . . . you know Charlie Turner—that cute boy in Celia's class—a couple others? They got very small parts or no part at all. In very bad taste, it seemed to me. After all, it's their religion."

"Ach," explained my mother, "what could Mr. Hilton do? They got very small voices; after all, why should they holler? The English language they know from the beginning by heart. They're blond like angels. You think it's so important they should get in the play? Christmas . . . the whole piece of goods . . . they own it."

I listened and listened until I couldn't listen anymore. Too sleepy, I climbed out of bed and kneeled. I made a little church of my hands and said, "Hear, O Israel . . ." Then I called out in Yiddish, "Please, good night, good night. Ssh." My father said, "Ssh yourself," and slammed the kitchen door.

I was happy. I fell asleep at once. I had prayed for everybody: my talking family, cousins far away, passersby, and all the lonesome Christians. I expected to be heard. My voice was certainly the loudest.

1959

MARI SANDOZ

The Christmas of the Phonograph Records

A RECOLLECTION

I T SEEMS to me that I remember it all quite clearly. The night was very cold, footsteps squeaking in the frozen snow that had lain on for over two weeks, the roads in our region practically unbroken. But now the holidays were coming and wagons had pushed out on the long miles to the railroad, with men enough to scoop a trail for each other through the deeper drifts.

My small brother and I had been asleep in our attic bed long enough to frost the cover of the feather tick at our faces when there was a shouting in the road before the house, running steps, and then the sound of the broom handle thumping against the ceiling below us, and father booming out, "Get up! The phonograph is here!"

The phonograph! I stepped out on the coyote skin at our bed, jerked on my woolen stockings and my shoes, buttoning my dress as I slipped down the outside stairs in the fading moon. Lamplight was pouring from the open door in a cloud of freezing mist over the back end of a loaded wagon, with three neighbors easing great boxes off, father limping back and forth shouting, "Don't break me my records!" his breath white around his dark beard.

Inside the house mother was poking sticks of wood into the firebox of the cookstove, her eyes meeting mine for a moment, shining, her concern about the extravagance of a talking machine when we needed overshoes for our chilblains apparently forgotten. The three largest boxes were edged through the doorway and filled much of the kitchen–living room floor. The neighbors stomped their felt boots at the stove and held their hands over the hot lids while father ripped at the boxes with his crowbar, the frozen nails squealing as they let go. First there was the machine, varnished oak, with a shining cylinder for the records, and then the horn, a great black, gilt-ribbed morning glory, and the crazy angled rod arm and chain to hold it in place.

By now a wagon full of young people from the Dutch community on

Mirage Flats turned into our yard. At a school program they had heard about the Edison phonograph going out to Old Jules Sandoz. They trooped in at our door, piled their wraps in the leanto and settled along the benches to wait.

Young Jule and James, the brothers next to me in age, were up too, and watching father throw excelsior aside, exposing a tight packing of round paper containers a little smaller than a middle-sized baking powder can, with more layers under these, and still more below. Father opened one and while I read out the instructions in my German-accented fifth-grade country school English, he slipped the brown wax cylinder on the machine, cranked the handle carefully, and set the needle down. Everybody waited, leaning forward. There was a rhythmic frying in the silence, and then a whispering of sound, soft and very, very far away.

It brought a murmur of disappointment and an escaping laugh, but gradually the whispers loudened into the sextet from *Lucia*, into what still seems to me the most beautiful singing in the world. We all clustered around, the visitors, fourteen, fifteen by now, and mother too, caught while pouring hot chocolate into cups, her long-handled pan still tilted in the air. Looking back I realize something of the meaning of the light in her face: the hunger for music she must have felt, coming from Switzerland, the country of music, to a western Nebraska government claim. True, we sang old country songs in the evenings, she leading, teaching us all she knew, but plainly it had not been enough, really nothing.

By now almost everybody pushed up to the boxes to see what there was to play, or called out some title hopefully. My place in this was established from the start. I was to run the machine, play the two-minute records set before me. There were violin pieces for father, among them *Alpine Violets* and *Mocking Bird* from the first box opened; *Any Rags*, *Red Wing*, and *I'm Trying so Hard to Forget You* for the young people; *Rabbit Hash* for my brothers, their own selection from the catalog; and Schubert's *Serenade* and *Die Kapelle* for mother, with almost everyone laughing over *Casey at the Telephone*, all except father. He claimed he could not understand such broken English, he who gave even the rankest westernism a French pronunciation.

With the trail broken to the main bridge of the region, just below our house, and this Christmas Eve, there was considerable travel on the road, people passing most of the night. The lighted windows, the music, the gathering of teams and saddlehorses in the yard, and the sub-zero weather tolled them in to the weathered little frame house with its leanto.

"You better set more yeast. We will have to bake again tomorrow," mother told me as she cut into a *zopf*, one of the braids of coffee cake baked in tins as large as the circle of both her arms. This was the last of five planned to carry us into the middle of holiday week.

By now the phonograph had been moved to the top of the washstand in our parents' kalsomined bedroom, people sitting on the two double beds, on the round-topped trunk and on benches carried in, some squatting on their heels along the wall. The little round boxes stood everywhere, on the dresser and on the board laid from there to the washstand and on the window sills, with more brought in to be played and father still shouting over the music, "Don't break me my records!" Some were broken, the boxes slipping out of unaccustomed or cold-stiffened hands, the brown wax perhaps already cracked by the railroad.

When the Edison Military Band started a gay, blaring galop, mother looked in at the bedroom door, pleased. Then she noticed all the records spread out there, and in the kitchen-living room behind her, and began to realize their number. "Three hundred!" she exclaimed in German, speaking angrily in father's direction, "Looks to me like more than three thousand!"

Father scratched under his bearded chin, laughing slyly. "I added to the order," he admitted. He didn't say how many, nor that there were other brands besides the Edison here, including several hundred foreign recordings obtained through a Swiss friend in New York, at a stiff price.

Mother looked at him, her blue eyes tragic, as she could make them. "You paid nothing on the mortgage! All the twenty-one-hundred-dollar inheritance wasted on a talking machine!"

No, father denied, puffing at his corncob pipe. Not all. But mother knew him well. "You did not buy the overshoes for the children. You forgot everything except your stamp collection, your guns, and the phonograph!"

"The overshoes are coming. I got them cheaper on time, with the guns."

"More debts!" she accused bitterly, but before she could add to this one of the young Swiss, Maier perhaps, or Paul Freye, grabbed her and, against the stubbornness of her feet, whirled her back into the kitchen in the galop from the Edison band. He raced mother from door to stove and back again and around and around, so her blue calico skirts flew out and the anger died from her face. Her eyes began to shine in an excitement I had never seen in them, and I realize now, looking back, all the fun our mother missed in her working life, even in her childhood in the old country, and during the much harder years later.

That galop started the dancing. Hastily the table was pushed against the wall, boxes piled on top of it, the big ones dragged into the leanto. Waltzes, two-steps, quadrilles, and schottisches were sorted out and set in a row ready for me to play while one of the men shaved a candle over the kitchen floor. There was room for only one set of square dancers but our bachelor neighbor, Charley Sears, called the turns with enthusiasm. The Peters girls, two school teachers, and several other young women whom I've forgotten were well outnumbered by the men, as is common in new communities. They waltzed, two-stepped, formed a double line for a Bohemian polka, or schottisched around the room, one couple close behind the other to, per-haps, *It Blew, Blew, Blew.* Once Charley Sears grabbed my hand and drew me out to try a quadrille, towering over me as he swung me on the corner and guided me through the allemande left. My heart pounded in shyness and my home-made shoes compounded my awkwardness. Later someone else dragged me out into a two-step, saying, "Like this: 'one, two; one, two.' Just let yourself go."

Ah, so that was how it was done. Here started a sort of craze that was to hold me for over twenty years, through the bear dance, the turkey trot, the Charleston, and into the Lindy hop. But that first night with the records even Old Jules had to try a round polka, even with his foot crippled in a long-ago well accident. When he took his pipe out of his mouth, dropped it lighted into his pocket, and whirled mother around several times we knew that this was a special occasion. Before this we had never seen him even put an arm around her.

After the boys had heard their selection again, and *The Preacher and the Bear*, they fell asleep on the floor and were carried to their bed in the leanto. Suddenly I remembered little Fritzlie alone in the attic, perhaps half-frozen. I hurried up the slippery, frosted steps. He was crying, huddled together under the feather tick, cold and afraid, deserted by the cat too, sleeping against the warm chimney. I brought the boy down, heavy hulk that he was, and laid him in with his brothers. By then the last people started to talk of leaving, but the moon had clouded over, the night-dark roads winding and treacherous through the drifts. Still, those who had been to town must get home with the Christmas supplies and such presents as they could manage for their children when they awoke in the morning.

Toward dawn father dug out *Sempach*, a song of a heroic Swiss battle, in which one of mother's ancestors fell, and *Andreas Hofer*, of another national hero. Hiding her pleasure at these records, mother hurried away to the cel-lar under the house for two big hams, one to boil while the Canada goose roasted for the Christmas dinner. From the second ham she sliced great red rounds for the frying pan and I mixed up a triple batch of baking powder biscuits and set on the two-gallon coffee pot. When the sun glistened on the frosted snow, the last of the horses huddled together in our yard were on the road. By then some freighters forced to camp out by an upset wagon came whipping their teams up the icy pitch from the Niobrara River and stopped in. Father was slumped in his chair, letting his pipe fall into his beard, but he looked up and recognized the men as from a ranch accused of driving out bona fide settlers. Instead of rising to order them off the place he merely said "How!" in the Plains greeting, and dropped back into his doze. Whenever the music stopped noticeably, he lifted his shaggy head, complaining, "Can't you keep the machine going?" even if I had my hands in the biscuits. "Play the *Mocking Bird* again," he might order, or a couple of the expensive French records of pieces he had learned to play indifferently in the violin lessons of his boyhood in Neuchatel. He liked *Spring Song* too, and *La Paloma*, an excellent mandolin rendition of *Come ye Disconsolate*, and several German love songs he had learned from his sweetheart, in Zurich, who had not followed him to America.

Soon my three brothers were up again and calling for their favorites as they settled to plates of ham with red gravy and biscuits, Fritzlie from the top of two catalogs piled on a chair shouting too, just to be heard. None of them missed the presents that we never expected on Christmas; besides, what could be finer than the phonograph?

While mother fed our few cattle and the hogs I worked at the big stack of dishes with one of the freighters to wipe them. Afterward I got away to the attic and slept a little, the music from below faint through my floating of dreams. Suddenly I awoke, remembering what day this was and that young Jule and I had hoped father might go cottontail hunting in the canyons up the river and help us drag home a little pine tree. Christmas had become a time for a tree, even without presents, a tree and singing, with at least one new song learned.

I dressed and hurried down. Father was asleep and there were new people in the bedroom and in the kitchen too, talking about the wonder of the music rolling steadily from the big horn. In our Swiss way we had prepared for the usual visitors during the holidays, with family friends on Christmas and surely some of the European homeseekers father had settled on free land, as well as passersby just dropping in to get warm and perhaps be offered a cup of coffee or chocolate or a glass of father's homemade wine if particularly privileged. Early in the forenoon the Syrian peddler we called Solomon drew up in the yard with his high four-horse wagon. I remember him every time I see a picture of Krishna Menon—the tufted hair, the same lean yellowish face and long white teeth. Solomon liked to strike our place for Christmas because there might be customers around and besides there was no display of religion to make him uncomfortable in his Mohammedanism, father said, although one might run into a stamp-collecting priest or a hungry preacher at our house almost any other time.

So far as I know, Solomon was the first to express what others must have thought. "Excuse it please, Mrs. Sandoz," he said, in the polite way of peddlers, "but it seem to uneducated man like me the new music is for fine palace—"

Father heard him. "Nothing's too good for my family and my neighbors," he roared out.

"The children have the frozen feet—" the man said quietly.

"Frozen feet heal! What you put in the mind lasts!"

The peddler looked down into his coffee cup, half full of sugar, and said no more.

It was true that we had always been money poor and plainly would go on so, but there was plenty of meat and game, plenty of everything that the garden, the young orchard, the field, and the open country could provide, and for all of which there was no available market. Our bread, dark and heavy, was from our hard macaroni wheat ground at a local water mill. The hams, sausage, and bacon were from our own smokehouse, the cellar full of our own potatoes, barrels of pickles and sauerkraut, and hundreds of jars of canned fruit and vegetables, crocks of jams and jellies, wild and tame, including buffalo berry, that wonderful, tart, golden-red jelly from the silvery bush that seems to retreat before close settlement much like the buffalo and the whooping crane. Most of the root crops were in a long pit outside, and the attic was strung with little sacks of herbs and poppy seed, bigger ones of dried green beans, sweetcorn, chokecherries, sandcherries, and wild plums. Piled along the low sides of the attic were bushel bags of popcorn, peas, beans, and lentils, the flour stacked in rows with room between for the mousing cat.

Sugar, coffee, and chocolate were practically all we bought for the table, with perhaps a barrel of blackstrap molasses for cookies and brown cake, all laid in while the fall roads were still open.

When the new batch of coffee cake was done and the fresh bread and buns, the goose in the oven, we took turns getting scrubbed at the heater in the leanto, and put on our best clothes, mostly made-over from some adult's but well-sewn. Finally we spread mother's two old country linen cloths over the table lengthened out by boards laid on salt barrels for twenty-two places. While mother passed the platters, I fed the phonograph with records that Mrs. Surber and her three musical daughters had selected, soothing music: Bach, Mozart, Brahms, and the *Moonlight Sonata* on two foreign records that father had hidden away so they would not be broken, along with an a capella *Stille Nacht* and some other foreign ones mother wanted saved. For lightness, Mrs. Surber had added *The Last Rose of Summer*, to please Elsa, the young soprano soon to be a professional singer in Cleveland, and a little Strauss and Puccini, while the young people wanted Ada Jones and *Monkey Land* by Collins and Harlan.

There was stuffed Canada goose with the buffalo berry jelly; ham boiled in a big kettle in the leanto; watercress salad; chow-chow and pickles, sweet and sour; dried green beans cooked with bacon and a hint of garlic; carrots, turnips, mashed potatoes and gravy, with coffee from the start to the pie, pumpkin and gooseberry. At the dishpan set on the high water bench, where I had to stand on a little box for comfort, the dishes were washed as fast as they came off the table, with a relay of wipers. There were also waiting young men and boys to draw water from the bucket well, to chop stove wood and carry it in.

As I recall now, there were people at the table for hours. A letter of mother's says that the later uninvited guests got sausage and sauerkraut, squash, potatoes, and fresh bread, with canned plums and cookies for dessert. Still later there was a big roaster full of beans and side-meat brought in by a lady homesteader, and some mince pies made with wild plums to lend tartness instead of apples, which cost money.

All this time there was the steady stream of music and talk from the bedroom. I managed to slip in the *Lucia* a couple of times until a tart-tongued woman from over east said she believed I was getting addled from all that hollering. We were not allowed to talk back to adults, so I put on the next record set before me, this one *Don't Get Married Any More, Ma*, selected for a visiting Chicago widow looking for her fourth husband, or perhaps her fifth. Mother rolled her eyes up at this bad taste, but father and the other old timers laughed over their pipes.

We finally got mother off to bed in the attic for her first nap since the records came. Downstairs the floor was cleared and the Surber girls showed their dancing-school elegance in the waltzes. There was a stream of young people later in the afternoon, many from the skating party at the bridge.

Father, red-eyed like the rest of us, limped among them, soaking up their praise, their new respect. By this time my brothers and I had given up having a tree. Then a big boy from up the river rode into the yard dragging a pine behind his horse. It was a shapely tree, and small enough to fit on a box in the window, out of the way. The youth was the son of father's worst enemy, the man who had sworn in court that Jules Sandoz shot at him, and got our father thirty days in jail, although everybody, including the judge, knew that Jules Sandoz was a crack shot and what he fired at made no further appearances.

As the son came in with the tree, someone announced loudly who he was. I saw father look toward his Winchester on the wall, but he was not the man to quarrel with an enemy's children. Then he was told that the boy's father himself was in the yard. Now Jules Sandoz paled above his bearding, paled so the dancers stopped, the room silent under the suddenly foolish noise of the big-horned machine. Helpless, I watched father jump toward the rifle. Then he turned, looked to the man's gaunt-faced young son.

"Tell your old man to come in. We got some good Austrian music."

So the man came in, and sat hunched over near the door. Father had left the room, gone to the leanto, but after a while he came out, said his "How!" to the man, and paid no attention when Mrs. Surber pushed me forward to make the proper thanks for the tree that we were starting to trim as usual. We played *The Blue Danube* and some other pieces long forgotten now for the man, and passed him the coffee and *küchli* with the others. He tasted the thin flaky frycakes. "Your mother is a good cook," he told me. "A fine woman."

When he left with the skaters all of father's friends began to talk at once, fast, relieved. "You could have shot him down, on your own place, and not got a day in the pen for it," one said.

Old Jules nodded. "I got no use for his whole outfit, but the music is for everybody."

As I recall now, perhaps half a dozen of us, all children, worked at the tree, looping my strings of red rose hips and popcorn around it, hanging the people and animal cookies with chokecherry eyes, distributing the few Christmas tree balls and the tinsel and candleholders that the Surbers had given us several years before. I brought out the boxes of candles I had made by dipping string in melted tallow, and then we lit the candles and with my schoolmates I ran out into the cold of the road to look. The tree showed fine through the glass.

Now I had to go to bed, although the room below me was alive with dancing and I remembered that Jule and I had not sung our new song, *Amerika ist ein schönes Land* at the tree.

Holiday week was much like Christmas, the house full of visitors as the news of the fine music and the funny records spread. People appeared from fifty, sixty miles away and farther so long as the new snow held off, for there was no other such collection of records in all of western Nebraska, and none with such an open door. There was something for everybody, Irishmen, Scots, Swedes, Danes, Poles, Czechs as well as the Germans and the rest, something pleasant and nostalgic. The greatest variety in tastes was among the Americans, from *Everybody Works but Father, Arkansas Traveler,* and *Finkelstein at the Seashore* to love songs and the sentimental *Always in the Way*; from home and native region pieces to the patriotic and religious. They had strong dislikes too, even in war songs. One settler, a GAR veteran, burst into tears and fled from the house at the first notes of *Tenting Tonight.* Perhaps it was the memories it awakened. Many Americans were as interested in classical music as any European, and it wasn't always a matter of cultivated taste. One illiterate little woman from down the river cried with joy at Rubinstein's *Melody in F.*

"I has heard me talkin' and singin' before," she said apologetically as she wiped her eyes, "but I wasn't knowin' there could be something sweet as that come from a horn."

Afternoons and evenings, however, were still the time for the dancers. Finally it was New Year, the day when the Sandoz relatives, siblings, uncles and cousins gathered, perhaps twenty of them immigrants brought in by the land locater, Jules. This year they were only a sort of eddy in the regular stream of outsiders. Instead of nostalgic jokes and talk of the family and the old country, there were the records to hear, particularly the foreign ones, and the melodies of the old violin lessons that the brothers had taken, and the guitar and mandolin of their one sister. Jules had to endure a certain amount of joking over the way he spent most of his inheritance. One brother was building a cement block home in place of his soddy with his, and a greenhouse. The sister was to have a fine large barn instead of a new home because her husband believed that next year Halley's comet would bring the end of the world. Ferdinand, the youngest of the brothers, had put his money into wild-cat oil stock and planned to become very wealthy.

Although most of their talk was in French, which mother did not speak, they tried to make up for this by complimenting her on the excellence of her chocolate and her golden fruit cake. Then they were gone, hot bricks at their feet, and calling back their adieus from the freezing night. It was a good thing they left early, mother told me. She had used up the last of the chocolate, the last cake of the two twenty-five pound caddies. We had baked up two sacks of flour, forty-nine pounds each, in addition to all that went into the Christmas preparations before the phonograph came. Three-quarters of a hundred pound bag of coffee had been roasted, ground, and used during the week, and all the winter's sausage and ham. The floor of the kitchen–living room, old and worn anyway, was much thinner for the week of dancing. New Year's night a man who had been there every day, all week, tilted back on one of the kitchen chairs and went clear through the floor.

"Oh, the fools!" father shouted at us all. "Had to wear out my floor dancing!"

But plainly he was pleased. It was a fine story to tell for years, all the story of the phonograph records. He was particularly gratified by the praise of those who knew something about music, people like the Surbers and a visitor from a Czech community, a relative of Dvorak, the great composer. The man wrote an item for the papers, saying, "This Jules Sandoz has not only settled a good community of homeseekers, but is enriching their cultural life with the greatest music of the world."

"Probably wants to borrow money from you," mother said. "He has come to the wrong door."

Gradually the records for special occasions and people were stored in the leanto. For those used regularly, father and a neighbor made a lot of flat boxes to fit under the beds, always handy, and a cabinet for the corner at the bedroom door. The best, the finest from both the Edison and the foreign recordings, were put into this cabinet, with a door that didn't stay closed. One warmish day when I was left alone with the smaller children, the water pail needed refilling. I ran out to draw a bucket from the well. It was a hard and heavy pull for a growing girl and I hated it, always afraid that I wouldn't last, and would have to let the rope slip and break the windlass.

Somehow, in my uneasy hurry, I left the door ajar. The wind blew it back and when I had the bucket started up the sixty-five foot well, our big old sow, loose in the yard, pushed her way into the house. Horrified, I shouted to Fritzlie to get out of her way, but I had to keep pulling and puffing until the bucket was at the top. Then I ran in. Fritzlie was up on a chair, safe, but the sow had knocked down the record cabinet and scattered the cylinders over the floor. Standing among them as in corn, she was chomping down the wax records that had rolled out of the boxes, eating some, box and all. Furiously I thrashed her out with the broom, amidst squealings and shouts. Then I tried to save what I could. The sow had broken at least thirty or thirty-five of the best records and eaten all or part of twenty more. *La Paloma* was gone, and *Träumerei* and *Spring Song*; *Evening Star* too, and half of the *Moonlight Sonata* and many others, foreign and domestic, including all of Brahms.

I got the worst whipping of my life for my carelessness, but the loss of the records hurt more, and much, much longer.

1965

JOAN DIDION

The Big Rock Candy Figgy Pudding Pitfall

YOU WILL PERHAPS have difficulty understanding why I conceived the idea of making 20 hard-candy topiary trees and 20 figgy puddings in the first place. The heart of it is that although I am frail, lazy and unsuited to doing anything except what I am paid to do, which is sit by myself and type with one finger, I like to imagine myself a "can-do" kind of woman, capable of patching the corral fence, pickling enough peaches to feed the hands all winter, and then winning a trip to Minneapolis in the Pillsbury Bake-Off. In fact, the day I stop believing that if put to it I could win the Pillsbury Bake-Off will signal the death of something.

It was late in September, about the time certain canny elves began strategically spotting their *Make it Yourself for Christmas* books near supermarket check-out counters, when I sensed the old familiar discontent. I would stand there in the Westward Ho market, waiting to check out my frozen chicken Tetrazzini and leafing through the books, and I would see how far I had drifted from the real pleasures. I did not "do" things. I did not sew spangles on potholders for my friends. I did not make branches of marzipan mistletoe for my hostesses. I did not give Corn Dog and Caroling Parties for neighborhood children (Did I know any neighborhood children? Were there any neighborhood children? What exactly was my neighborhood?), the Corn Dogs to be accompanied by Hot Santa's Grog.

Nor had it ever occurred to me to buy Styrofoam balls, cover them with hard candies, plant them on wooden stalks in small flowerpots, and end up with amusingly decorative hard-candy topiary trees, perfect for centerpieces or last-minute gifts. At the check-out counter, I recognized clearly that my plans for the Christmas season—making a few deadlines—were stale and unprofitable. Had my great-great-grandmother come west in a covered wagon and strung cranberries on scrub oaks so that I might sit by myself in a room typing with one finger and ordering Italian twinkle lights by mail from Hammacher Schlemmer?

I wanted to be the kind of woman who made hard-candy topiary trees and figgy puddings. The figgy puddings were not in the *Make it Yourself for Christmas* books but something I remembered from a carol. "Oh bring us a figgy pudding and a happy new year," the line went. I was unsure what a figgy pudding was, but it had the ring of the real thing.

"Exactly what kind of therapy are we up to this week?" my husband asked when I arrived home with 20 Styrofoam balls, 20 flowerpots and 60 pounds of, or roughly 6,000, hard candies, each wrapped in cellophane.

"Hard-candy topiary trees, if you don't mind," I said briskly, to gain the offensive before he could mention my last project, a hand-knitted sweater which would have cost $60 at Jax, the distinction being that, had I bought it at Jax, it would very probably be finished. "Twenty of them. Decorative. Amusing."

He said nothing.

"*Christmas* presents," I said.

There was a moment of silence as we contemplated the dining-room table, covered now with shifting dunes of lemon drops.

"Presents for whom?" he said.

"Your mother might like one."

"That leaves nineteen."

"All right. Let's just say they're centerpieces."

"Let's just say that if you're making twenty centerpieces, I hope you're under contract to Chasen's. Or maybe to Hilton."

"That's all *you* know," I countered, wittily.

Provisions for the figgy puddings were rather more a problem. *The Vogue Book of Menus and Recipes* made no mention of figgy pudding, nor did my cookbook, although the latter offered a recipe for "Steamed Date or Fig Pudding." This had a tentative sound, and so I merely laid in 20 pounds of dried figs and planned, when the time came, to improvise from there. I thought it unnecessary to mention the puddings to my husband just yet.

Meanwhile, work on the topiary trees proceeded. Pebbles were gathered from the driveway to line the flowerpots. ("Next time it rains and that driveway washes out," I was informed, "there's going to be one unhappy Santa's Helper around here.") Lengths of doweling to be used as stalks were wrapped with satin ribbons. The 20 Styrofoam balls glistened with candies, each affixed with an artfully concealed silk pin. (As it happened I had several thousand silk pins left from the time I planned to improvise a copy of a Grès evening dress.) There was to be a lemon-drop tree and an ice-mint tree and a cinnamon-lump tree. There was to be a delicate crystallized-violet tree. There was to be a witty-licorice tree.

All in all, the operation went more smoothly than any I had undertaken since I was 16 and won third prize in the Sacramento Valley Elimination Make-It-Yourself-With-Wool Contest. I framed graceful rejoinders to compliments. I considered the probability that I. Magnin or Neiman-Marcus would press me to make trees for them on an exclusive basis. All that remained was to set the candy balls upon their stalks—that and the disposition of the figs—and I had set an evening aside for this crowning of the season's achievement.

I suppose that it was about seven o'clock when I placed the first candy-covered ball on the first stalk. Because it did not seem overly secure, I drilled a deeper hole in the second ball. That one, too, once on its stalk, exhibited a certain tendency to sway, but then so does the Golden Gate Bridge. I was flushed with imminent success, visions of candy trees come true all around me. I suppose it was about eight o'clock when I placed the last ball on the last stalk, and I suppose it was about one minute after eight when I heard the first crack, and I suppose it was about 8:15 (there were several minutes of frantic shoring maneuvers) when my husband found me sitting on the dining-room floor, crying, surrounded by 60 pounds of scattered lemon drops and ice-mints and cinnamon lumps and witty licorice.

"I'll tell you what," he said. "Why don't we get the grout left over from when you were going to retile the bathroom, and make a ceramic candy floor."

"If you think you're going to get any figgy puddings," I said, "you'd better think again."

But I had stopped crying, and we went out for an expensive dinner. The next morning I gathered up the candies and took them to Girl Scout headquarters, presumably to be parceled into convalescents' nut cups by some gnome Brownie. The Styrofoam balls I saved. A clever woman should be able to do something very attractive for Easter with Styrofoam balls and 20 pounds of figs.

1966

JOHN UPDIKE

The Carol Sing

 SURELY ONE of the natural wonders of Tarbox was Mr. Burley at the Town Hall carol sing. How he would jubilate, how he would God-rest those merry gentlemen, how he would boom out when the male voices became Good King Wenceslas:

> Mark my footsteps, good my page;
> Tread thou in them boldly:
> Thou shalt find the winter's rage
> Freeze thy blood less co-*oh*-ldly.

When he hit a good "oh," standing beside him was like being inside a great transparent Christmas ball. He had what you'd have to call a God-given bass. This year, we other male voices just peck at the tunes: Wendell Huddlestone, whose hardware store has become the pizza place where the dropouts collect after dark; Squire Wentworth, who is still getting up petitions to protect the marsh birds from the atomic-power plant; Lionel Merson, lighter this year by about three pounds of gallstones; and that selectman whose freckled bald head looks like the belly of a trout; and that fireman whose face is bright brown all the year round from clamming; and the widow Covode's bearded son, who went into divinity school to avoid the draft; and the Bisbee boy, who no sooner was back from Vietnam than he grew a beard and painted his car every color of the rainbow; and the husband of the new couple that moved this September into the Whitman place on the beach road. He wears thick glasses above a little mumble of a mouth, but his wife appears perky enough.

> The-ey lo-okèd up and sa-haw a star,
> Shining in the east, beyond them far;
> And to the earth it ga-ave great light,
> And so it continued both da-hay and night.

She is wearing a flouncy little Christmassy number, red with white polka dots, one of those dresses so short that when she sits down on the old plush deacon's bench she has to help it with her hand to tuck under her behind, otherwise it wouldn't. A lively bit of a girl with long thighs as glossy as pond ice. She smiles nervously up over her cup of cinnamon-stick punch, wondering why she is here, in this dusty drafty public place. We must look monstrous to her, we Tarbox old-timers. And she has never heard Mr. Burley sing, but she knows something is missing this year; there is something failed, something hollow. Hester Hartner sweeps wrong notes into every chord: arthritis—arthritis and indifference.

> The first good joy that Mary had,
> It was the joy of one;
> To see the blessèd Jesus Christ
> When he was first her son.

The old upright, a Cickering, for most of the year has its keyboard locked; it stands beneath the town zoning map, its top piled high with rolled-up plot plans being filed for variances. The Town Hall was built, strange to say, as a Unitarian church, around 1830, but it didn't take around here, Unitarianism; the sea air killed it. You need big trees for a shady mystic mood, or at least a lake to see yourself in like they have over to Concord. So the town bought up the shell and ran a second floor through the air of the sanctuary, between the balconies: offices and the courtroom below, more offices and this hall above. You can still see the Doric pilasters along the walls, the top halves. They used to use it more; there were the Tarbox Theatricals twice a year, and political rallies with placards and straw hats and tambourines, and get-togethers under this or that local auspices, and town meetings until we went representative. But now not even the holly the ladies of the Grange have hung around can cheer it up, can chase away the smell of dust and must, of cobwebs too high to reach and rats' nests in the hot-air ducts and, if you stand close to the piano, that faint sour tang of blueprints. And Hester lately has taken to chewing eucalyptus drops.

> And him to serve God give us grace,
> *O lux beata Trinitas.*

The little wife in polka dots is laughing now: maybe the punch is getting to her, maybe she's getting used to the look of us. Strange people look ugly only for a while, until you begin to fill in those tufty monkey features with a little history and stop seeing their faces and start seeing their lives. Regardless, it does us good, to see her here, to see young people at the carol sing. We need new blood.

> This time of the year is spent in good cheer,
>   And neighbors together do meet,
> To sit by the fire, with friendly desire,
>   Each other in love to greet.
> Old grudges forgot are put in the pot,
>   All sorrows aside they lay;
> The old and the young doth carol this song,
>   To drive the cold winter away.

At bottom it's a woman's affair, a chance in the darkest of months to iron some man-fetching clothes and get out of the house. Those old holidays weren't scattered around the calendar by chance. Harvest and seedtime, seedtime and harvest, the elbows of the year. The women do enjoy it; they enjoy jostle of most any kind, in my limited experience. The widow Covode as full of rouge and purple as an old-time Scollay Square tart, when her best hope is burial on a sunny day, with no frost in the ground. Mrs. Hortense broad as a barn door, yet her hands putting on a duchess's airs. Mamie Nevins sporting a sprig of mistletoe in her neck brace. They miss Mr. Burley. He never married and was everybody's gallant for this occasion. He was the one to spike the punch, and this year they let young Covode do it, maybe that's why Little Polka Dots can't keep a straight face and giggles across the music like a pruning saw.

> Adeste, fideles,
> Laeti triumphantes;
> Venite, venite
> In Bethlehem.

Still that old tussle, "v" versus "wenite," the "th" as hard or soft. Education is what divides us. People used to actually resent it, the way Burley, with his education, didn't go to some city, didn't get out. Exeter, Dartmouth, a year at the Sorbonne, then thirty years of Tarbox. By the time he hit fifty he was fat and fussy. Arrogant, too. Last sing, he two or three times told Hester to pick up her tempo. "Presto, Hester, not andante!" Never married, and never really worked. Burley Hosiery, that his grandfather had founded, was shut down and the machines sold south before Burley got his manhood. He built himself a laboratory instead and was always about to come up with something perfect: the perfect synthetic substitute for leather, the perfectly harmless insecticide, the beer can that turned itself into mulch. Some said at the end he was looking for a way to turn lead into gold. That was just malice. Anything high attracts lightning, anybody with a name attracts malice. When it happened, the papers in Boston gave him six inches and a photograph ten years old. "After a long illness." It wasn't a long illness, it was cyanide, the Friday after Thanksgiving.

> The holly bears a prickle,
> As sharp as any thorn,
> And Mary bore sweet Jesus Christ
> On Christmas day in the morn.

They said the cyanide ate out his throat worse than a blowtorch. Such a detail is satisfying but doesn't clear up the mystery. Why? Health, money, hobbies, that voice. Not having that voice makes a big hole here. Without his lead, no man dares take the lower parts; we just wheeze away at the melody with the women. It's as if the floor they put in has been taken away and we're standing in air, halfway up that old sanctuary. We peek around guiltily, missing Burley's voice. The absent seem to outnumber the present. We feel insulted, slighted. The dead turn their backs. The older you get, the more of them snub you. He was rude enough last year, Burley, correcting Hester's tempo. At one point, he even reached over, his face black with impatience, and slapped her hands as they were still trying to make sense of the keys.

> Rise, and bake your Christmas bread:
> Christians, rise! The world is bare,
> And blank, and dark with want and care,
> Yet Christmas comes in the morning.

Well, why anything? Why do *we*? Come every year sure as the solstice to carol these antiquities that if you listened to the words would break your heart. Silence, darkness, Jesus, angels. Better, I suppose, to sing than to listen.

1970

TOMÁS RIVERA

The Night Before Christmas

CHRISTMAS EVE was approaching and the barrage of commercials, music and Christmas cheer over the radio and the blare of announcements over the loud speakers on top of the station wagon advertising movies at the Teatro Ideal resounded and seemed to draw it closer. It was three days before Christmas when Doña Maria decided to buy something for her children. This was the first time she would buy them toys. Every year she intended to do it but she always ended up facing up to the fact that, no, they couldn't afford it. She knew that her husband would be bringing each of the children candies and nuts anyway and, so she would rationalize that they didn't need to get them anything else. Nevertheless, every Christmas the children asked for toys. She always appeased them with the same promise. She would tell them to wait until the sixth of January, the day of the Magi, and by the time that day arrived the children had already forgotten all about it. But now she was noticing that each year the children seemed less and less taken with Don Chon's visit on Christmas Eve when he came bearing a sack of oranges and nuts.

"But why doesn't Santa Claus bring us anything?"

"What do you mean? What about the oranges and nuts he brings you?"

"No, that's Don Chon."

"No, I'm talking about what you always find under the sewing machine."

"What, Dad's the one who brings that, don't think we don't know that. Aren't we good like the other kids?"

"Of course, you're good children. Why don't you wait until the day of the Reyes Magos. That's when toys and gifts really arrive. In Mexico, it's not Santa Claus who brings gifts, but the Three

Wisemen. And they don't come until the sixth of January. That's the real date."

"Yeah, but they always forget. They've never brought us anything, not on Christmas Eve, not on the day of the Three Kings."

"Well, maybe this time they will."

"Yeah, well, I sure hope so."

That was why she made up her mind to buy them something. But they didn't have the money to spend on toys. Her husband worked almost eighteen hours a day washing dishes and cooking at a restaurant. He didn't have time to go downtown and buy toys. Besides, they had to save money every week to pay for the trip up north. Now they even charged for children too, even if they rode standing up the whole way to Iowa. So it cost them a lot to make the trip. In any case, that night when her husband arrived, tired from work, she talked to him about getting something for the children.

"Look, viejo, the children want something for Christmas."

"What about the oranges and nuts I bring them."

"Well, they want toys. They're not content anymore with just fruits and nuts. They're a little older now and more aware of things."

"They don't need anything."

"Now, you can't tell me you didn't have toys when you were a kid."

"I used to *make* my own toys, out of clay . . . little horses and little soldiers . . ."

"Yes, but it's different here. They see so many things . . . come on, let's go get them something . . . I'll go to Kress myself."

"You?"

"Yes, me."

"Aren't you afraid to go downtown? You remember that time in Wilmar, out in Minnesota, how you got lost downtown. Are you sure you're not afraid?"

"Yes, yes, I remember, but I'll just have to get my courage up. I've thought about it all day long and I've set my mind to it. I'm sure I won't get lost here. Look, I go out to the street. From here you can see the ice house. It's only four blocks away, so Doña Regina tells me. When I get to the ice house I turn to the right and

go two blocks and there's downtown. Kress is right there. Then, I come out of Kress, walk back towards the ice house and turn back on this street, and here I am."

"I guess it really won't be difficult. Yeah. Fine. I'll leave you some money on top of the table when I go to work in the morning. But be careful, vieja, there's a lot of people downtown these days."

The fact was that Doña Maria very rarely left the house. The only time she did was when she visited her father and her sister who lived on the next block. And she only went to church whenever someone died and, occasionally, when there was a wedding. But she went with her husband, so she never took notice of where she was going. And her husband always brought her everything. He was the one who bought the groceries and clothing. In reality she was unfamiliar with downtown even though it was only six blocks away. The cemetery was on the other side of downtown and the church was also in that direction. The only time that they passed through downtown was whenever they were on their way to San Antonio or whenever they were returning from up north. And this would usually be during the wee hours of the morning or at night. But that day she was determined and she started making preparations.

The next day she got up early as usual, and after seeing her husband and children off, she took the money from the table and began getting ready to go downtown. This didn't take her long.

"My God, I don't know why I'm so fearful. Why, downtown is only six blocks from here. I just go straight and then after I cross the tracks turn right. Then go two blocks and there's Kress. On the way back, I walk two blocks back and then I turn to the left and keep walking until I'm home again. God willing, there won't be any dogs on the way. And I just pray that the train doesn't come while I'm crossing the tracks and catches me right in the middle . . . I iust hope there's no dogs . . . I hope there's no train coming down the tracks."

She walked the distance from the house to the railroad tracks rapidly. She walked down the middle of the street all the way. She was afraid to walk on the sidewalk. She feared she might get bitten by a dog or that someone might grab her. In actuality there was only one dog along the entire stretch

and most of the people didn't even notice her walking toward downtown. She nevertheless kept walking down the middle of the street and, luckily, not a single car passed by, otherwise she would not have known what to do. Upon arriving at the crossing she was suddenly struck by intense fear. She could hear the sound of moving trains and their whistles blowing and this was unnerving her. She was too scared to cross. Each time she mustered enough courage to cross she heard the whistle of the train and, frightened, she retreated and ended up at the same place. Finally, overcoming her fear, she shut her eyes and crossed the tracks. Once she got past the tracks, her fear began to subside. She got to the corner and turned to the right.

The sidewalks were crowded with people and her ears started to fill up with a ringing sound, the kind that, once it started, it wouldn't stop. She didn't recognize any of the people around her. She wanted to turn back but she was caught in the flow of the crowd which shoved her onward toward downtown and the sound kept ringing louder and louder in her ears. She became frightened and more and more she was finding herself unable to remember why she was there amidst the crowd of people. She stopped in an alley way between two stores to regain her composure a bit. She stood there for a while watching the passing crowd.

"My God, what is happening to me? I'm starting to feel the same way I did in Wilmar. I hope I don't get worse. Let me see . . . the ice house is in that direction—no it's that way. No, my God, what's happening to me? Let me see . . . I came from over there to here. So it's in that direction. I should have just stayed home. Uh, can you tell me where Kress is, please? . . . Thank you."

She walked to where they had pointed and entered the store. The noise and pushing of the crowd was worse inside. Her anxiety soared. All she wanted was to leave the store but she couldn't find the doors anywhere, only stacks and stacks of merchandise and people crowded against one another. She even started hearing voices coming from the merchandise. For a while she stood, gazing blankly at what was in front of her. She couldn't even remember the names of the things. Some people stared at her for a few seconds, others just pushed her aside. She remained in this state for a while, then she started walking again. She finally made out some toys and put them in her bag. Then she saw a wallet and also put that in her bag. Suddenly she no longer heard the noise of the crowd. She only saw the people moving about—their legs, their arms, their mouths, their eyes. She finally asked where the door, the exit was. They told her and she started in that direction. She pressed through the crowd, pushing her way until she pushed open the door and exited.

She had been standing on the sidewalk for only a few seconds, trying to figure out where she was, when she felt someone grab her roughly by the arm. She was grabbed so tightly that she gave out a cry.

"Here she is . . . these damn people, always stealing something, stealing. I've been watching you all along. Let's have that bag."
"But . . ."

Then she heard nothing for a long time. All she saw was the pavement moving swiftly toward her face and a small pebble that bounced into her eye and was hurting a lot. She felt someone pulling her arms and when they turned her, face up, all she saw were faces far away. Then she saw a security guard with a gun in his holster and she was terrified. In that instant she thought about her children and her eyes filled with tears. She started crying. Then she lost consciousness of what was happening around her, only feeling herself drifting in a sea of people, their arms brushing against her like waves.

"It's a good thing my compadre happened to be there. He's the one who ran to the restaurant to tell me. How do you feel?"
"I think I must be insane, viejo."
"That's why I asked you if you weren't afraid you might get sick like in Wilmar."
"What will become of my children with a mother who's insane? A crazy woman who can't even talk, can't even go downtown."
"Anyway, I went and got the notary public. He's the one who went with me to the jail. He explained everything to the official. That you got dizzy and that you get nervous attacks whenever you're in a crowd of people."
"And if they send me to the insane asylum? I don't want to leave my children. Please, viejo, don't let them take me, don't let them. I shouldn't have gone downtown."
"Just stay here inside the house and don't leave the yard. There's no need for it anyway. I'll bring you everything you need. Look, don't cry anymore, don't cry. No, go ahead and cry, it'll make you feel better. I'm gonna talk to the kids and tell them to stop

bothering you about Santa Claus. I'm gonna tell them there's no Santa Claus, that way they won't trouble you with that anymore."

"No, viejo, don't be mean. Tell them that if he doesn't bring them anything on Christmas Eve, it's because the Reyes Magos will be bringing them something."

"But . . . well, all right, whatever you say. I suppose it's always best to have hope."

The children, who were hiding behind the door, heard everything, but they didn't quite understand it all. They awaited the day of the Reyes Magos as they did every year. When that day came and went with no arrival of gifts, they didn't ask for explanations.

1971

THOMAS M. DISCH

The Santa Claus Compromise

T HE FIRST REVELATIONS hit the headlines the day after
Thanksgiving, less than a year from the Supreme Court's
epochal decision to extend full civil liberties to five-year-
olds. After centuries of servitude and repression, the last minority
was finally free. Free to get married. Free to vote and hold office.
Free to go to bed at any hour they wanted. Free to spend their allowances
on whatever they liked.

For those services geared to the newly liberated young it was a period of
heady expansion. A typical example was Lord & Taylor's department stores,
which had gone deeply into the red in the two previous years, due to the
popularity of thermal body-paints. Changing its name to Dumb Dresses
and Silly Shoes, Lord & Taylor's profits soared to record heights in the second quarter of '89. In the field of entertainment the Broadway musical, *I
See London, I See France*, scored a similar success with audiences and critics
alike. "I think it shows," wrote *Our Own Times* Drama Critic Sandy Myers,
"how kids are really on the ball today. I think everyone who likes singing
and dancing and things like that should go and see it. But prudes should be
warned that some of the humor is pretty spicy."

It was the same newspaper's team of investigative reporters, Bobby Boyd
and Michelle Ginsberg, who broke the Santa Claus story one memorable
November morning. Under a banner headline that proclaimed:

THERE IS NO SANTA CLAUS!

Bobby told how months before, rummaging through various trunks and
boxes in his parents' home in Westchester, he had discovered a costume
identical in every respect with that worn by the "Santa Claus" who had
visited the Boyd household on the previous Christmas Eve. "My soul was
torn," wrote the young Pulitzer Prize winner, "between feelings of outrage
and fear. The thought of all the years of imposture and deceit that had been

practiced on me and my brothers and sisters around the world made me furious. Then, foreseeing all that I'd be up against, a shiver of dread went through me. If I'd known that the trail of guilt would lead me to the door of my father's bedroom, I can't be sure that I'd have followed it. I had my suspicions, of course."

But suspicions, however strong, weren't enough for Bobby and Michelle. They wanted evidence. Months of back-breaking and heart-breaking labor produced nothing but hearsay, innuendo, and conflicting allegations. Then, in mid-November, as the stores were already beginning to fill with Christmas displays, Michelle met the mysterious Clayton E. Forster. Forster claimed that he had repeatedly assumed the character and name of Santa Claus, and that this imposture had been financed from funds set aside for this purpose by a number of prominent New York businesses. When asked if he had ever met or spoken to the real Santa Claus, Forster declared outright that *there wasn't any*! Though prevented from confirming Forster's allegations from his own lips by the municipal authorities (Forster had been sent to prison on a vagrancy charge), reporters were able to listen to Michelle's tape recording of the interview, on which the self-styled soldier-of-fortune could be heard to say: "Santa Claus? Santa's just a pile of (expletive deleted), kid! Get wise—there ain't no (expletive deleted), and there never was one. It's nothing but your (expletive deleted) mother and father!"

The clincher, however, was Bobby's publication of a number of BankAmericard receipts, charging Mr. Oscar T. Boyd for, among much else, "2 rooty-toot-toots and 3 rummy-tum-tums." These purchases had been made in early December of the previous year and coincided *in all respects* with the Christmas presents that the Boyd children subsequently received, presumably from Santa Claus. "You could call it circumstantial evidence, sure," admitted *Our Own Times'* Senior Editor Barry "Beaver" Collins, "but we felt we'd reached the point when we had to let the public know."

The public reacted at first with sheer blank incomprehension. Only slowly did the significance and extent of the alleged fraud sink in. A Gallup poll, taken on December 1, asked voters aged 5 through 8: "Do you believe in Santa Claus?" The results: Yes, 26%; No, 38%; Not Sure, 36%. Older children were even more skeptical.

On December 12, an estimated 300,000 children converged on the Boyd residence in Westchester from every part of the city and the state. Chanting "Poop on the big fat hypocrites," they solemnly burned no less than 128 effigies of Santa Claus in the Boyds' front yard. Equivalent protests took place in every major city.

The real long-range consequences of the scandal did not become apparent for much longer, since they lay rather in what wasn't done than in what was. People were acting as though not only Santa but Christmas itself had been called in question. Log-jams of unsold merchandise piled up in stockrooms and warehouses, and the streets filled up with forests of brittle evergreens.

Any number of public figures tried, unavailingly, to reverse this portentous state of affairs. The Congress appropriated $3 million to decorate the Capitol and the White House with giant figures of Santa and his reindeer, and the Lincoln Memorial temporarily became the Santa Claus Memorial. Reverend Billy Graham announced that he was a personal friend of both Santa Claus and his wife, and had often led prayer meetings at Santa's workshop at the North Pole. But nothing served to restore the public's confidence. By December 18, one week before Christmas, the Dow-Jones industrial average had fallen to an all-time low.

In response to appeals from businessmen all over the country, a national emergency was declared, and Christmas was advanced one month, to the 25th of January, on which date it continues to be celebrated. An effort was made by the National Association of Manufacturers to substitute their own Grandma America for the disgraced Santa Claus. Grandma America had the distinct advantage over her predecessor that she was invisible and could walk through walls, thereby eliminating the age-old problem of how children living in chimneyless houses get their presents. There appeared to be hope that this campaign would succeed until a rival group of businesses, which had been excluded from the Grandma America franchise, introduced Aloysius the Magic Snowman, and the Disney Corporation premiered their new nightly TV series, *Uncle Scrooge and the Spirit of Christmas Presents*. The predictable result of the mutual recriminations of the various franchise-holders was an ever greater dubiety on the part of both children and grown-ups. "I used to be a really convinced believer in Santa," declared Bobby's mother in an exclusive interview with her son, "but now with all this foofaraw over Grandma America and the rest of them, I just don't know. It seems sordid, somehow. As for Christmas itself, I think we may just sit this one out."

"Bobby and I, we just felt *terrible*," pretty little (3' 11") Michelle Ginsberg said, recalling these dark mid-January days at the Pulitzer Prize ceremony. "We'd reported what we honestly believed were the facts. We never considered it could lead to a recession or anything so awful. I remember one Christmas morning, what *used* to be Christmas, that is, sitting there with my empty pantyhose hanging from the fireplace and just crying my heart out. It was probably the single most painful moment of my life."

Then, on January 21, *Our Own Times* received a telephone call from the President of the United States, who invited its two reporters, Billy and Michelle, to come with him on the Presidential jet, *Spirit of '76*, on a special surprise visit to the North Pole!

What they saw there, and whom they met, the whole nation learned on the night of January 24, the new Christmas Eve, during the President's momentous press conference. After Billy showed his Polaroid snapshots of the elves at work in their workshop, of himself shaking Santa's hand and sitting beside him in his sleigh, and of everyone—Billy, Michelle, Santa Claus and Mrs. Santa, the President and the First Lady—sitting down to a big turkey dinner, Michelle read a list of all the presents that she and Billy had received. Their estimated retail value: $18,599.95. As Michelle bluntly put it, "My father just doesn't make that kind of money."

"So would you say, Michelle," the President asked with a twinkle in his eye, "that you do believe in Santa Claus?"

"Oh, absolutely, there's no question."

"And you, Billy?"

Billy looked at the tips of his new cowboy boots and smiled. "Oh, sure. And not just 'cause he gave us such swell presents. His beard, for instance. I gave it quite a yank. I'd take my oath that that beard was real."

The President put his arms around the two children and gave them a big, warm squeeze. Then, becoming suddenly more serious, he looked right at the TV camera and said, "Billy, Michelle—your friends who told you that there is no Santa Claus were wrong. They have been affected by the skepticism of a skeptical age. They do not believe except they see. They think that nothing can be which is not comprehensible by their little minds. But all minds, Virginia—uh, that is to say, Billy and Michelle—whether they be men's or children's, are little. In this great universe of ours, man is a mere *insect*, an ant, in his intellect, as compared with the boundless world about him, as measured by the intelligence capable of grasping the *whole* of truth and knowledge.

"Not believe in Santa Claus? You might as well not believe in fairies. No Santa Claus! Thank God he lives, and he lives forever. A thousand years from now—nay, ten times ten thousand years from now, he will continue to make glad the heart of childhood."

Then, with a friendly wink, and laying his finger aside of his nose, he added, "In conclusion, I would like to say—to Billy and Michelle and to my fellow Americans of every age—Merry Christmas to all, and to all a good night!"

1974

PETE HAMILL

The Christmas Kid

I

IN THAT LOST CITY of memory, the wind is always blowing hard from the harbor and the snow is packed tightly on the hills of Prospect Park. They are skating on the Big Lake and the hallways of the tenements are wet with melted snow and the downtown stores are glad with blinking lights and the churches smell of pine and awe. And when I wander that lost Christmas city, I always think of Lev Augstein.

He was to become our Christmas kid. But he came among us one day in summer, a small, thin boy, nine years old, speaking a language we had never heard. His eyes were wide and brown and frightened, and he wore short pants that first day, and he stood on the corner near the Greek's coffee shop, staring at us as we finished a game of stickball. When the game was over, my brother, Tommy, asked him to play with us, but the boy's face trembled and he backed up, his eyes confused. Ralphie Boy handed him the Spaldeen and the boy shook his head in refusal and said something in that language and then ran away on toothpick legs to 11th Street.

"He don't speak English," Ralphie Boy said, in an amazed way. "He don't even speak Italian!"

Within days, we learned that the new kid was from Poland, which we located with precision in our geography books. Poland was wedged between Germany and Russia, and the language he spoke was called Yiddish. We also learned that the boy was living with his uncle, a cool, white-haired man named Barney Augstein.

"If he's related to Barney," my father said at the kitchen table, "then he's the salt of the earth."

Barney Augstein was one of the best men in that neighborhood, and one of the most important. He was the bookmaker. Each day, dressed like a dude, smiling and smoking a cigar, Barney would move from bar to bar, handling the action. Until Lev arrived, Barney lived alone in an apartment near the firehouse, and they said in the neighborhood that long ago, he had been married to a Broadway dancer. She had left him to go to Hollywood, and this gave Barney Augstein an aura of melancholy glamour. Ralphie Boy, Eddie Waits, Cheech, and the others all agreed that any nephew of Barney Augstein was okay with us.

We learned that the new kid's name was Lev. Ralphie Boy showed Lev how to hold a Spaldeen, throw it, catch it, hit it, and the rest of us taught him English. We told him the names of the important things: bat, ball, base; car, street, trolley; house, roof, yard, factory; store. Soda. Candy. Cops. Lev stood there while we pointed at things and he named them, proud when he got the word right, but trembling when he got it wrong. "I hate when he does that," Ralphie Boy said one morning. "It's like a dog that got beat too much." And we noticed two things about him. He never smiled. And he had a number tattooed on his wrist.

"A number on his wrist?" my mother said one night. "Oh, my God." She was silent for a while, then glanced out the window at the skyline glittering across the harbor. "Well, make sure you take care of that boy. Don't let anything happen to him. Ever."

The summer moved on. Lev put on weight, and Barney Augstein bought him clothes and Keds and a first baseman's mitt. We tried to explain all of life to him, particularly the Dodgers. Lev listened gravely to the story of the holy team, and if he didn't fully comprehend, he certainly tried. He recited the litany: Reiser, Reese, Walker . . .

"He play baseball good?" Lev said, pointing at a picture of Reiser in the *Daily News*. "He play stickball good?"

"Good?" Ralphie Boy said. "He's like Christmas every day."

"Christmas every day?" Lev said.

II

One afternoon, Barney Augstein came around with Charlie Flanagan. They were best friends, though Charlie was a cop. Their friendship was one reason Augstein could work openly as a bookmaker in the neighborhood without being arrested. My father said their friendship went back to Prohibition, when they lived on the Lower East Side and worked as guards on the whiskey runs to Canada. Now Charlie lived alone. He and Barney went to the fights together, and bought their clothes from the same tailor, and even went to Broadway shows. We were sitting on the cellar board of Roulston's grocery store when they came over together.

"Listen, you bozos," Augstein said. "One of yiz has been teachin' my nephew bad woids, and I want it to stop."

"Nah," Ralphie Boy said.

"Don't gimme 'nah,'" Augstein said. "I'm warnin' yiz. If yiz keep teaching Lev doity woids, I'll have yiz t'rown in fronta da Sevent' Avenue bus. Ya got that?"

"Dat goes for me, too," Flanagan said. "Barney wants his nephew to be a gent, not a hat rack like you guys. So teach the kid right. And if I hear he gets in trouble, I'll lock yiz all up."

They turned around and walked across the street to Rattigan's Bar and Grill, a couple of cool older dudes in sport shirts. They were laughing.

III

The trouble started around Labor Day weekend, and it all came from Nora McCarthy. She lived up the block from Rattigan's, almost directly across 11th Street from Barney Augstein's house. She was in her forties, a large, box-shaped woman with horn-rimmed glasses, and she was awful. Everybody's business was her business, and when she wasn't working at the Youth Board, a job she'd received from the Regular Democratic Club, she was policing private lives. My father called her Nora the Nose. Now she had begun investigating Lev Augstein. On Labor Day weekend, when we were feeling forlorn about the imminent return to school, she came over to us after a game.

"What's this new boy's name?" she said, pointing at Lev.

"Why?" Ralphie Boy said. "What business is it of yours?"

"I live in this neighborhood!" she snapped. "I have a right to know when strangers show up. Particularly if they live with a known criminal. And particularly if they are young. Young people are my job."

We all made rude noises and laughed. But Lev did not laugh. He looked up at Nora McCarthy, at her severe hairdo, her coarse skin, the mole on her chin, the square, blocky hands, the hard judgmental lines that bracketed her mouth, and he sensed danger. He backed away, but Nora McCarthy grabbed his wrist. She moved her thumb and saw the tattooed number and then she smiled.

"You're a Jew, aren't you?" she said. "You're one of those DPs. Those displaced persons. Aren't you?" She gave Lev's wrist a tug. "But I bet you don't have any papers. You got that look. That scared look. Tell me the truth."

Lev pulled away, but she held on. And then Ralphie Boy came around behind her and gave her a ferocious kick in the ass, and she let go, and then we were all running, Lev with us, and we didn't stop until we were deep in the bushes of Prospect Park. We sat there, aching from the run, and then laughing at what Ralphie Boy had done. Lev didn't laugh. He didn't know a lot of English but he sure knew what Nora the Nose meant when she said the word "Jew."

That night, my father came home angry because he'd run into a furious Nora McCarthy. He hated giving the Nose even a slight edge and wanted to know why we'd done what we did. We told him. He started laughing hard, and gave us each a hug and told us to dress quickly because we were going to Barney Augstein's to see a fight on Barney's new television set. We walked up 11th Street in the chilly evening to Barney's. Across the street, Nora McCarthy was at the window, inspecting the block. My father walked over, spit in her yard, and yelled up at her: "Benny Leonard was a Jew!" I didn't know who Benny Leonard was, but I knew from the way he said it that if Benny Leonard was a Jew, then being a Jew was a great thing. Nora McCarthy closed the window.

Barney Augstein's living room was packed. Charlie Flanagan was mixing drinks in the kitchen. A woman named Bridget Moynihan was cooking a beef stew. In the living room, seated in a large chair, there was a lean, sun-tanned, dark-haired man with an amused look on his face. Lev brought me over and said something in Yiddish to this man, and the man shook my hand politely, while Lev told me that the man was his Uncle Meyer.

"Nice to meet you, sport," Meyer said to me. "You take care of this kid, okay? He's been through a lot." He looked down at a diamond pinkie ring. "His mother, his father, the whole goddamn family, except him. They all got it. Know what I mean?"

Then he turned his attention to the TV, talking about Willie Pep with Charlie Flanagan, and about Ray Robinson with Barney Augstein, and then about baseball, and somehow the talk got around to Pete Reiser.

"Pete Reiser," Lev said. "Like Christmas every day."

"Now, *there's* a smart kid," said Meyer, and they all laughed. Meyer and Barney argued for a while about the fight on TV, and then Meyer produced the fattest roll of bills I'd ever seen. "Put your money where your mouth is," Meyer said, and smiled.

"Come," Lev said, and led me to his room. It was very small—a bed, a bureau, a chair. But it felt like a library. There were stacks of comic books everywhere, grammar books, two fat dictionaries. And drawings that Lev had made: Batman, the Green Lantern, Captain America, Donald Duck.

There were other drawings, too; buildings with spirals of black cloud issuing from chimneys; barefoot men with shaved heads and gray pajamas; watchtowers; barbed wire.

"You're an artist," I said.

"An artist?"

"Yeah, an artist."

"Pete Reiser is an artist?"

"Yeah," I said. "In a way."

"Like Christmas every day," Lev said. "An artist."

IV

Fall arrived. The days shortened. Most of us went to the Catholic school, but Lev enrolled in public school, where Ralphie Boy became his protector. Ralphie Boy had been kicked out of Catholic school.

"The kid is scared all the time," Ralphie Boy told me. "I gotta teach him how to fight."

Every day now, the woman named Bridget Moynihan was coming to Barney's house. She was about forty and lived with her mother and had a plain, sweet face. Barney hired her as a housekeeper, to make sure Lev ate properly and washed himself and always had clean clothes.

"I tried," Barney said to my father one day. "But I just got no talent for being a mother. This kid is family, you know. I'm his only living relative. But a mother I'm not."

They started to go to the movies together: Barney and Charlie and Bridget and Lev. They took walks, and went shopping together, too. Then at Thanksgiving, Barney prepared a big dinner. He asked us to come over after our own dinner and make Lev feel like he had a home. But Lev was in his room when we got there, and he was crying. Barney asked me to talk to him.

"Go 'way," Lev said, turning his back on me, sobbing into his pillow.

"What's the matter, Lev?"

"Go 'way, go 'way."

"You don't like turkey, Lev?" I said.

He whirled around, full of anger. "Too *much*! Is too *much*! All *food, food, food.* Too much!"

I was a kid then, but looking into the eyes of a boy who had survived a death camp, even I understood.

V

After Thanksgiving, the Christmas season began. Down on Fifth Avenue, store windows magically filled with toys and train sets and red stockings. Christmas banners stretched across the downtown streets, painted with the slogans of Christmas, about peace on earth and good will toward men. Christmas music played from the loudspeakers, and there were Salvation Army bands outside Abraham & Straus and men selling chestnuts and rummies dressed in Santa Claus costumes, ringing little bells. We took Lev with us as we wandered these streets, and he was full of amazement and wonder.

"But what is?" he said. "What is they mean, Christmas?"

"Hey, Lev, fig-*get* it," Ralphie Boy said. "You're a Jew. Christmas is for Catlicks."

"Explain, please."

A theological discussion of extraordinary complexity then took place. Was Santa Claus a saint? Did they have Christmas bells in the stable in Bethlehem, and who made them? Did Joseph and Mary put stockings over the mantelpiece, and was there a mantelpiece in that stable? How come the Three Wise Men didn't come on reindeer instead of camels, and, by the way, where did they come from? If Jesus was the son of God, why didn't God just show up in person? It got even worse as we roamed around. But Lev stayed with it, almost burning with intensity, as if torn between the images in those store windows and the fact that he was a Jew.

"Why is not for Jews?" he said.

"Because Jesus was a Catlick, Lev," Ralphie Boy explained.

"No, he wasn't," my brother, Tommy, said. "Jesus was a Jew."

"Come *on*," Ralphie Boy said. "Stop kiddin' around."

"I ain't kiddin'," Tommy said. "Jesus was a Jew. So was his mother and father."

"That's right," I said. "You could look it up."

"Well, when did he become a Catlick? After he *died*?"

"How do *I* know?" Tommy said. "All I know is, while he was here on earth he was a Jew."

"Ridiculous!" Ralphie Boy said.

If Lev had any doubts about the essential craziness of the goyim, they were not resolved by this version of the Council of Trent.

VI

Then Barney Augstein got sick and was taken to Methodist Hospital. There were whispered conversations about what was wrong with him, and then plans were made by Bridget and my mother and Charlie Flanagan. Bridget moved into Barney's house, and my mother and Tommy and I came over every night to help Lev with his homework, and the women decided they could give a Christmas party anyway. They would combine Hanukkah and Christmas, get a Christmas tree, hang pictures of Santa Claus around the house, but leave out all the mangers and statues of Jesus. Barney was part of the planning; he called each night from the hospital and talked to Lev and then Bridget, and later Bridget would talk to my mother.

"He wants to get the lad everything," Bridget would say. "Train sets, and chemistry sets, and a big easel so he can paint. A camera. A radio. And I have to keep stopping him, because he's gonna spoil that kid rotten."

Then on December 19, the first snowfall arrived in the city. Lev was in our house and we took him up to the roof and we stood there while the snow fell on the pigeon coops and the backyards, and obscured the skyline and the harbor, and clung to the trees, all of it pure and white and blinding. We scooped a handful from the roof of our pigeon coop, explained to Lev that it was "good packing," and started dropping snowballs into the street, hoping that we would see Nora the Nose. She wasn't there but others were, and soon Ralphie Boy was with us, too, and Eddie Waits, and Cheech, and we were all firing snowballs from the rooftops, as skillful as dive-bombers, and Lev was with us, joining in, one of the crowd at last.

"Good packing," he shouted. "*Good packing!*"

That night, while we all slept, Barney Augstein died.

VII

They took Lev away two days later. A man and a woman in a dirty Chevy arrived at Barney's house at eight in the morning, showed Bridget their credentials, and took Lev to the children's shelter. Somewhere downtown. Where the courthouses were. And the jails. Bridget swore that she looked across the street and saw Nora McCarthy at her window, smiling. We learned all this that afternoon, when Ralphie Boy told us that Lev wasn't at school. We went up to Barney's and Charlie Flanagan was there with Bridget.

"He didn't have papers," Charlie said. "Barney got him in through Canada. The kid never had papers."

"So what'll they do?"

"Ship him back."

"*To the concentration camp?*"

"No," Charlie said. "To Poland."

"Well, maybe not," Bridget said. "Maybe he'll just go to an orphanage."

"*An orphanage?*"

We were filled with horror. Poland was bad enough, over there between Germany and Russia. But an orphanage was right out of *Oliver Twist*. I could see Lev, like Oliver on the H-O Oats box, holding a wooden bowl, his clothes in rags, asking for more gruel. That's what the book said. Gruel. Some kind of gray paste, what they always fed orphans, and I thought it was awful that Lev would have to spend all his years until he was eighteen eating the stuff. Worse, he could be adopted by some ham-fisted jerk who beat him every night. Or, even worse, someone who hated Jews. And all of us, in that moment, seemed to agree on the same thing.

"We gotta get him outta there," Ralphie Boy whispered. "Fast."

The phone rang and Charlie answered it. He talked cop talk for a while, and mentioned the State Department, shook his head, and said he couldn't adopt a kid because he was single. He hung up the phone, lit a cigar, cursed, and stared at the wall. Then he turned on us.

"All right, you bozos," he said. "Beat it."

I was halfway down the block when I realized I'd left my gloves on the kitchen table. I went back. Bridget answered the door and I hurried past her to get the gloves. Charlie was on the phone again.

"Hello, Meyer?" he said. "This is Charlie . . ."

He glowered at me until I left.

That night it snowed, and kept snowing the next day, and on the day after that, they closed the public schools, and we listened in the morning to "Rambling with Gambling," praying for more snow and the closing of the Catholic schools, too. The snow piled up in the streets, and we burrowed tunnels through it, and made huge boulders that blocked the cars in the side streets. The park was like a wonderland, pure and innocent and white, the leafless trees like the handwriting Lev used when he showed us his own language, and kids were everywhere—on sleighs, barrel staves, sliding down the snow-packed hills. All the kids except Lev. He was in the children's shelter, eating gruel.

Then on the afternoon of Christmas Eve, Charlie Flanagan rang our bell.

My mother went out to the hall and met Charlie halfway down the stairs. There was a murmured conversation. Then she came up and told us to get dressed.

"Charlie's taking you to see Lev," she said. She gave us a present she had bought for him, a picture book about Thomas Jefferson, and down we went to the street. Ralphie Boy, Eddie Waits, and Cheech were already in Charlie's Plymouth, each carrying a present.

"Now, listen, you bozos," he said, "Don't do anything ridiculous when we see him. Got it straight? Just do what the hell we tell you to do."

We drove to downtown Brooklyn, where the government buildings rose in their mean, gaunt style from the snow-packed streets. Charlie pulled the car down a side street and parked. And in a few minutes, a Cadillac parked in front of him. He looked at his watch.

"The party for the orphans is already started," he said. "So you bozos just come in with us."

Two men dressed like Arabs got out of the Cadillac. They had head-dresses on and mustaches, and shoes that curled up, and pantaloons, and flowing green-and-orange capes. One of them was the largest human being I ever saw. The other one was Meyer.

"Hello, sports," Meyer said, pulling a drag on a cigar. "Hello, Charlie."

He handed Charlie a box, and Charlie opened it and took out an Arab costume, and put it on over his suit. In a minute he, too, was a Wise Man from the East, his face covered with a false beard and mustache. We followed the three of them around the corner and into the children's shelter. There was a scrawny Christmas tree in the lobby, and windows smeared with Bon Ami cleanser to look like they were covered with snow, and cut-outs of Santa Claus on the walls, and a few dying pieces of holly. A guard looked up when we walked in, his eyes widening at the sight of the three wild-looking Arabs.

"We're here for a Christmas party," the big guy said.

"Oh, yeah, yeah," the guard said. "Second floor."

We walked up a flight of stairs. The three Arabs glanced at each other, and Meyer chuckled and opened a door. They stepped into a room crowded with forlorn children, and then started to sing:

"We t'ree kings of Orient are . . ."

Everybody cheered and they kept on singing and patting the kids on the head, and looking angelic, and then Lev came running from a corner, right to Ralphie Boy, and hugged him and started to cry and then Ralphie Boy started to cry and then everybody was crying and the three Wise Men kept right on singing. They did "Jingle Bells" and "Silent Night" and "White Christmas." The two guards cheered, and the other kids sang along with them, and then Meyer couldn't stand it any longer and he lit a cigar, and then the other two lit up, and they were singing "Mairzy Doats," and the big guy slipped a bottle of whiskey to one of the guards and a cigar to the other, and they went into "Jingle Bells" again, and moved closer to Lev, and after a little while, we couldn't see Lev anymore. The singing went on. The guards were drinking. And then it was time to go. Meyer, Charlie, and the big guy backed out, doing one final chorus of "We t'ree kings of Orient are . . ." We followed them outside, waved good-bye, wished all the other kids a merry Christmas, came into the lobby, wished the guard a merry Christmas, too, and headed into the empty street.

Around the corner, Meyer stopped, lifted his whirling Arab costume, and let Lev out.

"Merry Christmas, sport," Meyer said to the kid. "Merry Christmas."

For the first time, Lev Augstein smiled.

VIII

That night, we sneaked Lev into our house, far from the eyes of Nora the Nose, and said our tearful good-byes. Then we all went down to Meyer's car. The trunk was packed with suitcases, but they wedged in a few more packages, and then Lev was driven out of our neighborhood, heading into Christmas Day, never to return. A few weeks later, Charlie Flanagan put in his papers, retired from the cops, married Bridget Moynihan, and moved to Florida to live on his pension and serve as a security boss in a certain hotel in Miami Beach. It's said that he and Bridget adopted a young boy soon after, and raised him as a Jew out of respect for the boy's uncle. Christmas was a big event in their house, but then so was Hanukkah.

I thought about Lev every year after that, when the snow fell through the Brooklyn sky and turned our neighborhood white, or when somebody told me that the snow was good packing, or when I heard certain songs from hidden speakers. I also thought about him when I met people with tattoos on their wrists, or saw barbed wire. But I didn't worry about him. I knew he was all right.

1979

GENE WOLFE

The War Beneath the Tree

"IT'S CHRISTMAS EVE, Commander Robin," the Spaceman
said. "You'd better go to bed, or Santa won't come."
Robin's mother said, "That's right, Robin. Time to say good
night."

The little boy in blue pajamas nodded, but made no move to rise.

"Kiss me," said Bear. Bear walked his funny, waddly walk around the tree
and threw his arms about Robin. "We have to go to bed. I'll come too." It
was what he said every night.

Robin's mother shook her head in amused despair. "Listen to them," she
said. "Look at him, Bertha. He's like a little prince surrounded by his court.
How is he going to feel when he's grown and can't have transistorized syco-
phants to spoil him all the time?"

Bertha the robot maid nodded her own almost human head as she put
the poker back in its stand. "That's right, Ms. Jackson. That's right for sure."

The Dancing Doll took Robin by the hand, making an *arabesque penché*
of it. Now Robin rose. His guardsmen formed up and presented arms.

"On the other hand," Robin's mother said, "they're children only such a
short time."

Bertha nodded again. "They're only young once, Ms. Jackson. That's for
sure. All right if I tell these little cute toys to help me straighten up after he's
asleep?"

The Captain of the Guardsmen saluted with his silver saber, the Largest
Guardsman beat the tattoo on his drum, and the rest of the guardsmen
formed a double file.

"He sleeps with Bear," Robin's mother said.

"I can spare Bear. There's plenty of others."

The Spaceman touched the buckle of his antigravity belt and soared to
a height of four feet like a graceful, broad-shouldered balloon. With the
Dancing Doll on his left and Bear on his right, Robin toddled off behind
the guardsmen. Robin's mother ground out her last cigarette of the evening,

winked at Bertha, and said, "I suppose I'd better turn in too. You needn't help me undress, just pick up my things in the morning."

"Yes'um. Too bad Mr. Jackson ain't here, it bein' Christmas Eve and you expectin' an' all."

"He'll be back from Brazil in a week—I've told you already. And Bertha, your speech habits are getting worse and worse. Are you sure you wouldn't rather be a French maid for a while?"

"Maize none, Ms. Jackson. I have too much trouble talkin' to the men that comes to the door when I'm French."

"When Mr. Jackson gets his next promotion, we're going to have a chauffeur," Robin's mother said. "He's going to be Italian, and he's going to *stay* Italian."

Bertha watched her waddle out of the room. "All right, you lazy toys! You empty them ashtrays into the fire an' get everythin' put away. I'm goin' to turn myself off, but the next time I come on, this room better be straight or there's goin' to be some broken toys around here."

She watched long enough to see the Gingham Dog dump the largest ashtray on the crackling logs, the Spaceman float up to straighten the magazines on the coffee table, and the Dancing Doll begin to sweep the hearth. "Put yourselfs in your box," she told the guardsmen, and turned off.

In the smallest bedroom, Bear lay in Robin's arm. "Be quiet," said Robin.

"I *am* quiet," said Bear.

"Every time I am almost gone to sleep, you squiggle."

"I don't," said Bear.

"You do."

"Sometimes you have trouble going to sleep too, Robin," said Bear.

"I'm having trouble *tonight*," Robin countered meaningfully.

Bear slipped from under his arm. "I want to see if it's snowing again." He climbed from the bed to an open drawer, and from the open drawer to the top of the dresser. It was snowing.

Robin said, "Bear, you have a circuit loose." It was what his mother sometimes said to Bertha.

Bear did not reply.

"Oh, Bear," Robin said sleepily, a moment later. "I know why you're antsy. It's your birthday tomorrow, and you think I didn't get you anything."

"Did you?" Bear asked.

"I will," Robin said. "Mother will take me to the store." In half a minute his breathing became the regular, heavy sighing of a sleeping child.

Bear sat on the edge of the dresser and looked at him. Then he said under his breath, "I can sing Christmas carols." It had been the first thing he had ever said to Robin, one year ago. He spread his arms. *All is calm. All is bright.* It made him think of the lights on the tree and the bright fire in the living room. The Spaceman was there, but because he was the only toy who could fly, none of the others liked the Spaceman much. The Dancing Doll was there too. The Dancing Doll was clever, but, well . . . He could not think of the word.

He jumped down into the drawer on top of a pile of Robin's undershirts, then out of the drawer, softly to the dark, carpeted floor.

"Limited," he said to himself. "The Dancing Doll is limited." He thought again of the fire, then of the old toys, the Blocks Robin had had before he and the Dancing Doll and the rest had come—the Wooden Man who rode a yellow bicycle, the Singing Top.

In the living room, the Dancing Doll was positioning the guardsmen, while the Spaceman stood on the mantel and supervised. "We can get three or four behind the bookcase," he called.

"Where they won't be able to see a thing," Bear growled.

The Dancing Doll pirouetted and dropped a sparkling curtsy. "We were afraid you wouldn't come," she said.

"Put one behind each leg of the coffee table," Bear told her. "I had to wait until he was asleep. Now listen to me, all of you. When I call, '*Charge!*' we must all run at them together. That's very important. If we can, we'll have a practice beforehand."

The Largest Guardsman said, "I'll beat my drum."

"You'll beat the enemy, or you'll go into the fire with the rest of us," Bear said.

Robin was sliding on the ice. His feet went out from under him and right up into the air so he fell down with a tremendous BUMP that shook him all over. He lifted his head, and he was not on the frozen pond in the park at all. He was in his own bed, with the moon shining in at the window, and it was Christmas Eve . . . no, Christmas Night now . . . and Santa was coming, maybe had already come. Robin listened for reindeer on the roof and did not hear reindeer steps. Then he listened for Santa eating the cookies his mother had left on the stone shelf by the fireplace. There was no munching or crunching. Then he threw back the covers and slipped down over the edge of his bed until his feet touched the floor. The good smells of tree and fire had come into his room. He followed them out of it ever so quietly, into the hall.

Santa was in the living room, bent over beside the tree! Robin's eyes opened until they were as big and as round as his pajama buttons. Then Santa straightened up, and he was not Santa at all, but Robin's mother in a new red bathrobe. Robin's mother was nearly as fat as Santa, and Robin had to put his fingers in his mouth to keep from laughing at the way she puffed, and pushed at her knees with her hands until she stood straight.

But Santa had come! There were toys—new toys!—everywhere under the tree.

Robin's mother went to the cookies on the stone shelf and ate half of one. Then she drank half the glass of milk. Then she turned to go back into her bedroom, and Robin retreated into the darkness of his own room until she was past. When he peeked cautiously around the door frame again, the toys—the new toys—were beginning to move.

They shifted and shook themselves and looked about. Perhaps it was because it was Christmas Eve. Perhaps it was only because the light of the fire had activated their circuits. But a Clown brushed himself off and stretched, and a Raggedy Girl smoothed her raggedy apron (with the heart embroidered on it), and a Monkey gave a big jump and chinned himself on the next-to-lowest limb of the Christmas tree. Robin saw them. And Bear, behind the hassock of Robin's father's chair, saw them too. Cowboys and Native Americans were lifting the lid of a box, and a Knight opened a cardboard door (made to look like wood) in the side of another box (made to look like stone), letting a Dragon peer over his shoulder.

"*Charge!*" Bear called. "*Charge!*" He came around the side of the hassock on all fours like a real bear, running stiffly but very fast, and he hit the Clown at his wide waistline and knocked him down, then picked him up and threw him halfway to the fire.

The Spaceman had swooped down on the Monkey; they wrestled, teetering, on top of a polystyrene tricycle.

The Dancing Doll had charged fastest of all, faster even than Bear himself, in a breathtaking series of *jetés*, but the Raggedy Girl had lifted her feet from the floor, and now she was running with her toward the fire. As Bear struck the Clown a second time, he saw two Native Americans carrying a guardsman—the Captain of the Guardsmen—toward the fire too. The Captain's saber had gone through one of the Native Americans and it must have disabled some circuit because the Native American walked badly; but in a moment more the Captain was burning, his red uniform burning, his hands thrown up like flames themselves, his black eyes glazing and crack-ing, bright metal running from him like sweat to harden among the ashes under the logs.

The Clown tried to wrestle with Bear, but Bear threw him down. The Dragon's teeth were sunk in Bear's left heel, but he kicked himself free. The Calico Cat was burning, burning. The Gingham Dog tried to pull her out, but the Monkey pushed him in. For a moment, Bear thought of the cellar stairs and the deep, dark cellar, where there were boxes and bundles and a hundred forgotten corners. If he ran and hid, the new toys might never find him, might never even try to find him. Years from now Robin would discover him, covered with dust.

The Dancing Doll's scream was high and sweet, and Bear turned to face the Knight's upraised sword.

When Robin's mother got up on Christmas Morning, Robin was awake al-ready, sitting under the tree with the Cowboys, watching the Native Amer-icans do their rain dance. The Monkey was perched on his shoulder, the Raggedy Girl (programmed, the store had assured Robin's mother, to begin Robin's sex education) in his lap, and the Knight and the Dragon were at his feet. "Do you like the toys Santa brought you, Robin?" Robin's mother asked.

"One of the Native Americans doesn't work."

"Never mind, dear, we'll take him back. Robin, I've got something impor-tant to tell you."

Bertha the robot maid came in with Corn Flakes and milk and vitamins, and café au lait for Robin's mother. "Where is those old toys?" she asked. "They done a picky-poor job of cleanin' up this room."

"Robin, your toys are just toys, of course—"

Robin nodded absently. A Red Calf was coming out of the chute, with a Cowboy on a Roping Horse after him.

"Where *is* those old toys, Ms. Jackson?" Bertha asked again.

"They're programmed to self-destruct, I understand," Robin's mother said. "But, Robin, you know how the new toys all came, the Knight and Dragon and all your Cowboys, almost by magic? Well, the same thing can happen with people."

Robin looked at her with frightened eyes.

"The same wonderful thing is going to happen here, in our home."

1979

Cynthia Felice

Track of a Legend

C HRISTMAS STARTED at school right after we returned from Thanksgiving holiday and took down the paper turkeys and pilgrims from the windows. The teacher sang "Jingle bells, Santa smells, Rudolph laid an egg" all the while that he was supposed to be reprogramming my December reading assignment, and the computer printed out MERRY CHRISTMAS every time I matched a vowel sound with the right word, and BAH, HUMBUG whenever I was wrong. And it said BAH, HUMBUG a lot and didn't light up the observation board. We used the gold math beads as garlands for the tree because we ate most of the popcorn, and paper chains were for kindergarteners who weren't smart enough to scheme to get out of lessons. Still, we had to listen to civic cassettes so that we would know it was also the anniversary of the Christmas Treaty of '55 that brought peace to all the world again. And to top it off, on the very last day before Christmas our teacher improvised a lecture about how whole stations full of people had nowhere to go but back to Earth, their way of life taken from them by the stroke of a pen. The cassettes didn't mention that part. I didn't think Earth was such a bad place to go, but I didn't speak up because I was eager to cut out prancing, round-humped reindeer with great racks of antlers from colored construction paper. I put glitter that was supposed to be used on the bells on the antlers and hooves, and the racks were so heavy that my reindeer's heads tore off when I hung them up. After lunch teacher said he didn't know why we were sitting around school on Christmas Eve day when it was snowing, and he told us to go build snowmen, and he swept up the scraps of construction paper and celluloid and glitter alone while we put our Christmas stars in plastic sacks and tucked them into our jackets so that our hands would be free to make snowballs.

My best friend, Timothy, and I took some of the gingerbread cookies sprinkled with red sugar to leave in the woods for Bigfoot, then ran out the door and got pelted with snowballs by upper-graders who must have sneaked out earlier.

Timothy and I ran over the new-fallen snow in the playground to duck behind the farthest fence, where we scooped up snow and fired back. We were evenly matched for a while, snowballs flying thick and heavy. Then the little kids came out of school and betrayed us by striking our flanks.

"The little brats," Timothy muttered, throwing down a slushball. I suspect he was less upset that the little ones had decided to team up with the big kids than that one of them was crying and making his way to the school building, and someone was sure to come checking to see who was making ice balls. "Come on," he said, still feigning disgust. "Let's go build our own fort and get ready for Bigfoot."

The creature of yore was not so legendary in our parts, where we kids often found footprints in mud after rainstorms and in the snows of winter, especially in the woods surrounding the school. The grown-ups just shook their heads and said someone was playing a joke, that nobody wore shoes that big and that a real Bigfoot would be barefoot, like in the video show. But no one really knew what Bigfoot's toes looked like. My dad said even the video maker just guessed. We kids figured Bigfoot's foot was full of matted hair or lumpy skin that left those strange-looking ridges. And we just knew that Bigfoot came out in the dark storms looking for a stray child to eat, and that gingerbread cookies merely whetted the creature's appetite.

Leaving the school behind us, we made our way toward the greenway along the hoverpath, where the freighters sprayed us with a blizzard of snow when they whooshed by.

"Look here," Timothy shouted, tugging at something he'd stepped on in the snow. Both of us scratched at the snow and pulled until we freed a great piece of cardboard. It was frozen stiff.

"Let's go to the hill," I said.

Dragging our cardboard sled behind us, we trudged along Bigfoot's own trail through the woods. You could tell the creature had passed here from time to time because branches were broken back wider than any kid could cause, and the path circled the hill outside a wire-and-picket fence, and the gate was always locked to keep Bigfoot and everyone else out. The hill was treeless, acres of grass manicured by robots with great rotary blades in summer and smooth as a cue ball in winter. Perfect for sledding. The only trouble with the hill was that Timothy's aunt lived in the shiny tin-can-lying-on-its-side house at the top. I knew she was weird because Timothy said she never came outside or went anywhere, and my parents would shake their heads when they talked about her. But we had the cardboard sled in our hands, and he was pulling strongly; so I guess he didn't care about his weird aunt.

The fence might keep clumsy Bigfoot out but delayed us only a few seconds when we snagged a ragged edge of the cardboard on it and had to stop to free it. Then we climbed what seemed to be fourteen thousand one hundred ten meters of elevation to a place a little below the odd house, where we finally rested, breathing as hard as ancient warriors who'd just dragged their elephant up the Alps.

Timothy's aunt's house whirred and clicked, and I looked up. There were no windows, but it had a thousand eyes hidden in the silver rivets that held the metal skirt over tungsten bones.

In the white snow it looked desolate, save for a trickle of smoke.

"Hey, your aunt's house is on fire," I said.

Timothy gave me a look that always made me feel stupid. "Her heat exchanger's broken. She's burning gas," he said. "I know because she asked my dad to get her a new one before Christmas."

"Does she come to your house for Christmas?"

"Nah. Sometimes she comes video, just like she used to when she lived up there." He gestured skyward, where snowflakes were crystallizing and falling on us, but I knew he meant higher, one of the space stations or orbiting cities. "It's better now because there's no delay when we talk. It's like she was in Portland or something."

"What's she like?" I said, suddenly wondering about this peculiar person who had been a fixture in my community since I was little, yet whom I'd never seen.

Timothy shrugged. "Like an aunt . . . always wanting to know if I ate my peas." Warrior Timothy was patting the cardboard elephant sled, making ready to resume our journey in the Alps.

"Why doesn't she come out of there?"

"My dad says she's got a complex or something from when she lived up there." He gestured skyward again.

"What's a complex?"

For a moment Timothy looked blank, then he said, "It's like what Joan-John and Lester-Linda Johnson have."

"You mean she goes to the clinic and comes back something else?" I said, wondering if his aunt used to be his uncle.

"I mean she doesn't go anywhere."

"But like to the consumer showcases down in the mall and the restaurant. She goes there, doesn't she?"

"Nope. Last year when her mux cable got cut and her video wasn't working she practically starved to death."

"But why? Is she crippled or something?" The teacher had said he knew a spacer who spent most of his time in a swimming pool, and when he did come out he had to use a wheelchair because he was too old to get used to gravity again.

"No, she's not crippled."

"What's she look like?"

"My mother."

Timothy's mother was regular looking; so whatever a complex was, it had nothing to do with getting ugly. The Johnsons weren't ugly either, but they went through what my dad called phases, which he said was all in their heads. Maybe Timothy's aunt's complex was like Lester Johnson's Linda phase, but that didn't seem right because Lester-Linda came outside all the time and Timothy's aunt never did.

"What does she do inside all the time?"

"Works."

I nodded, considerably wiser. The old public buildings were down in the woods with the school, mostly monuments to waste of space ever since we got our mux cable that fed into every building in the community. Most of the grown-ups stopped *going* to work, and they stopped coming to school on voting day, but we still had to go, and not just on voting day.

"Come on," Timothy said.

But the smoke fascinated me. It puffed out of a silver pipe and skittered down the side of the house as if the fluffy falling snow was pushing it down. It smelled strange. I formed a snowball, a good solid one, took aim at the silver pipe, and let it fly.

"Missed by at least a kilometer," Timothy said, scowling.

Undaunted I tried another, missed the pipe, but struck the house, which resounded with a metallic thud. I'd closed one of the house's eyes with a white patch of snow. Timothy grinned at me, his mind tracking with mine. She'd have to come out to get the snow off the sensors. Soon we had pasted a wavy line of white spots about midway up the silver wall.

"One more on the right," commanded Timothy. But he stopped mid-swing when we heard a loud whirring noise. Around the hill came a grass cutter, furiously churning snow with its blades.

"Retreat!" shouted Attila the Hun. Timothy grabbed the frozen cardboard sled.

We leaped aboard and the elephant sank to its knees. I didn't need Timothy to tell me to run.

At the fence we threw ourselves over the frozen pickets, miraculously not getting our clothes hung up in the wires. The grass cutter whirred along the fenced perimeter, frustrated, thank goodness, by the limits of its oxide-on-sand mind.

"Ever seen what one of those things does to a rabbit?" he asked me.

"No."

"Cuts them up into bits of fur and guts," Timothy said solemnly.

"Your aunt's weird," I said, grateful to be on the right side of the fence.

"Uh oh. You lost a glove," Timothy said.

I nodded unhappily and turned to look over at the wrong side of the fence. Shreds of felt and wire and red nylon lay in the grass cutter's swath.

We walked on, feeling like two dejected warriors in the Alpine woods without our elephant and minus one almost-new battery-operated glove until we spied Bigfoot's tracks in the snow—big, round splots leading up the side of the wash. Heartened by our discovery, we armed ourselves properly with snowballs and told each other this was the genuine article. The snowfall was heavier now, really Bigfoot weather, and we knew how much Bigfoot liked storms, or we'd find tracks all the time.

We followed the footprints all the way to the Wigginses' house, only to find little Bobby Wiggles in them, hand-me-down boots overheating and making great puddles with each step.

Bobby stood looking at us, cheeks flushed from heat or stinging wind. Then he or she—I couldn't tell if Bobby Wiggles was a boy or a girl—giggled and went running into the house.

Timothy and I stayed out in the snow searching for Bigfoot tracks but found only rabbit tracks, which we followed in hopes that Bigfoot might do likewise, since aside from children there was nothing else for it to eat in our neighborhood, and no children had ever been reported eaten. Bigfoot may not have been hungry, but we had had only a few gingerbread cookies since noon; so when the rabbit tracks zagged near my house, we didn't turn again. We forgot the rabbit and Bigfoot and walked the rest of the way through the ghost-white woods to my front door, where we kicked off our boots and threw down our jackets and gloves. Mom and Dad were in the media room in front of the kitchen monitor, checking the Christmas menu.

"Go back and plug your gloves into the recharger," Dad said without glancing up.

But Mom must have looked up because she said right away, "Both of them."

"I lost one," I said.

"Go back out and find it."

Timothy and I looked at each other.

Mom was still watching me. "It won't do any good," I said finally. "We were up on the hill, and Timothy's aunt sicced the grass cutter on us."

"Why would she do a thing like that?"

Timothy and I shrugged.

"Well, I'll call her and ask her to let you get your glove," Dad said, rolling his chair to the comm console.

"The grass cutter got it," I said, more willing to face punishment for losing a glove than what might happen if Dad found out the day before Christmas that we'd closed her house's eyes.

"I told you she was getting crazier by the minute," Dad said.

"She isn't dangerous."

"How do you know that? The grass cutter, of all things."

"She has too much dread to be deliberately mean. I don't doubt for a second that she knew a couple of kids could outrun the grass cutter, and what else could she do? Go outside and ask them to go away?" Mom shook her head. "Her heart would stop from the anxiety of leaving her little sanctuary."

"She left the clinic fast enough when it caught on fire, and when she first came back that was as much her sanctuary as her spaceship house is now."

"You can't expect her to have enough energy to treat every minor day-to-day incident like an emergency."

"I think she should go back where she came from."

"Hush, dear. We voted for the treaty."

"They ought to have sent them to L-5."

"Couldn't, and you know—"

Timothy and I left them talking about his aunt, but I knew I'd probably not heard the end of the glove. That was the problem with sexagenarian parents; they knew all the tricks from the first set of kids, and they had very good memories.

In the kitchen we had hot chocolate, slopping some on the puzzle my big sister had broken back into a thousand pieces before she gave it to me.

"What are you getting for Christmas?" Timothy asked me, his cheeks still pink from being outdoors and his eyes as bright as tinsel fluttering in the warm convection currents of the house.

I shrugged. My parents were firm about keeping the Christmas list up-to-date, and that started every year on December twenty-sixth. I still wanted the fighting kite I'd keyed into the list last March, and the bicycle sail and the knife and the Adventure Station with vitalized figures and voice control. I also wanted the two hundred and eighty other items on my list and knew I'd be lucky if ten were under the tree tomorrow morning and that some of them would be clothes, which I never asked for but always received. "An Adventure Station," I finally said, more hopeful than certain. It was the one thing I'd talked about a lot, but Dad kept saying it was too much like the Hovercraft Depot set I'd gotten last year.

"Me too," Timothy said, "and a sled. Which should we play with first?"

A sled! I didn't have to go to the terminal and ask for a display of my Christmas list to know that a sled was not on it. My old one had worked just fine all last winter, but I'd used it in June to dam up Cotton Creek to make a pond for my race boats, and a flood had swelled the creek waters and carried it off and busted the runners. Too late to be remembering on Christmas Eve, because I didn't believe in Santa Claus or Kriss Kringle. Only in Bigfoot, because I had seen the footprints with my own eyes.

"We should play with the sleds first," Timothy said, "before the other kids come out and ruin the snow."

"I'm going to get a knife with a real L-5 crystal handle."

Timothy shrugged. "My aunt's going to give me one of hers someday. She has lots of stuff from when she was a spacer."

"Yeah, but my knife will be new. Then I'd like to see Bigfoot get away from me!"

"We can bring Bigfoot back on my sled," Timothy said excitedly. He chugalugged the rest of his chocolate. "Early, right after presents. Meet me at the hill."

"Why at the hill?" I said suspiciously. But Timothy was already heading for the door and pulling on his boots.

"Best place for sledding."

"But what about your aunt's mower?" I said, whispering now.

"Early," he reminded me as he stepped out into the snow. I followed him, holding the door open. "And bring your sled."

"What time do you open presents?" I said. But if Timothy answered, I didn't hear.

The snow was falling in fat flakes, and the wind had come up and the snow was starting to drift over the hedges. Funny how it wasn't really dark with all that white around, and funny, too, how I wasn't so glad that it was coming down. What good was it without a sled? I could use the cardboard if I could find it again, which I doubted, for I could tell that if it kept snowing at the rate I was seeing from my doorway, there would be half a meter or more by morning, which also meant the grass cutter would get clogged before it got five meters from Timothy's crazy aunt's house. Timothy would let me try his sled if I pulled it up the hill, 'cause if he didn't I wouldn't let him hold my L-5 crystal-handled knife . . . if I got one.

"Close the door!" my father shouted, and I closed it and went to bed early, knowing I couldn't sleep but wanting to because morning would come sooner if I did, and when it did I would not have a sled—maybe not even an L-5 crystal-handled knife—only an old Adventure Station that Timothy didn't want to play until after lunch, and who cared about snow anyhow, even if it did come down so fast and hard that it was catching on my bedroom window like a blanket before my sleepy eyes.

I woke to silence and the sure knowledge that it was Christmas morning. I didn't know whether to look out the window or check under the tree first, until I heard my sister in the hall and made a dash to beat her to the living room, where my parents had piled all the packages, with their red bows and wrappings, under the tree.

The big one wrapped in red plastic had to be the Adventure Station, though my parents were famous for putting little items like L-5 crystal-handled knives in packages the size of CRTs, complete with rocks to weigh it down so you couldn't tell. I couldn't wait to find out for sure what was in it, but I had to because my parents came in muttering about coffee and asking if it was even dawn and not caring that it wasn't when they had their coffee and I put their first presents to open in their laps. I wanted to open the red plastic-covered package, but I couldn't tear the plastic, and my big sister was hogging the slitter; so I opened a smaller one with my name on it. A shiny blue crystal that was almost mirror bright but not quite, so I could see the steel blade was in the package, and suddenly I felt good about the snow, too, and about looking for Bigfoot even if we did have to carry it back on Timothy's sled. I got the slitter away from my sister and sliced open the Adventure Station, only it wasn't. I looked at my parents in complete amazement and saw that they both had that special knowing twinkle in their eyes that parents get when they've done something you don't expect them to do. In the packing popcorn was a new sled, the collapsible kind with a handle for carrying it back up the hill and a retractable towing cord and three runner configurations so that it could be used on hard-packed snow or powder. I extended it to its full length right there in the living room, awed by its metallic gleam and classy black racing stripes.

And then with my knife strapped around the outside of my jacket and my sled in hand, I was off to meet Timothy, determined to have Bigfoot in tow before lunchtime. The going was slow because the drifts were tall and I loved to break their peaks and feel the stuff collapse beneath my feet and to stand under the tallest pines and shake the snow off the branches, as if I were in a blizzard and not in the first sparkling rays of sunshine. I went the long way to the hill, sure I would find traces of Bigfoot so early in the morning, and I did. Huge prints that were bigger than I could make, even though they were filled in with new snow, and the stride sure wasn't kid-size. Besides, what grown-up would walk through the woods on Christmas Eve during a snowstorm? I'd follow them, I decided, until I had to turn off for the hill, then Timothy and I would come back and follow the tracks to Bigfoot's lair. But I didn't have to turn off. The fat tracks headed right off through the woods along the same shortcut Timothy and I had used yesterday.

Timothy wasn't there yet, and because I couldn't wait to try my sled on the hill and not because I was afraid to follow the tracks alone, I stopped at the place we'd climbed over yesterday. The snow had drifted along the inside of the fence, almost hiding the pickets from view. I figured that with just a little more accumulation it would have covered the top, then my silver sled could carry me all the way from the top of the hill, over the fence, and deep into the woods, where the trees would provide a test of steering skill or a fast stop. I climbed the fence, sled in hand, then carried armfuls of snow to the highest drift, scooping and shoving until the tops of the pickets were covered. When I was satisfied the sled would glide over, I looked around for Timothy, who might still be opening his presents for all I knew, then I started to the top of the hill. I was only a little bit wary about the grass cutter, for I figured it would get clogged if it came out in the snow, but you never know what else a crazy lady who sent out grass cutters to hack up kids might have. But the little house at the top was almost completely snow covered, and there was no sign of smoke. Either Timothy's father got her that new heat exchanger or she froze.

At the top of the hill, not too close to the house in case she was just sleeping and not dead, I extended the sled, putting the runners in their widest configuration to keep me atop the deep snow. I climbed on and took off, the Teflon bottom gliding like ice on ice, and the wind stinging my face, and my heart beating with joy at the sled's speed on its very first trial run. Only trouble was that the wide runners didn't steer very well as I picked up speed, and there being no beaten path in the snow, I wasn't completely certain I'd be on target to make my fence jump. I pulled hard to the right, and the sled came with it sluggishly, but enough so I started to think again that I would make the jump. I could see the pickets on either side, and those would make a painful stop, but I was going to make it and know what it was like to fly on a sled for a few meters, or I would have known if I hadn't overcorrected just before hitting the big drift. The sled skidded along the downside of the drift and into a hole. I hit on something that sent me flying. I came down hard, hurt and crying, upside down.

It took me a minute to realize that I wasn't badly hurt, just scraped and bumped here and there, and stuck. My head felt funny, almost like someone was choking me and pressing against my skull, but it wasn't so bad that I couldn't see once I stopped crying. But I couldn't get loose. I could get hold of the fence and turn a bit but not enough to unhook my foot, which was firmly wedged between two pickets as far as it could go. Try as I would, as nimble as I was, and as desperate in knowing that I was quite alone and there was no one to send for help, I could not get loose. I shouted for Timothy, prayed he would come out of the woods and get me loose, but he never came. I cried again, and my tears froze, and the plug in my mitten power pack must have come loose, because my fingers were cold, too. The woods were things with icy tentacles frozen to the sky, and the sun reflected brightly off the snow-topped world and made me cry again. The wide expanse of sky looked vast and forbidding and somehow confirmed my worst fears that there was no one but me within a million klicks. And I wondered how long a person could live upside down. Didn't they do that all the time out in space? It had made Timothy's aunt weird but, oh, Timothy's aunt! Maybe her house had ears as well as eyes, and I shouted and shouted, promising I'd never throw snowballs at her house again. I thought that all the blood in my body was pooled behind my eyeballs, and if I cried again my tears would be blood, and I wanted to cry again because I knew that Timothy's aunt never would come because she never went anywhere.

And then in the stillness of the morning, when there was nothing to hear in the snow-packed world but my crying, I heard what sounded like an animal breathing into a microphone—a very powerful microphone or a very big animal.

I held my breath and listened carefully, watching the woods, terrified that the creature was lurking there behind the snow-covered bushes. But I was hanging upside down, and it took me a moment to realize that the sound was coming from behind me, closer now, hissing. I turned wildly and pressed my face against the pickets to see what was on the other side.

A towering hulk.

Shoulders like a gorilla.

White as the snow.

Breath making great clouds.

Feet leaving massive tracks.

There wasn't a doubt at all in my mind that I'd finally found Bigfoot, and it was more awful than anything I had imagined.

I screamed and struggled, quite willing to leave my foot behind in the fence, if only that were possible. I tried to unsheathe my knife, and I dropped it in the snow. It was within reach, and I might have retrieved it, but the massive creature grabbed me by my coattails and hefted me up. With my foot free I kicked blindly, and I must have hurt it because it finally put me down. The fence was between us, but its hands still gripped me by the shoulders—smooth hands without fur, white and slightly slick looking, except there were wrinkles where the joints ought to have been, and those were like gray accordion pleats. I stood, dazed and dizzy from being on my head so long, staring up at Bigfoot's shiny eye. Her face was featureless but for the eye, and she still hissed angrily, and she had a vapor trail drifting out from her backside.

She let go of me, reached over to pick up the L-5 knife, and twirled it between her thumb and forefinger. The crystal flashed in the sunlight, just like the ads they'd filmed on L-5. She flipped it, and I caught it two-handed. I backed away toward where my sled lay, didn't bother to collapse it, but grabbed the cord. I ran for the woods.

When I looked back, Bigfoot was gone, but her tracks left a clear trail to the desolate little house at the top of the hill, where Christmas was wholly a video event, where Timothy's crazy aunt would rather starve to death than come out for food. And sometimes when it snowed, especially when it snowed on Christmas Day, I climbed over the fence of her universe to wipe the drifts of snow off the eyes of her house. It fell like glittering Christmas stars, peaceful again for all the world.

1983

ED McBAIN

And All Through the House

DETECTIVE STEVE CARELLA was alone in the squad room. It was very quiet for a Christmas Eve.

Normally, all hell broke loose the moment the stores closed. But tonight the squad room and the entire station house seemed unusually still. No phones ringing. No typewriters clacking away. No patrolmen popping upstairs to ask if any coffee was brewing in the clerical office down the hall. Just Carella, sitting at his desk and rereading the D.D. report he'd just typed, checking it for errors. He'd misspelled the "armed" in "armed robbery." It had come out "aimed robbery." He overscored the I with the ballpoint pen, giving the felony its true title. Armed robbery. Little liquor store on Culver Avenue. Guy walked in with a .357 Magnum and an empty potato sack. The owner hit a silent alarm and the two uniforms riding Boy One apprehended the thief as he was leaving the store.

Carella separated the carbons and the triplicate pages—white one in the uppermost basket, pink one in the basket marked for Miscolo in clerical, yellow one for the lieutenant. He looked up at the clock. Ten-thirty. The graveyard shift would be relieving at a quarter to twelve, maybe a bit earlier, since it was Christmas Eve.

God, it was quiet around here.

He got up from his desk and walked around the bank of high cabinets that partitioned the rest of the squad room from a small sink in the corner opposite the detention cage. Quiet night like this one, you could fall asleep on the job. He opened the faucet, filled his cupped hands with water and splashed it onto his face. He was a tall man and the mirror over the sink was set just a little too low to accommodate his height. The top of his head was missing. The mirror caught him just at his eyes, a shade darker than his brown hair and slanted slightly downward to give him a faintly Oriental appearance. He dried his face and hands with a paper towel, tossed the towel into the wastebasket under the sink and then yawned and looked at the clock again, unsurprised to discover that only two minutes had passed since the last time he'd looked at it. The silent nights got to you. He much preferred it when things were really jumping.

He walked to the windows at the far side of the squad room and looked down at the street. Things looked as quiet down there as they were up here. Not many cars moving, hardly a pedestrian in sight. Well, sure, they were all home already, putting the finishing touches on their Christmas trees. The forecasters had promised snow, but so far there wasn't so much as a flurry in the air. He was turning from the window when all of a sudden everything got bloody.

The first thing he saw was the blood streaming down the side of Cotton Hawes's face. Hawes was shoving two white men through the gate in the slatted rail divider that separated the squad room from the corridor outside. The men were cuffed at the wrist with a single pair of cuffs, right wrist to left wrist, and one of them was complaining that Hawes had made the cuff too tight.

"I'll give you tight," Hawes said and shoved again at both men. One of them went sprawling almost headlong into the squad room, dragging the other one with him. They were both considerably smaller than Hawes, who towered over them like a redheaded fury, his anger somehow pictorially exaggerated by the streak of white in the hair over his right temple, where a burglar had cut him and the hair had grown back white. The white was streaked with blood now from an open cut on his forehead. The cut streamed blood down the right side of his face. It seemed not to console Hawes at all that the two men with him were also bleeding.

"What the hell happened?" Carella asked.

He was already coming across the squad room as if someone had called in an assist officer, even though Hawes seemed to have the situation well in hand and this was, after all, a police station and not the big, bad streets outside. The two men Hawes had brought in were looking over the place as if deciding whether or not this was really where they wanted to spend Christmas Eve. The empty detention cage in the corner of the room did not look too terribly inviting to them. One of them kept glancing over his shoulder to see if Hawes was about to shove them again. Hawes looked as if he might throttle both of them at any moment.

"Sit down!" he yelled and then went to the mirror over the sink and looked at his face. He tore a paper towel loose from the holder, wet it and dabbed at the open cut on his forehead. The cut kept bleeding.

"I'd better phone for a meat wagon," Carella said.

"No, I don't need one," Hawes said.

"*We* need one," one of the two men said.

He was bleeding from a cut on his left cheek. The man handcuffed to him was bleeding from a cut just below his jawline. His shirt was stained with blood, too, where it was slashed open over his rib cage.

Hawes turned suddenly from the sink. "What'd I do with that bag?" he said to Carella. "You see me come in here with a bag?"

"No," Carella said. "What happened?"

"I must've left it downstairs at the desk," Hawes said and went immediately to the phone. He picked up the receiver, dialed three numbers and then said, "Dave, this is Cotton. Did I leave a shopping bag down there at the desk?" He listened and then said, "Would you send one of the blues up with it, please? Thanks a lot." He put the receiver back in the cradle. "Trouble I went through to make this bust," he said, "I don't want to lose the goddamn evidence."

"You ain't got no evidence," the man bleeding from the cheek said.

"I thought I told you to shut up," Hawes said, going to him. "What's your name?"

"I'm supposed to shut up, how can I give you my name?" the man said.

"How would you like to give me your name through a mouthful of broken teeth?" Hawes said. Carella had never seen him this angry. The blood kept pouring down his cheek, as if in visible support of his anger. "What's your goddamn name?" he shouted.

"I'm calling an ambulance," Carella said.

"Good," the man bleeding from under his jawline said.

"Who wants this?" a uniformed cop at the railing said.

"Bring it in here and put it on my desk," Hawes said. "What's your name?"

"Henry," the cop at the railing said.

"Not you," Hawes said.

"Which desk is yours?" the cop asked.

"Over there," Hawes said and gestured vaguely.

"What happened up here?" the cop asked, carrying the shopping bag in and putting it on the desk he assumed Hawes had indicated. The shopping bag was from one of the city's larger department stores. A green wreath and a red bow were printed on it. Carella, already on the phone, glanced at the shopping bag as he dialed Mercy General.

"Your name," Hawes said to the man bleeding from the cheek.

"I don't tell you nothing till you read me my rights," the man said.

"My name is Jimmy," the other man said.

"Jimmy what?"

"You dope, don't tell him nothin' till he reads you Miranda."

"You shut up," Hawes said. "Jimmy what?"

"Knowles. James Nelson Knowles."

"Now you done it," the man bleeding from the cheek said.

"It don't mean nothin' he's got my name," Knowles said.

"You gonna be anonymous all night?" Hawes said to the other man.

Into the phone, Carella said, "I'm telling you we've got three people bleeding up here."

"I don't need an ambulance," Hawes said.

"Well, make it as fast as you can, will you?" Carella said and hung up. "They're backed up till Easter, be a while before they can get here. Where's that first-aid kit?" he said and went to the filing cabinets. "Don't we have a first-aid kit up here?"

"This cut gets infected," the anonymous man said, "I'm gonna sue the city. I die in a police station, there's gonna be hell to pay. You better believe it."

"What name should we put on the death certificate?" Hawes asked.

"Who the hell filed this in the missing-persons drawer?" Carella said.

"Tell him your name already, willya?" Knowles said.

"Thomas Carmody, okay?" the other man said. He said it to Knowles, as if he would not allow himself the indignity of discussing it with a cop.

Carella handed the kit to Hawes. "Put a bandage on that, willya?" he said. "You look like hell."

"How about the *citizens*?" Carmody said. "You see that?" he said to Knowles. "They always take care of their own first."

"On your feet," Carella said.

"Here comes the rubber hose," Carmody said.

Hawes carried the first-aid kit to the mirror. Carella led Carmody and Knowles to the detention cage. He threw back both bolts on the door, took the cuffs off them and said, "Inside, boys." Carmody and Knowles went into the cage. Carella double-bolted the door again. Both men looked around the cage as if deciding whether or not the accommodations suited their taste. There were bars on the cage and protective steel mesh. There was no place to sit inside the cage. The two men walked around it, checking out the graffiti scribbled on the walls. Carella went to where Hawes was dabbing at his cut with a swab of cotton.

"Better put some peroxide on that," he said. "What happened?"

"Where's that shopping bag?" Hawes asked.

"On the desk there. What happened?"

"I was checking out a ten-twenty on Culver and Twelfth, guy went in and stole a television set this guy had wrapped up in his closet, he was giving it to his wife for Christmas, you know? They were next door with their friends, having a drink, burglar must've got in through the fire escape window; anyway, the TV's gone. So I take down all the information—fat chance of ever getting it back—and then I go downstairs, and I'm heading for the car when there's this yelling and screaming up the street, so I go see what's the matter, and these two jerks are arguing over the shopping bag there on the desk."

"It was all your fault," Carmody said to Knowles.

"You're the one started it," Knowles said.

"Anyway, it ain't our shopping bag," Carmody said.

"I figure it's just two guys had too much to drink," Hawes said, putting a patch over the cut, "so I go over to tell them to cool it, go home and sleep it off, this is Christmas Eve, right? All of a sudden, there's a knife on the scene. One of them's got a knife in his hand."

"Not me," Carmody said from the detention cage.

"Not me, either," Knowles said.

"I don't know who started cutting who first," Hawes said, "but I'm looking at a lot of blood. Then the other guy gets hold of the knife some way, and *he* starts swinging away with it, and next thing I know, I'm in the middle of it, and *I'm* cut, too. What it turns out to be—"

"What knife?" Carmody said. "He's dreaming."

"Yeah, what knife?" Knowles said.

"The knife you threw down the sewer on the corner of Culver and Eleventh," Hawes said, "which the blues are out searching in the muck for right this minute. I need this on Christmas Eve," he said, studying the adhesive patch on his forehead. "I really need it."

Carella went to the detention cage, unbolted the door and handed the first-aid kit to Carmody. "Here," he said. "Use it."

"I'm waiting for the ambulance to come," Carmody said. "I want real medical treatment."

"Suit yourself," Carella said. "How about you?"

"If he wants to wait for the ambulance, then I want to wait for the ambulance, too," Knowles said.

Carella bolted the cage again and went back to where Hawes was wiping blood from his hair with a wet towel. "What were they arguing about?" he asked.

"Nobody was arguing," Carmody said.

"We're good friends," Knowles said.

"The stuff in the bag there," Hawes said.

"I never saw that bag in my life," Carmody said.

"Me, either," Knowles said.

"What's in the bag?" Carella asked.

"What do you think?" Hawes said.

"Frankincense," Carmody said.

"Myrrh," Knowles said, and both men burst out laughing.

"My ass," Hawes said. "There's enough pot in that bag to keep the whole city happy through New Year's Day."

"Okay, let's go," a voice said from the railing.

Both detectives turned to see Meyer Meyer lead a kid through the gate in the railing. The kid looked about fourteen years old, and he had a sheep on a leash. The sheep's wool was dirty and matted. The kid looked equally dirty and matted. Meyer, wearing a heavy overcoat and no hat, looked pristinely bald and sartorial by contrast.

"I got us a shepherd," he said. His blue eyes were twinkling; his cheeks were ruddy from the cold outside. "Beginning to snow out there," he said.

"I ain't no shepherd," the kid said.

"No, what you are is a thief, is what you are," Meyer said, taking off his overcoat and hanging it on the rack to the left of the railing. "Sit down over there. Give your sheep a seat, too."

"Sheeps carry all kinds of diseases," Carmody said from the detention cage.

"Who asked you?" Meyer said.

"I catch some kind of disease from that animal, I'll sue the city," Carmody said.

In response, the sheep shit on the floor.

"Terrific," Meyer said. "Whyn't you steal something clean, like a snake, you dummy?"

"My sister wanted a sheep for Christmas," the kid said.

"Steals a goddamn sheep from the farm in the zoo, can you believe it?" Meyer said. "You know what you can get for stealing a sheep? They can send you to jail for twenty years, you steal a sheep."

"*Fifty* years," Hawes said.

"My sister wanted a sheep," the kid said and shrugged.

"His sister is Little Bo-peep," Meyer said. "What happened to your head?"

"I ran into a big-time dope operation," Hawes said.

"That ain't our dope in that bag there," Carmody said.

"That ain't even our bag there," Knowles said.

"When do we get a lawyer here?" Carmody said.

"Shut up," Hawes said.

"Don't tell them nothin' till they read you your rights, kid," Carmody said.

"Who's gonna clean up this sheep dip on the floor?" Carella asked.

"Anybody want coffee?" Miscolo said from outside the railing. "I got a fresh pot brewing in the office." He was wearing a blue sweater over regulation blue trousers, and there was a smile on his face until he saw the sheep. His eyes opened wide. "What's that?" he asked. "A deer?"

"It's Rudolph," Carmody said from the detention cage.

"No kidding, is that a *deer* in here?" Miscolo asked.

"It's a raccoon," Knowles said.

"It's my sister's Christmas present," the kid said.

"I'm pretty sure that's against regulations, a deer up here in the squad room," Miscolo said. "Who wants coffee?"

"I wouldn't mind a cup," Carmody said.

"I'd advise against it," Meyer said.

"Even on Christmas Eve, I have to take crap about my coffee," Miscolo said, shaking his head. "You want some, it's down the hall."

"I already told you I want some," Carmody said.

"You ain't in jail yet," Miscolo said. "This ain't a free soup kitchen."

"Christmas Eve," Carmody said, "he won't give us a cup of coffee."

"You better get that animal out of here," Miscolo said to no one and went off down the corridor.

"Why won't you let me take the sheep to my sister?" the kid asked.

"'Cause it ain't your sheep," Meyer said. "It belongs to the zoo. You stole it from the zoo."

"The zoo belongs to everybody in this city," the kid said.

"Tell 'im," Carmody said.

"What's this I hear?" Bert Kling said from the railing. "Inside, mister." His blond hair was wet with snow. He was carrying a huge valise in one hand, and his free hand was on the shoulder of a tall black man whose wrists were handcuffed behind his back. The black man was wearing a red plaid Mackinaw, its shoulders wet. Snowflakes still glistened in his curly black hair. Kling looked at the sheep. "Miscolo told me it was a deer," he said.

"Miscolo's a city boy," Carella said.

"So am I," Kling said, "but I know a sheep from a deer." He looked down. "Who made on the floor?" he asked.

"The sheep," Meyer said.

"My sister's present," the kid said.

Kling put down the heavy valise and led the black man to the detention cage. "Okay, back away," he said to Carmody and Knowles and waited for them to move away from the door. He unbolted the door, took the cuffs off his prisoner and said, "Make yourself at home." He bolted the door again. "Snowing up a storm out there," he said and went to the coatrack. "Any coffee brewing?"

"In the clerical office," Carella said.

"I meant *real* coffee," Kling said, taking off his coat and hanging it up.

"What's in the valise?" Hawes asked. "Looks like a steamer trunk you got there."

"Silver and gold," Kling said. "My friend there in the cage ripped off a pawnshop on The Stem. Guy was just about to close, he walks in with a sawed-off shotgun, wants everything in the store. I got a guitar downstairs in the car. You play guitar?" he asked the black man in the cage.

The black man said nothing.

"Enough jewelry in here to make the Queen of England happy," Kling said.

"Where's the shotgun?" Meyer asked.

"In the car," Kling said. "I only got two hands." He looked at Hawes. "What happened to your head?" he asked.

"I'm getting tired of telling people what happened to my head," Hawes said.

"When's that ambulance coming?" Carmody asked. "I'm bleeding to death here."

"So use the kit," Carella said.

"And jeopardize my case against the city?" Carmody said. "No way."

Hawes walked to the windows.

"Really coming down out there," he said.

"Think the shift'll have trouble getting in?" Meyer said.

"Maybe. Three inches out there already, looks like."

Hawes turned to look at the clock.

Meyer looked at the clock, too.

All at once, everyone in the squad room was looking at the clock.

The detectives were thinking the heavy snow would delay the graveyard shift and cause them to get home later than they were hoping. The men in the detention cage were thinking the snow might somehow delay the process of criminal justice. The kid sitting at Meyer's desk was thinking it was only half an hour before Christmas and his sister wasn't going to get the sheep she wanted. The squad room was almost as silent as when Carella had been alone in it.

And then Andy Parker arrived with his prisoners.

"Move it," he said and opened the gate in the railing.

Parker was wearing a leather jacket that made him look like a biker. Under the jacket, he was wearing a plaid woolen shirt and a red muffler. The blue woolen watch cap on his head was covered with snow. Even the three-day beard stubble on his face had snowflakes clinging to it. His prisoners looked equally white, their faces pale and frightened.

The young man was wearing a rumpled black suit, sprinkled with snow that was rapidly melting as he stood uncertainly in the opening to the squad room. Under the suit, he wore only a shirt open at the collar, no tie. Carella guessed he was twenty years old. The young woman with him—*girl*, more accurately—couldn't have been older than sixteen. She was wearing a lightweight spring coat open over what Carella's mother used to call a house dress, a printed cotton thing with buttons at the throat. Her long black hair was dusted with snow. Her brown eyes were wide in her face. She stood shivering just inside the railing, looking more terrified than any human being Carella had ever seen.

She also looked enormously pregnant.

As Carella watched her, she suddenly clutched her belly and grimaced in pain. He realized all at once that she was already in labor.

"I said *move* it," Parker said, and it seemed to Carella that he actually would *push* the pregnant girl into the squad room. Instead, he shoved past the couple and went directly to the coatrack. "Sit down over there," he said, taking off his jacket and hat. "What the hell is that, a sheep?"

"That's my sister's Christmas present," the kid said, though Parker hadn't been addressing him.

"Lucky her," Parker said.

There was only one chair alongside his desk. The young man in the soggy black suit held it out for the girl, and she sat in it. He stood alongside her as Parker took a seat behind the desk and rolled a sheaf of D.D. forms into the typewriter.

"I hope you all got chains on your cars," he said to no one and then turned to the girl. "What's your name, sister?" he asked.

"Maria Garcia Lopez," the girl said and winced again in pain.

"She's in labor," Carella said and went quickly to the telephone.

"You're a doctor all of a sudden?" Parker said and turned to the girl again. "How old are you, Maria?" he asked.

"Sixteen."

"Where do you live, Maria?"

"Well, thass the pro'lem," the young man said.

"Who's talking to you?" Parker said.

"You were assin' Maria—"

"Listen, you understand English?" Parker said. "When I'm talkin' to this girl here, I don't need no help from—"

"You wann' to know where we live—"

"I want an address for this *girl* here, is what I—"

"You wann' the address where we *s'pose'* to be livin'?" the young man said.

"All right, what's *your* name, wise guy?" Parker said.

"José Lopez."

"The famous bullfighter?" Parker said and turned to look at Carella, hoping for a laugh.

Carella was on the telephone. Into the receiver, he said, "I *know* I already called you, but now we've got a pregnant woman up here. Can you send that ambulance in a hurry?"

"I ain' no bullfighter," José said to Parker.

"What are you, then?"

"I wass cut sugar cane in Puerto Rico, but now I don' have no job. Thass why my wife an' me we come here this city, to fine a job. Before d' baby comes."

"So what were you doing in that abandoned building?" Parker said and turned to Carella again. "I found them in an abandoned building on South Sixth, huddled around this fire they built."

Carella had just hung up the phone. "Nothing's moving out there," he said. "They don't know *when* the ambulance'll be here."

"You know it's against the law to take up residence in a building owned by the city?" Parker said. "That's called squatting, José, you know what squatting is? You also know it's against the law to set fires inside buildings? That's called arson, José, you know what arson is?"

"We wass cold," José said.

"Ahhh, the poor kids were cold," Parker said.

"Ease off," Carella said softly. "It's Christmas Eve."

"So what? That's supposed to mean you can break the law, it's Christmas Eve?"

"The girl's in labor," Carella said. "She may have the baby any damn minute. Ease off."

Parker stared at him for a moment and then turned back to José. "Okay," he said, "you came up here from Puerto Rico looking for a job—"

"*Sí, señor.*"

"Talk English. And don't interrupt me. You came up here lookin' for a job; you think jobs grow on trees here?"

"My cousin says he hass a job for me. D' factory where he works, he says there's a job there. He says come up."

"Oh, now there's a cousin," Parker said to Hawes, hoping for a more receptive audience than he'd found in Carella. "What's your cousin's name?" he asked José.

"Cirilo Lopez."

"Another bullfighter?" Parker said and winked at Hawes. Hawes did not wink back.

"Whyn't you leave him alone?" Carmody said from the cage.

Parker swiveled his chair around to face the cage. "Who said that?" he asked and looked at the black man. "You the one who said that?"

The black man did not answer.

"I'm the one who said it," Carmody admitted.

"What are you in the cage for?"

"Holding frankincense and myrrh," Carmody said and laughed. Knowles laughed with him. The black man in the cage did not crack a smile.

"How about you?" Parker asked, looking directly at him.

"He's mine," Kling said. "That big valise there is full of hot goods."

"Nice little crowd we get here," Parker said and swiveled his chair back to the desk. "I'm still waitin' for an address from you two," he said. "A *legal* address."

"We wass s'pose' to stay with my cousin," José said. "He says he hass a room for us."

"Where's that?" Parker asked.

"Eleven twenny-four Mason Avenue, apar'men' thirty-two."

"But there's no room for us," Maria said. "Cirilo, he's—" She caught her breath. Her face contorted in pain again.

José took her hand. She looked up at him. "D' lady lives ness door," he said to Parker, "she tells us Cirilo hass move away."

"When's the last time you heard from him?"

"Lass' month."

"So you don't think to check, huh? You come all the way up from Puerto Rico without checkin' to see your cousin's still here or not? Brilliant. You hear this, Bert?" he said to Kling. "Jet-set travelers we got here; they come to the city in their summer clothes in December, they end up in an abandoned building."

"They thought the cousin was still here, that's all," Kling said, watching the girl, whose hands were now spread wide on her belly.

"Okay, what's the big emergency here?" someone said from the railing.

The man standing there was carrying a small black satchel. He was wearing a heavy black overcoat over white trousers and tunic. The snow on the shoulders of the coat and dusted onto his bare head was as white as the tunic and pants. "Mercy General at your service," he said. "Sorry to be so late; it's been a busy night. Not to mention two feet of snow out there. Where's the patient?"

"You'd better take a look at the girl," Carella said, "She's in—"

"Right here," Carmody said from the cage.

"Me, too," Knowles said.

"Somebody want to let them out?" the intern said. "One at a time, please."

Hawes went to the cage and threw back the bolts on the door.

"Who's first?" the intern said.

Carella started to say, "The girl over there is in la—"

"Free at last," Carmody interrupted, coming out of the cage.

"Don't hold your breath," Hawes said and bolted the door again.

The intern was passing Parker's desk when Maria suddenly gasped.

"You okay, miss?" he said at once.

Maria clutched her belly.

"Miss?" he said.

Maria gasped again and sucked in a deep breath of air.

Meyer rolled his eyes. He and Miscolo had delivered a baby right here in the squad room not too long ago, and he was grateful for the intern's presence.

"This woman is in *labor!*" the intern said.

"Comes the dawn," Carella said, sighing.

"Iss it d' baby comin'?" José asked.

"Looks that way, mister," the intern said. "Somebody get a blanket or something. You got any blankets up here?"

Kling was already on his way out of the squad room.

"Just take it easy, miss," the intern said. "Everything's gonna be fine." He looked at Meyer and said, "This is my first baby."

Terrific, Meyer thought, but he said nothing.

"You need some hot water?" Hawes asked.

"That's for the movies," the intern said.

"Get some hot water," Carmody said.

"I don't need hot water," the intern said. "I just need someplace for her to lie down." He thought about this for a moment. "Maybe I *do* need hot water," he said.

Hawes ran out of the squad room, almost colliding with Kling, who was on his way back with a pair of blankets he'd found in the clerical office. Miscolo was right behind him.

"Another baby coming?" he asked Meyer. He seemed eager to deliver it.

"We got a professional here," Meyer said.

"You need any help," Miscolo said to the intern, "just ask, okay?"

"I won't need any help," the intern said, somewhat snottily, Miscolo thought. "Put those blankets down someplace. You okay, miss?" He suddenly looked very nervous.

Maria nodded and then gasped again and clutched her belly and stifled a scream. Kling was spreading one of the blankets on the floor to the left of the detention cage, near the hissing radiator. Knowles and the black man moved to the side of the cage nearest the radiator.

"Give her some privacy," Carella said softly. "Over there, Bert. Behind the filing cabinets."

Kling spread the blanket behind the cabinets.

"She's gonna have her baby right here," Knowles said.

The black man said nothing.

"I never experienced nothin' like this in my life," Knowles said, shaking his head.

The black man still said nothing.

"Maria?" José said.

Maria nodded and then screamed.

"Try to keep it down, willya?" Parker said. He looked as nervous as the intern did.

"Just come with me, miss," the intern said, easing Maria out of the chair, taking her elbow and guiding her to where Kling had spread the blanket behind the cabinets. "Easy, now," he said. "Everything's gonna be fine."

Hawes was back with a kettle of hot water. "Where do you want—" he started to say, just as Maria and the intern disappeared from view behind the bank of high cabinets.

It was three minutes to midnight, three minutes to Christmas Day.

From behind the filing cabinets, there came only the sounds of Maria's labored breathing and the intern's gentle assurances that everything was going to be all right. The kid kept staring at the clock as it threw the minutes before Christmas into the room. Behind the filing cabinets, a sixteen-year-old girl and an inexperienced intern struggled to bring a life into the world.

There was a sudden sharp cry from behind the cabinets.

The hands of the clock stood straight up.

It was Christmas Day.

"Is it okay?" Parker asked. There was something like concern in his voice.

"Fine baby boy," the intern said, as if repeating a line he'd heard in a movie. "Where's that water? Get me some towels. You've got a fine, healthy boy, miss," he said to Maria and covered her with the second blanket.

Hawes carried the kettle of hot water to him.

Carella brought him paper towels from the rack over the sink.

"Just going to wash him off a little, miss," the intern said.

"You got a fine baby boy," Meyer said to José, smiling.

José nodded.

"What're you gonna name him?" Kling asked.

The black man, who'd been silent since he'd entered the squad room, suddenly said in a deep and sonorous voice, "'Behold, a virgin shall conceive and bear a son, and his name shall be called Emmanuel.'"

"Amen," Knowles said.

The detectives were gathered in a knot around the bank of filing cabinets now, their backs to Carmody. Carmody could have made a run for it, but he didn't. Instead, he picked up first the shopping bag of marijuana he and Knowles had been busted for and then the valise containing the loot Kling had recovered when he'd collared the black man. He carried them to where Maria lay behind the cabinets, the baby on her breast. He knelt at her feet. He dipped his hand into the bag, grabbed a handful of pot and sprinkled it onto the blanket. He opened the valise. There were golden rings and silver plates in the valise, bracelets and necklaces, rubies and diamonds and sapphires that glittered in the pale, snow-reflected light that streamed through the corner windows.

"*Gracias,*" Maria said softly. "*Muchas gracias.*"

Carella, standing closest to the windows, looked up at the sky, where the snow still swirled furiously.

"That's not a bad name," Meyer said to José. "Emmanuel."

"I will name him Carlos," José said. "After my father."

Carella turned from the windows.

"What'd you expect to see out there?" Parker asked. "A star in the East?"

1984

George V. Higgins

The Impossible Snowsuit of Christmas Past

THE DRESS-UP SNOWSUIT was made of coarse, scratchy, heavy brown tweed. It consisted of a cap, coat and leggings. The cap was pleated, with narrow visor and a brown button on the crown. It had earflaps that strapped under the chin and snapped together tightly. The coat was double-breasted, with three leather buttons; it had a narrow collar and the skirt of it was flared. It was lined in brown silk and had brown leather buttons on the sleeves. The leggings had a zipper fly and button closure. They were provided with side zippers to fit closely to the calves. They were held up by braces, and down by elastic stirrups which kept the leather bottoms tight to the tops of my shoes, like spats.

To this day, forty years or so later, that snowsuit springs to memory whenever I find myself tricked by the New England weather or a faulty thermostat in a room I cannot immediately leave into acute, sweaty discomfort attributable to my choice of a heavier apparel than has proved appropriate. When my vanity overrules the reality reported by the bathroom scales, and I venture forth in favorite three-piece suits that should remain on hangers until I have dropped ten pounds, or in a dinner jacket which will last the night only if I decline the dinner, I remember that snowsuit. In my personal dictionary, the text of the definition of *misery* is illustrated by a pen-and-ink drawing of a little boy in a heavy tweed snowsuit, his fat round face distorted by the strap of the earflaps under his pudgy chin. I hated that snowsuit then, and I hate it to this day.

This enduring obsession of mine demonstrates several things, I think. It suggests that my grandfather probably bought me the snowsuit, since a garment sufficiently elaborate to cause such discomfort would have been beyond the budget of my parents' earnings. It probably accounts in part for my resistance to attendance at occasions denominated "special," because when such events occurred in the winters of my childhood, I had to wear the snowsuit. It establishes, at least to my satisfaction, that the clothing preferences of children past the diaper stage should be ordinarily heeded, so long as their indulgence will not result in allegations of child neglect against their doting parents. And it surely proves beyond a reasonable doubt that my parents and grandfather knew how Christmas should be kept.

It proves that because each year there was one cold day when the despised dress-up snowsuit was brought from the closet and I was braced, zipped, buttoned and snapped into it without clamor or tears. That was December 24th. Late in the morning of December 24th, which in memory is always dry and cold and crisp, my father, released from teaching duties by the school vacation, would announce that he was ready for our luncheon trip to Boston, and I would get suited up. The trip was not for last-minute shopping; it was agreed, in fact, that no late petitions for gifts inadvertently omitted from the letter to Santa (who brought all of mine) would be entertained. The official explanation for the annual excursion was that my mother, like Santa, had many preparations to attend to before the next day's feast, and we were doing her a kindness by getting out from underfoot and leaving her alone. This had the merit of being so patent a pretext for our personal self-indulgence that I found it deliciously conspiratory, and for quite a few years remained surprised she let us get away with it.

In my childhood, as I recall, we seldom drove the 20 or so miles north to Boston on any of our trips, except in the summer, when we went to Fenway Park. These were the years of World War II, remember; gas and tires were rationed, and carefully husbanded. We went instead to the greystone station in North Abington and got on one of the frequent trains into South Station. We walked up Summer Street to Washington Street, and north on Washington to School Street, and then west up School to Patten's Restaurant next to what is now known as the Old City Hall. If the heater blasting in the 1941 blue and white DeSoto coupe and the warmth of the train had not before that enabled me to do so, keeping up with my father's stride on that stroll always enabled me to break a good sweat inside my brown snowsuit, but I did not complain.

This was because when we arrived for lunch, I was allowed to remove the cap and coat, and the leggings as well. That last represented one of the corporal works of mercy on my father's part, because getting me back into them was an ordeal by tweed. Released from that bondage, I went with him up the broad staircase to the second floor dining room, which in memory is dark wood and some sort of light wall covering, with green drapes framing views from tall windows. The tables were set in white and the place was filled with men who talked loudly and laughed a lot, and it seemed very busy and quite thrilling. My father knew some of these men, because in addition to teaching he was active in the Massachusetts NEA affiliate, and had weekly Boston meetings, and when we claimed our reservation he would pause at their tables and introduce me. Many of the men had cone-shaped glasses in front of their places, some filled with a clear, colorless, viscous fluid in which an olive or small onion was immersed, others with a clear brown liquid in which a maraschino cherry had been sunk; I was always curious about those beverages, which were not consumed in our house, and impressed as well by the hearty good cheer which their consumers displayed. Much later I did research which convinced me that the refreshments and the joviality were not unrelated.

My father and I usually had fried clams. He started with tomato juice and I had clam chowder. He had apple pie with vanilla ice cream for dessert. I had an ice cream clown, its features being represented by raisins and pieces of marinated fruit, accompanied by two repellent little vanilla waffle cookies. We both dawdled over dessert, partly because we both luxuriated in the hubbub of the place, and partly because finishing portended the next struggle with the snowsuit.

Out on School Street again in mid-afternoon, we went uphill to Tremont Street, to visit Eric Fuchs', then as now a shrine for devotees of model trains. My application to Santa in those days always included several items made by Lionel, invariably more numerous and costly than Santa was able to afford. My father bought me one small anticipatory gift—a box of lichen shrubbery, perhaps, or four more pieces of straight track—in order to prevent a frenzy of impatient greed. From Fuchs' we worked our way back to Washington Street, looking in the windows of the department stores where the workmen were already taking down the Christmas decorations, making both of us feel sad. My father and I agreed that they should be left up at least until New Year's. Then we got back on the train and went home in the dusk, some years in falling snow, but always with me convinced I had the best father in the world, and Christmas was the best time of the year.

Now of course I am lots older, tougher and realistic. No one in years has been rash enough to try to get me into a snowsuit. Now I realize the purpose of the trip on the day before Christmas was not only to get me out of the house but also to trot me all over Boston and wear me out so I would sleep when Santa came that night with a tree to decorate and trains to set up, and all his other chores. There's grass between the train rails now. The North Abington station burned; South Station was demolished. Patten's moved some years ago; there's a new City Hall. My father died in September of 1966, gypping me thus far out of nineteen more such lunches. There is no Santa Claus; I was being gently conned. Stern reality impinges: lives and Christmases are fleeting, and we have to deal with that.

This is one way I have dealt with that loss of innocence: The week before Christmas each year since my children were quite small, my daughter and I have been lunching at the Ritz, my son and I at Locke Ober. We walk through the Common and look at the lights, and keep every Christmas in that and other ways as though it could never last. Which means, of course, they have.

They have because although I've learned a lot since my snowsuit days, and dislike much of it, I still know now what I knew then, on those trains home through the snow. And what I knew then was right.

1985

RON CARLSON

The H Street Sledding Record

THE LAST THING I do every Christmas Eve is go out in the yard and throw the horse manure onto the roof. It is a ritual. After we return from making our attempt at the H Street Sledding Record, and we sit in the kitchen sipping Egg Nog and listening to Elise recount the sled ride, and Elise then finally goes to bed happily, reluctantly, and we finish placing Elise's presents under the tree and we pin her stocking to the mantel—with care—and Drew brings out two other wrapped boxes which anyone could see are for me, and I slap my forehead having forgotten to get her anything at all for Christmas (except the prizes hidden behind the glider on the front porch), I go into the garage and put on the gloves and then into the yard where I throw the horse manure on the roof.

Drew always uses this occasion to call my mother. They exchange all the Christmas news, but the main purpose of the calls the last few years has been for Drew to stand in the window where she can see me out there lobbing the great turds up into the snow on the roof, and describe what I am doing to my mother. The two women take amusement from this. They say things like: "You married him" and "He's your son." I take their responses to my rituals as a kind of fond, subtle support, which it is. Drew had said when she first discovered me throwing the manure on the roof, the Christmas that Elise was four, "You're the only man I've ever known who did that." See: a compliment.

But, now that Elise is eight, Drew has become cautious: "You're fostering her fantasies." I answer: "Kids grow up too soon these days." And then Drew has this: "What do you want her to do, come home from school in tears when she's fifteen? Some kid in her class will have said—*Oh, sure, Santa's reindeer shit on your roof, eh?*" All I can say to Drew then is: "Some kid in her class! Fine! I don't care what he says. I'm her father!"

I have thrown horse manure on our roof for four years now, and I plan to do it every Christmas Eve until my arm gives out. It satisfies me as a homeowner to do so, for the wonderful amber stain that is developing between the swamp cooler and the chimney and is visible all spring-summer-fall as you drive down the hill by our house, and for the way the two rosebushes by the gutterspout have raged into new and profound growth during the milder months. And as a father, it satisfies me as a ritual that keeps my family together.

Drew has said, "You want to create evidence? Let's put out milk and a cookie and then drink the milk and eat a bite out of the cookie."

I looked at her. "Drew," I had said, "I don't like cookies. I never ate a dessert in my life."

And like I said, Drew has been a good sport, even the year I threw one gob short and ran a hideous smear down the kitchen window screen that hovered over all us until March when I was able to take it down and go to the carwash.

I obtain the manure from my friend Bob, more specifically from his horse, Power, who lives just west of Heber. I drive out there the week before Christmas and retrieve about a bushel. I throw it on the roof a lump at a time, wearing a pair of welding gloves my father gave me.

I put the brake on the sled in 1975 when Drew was pregnant with Elise so we could still make our annual attempt on the H Street Record on Christmas Eve. It was the handle of a broken Louisville Slugger baseball bat, and still had the precise "34" stamped into the bottom. I sawed it off square and drilled and bolted it to the rear of the sled, so that when I pulled back on it, the stump would drag us to a stop. As it turned out, it was one of the two years when there was no snow, so we walked up to Eleventh Avenue and H Street (as we promised: rain or shine), sat on the Flexible Flyer in the middle of the dry street on a starry Christmas Eve, and I held her in my lap. We sat on the sled like two basketball players contesting possession of her belly. We talked a little about what it would be like when she took her leave from the firm and I had her home all day with the baby, and we talked remotely about whether we wanted any more babies, and we talked about the Record, which was set on December 24, 1969, the first Christmas of our marriage, when we lived in the neighborhood, on Fifth Avenue in an old barn of a house the total rent on which was seventy-two fifty, honest, and Drew had given me the sled that very night and we had walked out about midnight and been surprised by the blizzard. No wonder we took the sled and walked around the corner up H Street, up, up, up to Eleventh Avenue, and without speaking or knowing what we were doing, opening the door on the second ritual of our marriage, the annual sled ride (the first ritual was the word "condition" and the activities it engendered in our droopy old bed).

At the top we scanned the city blurred in snow, sat on my brand new Christmas sled, and set off. The sled rode high and effortlessly through the deep snow, and suddenly, as our hearts started and our eyes began to burn against the snowy air, we were going faster than we'd planned. We crossed Tenth Avenue, nearly taking flight in the dip, and then descended in a dark rush: Ninth, Eighth, Seventh, soaring across each avenue, my arms wrapped around Drew like a straitjacket to drag her off with me if a car should cross in front of us on Sixth, Fifth Avenue, Fourth (this all took seconds, do you see?) until a car did turn onto H Street, headed our way, and we veered the new sled sharply, up over the curb, dousing our speed in the snowy yard one house from the corner of Third Avenue. Drew took a real faceful of snow, which she squirmed around and pressed into my neck, saying the words: "Now, that's a record!"

And it was the Record: Eleventh to Third, and it stood partly because there had been two Christmas Eves with no snow, partly because of assorted spills brought on by too much speed, too much laughter, sometimes too much caution, and by a light blue Mercedes that crossed Sixth Avenue just in front of us in 1973. And though some years were flops, there was nothing about Christmas that Elise looked forward to as much as our one annual attempt at the H Street Sledding Record.

I think Drew wants another baby. I'm not sure, but I think she wants another child. The signs are so subtle they barely seem to add up, but she says things like, "Remember before Elise went to school?" and "There sure are a lot of women in their mid-thirties having babies." I should ask her. But for some reason, I don't. We talk about everything, *everything*. But I've avoided this topic. I've avoided talking to Drew about this topic because I want another child too badly to have her not want one. I want a little boy to come into the yard on Christmas morning and say: "See, there on the roof! The reindeers were there!" I want another kid to throw horse manure for. I'll wait. It will come up one of these days; I'll find a way to bring it up. Christmas is coming.

Every year on the day after Halloween, I tip the sled out of the rafters in the garage and Elise and I sponge it off, clean the beautiful dark blond wood with furniture polish, enamel the nicked spots on the runner supports with

black engine paint, and rub the runners themselves with waxed paper. It is a ritual done on the same plaid blanket in the garage and it takes all afternoon. When we are finished, we lean the sled against the wall, and Elise marches into the house. "Okay now," she says to her mother: "Let it snow."

On the first Friday night in December, every year, Elise and Drew and I go buy our tree. This too is ritual. Like those families that bundle up and head for the wilderness so they can trudge through the deep, pristine snow, chop down their own little tree, and drag it, step by step, all the way home, we venture forth in the same spirit. Only we take the old pickup down to South State and find some joker who has thrown up two strings of colored lights around the corner of the parking lot of a burned-out Safeway and is proffering trees to the general public.

There is something magical and sad about this little forest just sprung up across from City Tacos, and Drew and Elise and I wander the wooded paths, waiting for some lopsided pinon to leap into our hearts.

The winter Drew and I became serious, when I was a senior and she was already in her first year at law school, I sold Christmas trees during vacation. I answered a card on a dorm bulletin board and went to work for a guy named Geer, who had cut two thousand squat pinons from the hills east of Cedar City and was selling them from a dirt lot on Redwood Road. Drew's mother invited me to stay with them for the holidays, and it gave me the chance to help Drew make up her mind about me. I would sell trees until midnight with Geer, and then drive back to Drew's and watch every old movie in the world and wrestle with Drew until our faces were mashed blue. I wanted to complicate things wonderfully by having her sleep with me. She wanted to keep the couch cushions between us and think it over. It was a crazy Christmas; we'd steam up the windows in the entire living room, but she never gave in. We did develop the joke about "condition," which we still use as a code word for desire. And later, I won't say if it was spring or fall, when Drew said to me, "I'd like to see you about this condition," I knew everything was going to be all right, and that we'd spend every Christmas together for the rest of our lives.

One night during that period, I delivered a tree to University Village, the married students' housing off Sunnyside. The woman was waiting for me with the door open as I dragged the pine up the steps to the second floor. She was a girl, really, about twenty, and her son, about three, watched the arrival from behind her. When I had the tree squeezed into the apartment,

she asked if I could just hold it for a minute while she found her tree stand. If you ever need to stall for a couple of hours, just say you're looking for your tree stand; I mean the girl was gone for about twenty minutes. I stood and exchanged stares with the kid, who was scared; he didn't understand why some strange man had brought a tree into his home. "Christmas," I told him. "Christmas. Can you say 'Merry Christmas'?" I was an idiot.

When the girl returned with her tree stand, she didn't seem in any hurry to set it up. She came over to me and showed me the tree stand, holding it up for an explanation as to how it worked. Close up the girl's large eyes had an odd look in them, and then I understood it when she leaned through the boughs and kissed me. It was a great move; I had to hand it to her. There I was holding the tree; I couldn't make a move either way. It has never been among my policies to kiss strangers, but I held the kiss and the tree. Something about her eyes. She stepped back with the sweetest look of embarrassment and hope on her pretty face that I'd ever seen. "Just loosen the turn-screws in the side of that stand," I said, finally. "And we can put this tree up."

By the time I had the tree secured, she had returned again with a box of ornaments, lights, junk like that, and I headed for the door. "Thanks," I said. "Merry Christmas."

Her son had caught on by now and was fully involved in unloading the ornaments. The girl looked up at me, and this time I saw it all: her husband coming home in his cap and gown last June, saying, "Thanks for law school, honey, but I met Doris at the Juris-Prudence Ball and I gotta be me. Keep the kid."

The girl said to me, "You could stay and help."

It seemed like two statements to me, and so I answered them separately: "Thank you. But I can't stay; that's the best help. Have a good Christmas."

And I left them there together, decorating that tree; a ritual against the cold.

"How do you like it?" Elise says to me. She has selected a short broad bush which seems to have grown in two directions at once and then given up. She sees the look on my face and says, "If you can't say anything nice, don't say anything at all. Besides, I've already decided: this is the tree for us."

"It's a beautiful tree," Drew says.

"Quasimodo," I whisper to Drew. "This tree's name is Quasimodo."

"No whispering," Elise says from behind us. "What's he saying now, Mom?"

"He said he likes the tree, too."

Elise is not convinced and after a pause she says, "Dad. It's Christmas. Behave yourself."

When we go to pay for the tree, the master of ceremonies is busy negotiating a deal with two kids, a punk couple. The tree man stands with his hands in his change apron and says, "I gotta get thirty-five bucks for that tree." The boy, a skinny kid in a leather jacket, shrugs and says he's only got twenty-eight bucks. His girlfriend, a large person with a bowl haircut and a monstrous black overcoat festooned with buttons, is wailing, "Please! Oh no! Jimmy! Jimmy! I love that tree! I want that tree!" The tree itself stands aside, a noble pine of about twelve feet. Unless these kids live in a gymnasium, they're buying a tree bigger than their needs.

Jimmy retreats to his car, an old Plymouth big as a boat. "Police Rule" is spraypainted across both doors in balloon letters. He returns instantly and opens a hand full of coins. "I'll give you thirty-one bucks, fifty-five cents, and my watch." To our surprise, the wily tree man takes the watch to examine it. When I see that, I give Elise four dollars and tell her to give it to Kid Jimmy and say, "Merry Christmas." His girlfriend is still wailing but now a minor refrain of "Oh Jimmy, that tree! Oh Jimmy, etc." I haven't seen a public display of emotion and longing of this magnitude in Salt Lake City, ever. I watch Elise give the boy the money, but instead of saying, "Merry Christmas," I hear her say instead: "Here, Jimmy. Santa says keep your watch."

Jimmy pays for the tree, and his girl—and this is the truth—jumps on him, wrestles him to the ground in gratitude and smothers him for nearly a minute. There have never been people happier about a Christmas tree. We pay quickly and head out before Jimmy or his girlfriend can think to begin thanking us.

On the way home in the truck, I say to Elise, "Santa says keep your watch, eh?"

"Yes, he does," she smiles.

"How old are you, anyway?"

"Eight."

It's an old joke, and Drew finishes it for me: "When he was your age, he was seven."

We will go home and while the two women begin decorating the tree with the artifacts of our many Christmases together, I will thread popcorn onto a long string. It is a ritual I prefer for its uniqueness; the fact that once a year I get to sit and watch the two girls I am related to move about a tree inside our home, while I sit nearby and sew food.

*

On the morning of the twenty-fourth of December, Elise comes into our bedroom, already dressed for sledding. "Good news," she says. "We've got a shot at the record."

Drew rises from the pillow and peeks out the blind. "It's snowing," she says.

Christmas Eve, we drive back along the snowy Avenues, and park on Fifth, as always. "I know," Elise says, hopping out of the car. "You two used to live right over there before you had me and it was a swell place and only cost seventy-two fifty a month, honest."

Drew looks at me and smiles.

"How old are you?" I ask Elise, but she is busy towing the sled away, around the corner, up toward Eleventh Avenue. It is still snowing, petal flakes, teeming by the streetlamps, trying to carry the world away. I take Drew's hand and we walk up the middle of H Street behind our daughter. There is no traffic, but the few cars have packed the tender snow perfectly. It *could* be a record. On Ninth Avenue, Drew stops me in the intersection, the world still as snow, and kisses me. "I love you," she says.

"What a planet," I whisper. "To allow such a thing."

By the time we climb to Eleventh Avenue, Elise is seated on the sled, ready to go. "What are you guys waiting for, Christmas?" she says and then laughs at her own joke. Then she becomes all business: "Listen, Dad, I figure if you stay just a little to the left of the tire tracks we could go all the way. And no wobbling!" She's referring to last year's record attempt, which was extinguished in the Eighth Avenue block when we laughed ourselves into a fatal wobble and ended in a slush heap.

We arrange ourselves on the sled, as we have each Christmas Eve for eight years. As I reach my long legs around these two women, I sense their excitement. "It's going to be a record!" Elise whispers into the whispering snow.

"Do you think so?" Drew asks. She also feels this could be the night.

"Oh yeah!" Elise says. "The conditions are perfect!"

"What do you think?" Drew turns to me.

"Well, the conditions are perfect."

When I say *conditions*, Drew leans back and kisses me. So I press: "There's still room on the sled," I say, pointing to the "F" in Flexible Flyer that is visible between Elise's legs. "There's still room for another person."

"Who?" Elise asks.

"Your little brother," Drew says, squeezing my knees.

And that's about all that was said, sitting up there on Eleventh Avenue on Christmas Eve on a sled which is as old as my marriage with a brake that is as old as my daughter. Later tonight I will stand in my yard and throw this year's reindeer droppings on my very own home. I love Christmas.

Now the snow spirals around us softly. I put my arms around my family and lift my feet onto the steering bar. We begin to slip down H Street. We are trying for the record. The conditions, as you know by now, are perfect.

1985

STEVE RASNIC TEM

Buzz

H E FELT a trembling in his ears, like the passage of warm breath, and a buzzing high inside his brain, as if a tiny but persistent voice were trapped there.

"Paul, please."

"I'm up, dammit." After a few more minutes he kicked off the covers and rolled out of bed.

"The kids want you there when they open presents."

Paul had heard Alice cajole and threaten the three children all morning about how they *had* to wait, but he said nothing.

Annie got the usual assortment of dolls, with the celebrity addition this year of a Cabbage Patch Kid. Richard got a train set, a microscope, Lincoln Logs, G.I. Joe paraphernalia, the Christmas release accessories for his Masters of the Universe collection, and assorted other vicious personnae. Their oldest, Willy, got cash and a motorbike, something else Paul had disapproved of but had been skillfully pressured into accepting.

The kids' gifts were a bit stereotyped: he and his wife had finally given up on arranging for Santa to deliver "cross-gender" presents. This was the stuff they really wanted. But Paul found himself unable, as yet, to stop hoping their tastes in heroes and role-models might change. For now, any crudely-drawn animated figure with a good merchandizing arrangement might dazzle them.

The expensive motorized Erector set he'd bought Willy, on his own initiative, lay forgotten in its box, shrouded in white tissue.

"Kids have changed, Paul," Alice whispered behind him. "They don't always go for the toys their parents treasured as children."

He turned around. His wife wore her *Didn't I tell you?* look.

Paul shrugged. "I just wanted to please him . . . and please myself, too, I guess."

Annie was completely enthralled with her Cabbage Patch doll.

"Now, sit here, Lillie Beth. I don't want you fallin' off the table and gettin' hurted." Propped up on the table, the doll looked dim-witted. The expression on its face reminded Paul of a mutant biscuit. "Oh, I know," Annie said suddenly, "you want to go for a walk by the railroad tracks." Annie hopped the doll over the carpeting, slamming its feet down so hard the legs bent grotesquely. Richard aimed his rocket launchers their way and made popping noises, much to Annie's dismay, "*Leave* my baby *alone!*" She let the doll fall over onto the tracks. "Oh, my baby," she cried theatrically. "She's caught on the railroad thing!"

Richard, eager to play along, ran over to the train transformer and turned it on. Annie stood a few feet away, waiting, then suddenly ran toward the tracks. "I'll save you, Lillie Beth!" and picked up the doll before the train arrived.

As a child, Paul had always pretended to be his own father in such heroic games, playing out the John Wayne role. His father had been as distant and mysterious to him as these plastic heroes must be to his own kids.

He stood by the window, staring at the burned-out husk of the Reynolds house across the street. Two weeks ago Jay Reynolds had carried two of his children out of that fire, to safety. He was burnt over thirty percent of his body, Paul had heard. The neighbors seemed to be feeling a mixture of awe and abhorrence toward the man. Consequently, no one had visited Reynolds as yet.

He imagined a truck careening across his front yard, and his last minute dive and tackle that saved Annie and her doll.

He imagined Richard caught in a gas explosion, and his futile efforts to save his son dissolving within the flames.

Paul was always one of the last to open his presents. Not so much because he had grown disenchanted with Christmas—which he had—but because the kids' gifts blocked most of the tree and he had a hard time finding any marked for him.

He thought he'd opened them all—thanking his brood for socks and ties and belts and a heavy robe and two sets of metric wrenches—when Richard pulled out a small package from under the backside of the tree. "One more, Dad."

Richard brought it over and dropped it into his lap. The packaging was interesting: it looked like metallic red foil, but felt more like plastic. A small plastic card with his name in crisp black lettering graced the front. The wrapping was fastened in back by what looked like an irregular round seal of the same material as the wrapping.

"Who's it from?" He looked around the living room.

Everyone denied knowledge of it. Finally his wife said, "It's probably from one of your friends. They must have slipped it behind the tree during the party last night."

Paul gazed at the tree. Impossible. There'd been far too many packages piled in front for anyone to slip back there. He lifted the front of the card. Inside, in the same black lettering as his name, were the words:

WHAT YOU WANTED

He turned the package over and tried to peel the seal off with his fingernail. It didn't budge to his efforts, but then suddenly the wrapping straightened out, the sides of the box hinged, and a small object tumbled to the carpet.

Paul picked it up carefully. It was a miniature sculpture of some sort of fantastic insect, done in something like brass, something like copper, with jeweled eyes and a highly-burnished thorax.

"How cute!" Alice cried. Paul found he couldn't say anything for a moment.

"I think it's some sort of fancy Christmas tree ornament," he finally said. It was delicate, and so precise in its details that he wondered whether it was an exact replica of some exotic species of insect.

"Whatcha gonna do with it, Daddy?" Annie asked, without taking her eyes off her Cabbage Patch doll.

"Hang it on the tree," he said, almost laughing because of the sudden giddiness he was feeling.

He walked over to the tree and, reaching as far as he could, placed it near the top. He stepped back to admire it. It was amazing, the way its shiny surfaces caught the multicolored lights and seemed to blend them, hold them fast within its metal.

"Ooooh, pretty," Annie said.

"Yes. It *is* nice," Paul said proudly.

A couple of hours after lunch Paul was sitting by himself in the living room, gazing at his ornament, drinking again. He'd needed a break. Annie had temporarily lost one of her dolls (it would show up a couple of days later behind a piece of furniture), and Richard had broken one of the GI Joe pieces and lost several of the smaller "personal accessories" (which would *not* be found). Both were upstairs in their rooms, crying.

He looked at the bottle. Rolling Rock, the last of the year's stock. Maybe he'd had too much; his ears felt tender, ringing.

He looked up at the tree and watched as the ornament moved several inches to devour the head of a tinsel-haired angel. He put down his drink. The tree began to rustle, sprinkling dry pine needles out on his rug.

"Alice!" he shouted.

A few agonizing minutes later, during which Paul watched the ornament wander around the tree, disturbing ornaments, slipping garlands from branches, and chewing needles, Alice and the kids ran into the room, surrounding him, prodding him, asking what was wrong.

"The tree," he said, still watching it. "That *insect!*"

Alice walked over and began picking up the dislodged ornaments. "That cat!" she said. "You'd think after all these years she'd know better." She brushed the back of her hand through the branches. "I'm sorry, Paul. Looks like she knocked your new ornament somewhere."

Willy rolled his eyes in exaggerated fashion. "Jees, Dad. Thought it was a fire or something."

Paul just looked at the boy.

Paul went into the bedroom and got his nine iron out of the golf bag. The rest of the afternoon he wandered the house with it. He didn't find the thing. Just before dinner he put the club away.

Alice had gone all out on the dinner—both turkey and ham, broccoli in cheese sauce, deviled eggs, all his favorites. Annie had brought her Cabbage Patch Kid to the dinner table, where she'd set up a highchair for the thing. Paul was in a good enough mood that it didn't bother him, even when she pretended to feed it, and cheese sauce dripped over its chin.

As he watched the thin yellow drool drop onto the front of the doll's dress, a narrow black line, so like a crack, spread across the puffed cheeks, the idiot eyes, joined five other similar cracks spreading from points around the doll's head, and then the insect's ragged mouth parts appeared over the top of the orange yarn hair, sharp-edged jowls gnawing through soft plastic.

Annie was reaching to stroke the doll's hair.

"No!" he screamed, jumping up from the chair, bathrobe flopping like a giant, awkward bird. He jerked the carving knife out of the turkey and plunged it into the doll's head, where the black lines had just disappeared.

The force of Paul's lunge dragged him off-balance, over the chair and onto the floor. He could feel the table rocking under his hip, everybody jumping away, shouting, dishes falling and breaking. From his vantage point on the floor he could see small discarded piles of broccoli, mashed potatoes, and ham, and a long, articulated black carapace snaking its way over the orange rug that led back into the living room.

Paul sat alone in the dark parlor, staring through the partially-open door at Richard running his train set around the coffee table. He'd been there since the knife incident, planning, weighing the risk to his family's lives (after all, he didn't know for sure the thing would hurt anyone) against the risk to his own reputation (which seemed irretrievably lost at this point). He'd had to listen while in the other room Alice tried to explain that their father had been under a lot of pressure lately, that he'd been drinking too much, and reassuring Annie that Lillie Beth wasn't really dead, just wounded, and after Mom took her away to the doctor for awhile she'd come back looking brand new. (*Oh, great, Alice*, he thought. *Do you really think a new doll will fool her?*)

The train started up again. Paul could hear the electrical hum of the engine, louder than he would have expected.

There was an eighth car at the end of the train. There'd been only seven when Richard first set it up. The box said seven. A shiny black tank car with dingy yellow highlights and slick piping and a long hard tail that drew sparks when it struck the track.

Paul came roaring out into the room, fish net held high, imagining himself John Wayne, Indiana Jones, his father.

He scooped the net rapidly into the rear car, sending a chain of heavy plastic and cheap metal spinning over his son's head. He raised the net over his head triumphantly.

The black thing, a good thirty times larger than when he'd first seen it, snapped its back and hissed a stench from within the net. Then the net was tearing, and the collective voice of Paul's family was clawing at his ears.

A shelf ripped off the wall and swung with all his might didn't even slow the thing. Jagged glass, with Paul holding his foot on its back, didn't even scar.

Alice brought him a large pot. Paul slammed the mouth down over it. The black pot rocked, then flew off, cracking the plaster wall by the fireplace.

What next! What next! Paul began to imagine, and could not turn the imagining off. He started to cry, hating himself as the thing turned and turned on the living room rug, then flew toward Annie, glistening claws cocked, open.

"Daddy! Daddy! It's in my hair!" she screamed, and Paul could imagine no heroics, only a sick despair, as he heard his little girl wail and saw the dark fantasy of a spider, the cold fantasy of a serpent, the screaming fantasy of inhuman black appendage ripping through the yellow halo of her hair.

And looking around for something else to throw, to pry, or pound with, Paul spied the strange shiny wrap neatly stacked on top of all the others by the tree.

He didn't feel heroic as he lowered the shiny wrap over his sweet daughter's head, and felt the edges fold over the thing, the thing passively withdrawing inside the package, no more threat than an old man retiring early for the evening.

He felt like a fiend.

It was nearly dawn before Paul finally took his secret present out to the trash. There, with all the discarded wrappings and empty boxes promising more than a child was likely to receive, he placed the box, piling whatever he could on top, however unnecessary.

He glanced up and down the alley, with familiar backyards and familiar trashbins ranked as far as he could see in the dim morning light. He watched his friends, the other fathers, trying to hide their own presents, their own imaginings, beneath mountains of trash. The sirens began.

1985

AMY TAN

Fish Cheeks

I FELL IN LOVE with the minister's son the winter I turned fourteen. He was not Chinese, but as white as Mary in the manger.
For Christmas I prayed for this blond-haired boy, Robert, and a
slim new American nose.

When I found out that my parents had invited the minister's
family over for Christmas Eve dinner, I cried. What would Robert think of
our shabby Chinese Christmas? What would he think of our noisy Chinese
relatives who lacked proper American manners? What terrible disappointment would he feel upon seeing not a roasted turkey and sweet potatoes
but Chinese food?

On Christmas Eve, I saw that my mother had outdone herself in creating a strange menu. She was pulling black veins out of the backs of fleshy
prawns. The kitchen was littered with appalling mounds of raw food: A
slimy rock cod with bulging fish eyes that pleaded not to be thrown into
a pan of hot oil. Tofu, which looked like stacked wedges of rubbery white
sponges. A bowl soaking dried fungus back to life. A plate of squid, criss-
crossed with knife markings so they resembled bicycle tires.

And then they arrived—the minister's family and all my relatives in a
clamor of doorbells and rumpled Christmas packages. Robert grunted
hello, and I pretended he was not worthy of existence.

Dinner threw me deeper into despair. My relatives licked the ends of
their chopsticks and reached across the table, dipping into the dozen or
so plates of food. Robert and his family waited patiently for platters to be
passed to them. My relatives murmured with pleasure when my mother
brought out the whole steamed fish. Robert grimaced. Then my father
poked his chopsticks just below the fish eye and plucked out the soft meat.
"Amy, your favorite," he said, offering me the tender fish cheek. I wanted to
disappear.

At the end of the meal my father leaned back and belched loudly, thanking my mother for her fine cooking. "It's a polite Chinese custom, to show

you are satisfied," he explained to our astonished guests. Robert was looking down at his plate with a reddened face. The minister managed to muster a quiet burp. I was stunned into silence for the rest of the night.

After all the guests had gone, my mother said to me, "You want be same like American girls on the outside." She handed me an early gift. It was a miniskirt in beige tweed. "But inside, you must always be Chinese. You must be proud you different. You only shame is be ashame."

And even though I didn't agree with her then, I knew that she understood how much I had suffered during the evening's dinner. It wasn't until many years later—long after I had gotten over my crush on Robert—that I was able to appreciate fully her lesson and the true purpose behind our particular menu. For Christmas Eve that year, she had chosen all my favorite foods.

1987

Ann Petry

Checkup

H E WAS GOING down fast. He could feel the wind, the cold air, against his face. It gave him a wonderful sense of exhilaration, a feeling of power, absolute power. He looked up and the stars were further and further away, receding, receding. He looked down and the earth, a great dark mass seemed to be coming toward him, enlarging and enlarging. He went faster and faster.

And then, suddenly, he knew that something had gone wrong. He was no longer flying. He was falling. He closed his eyes thinking, How art thou fallen, O Lucifer, Son of the morning . . . how art thou fallen. He was so conscious of the words that he thought he had spoken them aloud or that someone had.

He shook his head. He was not Lucifer. He was Michael. He said a prayer, softly, under his breath, and felt the terrible force of the wind literally blow the words away, blow his breath away.

He stopped falling as suddenly as he had started. But he was not flying. He was suspended above the earth, held there. He opened his eyes. He was wrong about the earth being dark. It was a strangely luminous, light-reflecting white. He recognized the whiteness as snow. Then he landed on his feet. It was as though he had been picked up, held, and then placed on the earth very gently.

The air was damp and so cold that he shivered. His feet were numb. He began moving them to see if he could get the circulation started. They felt strangely heavy. He knew at once, from the heaviness, that he was earthbound and he was startled. When he had been selected to make this trip they had told him everything they thought he would need to know, but they had not told him, had either forgotten or deliberately omitted, or perhaps did not know themselves, that he would lose the ability to fly when he reached Earth. They had said, "Michael, you are the one to go, you have been Chosen, Michael, Michael. . . ."

He looked around because he thought someone had actually said,

"Michael . . . Michael. . . ." The words seemed to linger in the air. But there was no one anywhere in sight. The moon was at the full and the snow reflected the light from the moon so that he could see as clearly as though it were daylight. He was in a cornfield, or what had been a cornfield. The frozen ground was covered with the hard stubble where the stalks had been. Snow on them. Snow on everything, even clinging to the wire fence that enclosed the field.

Far off, in the distance, he saw the lights of a village or a town. He decided to go in that direction, and lifted his wings. Nothing happened. He felt for them. They were gone. He looked down at himself, frowning now. The shining robe was gone, too. His legs were much shorter, in fact they were so short they were obviously the undeveloped legs of a child. No wonder he was cold. He was now wearing pants made of faded blue cotton, ragged pants. Did he have shoes? Leaning over, he examined his feet. Well, shoes of a sort. They seemed to be made of canvas, and they were the same faded grayblue as his pants, and there were many holes in them. But he was wearing a dark brown leather jacket, very shabby, torn here and there but quite warm.

His hands were very cold. They had grown smaller, too, and they were so dirty they were indistinguishable from the dark brown color of the jacket. He sighed, thinking, well, my back is warm. The wind does not go through this jacket.

He headed toward the village, running, trying to keep warm, pausing now and then to see if by some miracle his wings had been returned. As he hurried along he became aware that he was hungry, not just the normal before-meals hunger, but a kind of sharp pinching of his stomach that told him it had been days since he had had enough to eat. He decided that he would ask for food at the first house he came to.

When he reached the village he kept staring at the houses: big houses, painted white, their windows blazing with light from candles, and from lights shaped like stars, the doorways decorated with strings of brilliant little lights.

He had had no idea that any place, anywhere, could look like this small snowcovered village in the moonlight. The colored lights from the houses made the snow under the windows and along the paths, pink and lavender, dark green and deep yellow. This bejewelled snow seemed to lead straight up to the big front doors of the houses and then it was reflected back into the street.

As he stood there, bemused, he became aware of the mouth-watering smell of meat being roasted. It made him remember how hungry he was. So he opened the picket gate, walked up the pathway, knocked on the front door of one of the largest of the houses.

A fat little girl opened the door. She smiled at him. There were dimples in her cheeks. "Hello," she said. "Come in."

He hesitated just inside the door.

"Come all the way in and see our Christmas tree."

It was warm inside the house. There was a smoky smell from wood being burned in a fireplace and the delicious spicy smell from something being baked elsewhere in the house. When he saw the tree he forgot that he was hungry. It was so tall it reached the ceiling and it was covered with lights and festooned with garlands of something that glittered. There was a small figure of an angel at the very top.

The little girl said, "What's your name?"

"Michael."

"Mine's Elisabeth." After she said this she started hopping about on one foot. He saw that she had long braids that swung back and forth as she hopped.

He heard voices from the back of the house. Someone said, quite clearly, "I thought I heard the front door."

Then another brisker voice said, "Who is she talking to? She's talking to someone."

Footsteps approached and then retreated and the first voice said, "She talking to a little boy."

"Who is he?"

"I don't know. I didn't say anything to him. I just caught a brief glimpse of him in the mirror."

"I'd better find out who he is . . . you never know. . . ."

Then a tall woman entered the room. She said sharply, "You're dripping all over my rug . . . your sneakers are dripping . . . you didn't wipe your feet."

Michael ignored her. There was a long mirror between the windows. The entire room was reflected in it. He could see the tree with its baubles and its glittering garlands, and at the very top of the tree the fragile wings of the tiny angel moved back and forth. He decided there was a current of air in the room just strong enough to make the gauzy wings flutter like the wings of a butterfly. He could see the fireplace and a deep dark red rug on the floor and the bluegreen walls of the room. There were prisms on a three-branched candelabra on a table near the fireplace, and the prisms caught the light from the fire, reflecting it, so that they seemed to be moving, too.

"Where did you come from?" the tall woman asked. "Do you live around here?"

Michael did not answer, could not answer, because he had seen something else reflected in that big sparkling mirror. There was a boy there, a little black boy, the skin on his face and hands dark dark brown, ashy from the cold. His hair was matted, tangled, uncared for. The child's eyes were enormous, frightened, like the eyes of a deer, terribly liquid, soft.

He looked down at his own hands, and he caught a movement in the mirror, touched his face, and the ragged little black boy lifted one of his small dark hands up to his face, too. Then he knew. He, Michael, was the boy in the mirror. He stared and stared.

"Here, run along," the woman said. "Run along—"

She opened the door. He went out slowly, reluctant to leave that warm fragrant room, and he turned and looked back.

The tall woman said, "Why he's a little black boy."

"What's the matter with him?" the little girl asked. "What did you say was the matter with him?"

The closing of the door cut off the sound of her voice. Michael walked away and then turned and looked back at the house. There were lights in all the rooms, upstairs and downstairs, and a great spray of evergreens on the door.

He stared up at the sky. It was full of stars. He thought that if he could reach up high enough he could touch them. He wondered if he could fly again. He tried his wings, holding his breath. Nothing happened. He thought, Christmas Eve, and I, Michael, am earthbound. I have no recollection of an earthly existence. If I ever had one it must have been so many years ago that I have forgotten it. I do not know what color my skin was then, no recollection of it and it has been a matter of no importance for so many years that—

But he had to go somewhere and quickly because he would not be able to survive in this frigid air. Where would he go?

He heard someone calling, and the sound of feet running behind him. He turned. The fat little girl was coming toward him, calling, "Little boy, little boy, Michael!"

She had no hat, no coat. She was holding something out to him. "This is for you," she said. "I brang it specially for you," and dropped something warm, and spicy smelling, in his hand and then ran back toward the house.

He could feel the warmth from whatever it was seeping into his hands, dispelling the numbness in his fingers, and the fragrant spicy smell was wonderful. He ate it quickly, stuffing it in his mouth thinking, it's ginger-bread. That was what they had been baking in the kitchen of that warm, brilliantly lit house. Gingerbread.

Suddenly he could fly again. His wings had been returned. He did not have to touch them to know this. There was a buoyancy about his body. He had to hold his feet on the ground they had become so light.

Yet when he rose in the air, he realized that his wings were not as big and strong as they had been. He supposed they were suited to the size of a child's body. He tired quickly, and the power, the sense of tremendous power, and the feeling of exultation had vanished.

He flew low over the town because he could no longer soar high up in the air. He heard the sound of music, of people singing. It was a song he had known somewhere but not the words; O Come all ye Faithful. The sound came from a nearby building. Then he remembered that he had known it as Adeste Fideles, and he hummed it under his breath, thinking, how beau-tiful the village is in the moonlight.

Almost immediately afterward he had the dreadful sensation of falling and he thought once again of the words, "How art thou fallen," what they must have meant and how it felt to be going down, down, down, down, unable to stop.

He saw a light, a white, brilliant light through the bare branches of trees. And then he was falling through the branches, rough bark and twigs scrap-ing his skin. He caught a quick glimpse of a building painted white, and something in his mind said, temple, Greek temple. No. A church. It was a church. It was somehow related to, suggested a temple—the columns, the rhythmic line of the steps, the utter simplicity of the structure suggested a temple. Then he saw the sidewalk, was looking straight down at it, and saw people standing below him, and for a split second knew what it would be like, falling fast and then crashing—he tried to slow his progress, to break the fall, and landed heavily on a flagstone walk.

But he was not hurt. Just his knee. He seemed to have scraped it a little.

There were people all around him. He supposed they must have been just coming out of the church. They brushed against him, and he heard excla-mations of surprise, and there was a kind of withdrawing motion as people moved back, away from him.

A woman said, "Oh, dear me!"

A man said, "What is it?"

Then there was a babble of voices, all speaking at once.

"Something fell—"

"Impossible—"

"Why it's a little black boy—"

"Where did he come from?"

"He fell out of one of the maple trees."

"The night before Christmas and he was up in a tree?"

"Someone should call the police."

"Yes, yes. Call the State Police."

Then a gentle voice said, "Are you hurt?"

Michael looked up and saw that a frail old man was bending over him. He was bareheaded and his hair was white. His skin looked translucent. His face was as gentle as his voice, as he said, "But you must not lie here. I will take you into my house."

Someone said, "But Reverend—"

The old man ignored the protesting voice. "Your hands are so cold," he said as he helped Michael to his feet. "You are probably hungry, too. Come, I will take you home with me."

As Michael walked beside him, holding on to his hand, he thought it was a warm, surprisingly strong hand for so old a man. To his astonishment he began to feel a kind of buoyancy rushing all through his body. He felt light as air. He was growing taller, and taller, and taller.

He murmured, "Thank you!" and then said softly, "I am going now. I must go now. I'm all right. Thank you!"

He soared straight up, aware that his wings were once again tremendous, aware that he was giving off light. For a fraction of a second he saw the minister, a tiny figure down on the sidewalk, his gentle old face turned upward, his expression one of wonder, and of expectancy, and then he could no longer see him.

Michael went up and up and up, thinking that he knew all he needed to know about Earth. He would report that on the eve of the Birthday, the celebration of it was purely pagan, largely a matter of the decoration of houses with evergreens, with candles, with shiny baubles. The air rushed past him, the stars were very close, the earth was so far that it was only a dark and shapeless void.

Then he thought, only Heaven knows when I'll be back again. It has been five hundred years since one of us visited Earth. Certainly he owed it to the others to see as much as he could. He sighed thinking of that snowcovered village with its big houses, and the beautiful simplicity of the church, and the pure and lovely light that streamed from the lantern hung over the doorway, but only a child and an old man had been concerned about him. The others were indifferent or coldly curious or hostile but not concerned. Would a great city be like that? He decided to find out.

He changed the direction of his flight, and started descending. He went down fast. Suddenly an airplane zoomed past on his right. He looked straight into the cockpit, and he saw the pilot, saw the expression of alarm on his face, saw his lips move, form words, read his lips, "What kind of damn thing is that—look—what is it—did you see it—" and Michael was out of sight.

A city lay just beneath him, a great city, a city of brilliant light. It stretched out for miles along the length of a waterfront. He had a quick look at it and then he started going down faster, falling, falling.

He landed on his back in the middle of a group of people. He lay there gasping. His back felt as though it had been broken in two separate pieces. People glanced down at him. No one stopped to ask whether he was hurt or why he was lying there. Feet and legs kept going past him, swiftly. He heard the sound of heels on the pavement, a hard staccato sound, high heels of women's shoes, low heels of men's shoes, tap, tap, tap, click, click, click and the roaring sound of traffic, the starting and stopping of cars and busses, the screech of brakes. As he lay on the sidewalk he thought, I might be a log in a river, and the water simply goes around me and then meets again once it has gone past me.

He got to his feet, slowly, painfully. His back ached so that for a moment he thought he would not be able to walk. He could tell by the awful heaviness of his feet that his wings had disappeared. He was earthbound again.

It seemed to him that he had walked for miles. When he stopped to rest he found that he was on a street lined with stores. He had never seen anything like them. There were angels and Santa Clauses and jewelry and toys and clothing on display in the shop windows. He assumed that these were the most precious, the most costly, the most beautiful things that it was possible to buy—the sum of the gold and frankincense and myrrh of the entire world.

He stopped in front of the stores attracted by the fact that the entire back wall of the window was a mirror. He could see the reflection of the people who were passing by, and the people who were standing near him.

Somewhere behind him a young woman said, "Oh, look he's a hunchback. He's a little nigger hunchback. Rub his hump, for luck. We're going to need all the luck we can get to-night."

Michael glanced in the mirror, stared in the mirror. It is I, he thought. I am the one she means. It had not occurred to him to wonder what he would be like this time. He was a small black boy again, but not the same one. He had been frightfully thin before, and very dirty, ragged. He still was. But something had changed. He was hunchbacked now. He turned slightly so that he could see himself in profile. No question about it. He had a hump on his back. Yes, but—not really. He could fly if he wanted to. His feet felt light. He had wings again. The wings made him look like that, wings folded under the brown leather jacket. He wondered if they were his own big powerful wings. He decided to find out. He went up, up, up. There was light all around him as he soared. He was aware that people in the street were staring up at him. He heard an astonished murmur, and then quite clearly, a child's voice, high, shrill, "Look, Mommy, look, it's Superman!"

A woman said, "Nonsense, it's one of those balloon things from Macy's. Come along, come along now."

Michael flew low over the city, trying to decide where he would land. He picked a dark side street, and landed lightly, on his feet.

The door of a nearby building opened and he heard loud voices, saw a lighted interior filled with men who were standing in front of a long counter drinking out of small glasses. There was a sudden gust of wind and his nostrils caught the noisome smell of fermented grain. He decided that it came from some foul earthly brew these men were drinking.

Then a man lurched out of the door. He came down the steps toward the street, a small black man, swaying back and forth. When he reached the sidewalk he stood still staring at Michael.

He put his arm in front of his eyes and then slowly removed it. "Oh, my God," he said and recovered his eyes. "I shouldn't have," he muttered, "I knew," and he took his arm away and looked at Michael again, "I knew I shouldn't have took that last drink."

Michael said, "I—"

"Go away," the man pleaded. "Go away. Just go away." He started backing up the steps, backing toward the door, opened it and shouted, "Call the law. Somebody call the law." His voice kept rising in pitch until it sounded like a scream, "Somebody call the law!"

Men crowded into the doorway shouting, "Whatsamatter with you?" "Whyn't you go on home and sleep it off?"

Then they saw Michael. There was silence.

As he walked back and forth, he was giving off light. The dark mean little side street was filled with a soft light that emanated from his wings, from his robe. People were coming to the windows of the houses, looking down at him, pointing.

Someone said softly, "What in hell is it?"

Michael walked slowly down the street, and a bottle smashed on the sidewalk just in front of him. A brick grazed his shoulder. The light he was emitting faded, faded, faded—was gone. By the time he turned the corner he had lost the power to fly, it had gone out of him.

He walked a long way and then suddenly he was on a long wide brilliantly lighted street. It was filled with people, all carrying bundles and packages, all walking with the same hurried gait that he had now come to recognize.

He stopped in front of one of the stores because he caught a glimpse of himself in the window. Or at least he assumed that his was the small white face quite close to the window, a kind of hunger in the eyes. He was a ragged boy again, dirty, unkempt. But this time his skin was white. He was freckled. His head looked too big for his emaciated body. His tow-colored hair was matted, obviously needed cutting, needed brushing, needed washing. He shivered from the cold and the child reflected in the window shivered, too.

A young black man inside the store saw him looking in the window and frowned at him, and then came to the door, and shouted, "Whyn' you damn honkey kids stay over on Amsterdam where you belong? Get away from here before I call a cop—" He mumbled something else that sounded like a threat, and Michael moved away, hurrying.

On an impulse he followed the sound of music down a flight of steps. It was beginning to snow and he was so cold that he knew he had to find shelter somewhere or freeze to death. Besides he was hungry and he could smell food cooking and he decided that he was going to eat even if he had to steal the food.

Opening a door at the foot of a short flight of stairs he found himself in a long narrow room. Once inside he saw there was a long counter that ran the length of the room. There was a man in a tall chef's cap and a white coat standing behind the counter, a man with skin so black that Michael stared at him.

He said, "Could you please give me something to eat?"

The black man said, "Sure, wait a minute." He moved so quickly that Michael could scarcely follow all the motions he made, and then the man put two thick sandwiches down on the counter, sandwiched with big juicy looking pieces of meat inside them, and a glass of milk, and then he leaned on the counter.

Michael said, "I haven't any money," and one thin white hand was already reaching towards the thick sandwiches.

"It's on the house," the counterman said. "Night before Christmas everybody in the whole wide world oughtta have more'n they can eat."

The sandwiches were good. Michael finished them quickly and then gulped down the milk.

The counterman had watched him eat with a kind of satisfaction. When he had finished the man said, "Your folks all right?" And without waiting for an answer said, "That's fine. Well, Merry Christmas to you. Here you better take along somethin' sweet for the road." He handed Michael a candy bar.

Michael looked around the room as he slowly unwrapped the candy bar. There were signs on the wall, "No Trust," and "Let's Be Friends," and close by there was a huge yellow cat sitting on a chair. He was certain the cat was purring from the way it was sitting, its feet tucked under it, its back humped over in a big fat curve. There was a wreath on the wall with Merry Christmas spelled out in red letters. It was a snug place filled with a steamy warmth and the mouth-watering smell of food. He hated to leave. He kept thinking, What if I can't fly? Where will I go? What will I do?

The man behind the counter said, "Where you bound for?"

"I don't know. I—"

"I got a cot in the back. You can stay here if you want to."

Michael thought, enough to report on? Well, of course, yes. And what will I say? Simply the mixture as before: neither all good nor all evil. The good sometimes outweighs the evil and sometimes it doesn't.

He headed towards the door because that old familiar feeling of buoyancy had returned. He was growing taller and taller and he had to hurry before he got too tall for the doorway.

He said, "I'm all right now. I've got a place to stay. Good-bye and thank you very kindly."

As he left he saw that the counterman was staring at him, mouth open. Michael knew that it must be a frightening experience for a mortal to witness a transformation like this, watch it take place, watch the big powerful wings begin to expand, watch the light that was emanating from them.

"What—what—" the counterman said.

Michael thought there ought to be something he could say to the man that would explain this transformation.

Outside on the street, just before he soared straight up he shouted, "Home! I'm going home!"

Then he was gone up, up into the cold air, with the wind against his face, exulting in his own power and speed.

1989

SANDRA CISNEROS

Three Wise Guys

THE BIG BOX came marked DO NOT OPEN TILL XMAS, but the mama said not until the Day of the Three Kings. Not until *Dia de los Reyes*, the sixth of January, do you hear? That is what the mama said exactly, only she said it all in Spanish. Because in Mexico where she was raised, it is the custom for boys and girls to receive their presents on January sixth, and not Christmas, even though they were living on the Texas side of the river now. Not until the sixth of January.

Yesterday the mama had risen in the dark same as always to reheat the coffee in a tin saucepan and warm the breakfast tortillas. The papa had gotten up coughing and spitting up the night, complaining how the evening before the buzzing of the insects had kept him from sleeping. By the time the mama had the house smelling of oatmeal and cinnamon, the papa would be gone to the fields, the sun already tangled in the trees and the *urracas* screeching their rubber-screech cry. The boy Ruben and the girl Rosalinda would have to be shaken awake for school. The mama would give the baby Gilberto his bottle and then she would go back to sleep before getting up again to the chores that were always waiting. That is how the world had been.

But today the big box had arrived. When the boy Ruben and the girl Rosalinda came home from school, it was already sitting in the living room in front of the television set that no longer worked. Who had put it there? Where had it come from? A box covered with red paper with green Christmas trees and a card on top that said "Merry Christmas to the Gonzalez Family. Frank, Earl, and Dwight Travis. P.S. DO NOT OPEN TILL XMAS." That's all.

Two times the mama was made to come into the living room, first to explain to the children and later to their father how the brothers Travis had arrived in the blue pickup, and how it had taken all three of those big men to lift the box off the back of the truck and bring it inside, and how she had

had to nod and say thank-you thank-you thank-you over and over because those were the only words she knew in English. Then the brothers Travis had nodded as well, the way they always did when they came and brought the boxes of clothes, or the turkey each November, or the canned ham on Easter, ever since the children had begun to earn high grades at the school where Dwight Travis was the principal.

But this year the Christmas box was bigger than usual. What could be in a box so big? The boy Ruben and the girl Rosalinda begged all afternoon to be allowed to open it, and that is when the mama had said the sixth of January, the Day of the Three Kings. Not a day sooner.

It seemed the weeks stretched themselves wider and wider since the arrival of the big box. The mama got used to sweeping around it because it was too heavy for her to push in a corner. But since the television no longer worked ever since the afternoon the children had poured iced tea through the little grates in the back, it really didn't matter if the box obstructed the view. Visitors that came inside the house were told and told again the story of how the box had arrived, and then each was made to guess what was inside.

It was the *comadre* Elodia who suggested over coffee one afternoon that the big box held a portable washing machine that could be rolled away when not in use, the kind she had seen in her Sears Roebuck catalog. The mama said she hoped so because the wringer washer she had used for the last ten years had finally gotten tired and quit. These past few weeks she had had to boil all the clothes in the big pot she used for cooking the Christmas tamales. Yes. She hoped the big box was a portable washing machine. A washing machine, even a portable one, would be good.

But the neighbor man Cayetano said, What foolishness, *comadre*. Can't you see the box is too small to hold a washing machine, even a portable one. Most likely God has heard your prayers and sent a new color TV. With a good antenna you could catch all the Mexican soap operas, the neighbor man said. You could distract yourself with the complicated troubles of the rich and then give thanks to God for the blessed simplicity of your poverty. A new TV would surely be the end to all your miseries.

Each night when the papa came home from the fields, he would spread newspapers on the cot in the living room, where the boy Ruben and the girl Rosalinda slept, and sit facing the big box in the center of the room. Each night he imagined the box held something different. The day before yesterday he guessed a new record player. Yesterday an ice chest filled with beer.

Today the papa sat with his bottle of beer, fanning himself with a magazine, and said in a voice as much a plea as a prophecy: air conditioner.

But the boy Ruben and the girl Rosalinda were sure the big box was filled with toys. They had even punctured it in one corner with a pencil when their mother was busy cooking, but they could see nothing inside but blackness.

Only the baby Gilberto remained uninterested in the contents of the big box and seemed each day more fascinated with the exterior of the box rather than the interior. One afternoon he tore off a fistful of paper, which he was chewing when his mother swooped him up with one arm, rushed him to the kitchen sink, and forced him to swallow handfuls of lukewarm water in case the red dye of the wrapping paper might be poisonous.

When Christmas Eve finally came, the family Gonzalez put on their good clothes and went to Midnight Mass. They came home to a house that smelled of tamales and *atole*, and everyone was allowed to open one present before going to sleep. But the big box was to remain untouched until the sixth of January.

On New Year's Eve the little house was filled with people, some related, some not, coming in and out. The friends of the papa came with bottles, and the mama set out a bowl of grapes to count off the New Year. That night the children did not sleep in the living room cot as they usually did, because the living room was crowded with big-fannied ladies and fat-stomached men sashaying to the accordion music of the dwarf twins from McAllen. Instead the children fell asleep on a lump of handbags and crumpled suit jackets on top of the mama and the papa's bed, dreaming of the contents of the big box.

Finally, the fifth of January. And the boy Ruben and the girl Rosalinda could hardly sleep. All night they whispered last-minute wishes. The boy thought perhaps if the big box held a bicycle, he would be the first to ride it, since he was the oldest. This made his sister cry until the mama had to yell from her bedroom on the other side of the plastic curtains, Be quiet or I'm going to give you each the stick, which sounds worse in Spanish than it does in English. Then no one said anything. After a very long time, long after they heard the mama's wheezed breathing and the papa's piped snoring, the children closed their eyes and remembered nothing.

The papa was already in the bathroom coughing up the night before from his throat when the *urracas* began their clownish chirping. The boy Ruben awoke and shook his sister. The mama, frying the potatoes and beans for breakfast, nodded permission for the box to be opened.

With a kitchen knife the boy Ruben cut a careful edge along the top. The girl Rosalinda tore the Christmas wrapping with her fingernails. The papa and the mama lifted the cardboard flaps and everyone peered inside to see what it was the brothers Travis had brought them on the Day of the Three Kings.

There were layers of balled newspaper packed on top. When these had been cleared the boy Ruben looked inside. The girl Rosalinda looked inside. The papa and the mama looked.

This is what they saw: the complete Britannica Junior Encyclopaedia, twenty-four volumes in red imitation leather with gold-embossed letters, beginning with Volume I, Aar–Bel and ending with Volume XXIV, Yel–Zyn. The girl Rosalinda let out a sad cry, as if her hair was going to be cut again. The boy Ruben pulled out Volume IV, Ded–Fem. There were many pictures and many words, but there were more words than pictures. The papa flipped through Volume XXII, but because he could not read English words, simply put the book back and grunted.

What can we do with this? No one said anything, and shortly after, the screen door slammed.

Only the mama knew what to do with the contents of the big box. She withdrew Volumes VI, VII, and VIII, marched off to the dinette set in the kitchen, placed two on Rosalinda's chair so she could better reach the table, and put one underneath the plant stand that danced.

When the boy and the girl returned from school that day they found the books stacked into squat pillars against one living room wall and a board placed on top. On this were arranged several plastic doilies and framed family photographs. The rest of the volumes the baby Gilberto was playing with, and he was already rubbing his sore gums along the corners of Volume XIV.

The girl Rosalinda also grew interested in the books. She took out her colored pencils and painted blue on the eyelids of all the illustrations of women and with a red pencil dipped in spit she painted their lips and fingernails red-red. After a couple of days, when all the pictures of women had been colored in this manner, she began to cut out some of the prettier pictures and paste them on loose-leaf paper.

One volume suffered from being exposed to the rain when the papa improvised a hat during a sudden shower. He forgot it on the hood of the car when he drove off. When the children came home from school they set it on the porch to dry. But the pages puffed up and became so fat, the book was impossible to close.

Only the boy Ruben refused to touch the books. For several days he avoided the principal because he didn't know what to say in case Mr. Travis were to ask how they were enjoying the Christmas present.

On the Saturday after New Year's the mama and the papa went into town for groceries and left the boy in charge of watching his sister and baby brother. The girl Rosalinda was stacking books into spiral staircases and making her paper dolls descend them in a fancy manner.

Perhaps the boy Ruben would not have bothered to open the volume left on the kitchen table if he had not seen his mother wedge her name-day corsage in its pages. On the page where the mama's carnation lay pressed between two pieces of Kleenex was a picture of a dog in a space ship. FIRST DOG IN SPACE the caption said. The boy turned to another page and read where cashews came from.

And then about the man who invented the guillotine. And then about Bengal tigers. And about clouds.

All afternoon the boy read, even after the mama and the papa came home. Even after the sun set, until the mama said time to sleep and put the light out.

In their bed on the other side of the plastic curtain the mama and the papa slept. Across from them in the crib slept the baby Gilberto. The girl Rosalinda slept on her end of the cot. But the boy Ruben watched the night sky turn from violet. To blue. To gray. And then from gray. To blue. To violet once again.

1990

Inn

CHRISTMAS EVE. *The organ played the last notes of "O Come, O Come, Emmanuel," and the choir sat down. Reverend Wall hobbled slowly to the pulpit, clutching his sheaf of yellowed typewritten sheets.*

In the choir, Dee leaned over to Sharon and whispered, "Here we go. Twenty-four minutes and counting."

On Sharon's other side, Virginia murmured, "'And all went to be taxed, every one into his own city.'"

Reverend Wall set the papers on the pulpit, looked rheumily out over the congregation, and said, "'And all went to be taxed, every one into his own city. And Joseph also went up from Galilee, out of the city of Nazareth, into Judea, unto the city of David, which is called Bethlehem, because he was of the house and lineage of David. To be taxed with Mary, his espoused wife, being great with child.'" He paused.

"We know nothing of that journey up from Nazareth," Virginia whispered.

"We know nothing of that journey up from Nazareth," Reverend Wall said, in a wavering voice, "what adventures befell the young couple, what inns they stopped at along the way. All we know is that on a Christmas Eve like this one they arrived in Bethlehem, and there was no room for them at the inn."

Virginia was scribbling something on the margin of her bulletin. Dee started to cough. "Do you have any cough drops?" she whispered to Sharon.

"What happened to the ones I gave you last night?" Sharon whispered back.

"Though we know nothing of their journey," Reverend Wall said, his voice growing stronger, "we know much of the world they lived in. It was a world of censuses and soldiers, of bureaucrats and politicians, a world busy with property and rules and its own affairs."

Dee started to cough again. She rummaged in the pocket of her music folder and came up with a paper-wrapped cough drop. She unwrapped it and popped it into her mouth.

"*. . . a world too busy with its own business to even notice an insignificant couple from far away,*" *Reverend Wall intoned.*

Virginia passed her bulletin to Sharon. Dee leaned over to read it, too. It read, "What happened here last night after the rehearsal? When I came home from the mall, there were police cars outside."

Dee grabbed the bulletin and rummaged in her folder again. She found a pencil, scribbled, "Somebody broke into the church," and passed it across Sharon to Virginia.

"You're kidding," Virginia whispered. "Were they caught?"

"No," Sharon said.

The rehearsal on the twenty-third was supposed to start at seven. By a quarter to eight the choir was still standing at the back of the sanctuary waiting to sing the processional, the shepherds and angels were bouncing off the walls, and Reverend Wall, in his chair behind the pulpit, had nodded off. The assistant minister, Reverend Lisa Farrison, was moving poinsettias onto the chancel steps to make room for the manger, and the choir director, Rose Henderson, was on her knees, hammering wooden bases onto the cardboard palm trees. They had fallen down twice already.

"What do you think are the chances we'll still be here when it's time for the Christmas Eve service to start tomorrow night?" Sharon said, leaning against the sanctuary door.

"I can't be," Virginia said, looking at her watch. "I've got to be out at the mall before nine. Megan suddenly announced she wants Senior Prom Barbie."

"My throat feels terrible," Dee said, feeling her glands. "Is it hot in here, or am I getting a fever?"

"It's hot in these *robes*," Sharon said. "Why *are* we wearing them? This is a rehearsal."

"Rose wanted everything to be exactly like it's going to be tomorrow night."

"If I'm exactly like this tomorrow night, I'll be dead," Dee said, trying to clear her throat. "I *can't* get sick. I don't have any of the presents wrapped, and I haven't even *thought* about what we're having for Christmas dinner."

"At least you *have* presents," Virginia said. "I have eight people left to buy for. Not counting Senior Prom Barbie."

"I don't have anything done. Christmas cards, shopping, wrapping, baking, nothing, and Bill's parents are coming," Sharon said. "Come *on*, let's get this show on the road."

Rose and one of the junior choir angels hoisted the palm trees to standing. They listed badly to the right, as if Bethlehem were experiencing a
hurricane. "Is that straight?" Rose called to the back of the church.

"Yes," Sharon said.

"Lying in church," Dee said. "Tsk, tsk."

"All right," Rose said, picking up a bulletin. "Listen up, everybody. Here's
the order of worship. Introit by the brass quartet, processional, opening
prayer, announcements—Reverend Farrison, is that where you want to talk
about the 'Least of These' Project?"

"Yes," Reverend Farrison said. She walked to the front of the sanctuary.
"And can I make a quick announcement right now?" She turned and faced
the choir. "If anybody has anything else to donate, you need to bring it to
the church by tomorrow morning at nine," she said briskly. "That's when
we're going to deliver the donations to the homeless. We still need blankets
and canned goods. Bring them to the Fellowship Hall."

She walked back down the aisle, and Rose started in on her list again. "Announcements, 'O Come, O Come, Emmanuel,' Reverend Wall's sermon—"

Reverend Wall nodded awake at his name. "Ah," he said, and hobbled
toward the pulpit, clutching a sheaf of yellowed typewritten papers.

"Oh, no," Sharon said. "Not a Christmas pageant *and* a sermon. We'll be
here forever."

"Not *a* sermon," Virginia said. "*The* sermon. All twenty-four minutes of
it. I've got it memorized. He's given it every year since he came."

"Longer than that," Dee said. "I swear last year I heard him say something in it about World War I."

"'And all went to be taxed, every one into his own city,'" Reverend Wall
said. "'And Joseph also went up from Galilee, out of the city of Nazareth.'"

"Oh, *no*," Sharon said. "He's going to give the whole sermon right now."

"We know nothing of that journey up from Bethlehem," he said.

"Thank you, Reverend Wall," Rose said. "After the sermon, the choir
sings 'O Little Town of Bethlehem' and Mary and Joseph—"

"What message does the story of their journey hold for us?" Reverend
Wall said, picking up steam.

Rose was hurrying up the aisle and up the chancel steps. "Reverend Wall,
you don't need to run through your sermon right now."

"What does it say to us," he asked, "struggling to recover from a world
war?"

Dee nudged Sharon.

"Reverend *Wall*," Rose said, reaching the pulpit. "I'm afraid we don't have time to go through your whole sermon right now. We need to run through the pageant now."

"Ah," he said, and gathered up his papers.

"All right," Rose said. "The choir sings 'O Little Town of Bethlehem' and Mary and Joseph, you come down the aisle."

Mary and Joseph, wearing bathrobes and Birkenstocks, assembled themselves at the back of the sanctuary and started down the center aisle.

"No, no, Mary and Joseph, not that way," Rose said. "The wise men from the East have to come down the center aisle, and you're coming up from Nazareth. You two come down the side aisle."

Mary and Joseph obliged, taking the aisle at a trot.

"No, no, slow *down*," Rose said. "You're tired. You've walked all the way from Nazareth. Try it again."

They raced each other to the back of the church and started again, slower at first and then picking up speed.

"The congregation won't be able to see them," Rose said, shaking her head. "What about lighting the side aisle? Can we do that, Reverend Farrison?"

"She's not here," Dee said. "She went to get something."

"I'll go get her," Sharon said, and went down the hall.

Miriam Hoskins was just going into the adult Sunday school room with a paper plate of frosted cookies. "Do you know where Reverend Farrison is?" Sharon asked her.

"She was in the office a minute ago," Miriam said, pointing with the plate.

Sharon went down to the office. Reverend Farrison was standing at the desk, talking on the phone. "How soon can the van be here?" She motioned to Sharon she'd be a minute. "Well, can you find out?"

Sharon waited, looking at the desk. There was a glass dish of paper-wrapped cough drops next to the phone, and beside it a can of smoked oysters and three cans of water chestnuts. *Probably for the "Least of These" Project*, she thought ruefully.

"Fifteen minutes? All right. Thank you," Reverend Farrison said, and hung up. "Just a minute," she told Sharon, and went to the outside door. She opened it and leaned out. Sharon could feel the icy air as she stood there. She wondered if it had started snowing.

"The van will be here in a few minutes," Reverend Farrison said to someone outside.

Sharon looked out the stained-glass panels on either side of the door, trying to see who was out there.

"It'll take you to the shelter," Reverend Farrison said. "No, you'll have to wait outside." She shut the door. "Now," she said, turning to Sharon, "what did *you* want, Mrs. Englert?"

Sharon said, still looking out the window, "They need you in the sanctuary." It *was* starting to snow. The flakes looked blue through the glass.

"I'll be right there," Reverend Farrison said. "I was just taking care of some homeless. That's the second couple we've had tonight. We always get them at Christmas. What's the problem? The palm trees?"

"What?" Sharon said, still looking at the snow.

Reverend Farrison followed her gaze. "The shelter van's coming for them in a few minutes," she said. "We can't let them stay in here unsupervised. First Methodist's had their collection stolen twice in the last month, and we've got all the donations for the 'Least of These' Project in there." She gestured toward the Fellowship Hall.

I thought they were *for the homeless*, Sharon thought. "Couldn't they just wait in the sanctuary or something?" she said.

Reverend Farrison sighed. "Letting them in isn't doing them a kindness. They come here instead of the shelter because the shelter confiscates their liquor." She started down the hall. "What did they need me for?"

"Oh," Sharon said, "the lights. They wanted to know if they could get lights over the side aisle for Mary and Joseph."

"I don't know," she said. "The lights in this church are such a mess." She stopped at the bank of switches next to the stairs that led down to the choir room and the Sunday school rooms. "Tell me what this turns on."

She flicked a switch. The hall light went off. She switched it back on and tried another one.

"That's the light in the office," Sharon said, "and the downstairs hall, and that one's the adult Sunday school room."

"What's this one?" Reverend Farrison said. There was a yelp from the choir members. Kids screamed.

"The sanctuary," Sharon said. "Okay, that's the side aisle lights." She called down to the sanctuary. "How's that?"

"Fine," Rose called. "No, wait, the organ's off."

Reverend Farrison flicked another switch, and the organ came on with a groan.

"Now the side lights are off," Sharon said, "and so's the pulpit light."

"I told you they were a mess," Reverend Farrison said. She flicked another switch. "What did that do?"

"It turned the porch light off."

"Good. We'll leave it off. Maybe it will discourage any more homeless from coming," she said. "Reverend Wall let a homeless man wait inside last week, and he relieved himself on the carpet in the adult Sunday school room. We had to have it cleaned." She looked reprovingly at Sharon. "With these people, you can't let your compassion get the better of you."

No, Sharon thought. *Jesus did, and look what happened to him.*

"The innkeeper could have turned them away," Reverend Wall intoned. "He was a busy man, and his inn was full of travelers. He could have shut the door on Mary and Joseph."

Virginia leaned across Sharon to Dee. "Did whoever broke in take anything?"

"No," Sharon said.

"Whoever it was urinated on the floor in the nursery," Dee whispered, and Reverend Wall trailed off confusedly and looked over at the choir.

Dee began coughing loudly, trying to smother it with her hand. He smiled vaguely at her and started again. "The innkeeper could have turned them away."

Dee waited a minute, and then opened her hymnal to her bulletin and began writing on it. She passed it to Virginia, who read it and then passed it back to Sharon.

"Reverend Farrison thinks some of the homeless got in," it read. "They tore up the palm trees, too. Ripped the bases right off. Can you imagine anybody doing something like that?"

"As the innkeeper found room for Mary and Joseph that Christmas Eve long ago," Reverend Wall said, building to a finish, "let us find room in our hearts for Christ. Amen."

The organ began the intro to "O Little Town of Bethlehem," and Mary and Joseph appeared at the back with Miriam Hoskins. She adjusted Mary's white veil and whispered something to them. Joseph pulled at his glued-on beard.

"What route did they finally decide on?" Virginia whispered. "In from the side or straight down the middle?"

"Side aisle," Sharon whispered.

The choir stood up. "'O little town of Bethlehem, how still we see thee lie,'" they sang. "'Above thy deep and dreamless sleep, the silent stars go by.'"

Mary and Joseph started up the side aisle, taking the slow, measured steps Rose had coached them in, side by side. No, Sharon thought. That's not right. They didn't look like that. Joseph should be a little ahead of Mary, protecting her, and her hand should be on her stomach, protecting the baby.

*

They eventually decided to wait on the decision of how Mary and Joseph would come, and started through the pageant. Mary and Joseph knocked on the door of the inn, and the innkeeper, grinning broadly, told them there wasn't any room.

"Patrick, don't look so happy," Rose said. "You're supposed to be in a bad mood. You're busy and tired, and you don't have any rooms left."

Patrick attempted a scowl. "I have no rooms left," he said, "but you can stay in the stable." He led them over to the manger, and Mary knelt down behind it.

"Where's the baby Jesus?" Rose said.

"He's not due till tomorrow night," Virginia whispered.

"Does anybody have a baby doll they can bring?" Rose asked.

One of the angels raised her hand, and Rose said, "Fine. Mary, use the blanket for now, and, choir, you sing the first verse of 'Away in a Manger.' Shepherds," she called to the back of the sanctuary, "as *soon* as 'Away in a Manger' is over, come up and stand on *this* side." She pointed.

The shepherds picked up an assortment of hockey sticks, broom handles, and canes taped to one-by-twos and adjusted their headcloths.

"All right, let's run through it," Rose said. "Organ?"

The organ played the opening chord, and the choir stood up.

"A-way," Dee sang and started to cough, choking into her hand.

"Do—cough—drop?" she managed to gasp out between spasms.

"I saw some in the office," Sharon said, and ran down the chancel steps, down the aisle, and out into the hall.

It was dark, but she didn't want to take the time to try to find the right switch. She could more or less see her way by the lights from the sanctuary, and she thought she knew right where the cough drops were.

The office lights were off, too, and the porch light Reverend Farrison had turned off to discourage the homeless. She opened the office door, felt her way over to the desk, and patted around till she found the glass dish. She grabbed a handful of cough drops and felt her way back out into the hall.

The choir was singing "It Came Upon a Midnight Clear," but after two measures they stopped, and in the sudden silence Sharon heard knocking.

She started for the door and then hesitated, wondering if this was the same couple Reverend Farrison had turned away earlier, coming back to make trouble, but the knocking was soft, almost diffident, and through the stained-glass panels she could see it was snowing hard.

She switched the cough drops to her left hand, opened the door a little, and looked out. There were two people standing on the porch, one in front of the other. It was too dark to do more than make out their outlines, and at first glance it looked like two women, but then the one in front said in a young man's voice, "*Erkas.*"

"I'm sorry," Sharon said. "I don't speak Spanish. Are you looking for a place to stay?" The snow was turning to sleet, and the wind was picking up.

"*Kumrah,*" the young man said, making a sound like he was clearing his throat, and then a whole string of words she didn't recognize.

"Just a minute," she said, and shut the door. She went back into the office, felt for the phone, and, squinting at the buttons in the near-darkness, punched in the shelter number.

It was busy. She held down the receiver, waited a minute, and tried again. Still busy. She went back to the door, hoping they'd given up and gone away.

"*Erkas,*" the man said as soon as she opened it.

"I'm sorry," she said. "I'm trying to call the homeless shelter," and he began talking rapidly, excitedly.

He stepped forward and put his hand on the door. He had a blanket draped over him; which was why she'd mistaken him for a woman. "*Erkas,*" he said, and he sounded upset, desperate, and yet somehow still diffident, timid.

"*Bott lom,*" he said, gesturing toward the woman, who was standing back almost to the edge of the porch, but Sharon wasn't looking at her. She was looking at their feet.

They were wearing sandals. At first she thought they were barefoot and she squinted through the darkness, horrified. Barefoot in the snow! Then she glimpsed the dark line of a strap, but they still might as well be. And it was snowing hard.

She couldn't leave them outside, but she didn't dare bring them into the hall to wait for the van either, not with Reverend Farrison around.

The office was out—the phone might ring—and she couldn't put them in the Fellowship Hall with all the stuff for the homeless in there.

"Just a minute," she said, shutting the door, and went to see if Miriam was still in the adult Sunday school room. It was dark, so she obviously wasn't, but there was a lamp on the table by the door. She switched it on. No, this wouldn't work either, not with the communion silver in a display case against the wall, and anyway, there was a stack of paper cups on the table, and the plates of Christmas cookies Miriam had been carrying, which meant there'd be refreshments in here after the rehearsal. She switched off the light, and went out into the hall.

Not Reverend Wall's office—it was locked anyway—and certainly not Reverend Farrison's, and if she took them downstairs to one of the Sunday school rooms, she'd just have to sneak them back up again.

The furnace room? It was between the adult Sunday school room and the Fellowship Hall. She tried the doorknob. It opened, and she looked in. The furnace filled practically the whole room, and what it didn't was taken up by a stack of folding chairs. There wasn't a light switch she could find, but the pilot light gave off enough light to maneuver by. And it was warmer than the porch.

She went back to the door, looked down the hall to make sure nobody was coming, and let them in. "You can wait in here," she said, even though it was obvious they couldn't understand her.

They followed her through the dark hall to the furnace room, and she opened out two of the folding chairs so they could sit down, and motioned them in.

"It Came Upon a Midnight Clear" ground to a halt, and Rose's voice came drifting out of the sanctuary. "Shepherd's crooks are not weapons. All right. Angel?"

"I'll call the shelter," Sharon said hastily, and shut the door on them.

She crossed to the office and tried the shelter again. "Please, please answer," she said, and when they did, she was so surprised, she forgot to tell them the couple would be inside.

"It'll be at least half an hour," the man said. "Or forty-five minutes."

"Forty-five minutes?"

"It's like this whenever it gets below zero," the man said. "We'll try to make it sooner."

At least she'd done the right thing—they couldn't possibly stand out in that snow for forty-five minutes. The right thing, she thought ruefully, sticking them in the furnace room. But at least it was warm in there and out of the snow. And they were safe, as long as nobody came out to see what had happened to her.

"Dee," she said suddenly. Sharon was supposed to have come out to get her some cough drops.

They were lying on the desk where she'd laid them while she phoned. She snatched them up and took off down the hall and into the sanctuary.

The angel was on the chancel steps, exhorting the shepherds not to be afraid. Sharon threaded her way through them up to the chancel and sat down between Dee and Virginia.

She handed the cough drops to Dee, who said, "What took you so long?"

"I had to make a phone call. What did I miss?"

"Not a thing. We're still on the shepherds. One of the palm trees fell over and had to be fixed, and then Reverend Farrison stopped the rehearsal to tell everybody not to let homeless people into the church, that Holy Trinity had had its sanctuary vandalized."

"Oh," she said. She gazed out over the sanctuary, looking for Reverend Farrison.

"All right, now, after the angel makes her speech," Rose said, "she's joined by a multitude of angels. That's *you*, junior choir. No. Line up on the steps. Organ?"

The organ struck up "Hark, the Herald Angels Sing," and the junior choir began singing in piping, nearly inaudible voices.

Sharon couldn't see Reverend Farrison anywhere. "Do you know where Reverend Farrison went?" she whispered to Dee.

"She went out just as you came in. She had to get something from the office."

The office. What if she heard them in the furnace room and opened the door and found them in there? She half stood.

"Choir," Rose said, glaring directly at Sharon. "Will you help the junior choir by humming along with them?"

Sharon sat back down, and after a minute Reverend Farrison came in from the back, carrying a pair of scissors.

"'Late in time, behold Him come,'" the junior choir sang, and Miriam stood up and went out.

"Where's Miriam going?" Sharon whispered.

"How would I know?" Dee said, looking curiously at her. "To get the refreshments ready, probably. Is something the matter?"

"No," she said.

Rose was glaring at Sharon again. Sharon hummed, "'Light and life to all He brings,'" willing the song to be over so she could go out, but as soon as it was over, Rose said, "All right, wise men," and a sixth-grader carrying a jewelry box started down the center aisle. "Choir, 'We Three Kings.' Organ?"

There were four long verses to "We Three Kings of Orient Are." Sharon couldn't wait.

"I have to go to the bathroom," she said. She set her folder on her chair and ducked down the stairs behind the chancel and through the narrow room that led to the side aisle. The choir called it the flower room because that was where they stored the out-of-season altar arrangements. They used it for sneaking out when they needed to leave church early, but right now there was barely room to squeeze through. The floor was covered with music stands and pots of silk Easter lilies, and a huge spray of red roses stood in front of the door to the sanctuary.

Sharon shoved it into the corner, stepping gingerly among the lilies, and opened the door.

"Balthazar, lay the gold in front of the manger, don't drop it. Mary, you're the Mother of God. Try not to look so scared," Rose said.

Sharon hurried down the side aisle and out into the hall, where the other two kings were waiting, holding perfume bottles.

"'Westward leading, still proceeding, guide us to thy perfect light,'" the choir sang.

The hall and office lights were still off, but light was spilling out of the adult Sunday school room all the way to the end of the hall. She could see that the furnace room door was still shut.

I'll call the shelter again, she thought, *and see if I can hurry them up, and if I can't, I'll take them downstairs till everybody's gone, and then take them to the shelter myself.*

She tiptoed past the open door of the adult Sunday school room so Miriam wouldn't see her, and then half sprinted down to the office and opened the door.

"Hi," Miriam said, looking up from the desk. She had an aluminum pitcher in one hand and was rummaging in the top drawer with the other. "Do you know where the secretary keeps the key to the kitchen? It's locked, and I can't get in."

"No," Sharon said, her heart still pounding.

"I need a spoon to stir the Kool-Aid," Miriam said, opening and shutting the side drawers of the desk. "She must have taken them home with her. I don't blame her. First Baptist had theirs stolen last month. They had to change all the locks."

Sharon glanced uneasily at the furnace room door.

"Oh, well," Miriam said, opening the top drawer again. "I'll have to make do with this." She pulled out a plastic ruler. "The kids won't care."

She started out and then stopped. "They're not done in there yet, are they?"

"No," Sharon said. "They're still on the wise men. I needed to call my husband to tell him to take the turkey out of the freezer."

"I've got to do that when I get home," Miriam said. She went across the hall and into the library, leaving the door open. Sharon waited a minute and then called the shelter. It was busy. She held her watch to the light from the hall. They'd said half an hour to forty-five minutes. By that time the rehearsal would be over and the hall would be full of people.

Less than half an hour. They were already singing "Myrrh is mine, its bitter perfume." All that was left was "Silent Night" and then "Joy to the World," and the angels would come streaming out for cookies and Kool-Aid.

She went over to the front door and peered out. Below zero, the woman at the shelter had said, and now there was sleet, slanting sharply across the parking lot.

She couldn't send them out in that without any shoes. And she couldn't keep them up here, not with the kids right next door. She was going to have to move them downstairs.

But where? Not the choir room. The choir would be taking their folders and robes back down there, and the pageant kids would be getting their coats out of the Sunday school rooms. And the kitchen was locked.

The nursery? That might work. It was at the other end of the hall from the choir room, but she would have to take them past the adult Sunday school room to the stairs, and the door was open.

"'Si-i-lent night, ho-oh-ly night,'" came drifting out of the sanctuary, and then was cut off, and she could hear Reverend Farrison's voice lecturing, probably about the dangers of letting the homeless into the church.

She glanced again at the furnace room door and then went into the adult Sunday school room. Miriam was setting out the paper cups on the table. She looked up. "Did you get through to your husband?"

"Yes," Sharon said. Miriam looked expectant.

"Can I have a cookie?" Sharon said at random.

"Take one of the stars. The kids like the Santas and the Christmas trees the best."

She grabbed up a bright yellow-frosted star. "Thanks," she said, and went out, pulling the door shut behind her.

"Leave it open," Miriam said. "I want to be able to hear when they're done."

Sharon opened the door back up half as far as she'd shut it, afraid any less would bring Miriam to the door to open it herself, and walked quietly to the furnace room.

The choir was on the last verse of "Silent Night." After that there was only "Joy to the World" and then the benediction. Open door or no open door, she was going to have to move them now. She opened the furnace room door.

They were standing where she had left them between the folding chairs, and she knew, without any proof, that they had stood there like that the whole time she had been gone.

The young man was standing slightly in front of the woman, the way he had at the door, only he wasn't a man, he was a boy, his beard as thin and wispy as an adolescent's, and the woman was even younger, a child of ten maybe, only she had to be older, because now that there was light from the half-open door of the adult Sunday school room Sharon could see that she was pregnant.

She regarded all this—the girl's awkward bulkiness and the boy's beard, the fact that they had not sat down, the fact that it was the light from the adult Sunday school room that was making her see now what she hadn't before—with some part of her mind that was still functioning, that was still thinking how long the van from the shelter would take, how to get them past Reverend Farrison, some part of her mind that was taking in the details that proved what she had already known the moment she opened the door.

"What are you *doing* here?" she whispered, and the boy opened his hands in a gesture of helplessness. "*Erkas,*" he said.

And that still-functioning part of her mind put her fingers to her lips in a gesture he obviously understood because they both looked instantly frightened. "You have to come with me," she whispered.

But then it stopped functioning altogether, and she was half running them past the open door and onto the stairs, not even hearing the organ blaring out "Joy to the world, the Lord is come," whispering, "Hurry! Hurry!" and they didn't know how to get down the steps, the girl turned around and came down backwards, her hands flat on the steps above, and the boy helped her down, step by step, as if they were clambering down rocks, and she tried to pull the girl along faster and nearly made her stumble, and even that didn't bring her to her senses.

She hissed, "Like this," and showed them how to walk down the steps, facing forward, one hand on the rail, and they paid no attention, they came down backwards like toddlers, and it took forever, the hymn she wasn't hearing was already at the end of the third verse and they were only halfway down, all of them panting hard, and Sharon scurrying back up above them as if that would hurry them, past wondering how she would ever get them up the stairs again, past thinking she would have to call the van and tell them not to come, thinking only, *Hurry, hurry,* and *How did they* get *here?*

She did not come to herself until she had herded them somehow down the hall and into the nursery, thinking, *It can't be locked, please don't let it be locked*, and it wasn't, and gotten them inside and pulled the door shut and tried to lock it, and it didn't have a lock, and she thought, *That must be why it wasn't locked*, an actual coherent thought, her first one since that moment when she opened the furnace room door—and seemed to come to herself.

She stared at them, breathing hard, and it *was* them, their never having seen stairs before was proof of that, if she needed any proof, but she didn't, she had known it the instant she saw them, there was no question.

She wondered if this was some sort of vision, the kind people were always getting where they saw Jesus's face on a refrigerator, or the Virgin Mary dressed in blue and white, surrounded by roses. But their rough brown cloaks were dripping melted snow on the nursery carpet, their feet in the useless sandals were bright red with cold, and they looked too frightened.

And they didn't look at all like they did in religious pictures. They were too short, his hair was greasy and his face was tough-looking, like a young punk's, and her veil looked like a grubby dishtowel and it didn't hang loose, it was tied around her neck and knotted in the back, and they were too young, almost as young as the children upstairs dressed like them.

They were looking around the room frightenedly, at the white crib and the rocking chair and the light fixture overhead. The boy fumbled in his sash and brought out a leather sack. He held it out to Sharon.

"How did you *get* here?" she said wonderingly. "You're supposed to be on your way to Bethlehem."

He thrust the bag at her, and when she didn't take it, untied the leather string and took out a crude-looking coin and held it out.

"You don't have to pay me," she said, which was ridiculous. He couldn't understand her. She held a flat hand up, pushing the coin away and shaking her head. That was a universal sign, wasn't it? And what was the sign for welcome? She spread her arms out, smiling at the youngsters. "You are welcome to stay here," she said, trying to put the meaning of the words into her voice. "Sit down. Rest."

They remained standing. Sharon pulled the rocking chair. "Sit, please."

Mary looked frightened, and Sharon put her hands on the arms of the chair and sat down to show her how. Joseph immediately knelt, and Mary tried awkwardly to.

"No, no!" Sharon said, and stood up so fast she set the rocking chair swinging. "Don't kneel. I'm nobody." She looked hopelessly at them. "How did you *get* here? You're not supposed to be here."

Joseph stood up. "*Erkas*," he said, and went over to the bulletin board.

It was covered with colored pictures from Jesus's life: Jesus healing the lame boy, Jesus in the temple, Jesus in the Garden of Gethsemane.

He pointed to the picture of the Nativity scene. "*Kumrah*," he said.

Does he recognize himself? she wondered, but he was pointing at the donkey standing by the manger. "*Erkas*," he said. "*Erkas*."

Did that mean "donkey," or something else? Was he demanding to know what she had done with theirs, or trying to ask her if she had one? In all the pictures, all the versions of the story, Mary was riding a donkey, but she had thought they'd gotten that part of the story wrong, as they had gotten everything else wrong, their faces, their clothes, and above all their youth, their helplessness.

"*Kumrah erkas*," he said. "*Kumrah erkas. Bott lom?*"

"I don't know," she said. "I don't know where Bethlehem is."

Or what to do with you, she thought. Her first instinct was to hide them here until the rehearsal was over and everybody had gone home. She couldn't let Reverend Farrison find them.

But surely as soon as she saw who they were, she would—what? Fall to her knees? Or call for the shelter's van? "That's the second couple tonight," she'd said when she shut the door. Sharon wondered suddenly if it was them she'd turned away, if they'd wandered around the parking lot, lost and frightened, and then knocked on the door again.

She couldn't let Reverend Farrison find them, but there was no reason for her to come into the nursery. All the children were upstairs, and the refreshments were in the adult Sunday school room. But what if she checked the rooms before she locked up?

I'll take them home with me, Sharon thought. *They'll be safe there.* If she could get them up the stairs and out of the parking lot before the rehearsal ended.

I got them down here without anybody seeing them, she thought. But even if she could manage it, which she doubted, if they didn't die of fright when she started the car and the seat belts closed down over them, home was no better than the shelter.

They had gotten lost through some accident of time and space, and ended up at the church. The way back—if there was a way back, there had to be a way back, they had to be at Bethlehem by tomorrow night—was here.

It occurred to her suddenly that maybe she shouldn't have let them in, that the way back was outside the north door. *But I couldn't not let them in,* she protested, *it was snowing, and they didn't have any shoes.*

But maybe if she'd turned them away, they would have walked off the porch and back into their own time. Maybe they still could.

She said, "Stay here," putting her hand up to show them what she meant, and went out of the nursery into the hall, shutting the door tightly behind her.

The choir was still singing "Joy to the World." They must have had to stop again. Sharon ran silently up the stairs and past the adult Sunday school room. Its door was still half open, and she could see the plates of cookies on the table. She opened the north door, hesitating a moment as if she expected to see sand and camels, and leaned out. It was still sleeting, and the cars had an inch of snow on them.

She looked around for something to wedge the door open with, pushed one of the potted palms over, and went out on the porch. It was slick, and she had to take hold of the wall to keep her footing. She stepped carefully to the edge of the porch and peered into the sleet, already shivering, looking for what? A lessening of the sleet, a spot where the darkness was darker, or not so dark? A light?

Nothing. After a minute she stepped off the porch, moving as cautiously as Mary and Joseph had going down the stairs, and made a circuit of the parking lot.

Nothing. If the way back had been out here, it wasn't now, and she was going to freeze if she stayed out here. She went back inside, and then stood there, staring at the door, trying to think what to do. *I've got to get help*, she thought, hugging her arms to herself for warmth. *I've got to tell somebody.* She started down the hall to the sanctuary.

The organ had stopped. "Mary and Joseph, I need to talk to you for a minute," Rose's voice said. "Shepherds, leave your crooks on the front pew. The rest of you, there are refreshments in the adult Sunday school room. Choir, don't leave. I need to go over some things with you."

There was a clatter of sticks and then a stampede, and Sharon was overwhelmed by shepherds elbowing their way to the refreshments. One of the wise men caught his Air Jordan in his robe and nearly fell down, and two of the angels lost their tinsel halos in their eagerness to reach the cookies.

Sharon fought through them and into the back of the sanctuary. Rose was in the side aisle, showing Mary and Joseph how to walk, and the choir was gathering up their music. Sharon couldn't see Dee.

Virginia came down the center aisle, stripping off her robe as she walked. Sharon went to meet her. "Do you know where Dee is?" she asked her.

"She went home," Virginia said, handing Sharon a folder. "You left this on your chair. Dee's voice was giving out completely, and I said, 'This is silly. Go home and go to bed.'"

"Virginia . . ." Sharon said.

"Can you put my robe away for me?" Virginia said, pulling her stole off her head. "I've got exactly ten minutes to get to the mall."

Sharon nodded absently, and Virginia draped it over her arm and hurried out. Sharon scanned the choir, wondering who else she could confide in.

Rose dismissed Mary and Joseph, who went off at a run, and crossed to the center aisle. "Rehearsal tomorrow night at 6:15," she said. "I need you in your robes and up here right on time, because I've got to practice with the brass quartet at 6:40. Any questions?"

Yes, Sharon thought, looking around the sanctuary. *Who can I get to help me?*

"What are we singing for the processional?" one of the tenors asked.

"'*Adeste Fideles*,'" Rose said. "Before you leave, let's line up so you can see who your partner is."

Reverend Wall was sitting in one of the back pews, looking at the notes to his sermon. Sharon sidled along the pew and sat down next to him.

"Reverend Wall," she said, and then had no idea how to start. "Do you know what *erkas* means? I think it's Hebrew."

He raised his head from his notes and peered at her. "It's Aramaic. It means 'lost.'"

"Lost." He'd been trying to tell her at the door, in the furnace room, downstairs. "We're lost."

"'Forgotten,'" Reverend Wall said. "'Misplaced.'"

Misplaced, all right. By two thousand years, an ocean, and how many miles?

"When Mary and Joseph journeyed up to Bethlehem from Nazareth, how did they go?" she asked, hoping he would say, "Why are you asking all these questions?" so she could tell him, but he said, "Ah. You weren't listening to my sermon. We know nothing of that journey, only that they arrived in Bethlehem."

Not at this rate, she thought.

"Pass in the anthem," Rose said from the chancel. "I've only got thirty copies, and I don't want to come up short tomorrow night."

Sharon looked up. The choir was leaving. "On this journey, was there anyplace where they might have gotten lost?" she said hurriedly.

"*Erkas* can also mean 'hidden, passed out of sight,'" he said. "Aramaic is very similar to Hebrew. In Hebrew, the word—"

"Reverend Wall," Reverend Farrison said from the center aisle. "I need to talk to you about the benediction."

"Ah. Do you want me to give it now?" he said, and stood up, clutching his papers.

Sharon took the opportunity to grab her folder and duck out. She ran downstairs after the choir.

There was no reason for any of the choir to go into the nursery, but she stationed herself in the hall, sorting through the music in her folder as if she were putting it in order, and trying to think what to do.

Maybe, if everyone went into the choir room, she could duck into the nursery or one of the Sunday school rooms and hide until everybody was gone. But she didn't know whether Reverend Farrison checked each of the rooms before leaving. Or worse, locked them.

She could tell her she needed to stay late, to practice the anthem, but she didn't think Reverend Farrison would trust her to lock up, and she didn't want to call attention to herself, to make Reverend Farrison think, "Where's Sharon Englert? I didn't see her leave." Maybe she could hide in the chancel, or the flower room, but that meant leaving the nursery unguarded.

She had to decide. The crowd was thinning out, the choir handing Rose their music and putting on their coats and boots. She had to do something. Reverend Farrison could come down the stairs any minute to search the nursery. But she continued to stand there, sorting blindly through her music, and Reverend Farrison came down the steps, carrying a ring of keys.

Sharon stepped back protectively, the way Joseph had, but Reverend Farrison didn't even see her. She went up to Rose and said, "Can you lock up for me? I've got to be at Emmanuel Lutheran at 9:30 to collect their 'Least of These' contributions."

"I was supposed to go meet with the brass quartet—" Rose said reluctantly.

Don't let Rose talk you out of it, Sharon thought.

"Be sure to lock *all* the doors, including the Fellowship Hall," Reverend Farrison said, handing her the keys.

"No, I've got mine," Rose said. "But—"

"And check the parking lot. There were some homeless hanging around earlier. Thanks."

She ran upstairs, and Sharon immediately went over to Rose. "Rose," she said.

Rose held out her hand for Sharon's anthem.

Sharon shuffled through her music and handed it to her. "I was wondering," she said, trying to keep her voice casual, "I need to stay and practice the music for tomorrow. I'd be glad to lock up for you. I could drop the keys by your house tomorrow morning."

"Oh, you're a godsend," Rose said. She handed Sharon the stack of music and got her keys out of her purse. "These are the keys to the outside doors, north door, east door, Fellowship Hall," she said, ticking them off so fast, Sharon couldn't see which was which, but it didn't matter. She could figure them out after everybody left.

"This is the choir room door," Rose said. She handed them to Sharon. "I *really* appreciate this. The brass quartet couldn't come to the rehearsal, they had a concert tonight, and I really need to go over the introit with them. They're having a terrible time with the middle part."

So am I, Sharon thought.

Rose yanked on her coat. "And after I meet with them, I've got to go over to Sara Berg's and pick up the baby Jesus." She stopped, her arm half in her coat sleeve. "Did you need me to stay and go over the music with you?"

"No!" Sharon said, alarmed. "No, I'll be fine. I just need to run through it a couple of times."

"Okay. Great. Thanks again," she said, patting her pockets for her keys. She took the key ring away from Sharon and unhooked her car keys. "You're a godsend, I mean it," she said, and took off up the stairs at a trot.

Two of the altos came out, pulling on their gloves. "Do you know what I've got to face when I get home?" Julia said. "Putting up the tree."

They handed their music to Sharon.

"I hate Christmas," Karen said. "By the time it's over, I'm worn to a frazzle."

They hurried up the stairs, still talking, and Sharon leaned into the choir room to make sure it was empty, dumped the music and Rose's robe on a chair, took off her robe, and went upstairs.

Miriam was coming out of the adult Sunday school room, carrying a pitcher of Kool-Aid. "Come on, Elizabeth," she called into the room. "We've got to get to Buymore before it closes. She managed to completely destroy her halo," she said to Sharon, "so now I've got to go buy some more tinsel. Elizabeth, we're the last ones *here*."

Elizabeth strolled out, holding a Christmas tree cookie in her mittened hand. She stopped halfway to the door to lick the cookie's frosting.

"Elizabeth," Miriam said. "Come on."

Sharon held the door for them, and Miriam went out, ducking her head against the driving sleet. Elizabeth dawdled after her, looking up at the sky.

Miriam waved. "See you tomorrow night."

"I'll be here," Sharon said, and shut the door. *I'll* still *be here*, she thought. *And what if they are? What happens then? Does the Christmas pageant disappear, and all the rest of it? The cookies and the shopping and the Senior Prom Barbies? And the church?*

She watched Miriam and Elizabeth through the stained-glass panel till she saw the car's taillights, purple through the blue glass, pull out of the parking lot, and then tried the keys one after the other, till she found the right one, and locked the door.

She checked quickly in the sanctuary and the bathrooms, in case somebody was still there, and then ran down the stairs to the nursery to make sure *they* were still there, that they hadn't disappeared.

They were there, sitting on the floor next to the rocking chair and sharing what looked like dried dates from an unfolded cloth. Joseph started to stand up as soon as he saw her poke her head in the door, but she motioned him back down. "Stay here," she said softly, and realized she didn't need to whisper. "I'll be back in a few minutes. I'm just going to lock the doors."

She pulled the door shut, and went back upstairs. It hadn't occurred to her they'd be hungry, and she had no idea what they were used to eating—unleavened bread? Lamb? Whatever it was, there probably wasn't any in the kitchen, but the deacons had had an Advent supper last week. With luck, there might be some chili in the refrigerator. Or, better yet, some crackers.

The kitchen was locked. She'd forgotten Miriam had said that, and anyway, one of the keys must open it. None of them did, and after she'd tried all of them twice she remembered they were Rose's keys, not Reverend Farrison's, and turned the lights on in the Fellowship Hall. There was tons of food in there, stacked on tables alongside the blankets and used clothes and toys. And all of it was in cans, just the way Reverend Farrison had specified in the bulletin.

Miriam had taken the Kool-Aid home, but Sharon hadn't seen her carrying any cookies. *The kids probably ate them all*, she thought, but she went into the adult Sunday school room and looked. There was half a paper plateful left, and Miriam had been right—the kids liked the Christmas trees and Santas the best—the only ones left were yellow stars. There was a stack of paper cups, too. She picked them both up and took them downstairs.

"I brought you some food," she said, and set the plate on the floor between them.

They were staring in alarm at her, and Joseph was scrambling to his feet.

"It's food," she said, bringing her hand to her mouth and pretending to chew. "Cakes."

Joseph was pulling on Mary's arm, trying to yank her up, and they were both staring, horrified, at her jeans and sweatshirt. She realized suddenly they must not have recognized her without her choir robe. Worse, the robe looked at least a little like their clothes, but this getup must have looked totally alien.

"I'll bring you something to drink," she said hastily, showing them the paper cups, and went out. She ran down to the choir room. Her robe was still draped over the chair where she'd dumped it, along with Rose's and the music. She put the robe on and then filled the paper cups at the water fountain and carried them back to the nursery.

They were standing, but when they saw her in the robe, they sat back down. She handed Mary one of the paper cups, but she only looked at her fearfully. Sharon held it out to Joseph. He took it, too firmly, and it crumpled, water spurting onto the carpet.

"That's okay, it doesn't matter," Sharon said, cursing herself for being an idiot. "I'll get you a real cup."

She ran upstairs, trying to think where there would be one. The coffee cups were in the kitchen, and so were the glasses, and she hadn't seen anything in the Fellowship Hall or the adult Sunday school room.

She smiled suddenly. "I'll get you a real cup," she repeated, and went into the adult Sunday school room and took the silver Communion chalice out of the display case. There were silver plates, too. She wished she'd thought of it sooner.

She went into the Fellowship Hall and got a blanket and took the things downstairs. She filled the chalice with water and took it in to them, and handed Mary the chalice, and this time Mary took it without hesitation and drank deeply from it.

Sharon gave Joseph the blanket. "I'll leave you alone so you can eat and rest," she said, and went out into the hall, pulling the door nearly shut again.

She went down to the choir room and hung up Rose's robe and stacked the music neatly on the table. Then she went up to the furnace room and folded up the folding chairs and stacked them against the wall. She checked the east door and the one in the Fellowship Hall. They were both locked.

She turned off the lights in the Fellowship Hall and the office, and then thought, *I should call the shelter,* and turned them back on. It had been an hour since she'd called. They had probably already come and not found anyone, but in case they were running really late, she'd better call.

The line was busy. She tried it twice and then called home. Bill's parents were there. "I'm going to be late," she told him. "The rehearsal's running long," and hung up, wondering how many lies she'd told so far tonight.

Well, it went with the territory, didn't it? Joseph lying about the baby being his, and the wise men sneaking out the back way, the Holy Family hightailing it to Egypt and the innkeeper lying to Herod's soldiers about where they'd gone.

And in the meantime, more hiding. She went back downstairs and opened the door gently, trying not to startle them, and then just stood there, watching.

They had eaten the cookies. The empty paper plate stood on the floor next to the chalice, not a crumb on it. Mary lay curled up like the child she was under the blanket, and Joseph sat with his back to the rocking chair, guarding her.

Poor things, she thought, leaning her cheek against the door. *Poor things. So young, and so far away from home.* She wondered what they made of it all. Did they think they had wandered into a palace in some strange kingdom? *There's stranger yet to come*, she thought, *shepherds and angels and old men from the east, bearing jewelry boxes and perfume bottles. And then Cana. And Jerusalem. And Golgotha.*

But for the moment, a place to sleep, out of the weather, and something to eat, and a few minutes of peace. How still we see thee lie. She stood there a long time, her cheek resting against the door, watching Mary sleep and Joseph trying to stay awake.

His head nodded forward, and he jerked it back, waking himself up, and saw Sharon. He stood up immediately, careful not to wake Mary, and came over to her, looking worried. "*Erkas kumrah*," he said. "*Bott lom?*"

"I'll go find it," she said.

She went upstairs and turned the lights on again and went into the Fellowship Hall. The way back wasn't out the north door, but maybe they had knocked at one of the other doors first and then come around to it when no one answered. The Fellowship Hall door was on the northwest corner. She unlocked it, trying key after key, and opened it. The sleet was slashing down harder than ever. It had already covered up the tire tracks in the parking lot.

She shut the door and tried the east door, which nobody used except for the Sunday service, and then the north door again. Nothing. Sleet and wind and icy air.

Now what? They had been on their way to Bethlehem from Nazareth, and somewhere along the way they had taken a wrong turn. But how? And where? She didn't even know what direction they'd been heading in. Up. Joseph had gone *up* from Nazareth, which meant north, and in "The First Nowell" it said the star was in the northwest.

She needed a map. The ministers' offices were locked, but there were books on the bottom shelf of the display case in the adult Sunday school room. Maybe one was an atlas.

It wasn't. They were all self-help books, about coping with grief and codependency and teenage pregnancy, except for an ancient-looking concordance and a Bible dictionary.

The Bible dictionary had a set of maps at the back. Early Israelite Settlements in Canaan, The Assyrian Empire, The Wanderings of the Israelites in the Wilderness. She flipped forward. The Journeys of Paul. She turned back a page. Palestine in New Testament Times.

She found Jerusalem easily, and Bethlehem should be northwest of it. There was Nazareth, where Mary and Joseph had started from, so Bethlehem had to be farther north.

It wasn't there. She traced her finger over the towns, reading the tiny print. Cana, Kedesh, Jericho, but no Bethlehem. Which was ridiculous. It had to be there. She started down from the north, marking each of the towns with her finger.

When she finally found it, it wasn't at all where it was supposed to be. Like them, she thought. It was south and a little west of Jerusalem, so close it couldn't be more than a few miles from the city.

She looked down at the bottom of the page for the map scale, and there was an inset labeled "Mary and Joseph's Journey to Bethlehem," with their route marked in broken red.

Nazareth was almost due north of Bethlehem, but they had gone east to the Jordan River, and then south along its banks. At Jericho they'd turned back west toward Jerusalem through an empty brown space marked Judean Desert.

She wondered if that was where they had gotten lost, the donkey wandering off to find water and them going after it and losing the path. If it was, then the way back lay southwest, but the church didn't have any doors that opened in that direction, and even if it did, they would open on a twentieth-century parking lot and snow, not on first-century Palestine.

How had they gotten here? There was nothing in the map to tell her what might have happened on their journey to cause this.

She put the dictionary back and pulled out the concordance.

There was a sound. A key, and somebody opening the door. She slapped the book shut, shoved it back into the bookcase, and went out into the hall. Reverend Farrison was standing at the door, looking scared. "Oh, Mrs. Englert," she said, putting her hand to her chest. "What are you still doing here? You scared me half to death."

That makes two of us, Sharon thought, her heart thumping. "I had to stay and practice," she said. "I told Rose I'd lock up. What are you doing here?"

"I got a call from the shelter," she said, opening the office door. "They got a call from us to pick up a homeless couple, but when they got here there was nobody outside."

She went in the office and looked behind the desk, in the corner next to the filing cabinets. "I was worried they got into the church," she said, coming out. "The last thing we need is someone vandalizing the church two days before Christmas." She shut the office door behind her. "Did you check all the doors?"

Yes, she thought, *and none of them led anywhere*. "Yes," she said. "They were all locked. And anyway, I would have heard anybody trying to get in. I heard you."

Reverend Farrison opened the door to the furnace room. "They could have sneaked in and hidden when everyone was leaving." She looked in at the stacked folding chairs and then shut the door. She started down the hall toward the stairs.

"I checked the whole church," Sharon said, following her.

She stopped at the stairs, looking speculatively down the steps.

"I was nervous about being alone," Sharon said desperately, "so I turned on all the lights and checked all the Sunday school rooms and the choir room and the bathrooms. There isn't anybody here."

She looked up from the stairs and toward the end of the hall. "What about the sanctuary?"

"The sanctuary?" Sharon said blankly.

She had already started down the hall toward it, and Sharon followed her, relieved, and then, suddenly, hopeful. Maybe there was a door she'd missed. A sanctuary door that faced southwest. "Is there a door in the sanctuary?"

Reverend Farrison looked irritated. "If someone went out the east door, they could have gotten in and hidden in the sanctuary. Did you check the pews?" She went into the sanctuary. "We've had a lot of trouble lately with homeless people sleeping in the pews. You take that side, and I'll take this one," she said, going over to the side aisle. She started along the rows of padded pews, bending down to look under each one. "Our Lady of Sorrows had their Communion silver stolen right off the altar."

The Communion silver, Sharon thought, working her way along the rows. She'd forgotten about the chalice.

Reverend Farrison had reached the front. She opened the flower room door, glanced in, closed it, and went up into the chancel. "Did you check the adult Sunday school room?" she said, bending down to look under the chairs.

"Nobody could have hidden in there. The junior choir was in there, having refreshments," Sharon said, and knew it wouldn't do any good. Reverend Farrison was going to insist on checking it anyway, and once she'd found the display case open, the chalice missing, she would go through all the other rooms, one after the other. Till she came to the nursery.

"Do you think it's a good idea us doing this?" Sharon said. "I mean, if there is somebody in the church, they might be dangerous. I think we should wait. I'll call my husband, and when he gets here, the three of us can check—"

"I called the police," Reverend Farrison said, coming down the steps from the chancel and down the center aisle. "They'll be here any minute."

The police. And there they were, hiding in the nursery, a bearded punk and a pregnant teenager, caught red-handed with the Communion silver.

Reverend Farrison started out into the hall.

"I didn't check the Fellowship Hall," Sharon said rapidly. "I mean, I checked the door, but I didn't turn on the lights, and with all those presents for the homeless in there . . ."

She led Reverend Farrison down the hall, past the stairs. "They could have gotten in the north door during the rehearsal and hidden under one of the tables."

Reverend Farrison stopped at the bank of lights and began flicking them. The sanctuary lights went off, and the light over the stairs came on.

Third from the top, Sharon thought, watching Reverend Farrison hit the switch. *Please. Don't let the adult Sunday school room come on.*

The office lights came on, and the hall light went out. "This church's top priority after Christmas is labeling these lights," Reverend Farrison said, and the Fellowship Hall light came on.

Sharon followed her right to the door and then, as Reverend Farrison went in, Sharon said, "You check in here. I'll check the adult Sunday school room," and shut the door on her.

She went to the adult Sunday school room door, opened it, waited a full minute, and then shut it silently. She crept down the hall to the light bank, switched the stairs light off and shot down the darkened stairs, along the hall, and into the nursery.

They were already scrambling to their feet. Mary had put her hand on the seat of the rocking chair to pull herself up and had set it rocking, but she didn't let go of it.

"Come with me," Sharon whispered, grabbing up the chalice. It was half full of water, and Sharon looked around hurriedly, and then poured it out on the carpet and tucked it under her arm.

"Hurry!" Sharon whispered, opening the door, and there was no need to motion them forward, to put her fingers to her lips. They followed her swiftly, silently, down the hall, Mary's head ducked, and Joseph's arms held at his sides, ready to come up defensively, ready to protect her.

Sharon walked to the stairs, dreading the thought of trying to get them up them. She thought for a moment of putting them in the choir room and locking them in. She had the key, and she could tell Reverend Farrison she'd checked it and then locked it to make sure no one got in. But if it didn't work, they'd be trapped, with no way out. She had to get them upstairs.

She halted at the foot of the stairs, looking up around the landing and listening. "We have to hurry," she said, taking hold of the railing to show them how to climb, and started up the stairs.

This time they did much better, still putting their hands on the steps in front of them instead of the rail, but climbing up quickly. Three-fourths of the way up, Joseph even took hold of the rail.

Sharon did better, too, her mind steadily now on how to escape Reverend Farrison, what to say to the police, where to take them.

Not the furnace room, even though Reverend Farrison had already looked in there. It was too close to the door, and the police would start with the hall. And not the sanctuary. It was too open.

She stopped just below the top of the stairs, motioning them to keep down, and they instantly pressed themselves back into the shadows. Why was it those signals were universal—danger, silence, run? *Because it's a dangerous world*, she thought, *then and now, and there's worse to come. Herod, and the flight into Egypt. And Judas. And the police.*

She crept to the top of the stairs and looked toward the sanctuary and then the door. Reverend Farrison must still be in the Fellowship Hall. She wasn't in the hall, and if she'd gone in the adult Sunday school room, she'd have seen the chalice was missing and sent up a hue and cry.

Sharon bit her lip, wondering if there was time to put it back, if she dared leave them here on the stairs while she sneaked in and put it in the display case, but it was too late. The police were here. She could see their red and blue lights flashing purply through the stained-glass door panels. In another minute they'd be at the door, knocking, and Reverend Farrison would come out of the Fellowship Hall, and there'd be no time for anything.

She'd have to hide them in the sanctuary until Reverend Farrison took the police downstairs, and then move them—where? The furnace room? It was still too close to the door. The Fellowship Hall?

She waved them upward, like John Wayne in one of his war movies, along the hall and into the sanctuary. Reverend Farrison had turned off the lights, but there was still enough light from the chancel cross to see by. She laid the chalice in the back pew and led them along the back row to the shadowed side aisle, and then pushed them ahead of her to the front, listening intently for the sound of knocking.

Joseph went ahead with his eyes on the ground, as if he expected more sudden stairs, but Mary had her head up, looking toward the chancel, toward the cross.

Don't look at it, Sharon thought. *Don't look at it*. She hurried ahead to the flower room.

There was a muffled sound like thunder, and the bang of a door shutting.

"In here," she whispered, and opened the flower room door.

She'd been on the other side of the sanctuary when Reverend Farrison checked the flower room. Sharon understood now why she had given it only the most cursory of glances. It had been full before. Now it was crammed with the palm trees and the manger. They'd heaped the rest of the props in it—the innkeeper's lantern and the baby blanket. She pushed the manger back, and one of its crossed legs caught on a music stand and tipped it over. She lunged for it, steadied it, and then stopped, listening.

Knocking out in the hall. And the sound of a door shutting. Voices. She let go of the music stand and pushed them into the flower room, shoving Mary into the corner against the spray of roses and nearly knocking over another music stand.

She motioned to Joseph to stand on the other side and flattened herself against a palm tree, shut the door, and realized the moment she did that it was a mistake.

They couldn't stand here in the dark like this—the slightest movement by any of them would bring everything clattering down, and Mary couldn't stay squashed uncomfortably into the corner like that for long.

She should have left the door slightly open, so there was enough light from the cross to see by, so she could hear where the police were. She couldn't hear anything with the door shut except the sound of their own light breathing and the clank of the lantern when she tried to shift her weight, and she couldn't risk opening the door again, not when they might already be in the sanctuary, looking for her. She should have shut Mary and Joseph in here and gone back into the hall to head the police off. Reverend Farrison would be looking for her, and if she didn't find her, she'd take it as one more proof that there was a dangerous homeless person in the church and insist on the police searching every nook and cranny.

Maybe she could go out through the choir loft, Sharon thought, if she could move the music stands out of the way, or at least shift things around so they could hide behind them, but she couldn't do either in the dark.

She knelt carefully, slowly, keeping her back perfectly straight, and put her hand out behind her, feeling for the top of the manger. She patted spiky straw till she found the baby blanket and pulled it out. They must have put the wise men's perfume bottles in the manger, too. They clinked wildly as she pulled the blanket out.

She knelt farther, feeling for the narrow space under the door, and jammed the blanket into it. It didn't quite reach the whole length of the door, but it was the best she could do. She straightened, still slowly, and patted the wall for the light switch.

Her hand brushed it. *Please*, she prayed, *don't let this turn on some other light*, and flicked it on.

Neither of them had moved, not even to shift their hands. Mary, pressed against the roses, took a caught breath, and then released it slowly, as if she had been holding it the whole time.

They watched Sharon as she knelt again to tuck in a corner of the blanket and then turned slowly around so she was facing into the room. She reached across the manger for one of the music stands and stacked it against the one behind it, working as gingerly, as slowly, as if she were defusing a bomb. She reached across the manger again, lifted one of the music stands, and set it on the straw so she could push the manger back far enough to give her space to move. The stand tipped, and Joseph steadied it.

Sharon picked up one of the cardboard palm trees. She worked the plywood base free, set it in the manger, and slid the palm tree flat along the wall next to Mary, and then did the other one.

That gave them some space. There was nothing Sharon could do about the rest of the music stands. Their metal frames were tangled together, and against the outside wall was a tall metal cabinet, with pots of Easter lilies in front of it. She could move the lilies to the top of the cabinet at least.

She listened carefully with her ear to the door for a minute, and then stepped carefully over the manger between two lilies. She bent and picked up one of them and set it on top of the cabinet and then stopped, frowning at the wall. She bent down again, moving her hand along the floor in a slow semicircle.

Cold air, and it was coming from behind the cabinet. She stood on tiptoe and looked behind it. "There's a door," she whispered. "To the outside."

"Sharon!" a muffled voice called from the sanctuary.

Mary froze, and Joseph moved so he was between her and the door. Sharon put her hand on the light switch and waited, listening.

"Mrs. Englert?" a man's voice called. Another one, farther off, "Her car's still here," and then Reverend Farrison's voice again, "Maybe she went downstairs."

Silence. Sharon put her ear against the door and listened, and then edged past Joseph to the side of the cabinet and peered behind it. The door opened outward. They wouldn't have to move the cabinet out very far, just enough for her to squeeze through and open the door, and then there'd be enough space for all of them to get through, even Mary. There were bushes on this side of the church. They could hide underneath them until after the police left.

She motioned Joseph to help her, and together they pushed the cabinet a few inches out from the wall. It knocked one of the Easter lilies over, and Mary stooped awkwardly and picked it up, cradling it in her arms.

They pushed again. This time it made a jangling noise, as if there were coat hangers inside, and Sharon thought she heard voices again, but there was no help for it. She squeezed into the narrow space, thinking, *What if it's locked?* and opened the door.

Onto warmth. Onto a clear sky, black and pebbled with stars.

"How—" she said stupidly, looking down at the ground in front of the door. It was rocky, with bare dirt in between. There was a faint breeze, and she could smell dust and something sweet. Oranges?

She turned to say, "I found it. I found the door," but Joseph was already leading Mary through it, pushing at the cabinet to make the space wider. Mary was still carrying the Easter lily, and Sharon took it from her and set it against the base of the door to prop it open and went out into the darkness.

The light from the open door lit the ground in front of them and at its edge was a stretch of pale dirt. The path, she thought, but when she got closer, she saw it was the dried bed of a narrow stream. Beyond it the rocky ground rose up steeply. They must be at the bottom of a draw, and she wondered if this was where they had gotten lost.

"*Bott lom?*" Joseph said behind her.

She turned around. "*Bott lom?*" he said again, gesturing in front and to the sides, the way he'd done in the nursery. Which way?

She had no idea. The door faced west, and if the direction held true, and if this was the Judean Desert, it should lie to the southwest. "That direction," she said, and pointed up the steepest part of the slope. "You go that way, I think."

They didn't move. They stood watching her, Joseph standing slightly in front of Mary, waiting for her to lead them.

"I'm not—" she said, and stopped. Leaving them here was no better than leaving them in the furnace room. Or out in the snow. She looked back at the door, almost wishing for Reverend Farrison and the police, and then set off toward what she hoped was the southwest, clambering awkwardly up the slope, her shoes slipping on the rocks.

How did they do this, she thought, grabbing at a dry clump of weed for a handhold, *even with a donkey*? There was no way Mary could make it up this slope. She looked back, worried.

They were following easily, sturdily, as certain of themselves as she had been on the stairs.

But what if at the top of this draw there was another one, or a dropoff? And no path. She dug in her toes and scrambled up.

There was a sudden sound, and Sharon whirled around and looked back at the door, but it still stood half open, with the lily at its foot and the manger behind.

The sound scraped again, closer, and she caught the crunch of footsteps and then a sharp wheeze.

"It's the donkey," she said, and it plodded up to her as if it were glad to see her.

She reached under it for its reins, which were nothing but a ragged rope, and it took a step toward her and blared in her ear, "Haw!" and then a wheeze that was practically a laugh.

She laughed, too, and patted his neck. "Don't wander off again," she said, leading him over to Joseph, who was waiting where she'd left them. "Stay on the path." She scrambled on up to the top of the slope, suddenly certain the path would be there, too.

It wasn't, but it didn't matter. Because there to the southwest was Jerusalem, distant and white in the starlight, lit by a hundred hearthfires, a thousand oil lamps, and beyond it, slightly to the west, three stars low in the sky, so close they were almost touching.

They came up beside her, leading the donkey. "*Bott lom*," she said, pointing. "There, where the star is."

Joseph was fumbling in his sash again, holding out the little leather bag.

"No," she said, pushing it back to him. "You'll need it for the inn in Bethlehem."

He put the bag back reluctantly, and she wished suddenly she had something to give them. Frankincense. Or myrrh.

"*Hunh-haw*," the donkey brayed, and started down the hill. Joseph lunged after him, grabbing for the rope, and Mary followed them, her head ducked.

"Be careful," Sharon said. "Watch out for King Herod." She raised her hand in a wave, the sleeve of her choir robe billowing out in the warm breeze like a wing, but they didn't see her. They went on down the hill, Mary with her hand on the donkey for steadiness, Joseph a little ahead. When they were nearly at the bottom, Joseph stopped and pointed at the ground and led the donkey off at an angle out of her sight, and Sharon knew they'd found the path.

She stood there for a minute, enjoying the scented breeze, looking at the almost-star, and then went back down the slope, skidding on the rocks and loose dirt, and took the Easter lily out of the door and shut it. She pushed the cabinet back into position, took the blanket out from under the door, switched off the light, and went out into the darkened sanctuary.

There was no one there. She went and got the chalice, stuck it into the wide sleeve of her robe, and looked out into the hall. There was no one there, either. She went into the adult Sunday school room and put the chalice back into the display case and then went downstairs.

"*Where* have you been?" Reverend Farrison said. Two uniformed policemen came out of the nursery, carrying flashlights.

Sharon unzipped her choir robe and took it off. "I checked the Communion silver," she said. "None of it's missing." She went into the choir room and hung up her robe.

"We looked in there," Reverend Farrison said, following her in. "You weren't there."

"I thought I heard somebody at the door," she said.

*

By the end of the second verse of "O Little Town of Bethlehem," Mary and Joseph were only three-fourths of the way to the front of the sanctuary.

"At this rate, they won't make it to Bethlehem by Easter," Dee whispered. "Can't they get a move on?"

"They'll get there," Sharon whispered, watching them. They paced slowly, unperturbedly, up the aisle, their eyes on the chancel. "'How silently, how silently,'" Sharon sang, "'the wondrous gift is given.'"

They went past the second pew from the front and out of the choir's sight. The innkeeper came to the top of the chancel steps with his lantern, determinedly solemn.

"'So God imparts to human hearts,
The blessings of his heaven.'"

"Where did they go?" Virginia whispered, craning her neck to try and see them. "Did they sneak out the back way or something?"

Mary and Joseph reappeared, walking slowly, sedately, toward the palm trees and the manger. The innkeeper came down the steps, trying hard to look like he wasn't waiting for them, like he wasn't overjoyed to see them.

"'No ear may hear his coming,
But in this world of sin . . .'"

At the back of the sanctuary, the shepherds assembled, clanking their staffs, and Miriam handed the wise men their jewelry box and perfume bottles. Elizabeth adjusted her tinsel halo.

"'Where meek souls will receive him still,
The dear Christ enters in.'"

Joseph and Mary came to the center and stopped. Joseph stepped in front of Mary and knocked on an imaginary door, and the innkeeper came forward, grinning from ear to ear, to open it.

1993

JOSÉ R. NIETO

Ixchel's Tears

I

WALKING STEADILY over packed snow, frigid water seeping into his inadequate boots, Francisco found that he couldn't stop thinking about the argument. It had started over nothing; an errand forgotten by Elizabeth, his fiancée; a piece of mail undelivered. Annoyed by her calm disposition, he made the mistake of accusing her of not apologizing enough. Elizabeth in turn accused him of always accepting her apologies.

"What am I supposed to do?" Francisco said, incredulously.

"You're supposed to say that it's okay," Elizabeth responded, "that I shouldn't worry about it. You should say that you love me, no matter what I do. When you tell me 'I accept your apology' in that tone of yours—you know, that official voice you put on—it makes me feel awful, like I've done something beyond forgiveness. I mean, does a letter really matter that much to you?" While she spoke Elizabeth squinted her eyes, as if she had trouble focusing.

Francisco shook his head. "It's just cultural," he said to dismiss the issue. Often when they disagreed, when he was tired or horny and did not feel like going at length, he was quick to raise the spectre of ethnic difference. It saved the effort of a good argument. Because of their disparate backgrounds—he, the product of a large working-class San Juan family; she, from a privileged Boston suburb—the subject carried the weight and significance of a veiled threat. In normal circumstances the mere mention of culture would serve to stymie the most heated debate, almost as if he had drawn a line on the ground, a fragile border that Elizabeth did not dare cross.

This time, though, maybe because of the holidays, or possibly due to the impending nuptials (still six months away), the two of them went on to rehash the rest of their disagreements: city or country residence, casual wedding or formal reception. Foolishly, Francisco revived an old fight about the language and religion of their future children. That one kept them at it until Elizabeth crossed her arms, glanced down at her shoes and started to cry.

"I don't think we're ready for this," she said. It was those words and that image—Elizabeth closed off, tears flowing in thin rivulets, her face flushed to a pale red—that had sent Francisco out carelessly into the brutal winter, thinly clad. His shoes leaked, the overcoat had small rodent-type holes on the back. Its lining had ripped weeks after he'd bought it at a fancy second-hand store. He wished he'd forgone style and bought sensible winter wear; as a graphic designer he made enough to afford it. As it was, he usually wore the ragged coat with a number of layers, or at least a sweater. Tonight he had on only a T-shirt and cotton sweatpants.

His flight, Francisco now understood, had been propelled by guilt and apprehension. For all their arguments he still cared deeply for Elizabeth. They shared a history, a passage through time. Their relationship (and he thought of it as an individual entity, a growing, living thing) had withstood passion and indifference, conflict and resolution, even a year of separation while Francisco attended art school in Madrid. When he'd first seen her, calmly sipping Grand Marnier from a brandy snifter at a friend's dinner party, he had become convinced that they would end up together. That was three years ago, but he could still picture her perfectly; wrist turned awkwardly, moist lips barely touching the contoured crystal as if she were kissing a relic, bare legs crossed under the kitchen chair, face and glass lit subtly by flickering candlelight. Right then he had fallen in love with her.

The blustering wind sprinkled loose snowflakes on his beard and hair, then swirled around his feet and crawled up his legs to fill his clothes. Even inside the deep pockets his fingers felt stiff and painfully dry. Across Cambridge Street he noticed the colorful lights of a flower shop, gaudily decorated for the holidays. It was then that it hit him: a gift for Elizabeth, that was precisely what he was after. The window display looked like a magic screen, a tempting portal to a lush tropical paradise. Improbable greens mingled with rich reds, purples and yellows, tones made brighter by the dirgeful gray of winter. Most of all, though, the plants promised soothing temperatures. They reminded him of home. Francisco could think of nothing better right now.

Christmas in Puerto Rico: *Noche Buena* up in the mountains, the family gathering as heavy raindrops played a quick rhythm on the tin roof, heavy smell of roasted pork and *gandules* hovering around Francisco like thick cigar smoke. Loud, dissonant conversations over rum and watery beer . . .

The light changed and Francisco rushed across the street, almost slipping into a pool of dirty slush. When he reached the shop he opened the door so abruptly that the counter person—a short brown man with shiny black hair and inset eyes—jumped from his stool as if startled. The warmth and green scent hit Francisco like a Caribbean wave; for a moment he stood at the entrance and let himself be enveloped. He shook the snow from his face and clothes, then stomped his feet.

"How can I help you?" said the man behind the counter. His words came out with difficulty, twisted by a heavy accent.

"I'm so glad you're still open," Francisco said, "being like it is Christmas Eve and all."

The man didn't respond. His leathery face showed a tentativeness that Francisco thought he recognized. He tried again, this time in Spanish. The man smiled and perked up, as if a weight had been removed from his back.

"Last minute we usually do good business," he said, "*plantas y flores*, people don't want to buy them too early. But I was going to close up soon."

"Well, I'm glad you didn't because I am in serious need of something nice for my *prometida*. It's kind of an emergency, really."

"Go ahead, look around. I can wait."

"*Gracias, hermano*," Francisco said, turning toward a majestic display by the left wall. The plants were arranged in shelves, stacked all the way to the ceiling; giant succulent leaves shared space with delicate orchids and spindly lilies. On the floor, plastic buckets held cut flowers: carnations, violets, daffodils and many others Francisco had never seen before. A whole corner was crowded with red poinsettias—*Flor de Pascuas*, as they called them back home.

The possibilities baffled Francisco. He had no idea what would best serve as a peace offering, what would once again open the channels of communication.

"Is this all you have?" he said.

"No, no, no, we have a refrigerator in the back, you know, with the delicate ones, roses and things."

Roses, that sounded better to Francisco.

"Could I see them? That might be more appropriate."

"Sure, hold on a minute." The man got off the stool and walked to the front door. Immediately Francisco noticed a significant limp; he seemed to drag his right leg rather than step with it. He took a key chain from his stained orange apron and locked the door with some difficulty.

"I'm by myself here," he explained as he fumbled with the lock.

"No problem," Francisco said. The short man turned around and led him to the rear of the store. As they pushed through a little swinging gate behind the counter Francisco wondered if the limp was due to a war wound. The man's accent placed him someplace in Central America, where crippling violence seemed a likely possibility. Francisco considered asking, but thought better of the idea.

"So you're doing the Anglo thing," the man said, "giving Christmas presents, *Santa Clos* and such."

"Yes," Francisco said, then reconsidered. "Well, no, actually. See, I got into a big fight with my *prometida* tonight, that's what happened. Probably holiday stress, I think, combined with the wedding it's making us kind of edgy."

"That's what I've been telling people, why do they go crazy with the gift-giving thing on Christmas? I mean, isn't the baby Jesus gift enough for everybody? Take it easy, I tell them, wait until the sixth. . . ."

Francisco shrugged. "Well, I'm from Puerto Rico," he said, "and we give presents on both Christmas and Three Kings Day. We kind of play it both ways, I guess."

"Oh," the man said, as if disappointed, "I didn't know they did that in Puerto Rico."

For a moment Francisco expected to become enmeshed in an argument about the Americanization of Puerto Rican culture (Lord knew that he'd heard them before), but as the man limped down the hallway he did not say another word.

They walked past a cluttered supply room—black bags of potting soil, miniature hoes, fertilizer—then through a glass sliding door covered with mist. From inside, the refrigerated case reminded Francisco of a small *bodega* aisle, if slightly colder. Harsh fluorescent lights illuminated the space, somewhat diminishing the impact of the colorful arrangement. Still, the packed shelves were stunning. Each level displayed hundreds of flowers: roses, cut orchids, tulips. As an artist Francisco was quick to detect subtle permutations of hues and shapes, careful patterns that served to enhance the visual experience; round petals mingled with insectlike blossoms, wiry stigmas hung from bright red poppies and reached lovingly into the adjacent bellflowers.

"Did you do this?" Francisco asked.

"What do you mean?"

"I mean, did you put this room together?"

The man looked around and smiled. "Yes," he said, "that was me. My cousin Eriberto, he owns the store and he used to keep the place in such a mess, but I straightened it out."

"It's beautiful," Francisco said absently. The man smiled again and nodded, but did not speak.

"Why don't we do this," Francisco said, "why don't you put together an arrangement for me. Put your nicest flowers together in a bouquet, I'll pay whatever it costs."

"We've got catalogues if you want to see them. . . ."

"No, that's fine, I trust you."

"*Bueno*," the man said, then with a quick wave of his arms sent Francisco out to the front of the store.

While he waited for the flowers Francisco paced back and forth, framed by walls of greenery, and in his mind he kept running Elizabeth's words—"I don't think we're ready for this . . ."—and with every repetition they became more definite, until, after a couple of turns, they had changed to "I know we're not ready for marriage . . ." and finally "We shouldn't get married." The weight of the imagined statement stopped him in midstep and made him shudder.

A few minutes later the man came forth with the finished bouquet. To his surprise Francisco found it rather disappointing. Not that the arrangement itself was ugly, far from it. The lavender orchids looked sublime nestled within a bunch of yellow chrysanthemums, and the single, central rose, red like a burning torch, conveyed a sense of longing and desire. But as he cradled the flowers in his arms Francisco wondered if such a gift was really suitable. Within weeks, he realized, the blooms would be nothing but wilted stems and dried petals—not exactly the message he'd wanted to deliver to his fiancée.

Francisco stared at the bouquet for a moment, then glanced quickly at the man. He was smiling, apparently satisfied with his work. Francisco couldn't blame him; he'd really done a good job.

"This is fine," he said as convincingly as possible, "they're beautiful. Now, how much do I owe you?"

The man dropped his smile just as Francisco finished the question. "Make it twenty," he said in a dry voice, "that'll be fine, twenty."

Francisco paid the man, thanked him, then headed for the door. Outside it started snowing again; thick clumps slid slowly down the tempered glass, leaving watery trails like tears. People walked hurriedly on the frozen sidewalk, wrapped tightly in bright ski jackets and woolen hats. Francisco paused just as he was about to push the door open, right hand stuck to the cold glass. Suddenly he couldn't face the prospect of going back to the apartment, of stepping nakedly into the sharp wind, carrying with him such a slight offering.

"What is it?" the man asked.

Francisco said the first thing that came to mind: "It's the cold, I just can't stand this freezing weather."

After a moment the man said, "Why don't you come out back to the office, I'll make some *café con leche* so we can heat up your insides. It's not like I want to head out there either."

"My name's Agustín Irriñosa," the man began. He held the coffee cup right under his nose and took a deep breath.

"Francisco Arriví."

"You said you're from Puerto Rico, is that right?"

"I live here in Cambridge now, but that's where I'm originally from. I left the island when I was eighteen. . . ."

"I've heard it's nice down there," Agustín said, smiling.

"Well you know," Francisco said, then paused to take a sip. The liquid burned his tongue but felt good going down; he could feel it drip all the way to his belly. "It's home so you don't really think about it much until you're gone."

"Bet you think about it now," Agustín said, "with this weather I mean."

"Yes I do," Francisco said plainly.

"I think about home too, Guatemala." Agustín stroked his chin, then leaned back on the chair. Francisco rested his elbows on the crowded desk and sighed.

"Must've been rough," he said. "I've read horrible things about the war."

"The war was one thing," Agustín said, his free hand fluttering, "but there was so much more to life than that. People think it's hell, but we had our share of happiness, me and my family, when the fighting stopped we made *milpe* grow with our hands, we drank *balche* and watched the sun being smothered by the rubber trees. And when the stars came out we told stories to each other, tales of *Cha-Chaac* and *Kukulcan*, but most of all, no matter what the soldiers did to us, we were always warm, and the trees never died and in the river the water always flowed."

Francisco nodded hesitantly and drank from the steaming cup. At first he did not know how to respond; what Agustín described was so far from his staid urban experience. Instead he stared at a small framed picture of

Jesus hanging on the opposite wall. Between his pierced hands he held a realistic-looking heart, like an Azteca sacrifice. *Sagrado Corazón*, Francisco thought.

"What about snow," he said after a moment, "what did you think of it when you first saw it?"

Agustín turned away like he'd smelled something awful.

"Bah," he said, "it's just frozen water, that's all it is."

Francisco chuckled, splashing coffee onto the desk. "I was never too hot on it myself," he said as he reached for a napkin to clean the mess. Soon Agustín was laughing as well.

"You hate it here too, huh?" he asked.

While considering the question Francisco ran a hand through his hair and glanced blankly at the paneled ceiling. Originally he'd come to Boston only for school, fully intending to return to the island. But then his parents divorced and going to Puerto Rico lost some of its urgency. He got a lucrative job, he made good friends in the city, he met Elizabeth. He fell in love.

He remembered the walk to the flower shop, icy gusts running through his flimsy clothes like needles.

"I don't know," he said, "sometimes. I miss a lot of things about Puerto Rico; the language, old San Juan, my family. Adjuntas, up in the mountains where my grandparents lived. I miss the sea, I guess, water warm like from a bathtub. Not like here, *verdad*? Anyway, my fiancée and I talked once about moving down, but you know, Elizabeth has her career, she doesn't speak any Spanish, she's real close to her family—"

Agustín seemed taken aback for a moment. "Elizabeth?" he said like it was a mouthful. "You mean she's a *gringa*?"

"She's Anglo," Francisco said, annoyed by the man's reaction. He'd gotten the same words, the same expression from a number of Latino acquaintances. In his mind Francisco dusted off a long list of arguments to explain his decision.

"I'm sorry," Agustín said, quickly regaining his composure, "I didn't mean to—"

"I understand," Francisco said, and was immediately brought back to his argument with Elizabeth. The thought made something twist uncomfortably in his chest. It was time to go home, he'd been away long enough, almost an hour. Though he wasn't looking forward to facing his fiancée, Francisco realized that gift or not he had little choice. There were, after all, matters left unresolved.

"Listen," he said as he pushed away from the desk, "I really should go back to my *prometida*. Thanks for your hospitality—"

"*Espérese un momentito*," Agustín said quickly, "are you sure that's what you want to take to your fiancée?" He pointed at the bouquet on Francisco's lap. "The way you looked at it," he continued, "you know, when I handed it to you, it was like you didn't care for it at all."

"Well it's beautiful," Francisco said, gently stroking the rose petals, "but . . . I don't know, maybe I should get her something that's going to last. I thought of getting a plant, but that just wouldn't have the same effect as the flowers. I mean, I already got her a Christmas present, a really nice bracelet in fact, but this, this has to be different. . . ."

Francisco paused, then looked down to the coffee cup. "We really went at it tonight," he said. "Jesus, you should have heard us! And, well, I have a feeling that when I get home tonight, I think there's a chance she's going to tell me that it's over. So you see, what I want, it has to be something special. . . ."

Excited, almost laughing, Agustín stood up and walked to Francisco's side. "I think I have exactly what you need," he said.

With quick steps (considering the man's prominent limp) Agustín led Francisco down a dusty stairwell, past heating ducts and clanking water pipes, then through an iron gate and into the tiny basement. Right across from the entrance, standing slightly askew against the cracked wall, stood a smaller version of the refrigerator upstairs; this one could have actually been a soda dispenser. On the middle shelf there was a delicate ceramic vase decorated with jaguar paws and proud quetzal birds. Within it lay a sole cut orchid, unlike any Francisco had ever seen. Huge silver-colored petals reflected the fluorescent glare like distorted mirrors.

"It's an Ixchel's tear, a moon orchid," Agustín explained, "it came from El Petén, near my home in Guatemala."

"I've never . . ." Francisco began, but let his voice trail off as he approached the refrigerator door.

"Most people haven't. Only a few of them grow in the entire Yucatán peninsula."

Francisco opened the door and knelt down in front of the flower. For up close the orchid's reddish center seemed to glow, as if it contained a dying ember. Had it not been for the way the petals quivered under his breath, he would have sworn they were made of steel.

"This is," he said, stumbling with the words, "this is unbelievable. Why, I mean, why would you keep it down here, hidden away?"

"Because it's not for sale," Agustín said, looking at the floor. "Eriberto, he doesn't know what to do with it, he doesn't even have a price for it yet."

"If you're not selling it then why are you showing it to me?"

Agustín paused and stroked his cheek and walked closer to Francisco. He put a heavy hand on his shoulder. "Because I'm giving it to you, that's what I'm doing."

"I don't understand," Francisco said.

"It's Christmas," Agustín said with a forced grin, "and that's what you do for Christmas, right?"

"But won't your boss—"

"What is he going to do, fire me? I'm his cousin and I work for nothing, just room and board. Besides, that orchid didn't cost him a cent. It was me who got it, you see. I brought it with me when I came from Guatemala." For a moment Agustín seemed angry, but at what Francisco could not tell.

The thought of receiving such a gift seemed unreal to Francisco. It was as if a stranger had offered to buy him a house or a car; it just didn't happen. He stepped away from the flower and pursed his lips, then slowly shook his head.

"Take it," Agustín said with some urgency, "I'm telling you, that's what you want."

"How long will it last?" Francisco asked sheepishly.

"That's the thing," Agustín said, "my Quiché *mama*, she used to tell me tales of the moon orchid, and what she said to me was that the blossoms, even if they're torn from the plant, they last forever. They never die. This one my mother got years ago, I carried it with me in an ammunition box. I waded across wide rivers and pushed through thick forests, I ran with it across two borders, and now look at it, it's still as beautiful as when she found it."

Perhaps because Agustín seemed to him like a kindred spirit—as much of an artist with flowers as he was with brushes and pens—Francisco found it natural to believe his story about the undying orchid. Aesthetically it made sense; blossoms had always been used to represent feelings of love and affection. Why should they, then, perish?

Reverently, Francisco reached into the refrigerator and took the vase in his hands. To his surprise there was no water inside. He rested it against his chest and felt a strange warmth exuding from the blossom—almost like a living thing—and he thought, Agustín's right: this is exactly what I need.

When Elizabeth sees the orchid she will be overwhelmed by its beauty, by the utter perfection of its form, and she will see, actually see, what I truly feel for her. In her slim hands she will hold the full extent of my devotion.

Before, he had told Agustín that he wasn't looking for a Christmas present. He'd been wrong, The moon orchid was the perfect Christmas gift, not just for Elizabeth, but for their relationship; a symbol concretized, like the baby Jesus, an embodiment of the permanence of love.

"Thank you," he said, "thank you. You don't know how much you've helped us. I think with this you've given us a future."

Agustín opened his mouth but did not say a word. Instead he took Francisco's left hand and shook it vigorously. With visible effort he lifted his fused leg and limped to the cement stairs. Still in awe, Francisco followed.

Once upstairs the man spent a few seconds playing with the lock, then pushed the door open. Immediately, the arctic wind rushed in, tussling the poinsettia leaves and stinging Francisco's face and bare hands.

"*Feliz Navidad*," he said and stepped into the cold. Through the glass window he saw Agustín mouth the same words.

After tucking the orchid under his coat, he walked to the curb and hailed a cab.

II

From the street the second-floor apartment appeared empty; there were no lights on in the windows and at eight-thirty Francisco thought it too early for Elizabeth to have gone to bed. Could she have moved out of the house so quickly? He shook his head to dispel the painful thought; his *prometida* would have never acted so rashly.

As soon as he'd stepped inside Francisco flicked the light switch and yelled "Elizabeth!" but there was no response. Out of habit, he reached behind the couch and plugged in the Christmas tree. The bulbs lit up immediately, but took a few minutes to start alternating. This year, because of all the wedding preparations, the smallish fir had ended up sparsely decorated. A single long strand of colored lights clung awkwardly to the abundant needles. Under the tree they kept a wooden manger scene complete with mother, father, baby and animals. The Three Kings—small stubs with golden crowns—stood impassively on the other side of the room. Every night before going to bed Francisco would move them closer to their destination.

He walked with a quick gait to the kitchen and carefully placed the moon orchid on the counter, right by the maple-wood cutting board. Taped to the pantry, Francisco found a hurriedly scrawled note from Elizabeth. In it she explained that she had not felt like being alone tonight, so she'd gone to her sister's, who lived only a few minutes away. At the bottom of the torn sheet she wrote down the phone number (as if he could forget that number) and next to it she inscribed in tall letters CALL ME.

Immediately Francisco reached for the wall-mounted phone and picked up the receiver. He'd already pressed the first digit when he thought, No, no, there you go again, acting, talking without thinking. That's what got you in trouble in the first place, *idiota*!

What was he going to say? He'd placed all his hopes in the orchid, in the meaningful act of gift giving. How could he have known that he would first have to talk to Elizabeth? Once again he felt the familiar sting of muted panic. It was as if he were standing in front of an empty canvas, pencil tip pressed lightly against the smooth surface, images turning fast inside his head, too fluid to capture in a single frame. The words were all there, but not quite in the right combination.

He sat on the kitchen stool, cracked his knuckles, then shook his arms to loosen up. Obviously he needed a clear mind, and patience. Much patience.

All of a sudden a thought crossed Francisco's mind that he tried hard to ignore; in Spanish he would know exactly what to say to Elizabeth. For all his years in Boston, he still found it easier to communicate emotions in his native language. Even the word *amor* seemed to hold more significance than its English equivalent. In Spanish, after all, he would never say "I love pizza," or "I loved that movie," uses that served to cheapen the expression, making it less meaningful. The phrase *te amo* implied a certain level of passion, a careless ardor that could never be conveyed in English; to Francisco it was almost magical. He'd only used it frivolously once—in an ill-fated attempt to bed a stunning classmate—and he had immediately regretted it.

He closed his eyes for a moment. Rubbing his forehead, he said out loud, "Maybe I should wait for her to call me." Yes, that was the rational thing to do, make sure she has had a chance to cool off. Taking the initiative could only make things worse.

Francisco took a cookie from a porcelain jar in the pantry and began to bite methodically around the sprinkled center. Soon he was staring at the moon orchid. The glittering petals reminded Francisco of his conversation with Agustín, of how easy it'd been to talk to him about his life in the island. When he blurted in Spanish that he missed Puerto Rico the man simply nodded and accepted the statement. If he'd been talking to Elizabeth he would have had to explain so much that in the end he would have given up and said nothing. Sitting as he was on that wobbly stool, staring deep into the fiery heart of Ixchel's tear, Francisco could not deny the attractiveness of cultural symmetry; one person talking in precise, descriptive terms, another listening intently, comprehending fully. How he wished it were that easy with Elizabeth.

He remained still on the stool more than an hour, absorbed by the blossom's delicate curvature. Inside the folds he could see twisted reflections of himself and the kitchen—light particles dancing in swirling, concentric patterns, like water down an open drain. Yes, that was the image; a tiny but powerful maelstrom, its flow drawing the fear and discomfort from him, leaving behind a strange but satisfying emptiness.

He was roused by the persistent ringing of the buzzerlike doorbell. Annoyed by the interruption, he stood up slowly and headed for the downstairs foyer. As he walked through the living room, Francisco discovered that the strand of colored lights had slipped from the Christmas fir. It now lay coiled around the tree's base, blinking arrhythmically.

"Jesus," he said. Before he could take a closer look the doorbell rang again.

He climbed down the stairs as quietly as possible since he didn't want to disturb the Portuguese family on the first floor. The two little girls had to be asleep already. After only eight months in the states they had come to take Santa Claus very seriously.

In the tiny viewer Francisco saw the man from the flower shop. Agustín stood on the porch shivering, even though he was wrapped in a large padded coat that looked like a comforter. Without hesitation, Francisco opened the door.

"Well, this is a surprise," he said. Agustín paid no heed to the pleasantry and pushed past him, then limped fast up the wooden staircase. Hanging from his left hand there was a rusted-green ammunition box. Francisco turned to look at the curious sight but did not move from the foyer.

"Where's the flower, the moon blossom?" the man yelled from upstairs. Francisco reacted like he'd just been shaken from a fond reminiscence. He rushed up the stairs after Agustín. By the time he made it to the kitchen the man had already taken Ixchel's tear from the ceramic vase and was placing it tenderly inside the box.

"Tell me," he said, closing the metal lid, "are you still in love with your fiancée?"

"Of course," Francisco said. As if to convince himself he repeated, "Of course I love her."

Shaking his head, Agustín ran stubby hands over his face and drew closer to him.

"Where's Elizabeth, Francisco?" he said.

"At her sister's, she went to her sister's after our fight this afternoon. Anyway, what does that have to do with my orchid?"

Agustín pulled on a small metal handle to close the latch on the ammunition box. He took off his coat and laid it out on the kitchen stool, then with one smooth motion lifted himself and sat on top of it.

"In the jungle we believe in circles," he began, "for many years my *mama* tried to explain that to me. Strange that it's in the States where I finally understood."

"Circles?" Francisco asked.

"We Quiché believe that Ixchel's tears are a gift from *la luna*, the sun's consort. So sad is she when she's alone in the sky that she cries, and her tears, when they hit the ground they turn to beautiful things, moon blossoms. So you see, from sadness comes something of beauty.

"But the thing is, it doesn't stop there, because the moon orchids live by sucking the life out of plants around them, they pull *la esencia*, that's why the flowers can live forever. When you find them they're almost always in the middle of an open clearing, surrounded by rotten trees. The Mayas, they used the tears to open up the forest for the *milpe* fields. Better than burning, I'm sure. So you see, death leads to food, to life."

Francisco was reminded of the scene in the living room. "That's what happened to my Christmas tree," he said, "that's why you kept the flower all by itself in that tiny basement. Well, if that's all, we'll just keep it someplace—"

"Do you realize that Elizabeth is still waiting for you?" Agustín interrupted. The harsh tone made it sound less like a question than an accusation.

Francisco felt like he'd just slipped underwater. All of a sudden he became aware of the stupidity of his thought and behavior since he'd arrived at home with the flower. How could he have waited so long to go after his fiancée? Pointing tentatively at the box he said, "Was that, I mean could that have been . . . ?"

Agustín nodded. His eyes were covered with red lines, like cracked marbles.

"But how?" Francisco said.

"After the empire fell apart, *curanderas* like my *mama* found out that Ixchel's tears could also drain strong feelings from people; hate, anger, jeal-

ousy. They can soothe someone who's in pain, or end a fight between brothers." He paused for a second, then said, "They can suck the love from even
the most passionate couple. . . ."

Francisco took a step back and glared intently at Agustín. The man lowered his head and began to speak in a low, pleading voice. Throughout his
hands remained on his lap, still.

"It was the cold, that's what it was. You walked into the shop and your
face was the color of snow and your hands were shaking and you told me
how much you hated the cold, how much you wished you were back home,
and the thing is, you *can* go home, you can take a plane tomorrow and
you'll be there. Me, I'm stuck here. You see, about a year ago I struck a
soldier who'd been trying to burn our fields, and since then my life's been
worthless in Guatemala. That's why I ran away, that's why I had to come to
this frozen hell to work for my cousin.

"I long for my home as much as you do, but I can't go anywhere, you
understand, I don't have a green card, no permits or anything, and if I'm
caught they'll send me back to die. But you, all that keeps you here's a
woman, a *gringa*. . . ."

"You had no right," Francisco began in anger, but stopped when he realized that Agustín was quietly weeping.

"I know, I know," he said, "but the thing is, I thought I was helping you.
I thought I was giving you the warm beaches and the green mountains, I
thought I was giving you back to your family. I mean, what better gift is
there than something you wish you could give to yourself?"

Francisco leaned against the counter and put his hands in his pockets. He
took a couple of deep breaths, then said calmly, "Why are you here then?"

Agustín looked up. His face glistened with tears.

"Before you left, you said something that stuck in my mind, even after I
locked up the store and headed home I just couldn't stop thinking about it.
You said that I had given you your future, and I kept thinking about what
my Quiché *mama* said to me when she handed me the Ixchel's tear, right
before I left. She handed me that ammunition box, and she told me, if you
want to feel better, if you miss us too much, open the box and let it clean
your mind. I never did though, even when I was starving in refugee camps,
even when I broke my knee and spent months in a leper's hospital. You see,
she gave me a choice—"

"Which you are now giving me," Francisco interjected. Agustín closed
his eyes and nodded quickly.

"The moon orchid can help you," he said, almost whispering. "It can drain the things that make you fight with your *prometida*. But the thing is, it would also let you think, and maybe then you'll decide that it's better to go back home, that you belong in your *islita*. The question is, do you want to take that chance?"

For an instant—perhaps because of his tears and the blue glimmer of the fluorescent lights—Agustín's eyes looked blank, as if he were blind. Francisco was momentarily taken aback by the illusion. Then a curious thought crossed his mind: Agustín's mother, she must have been a wise, wise woman. Right then and there he knew he had the answer.

"Take it away. Please take the flower with you."

Agustín nodded and jumped down from the stool. He slipped on his coat, took the ammunition box and put it under his arm and walked out of the kitchen. The limp made his body bounce awkwardly, like a needle on a scratched record. A minute later Francisco heard the muffled bang of the outside door being shut and knew that Agustín and Ixchel's tear were gone.

Back to square one, he thought. Guess the man was right about circles.

Elizabeth's note was still where he'd found it, taped to the pantry. The last line—CALL ME—seemed larger than before, as if in the ensuing hours it'd grown in importance. Instinctively Francisco looked at his watch. Five minutes past midnight; maybe it was too late to call.

He picked up the phone anyway. As he dialed his heart beat as if his chest were empty; every palpitation seemed to echo against his ribs and slowly fade away.

"Hello?" The voice took him by surprise; there had barely been a ring. Elizabeth must have been sitting right by the phone.

"It's me," he said.

"Where have you been?" she said angrily. "I've been waiting here for hours! How could you walk away like—"

Francisco blurted out, "*Te amo, Elizabeth.*"

Elizabeth was quiet for a minute. "Francisco," she finally said, and the way she said it—the tenderness in her voice, the music in her inflection—made it clear that she understood.

1995

NATHAN ENGLANDER

Reb Kringle

BUNA MICHLA stuck her head into the men's section of the sanctuary, hesitant, even though her husband was the only man there.

"Itzi," she said.

He was over by the ark, changing the bulb in the eternal light, pretending that he hadn't heard.

"Itzi, the children. Think of all the children."

"Bah!" He screwed in the bulb with his handkerchief and the eternal light flickered once before resuming its usual glow. Reb Yitzhak folded his hankie carefully and, slipping a hand under his caftan, stuffed it into his back pocket.

"Itzi!"

He turned to face her. "I should worry over the children? These are my children, all of them, that I should worry over them and their greed?"

She walked to the heart of the sanctuary and sat in the front row of the easterly-facing benches. "You should worry maybe over your shul. You should worry over the mortgage that is due." Buna took a deep breath. It was satisfying to yell at this stubborn man.

"How many people pray here, Yitzeleh? How many prayers go up to heaven from under this roof?"

"There are thirty-one people who pray here three times a day, and I don't know how many prayers reach heaven. If I knew such things I would also know a better way to pay the rent."

"And what of the roof under which we sleep?"

"Yes, Buna. And I would know also how to pay for the roof."

"How to pay you already know," she said. "Four weeks' work is food in our mouths, so what's the question? For eleven months you won't be forced to smile."

Reb Yitzhak considered his wife's statement. Every year it was the same argument and every year he lost. If only he had been born a wiser man—or married a simpler woman. He put his fingers into his long white beard and slowly worked them down toward its jagged end.

"It's a sin, this job," was all he came up with.

"It is absolutely not a sin. Where does it say that playing with goyishe children is a sin? There is no rule against playing games with them."

"Playing! You haven't seen, Buna. Anyone who has seen would never call such mayhem playing. Not since the time of Noah has the world seen such boundless greed."

"So it's not playing. Fine. But you're going. And you will be jolly and laugh like the bride's father at a wedding—miserable or not."

Reb Yitzhak took off his caftan and made his way down to the basement, leaning against the banister with every step. He was a heavy man, big in the belly, and his sciatica was acting up. The rickety wood stairs groaned as he headed down into the darkness, where he grabbed at the air in search of the frayed string and the lone sixty-watt bulb.

The oil burner sat under a web of rusted pipes that spread across the low ceiling. Behind the burner, there was a turn in the basement leading to a narrow dead end of storage space. It was the farthest place from anything, the best place to keep the Passover dishes so that they shouldn't be contaminated during the rest of the year.

He pulled the sheets off the boxes, all of which were marked PESACH, in Hebrew, with a big black marker. He couldn't make out the word since the light from the bulb barely reached that part of the room. But Reb Yitzhak didn't need to see so well. What he was looking for was recognizable by feel. The box he needed was fancy, not like the kind one brings home from the alley behind the supermarket, the sides advertising cereals and toilet paper, boxes living already a second life. This one had a top to it, the kind that could be lifted off, like a hatbox but square. This box felt smooth to the touch, overlaid with satin. When his fingers brushed against it he knew.

As he picked up the box, Reb Itzik employed the Back-Saver Erect Spine Lift, counting out the positions, "One, feet apart; two, bend knees," exactly as Dr. Mittleman had shown him.

Trudging up the stairs and directly to the front door, Itzik stopped and put the cumbersome package down.

"Ach," he said, "subway tokens."

"They're on the shelf in the foyer where they sit every day for the last forty years." Buna came in from the kitchen, wringing her hands on a towel and ready to show this mule of a man where was a token and the shelf and also, if need be, the front door.

"To get to the subway you remember?" she asked, daring him to show even the slightest bit of resistance. "You want I should get dressed and ride all the way into the city with you?"

Reb Yitzhak didn't want that at all.

Putting on caftan and coat and lifting the satin box, he gave Buna Michla his best look of despair—a look she saw only twice a year. First when it came time to carry up all the Passover dishes from the basement and, second, from the doorway, when he went off to the department store at the start of the holiday rush. So sad was the look that she lost her resolve not to chide him—she could not stand when he indulged himself to such a degree.

"Do they make you work on Shabbos?" she said. "Do they force you to go around with your head uncovered or deny you proper respect?" She undid the lock for him. "Like a king on a throne they treat you."

Itzik lifted up his box and fumbled with the door. "I pity such a king."

Leaning against a public telephone on the sidewalk and taking a moment to catch his breath, Itzik was surprised to see a new man yank open the gate of the service elevator at the department store. Ramirez, who had been there every year from the start, from the day Reb Itzik had surfaced with the employment agency slip in his hand, was now gone. He had been Reb Itzik's one friend at the job and had always kept an eye out on "the rabbi's" behalf. Without Ramirez there chewing on a cigar and offering immediate consolation, Itzik gave in to a moment of virtual despair. He felt abandoned. But at least one of them was free of the place.

Itzik approached the freight elevator, scowling at the Salvation Army worker who shook out Christmas tunes with wooden-handled bells—his last chance to be grumpy that day. The elevator man, not much older than a boy, gave Itzik a slow looking over, working his way up from the orthopedic shoes and taking his time with the long white beard. Itzik didn't flinch. He was used to it, prepared for the thousands of looks and inane questions, tugs and sticky fingers, that he was in for during the coming days.

"Floor?" the man asked, motioning with his thumb.

"Eight," Reb Itzik said.

"I heard about you," the elevator man told him, shoving the empty garbage dollies to the back wall. "You that Rabbi Santa."

"Yes," Itzik answered. "I'm the infamous Reb Santa."

The elevator man began to cough into his fist.

"Damn," he said. "I thought they were shitting me. That you was a myth."

"I exist, yes, for real," Reb Itzik said.

"Seems so," the man said. He began to pull the gate closed behind Reb Itzik and hesitated midway. "Don't you want to go in through the chimney?"

Reb Itzik turned to face the street.

"Such jokes my friend Ramirez got tired of making when you were still too small to reach the buttons."

The elves were in place, stationed every few feet throughout the giant room and continuing along the line of children that reached out into the hallway and past the tiny café, then snaked around the back of the passenger elevators and onto the staircase to the seventh floor. The room itself was decked with flashing lights and fake trees, hollow gifts with colored bows and giant paper candy canes that all the curious children ventured to lick, one germy tongue after another. There were elves posted on each side of Itzik; one—a humorless, muscular midget—wore a pair of combat boots that gave him the look of elf-at-arms. His companion might have been a twin. He wore black high-tops but had the same vigilant paramilitary demeanor.

Sitting in the chair, resting his hands on the golden armrests and leaning back against the plush cushions, Itzik was forced to admit that Buna was right. Poised in front of hundreds of worshiping faces and with a staff of thirty at his beck and call, it did indeed seem, looking down from his giant gilt chair, that he was a king on a throne.

Itzik had arranged for his support elves to keep up a steady stream of Merry Christmases. He was not one of the provincial Jews who had never crossed the Royal Hills bridge into Manhattan, the naives who'd never dealt with the secular world; it was not the first time that he'd put on the suit, and he very well knew the holiday kept him afloat. But even after all those years, the words "Merry Christmas" remained obscene to him.

The first child was an excited little girl. Small enough that she was there to see Santa, to get a pinch on the cheeks and a picture to put up on the refrigerator door—not yet a rapacious little beast with a list of demands who would have a seizure if he did not promise everything he was asked.

Itzik fell into character and gave a nod to the elf manning the crimson cord. The little girl rushed toward him like a bull in a chute, her mother prodding her regardless, and the immense crowd taking a baby step toward him, beginning with the front and then spreading backward in a seemingly endless wave.

"Ho, ho, ho," Itzik said, offering a hand as the girl was lowered into his lap. The girl beamed appropriately, bathed in the light of popping flashes and the glory of receiving the first ho, ho, ho of the year.

"What's your name?"

"It's Emily, Santa. I wrote you a letter."

"Yes, of course. The letter from Emily." He tapped his foot against the platform. "Well, remind Santa again: Have you been a good little girl?"

By twenty minutes to lunch, Itzik was sure that his very spirit was being challenged, as if God had become sadistic in his tests of the human soul. Both his pant legs were wet with the accidents of children who showed their excitement like puppies. The sciatica was broken glass running up and down the nerve in the back of his thigh. And one boy—a little Nazi, that one—had pulled out a pair of safety scissors and gone after his beard.

"Get on up there," said the elf on winter break from Tulane. She lowered a curly-headed tyke onto Itzik's left knee, his bottom lip flapping as he primed his crying machine.

"Don't cry, boychik. Tell me where's your mother."

"She's waiting for me at the Lancôme counter." And then, after a pause, "She's getting her face done."

"Her face done?" Itzik said.

"Yes," the boy said.

"So, nu?" Itzik said. "Have you been good this year?"

The boy nodded.

"Did you pay federal and state taxes, both?"

The boy shook his head, no.

"I can find it in my heart to forgive you," Itzik said. "But Santa isn't the IRS."

The boy didn't laugh. The elves didn't laugh. Tulane actually sneered.

Reb Itzik ran his hand along the length of his beard and extended his free leg.

"What can I do you for?" he asked.

"Mountain bike," said the boy.

"And?"

"Force Five Action Figures."

"And?"

"Doom—the Return of the Deathbot; Man Eater; Stop That Plague; and Gary Barry's All Star Eye on the Prize—all on CD-ROM."

"Anything else?" This appeared to be, aside from the sappy children in search of world peace, the shortest appointment of the day.

"Come on," Itzik said, "out with it." The lip was starting to move again and Itzik knew if he didn't get that last wish soon, he was in for a tantrum. "How about it?"

"A menorah," said the boy, and the tears started anyway and then stopped in a fine show of strength. It was Santa, at first stunned, then desperately trying to recall a toy by that name, who found himself bordering on a fit.

"A what?" he said, way too loudly. Then, sweet, nice, playing the part of Mr. Kringle: "A what-did-you-say?"

"A menorah."

"And what would a nice Christian boy want with a menorah?"

"I'm Jewish, not Christian. My new father says we're having a real Christmas and a tree, and not any candles at all—which isn't fair because my last father let me have a menorah and he wasn't Jewish." And the tears started running along with his nose.

"Why won't this new daddy let you light candles?"

"Because he says there's not going to be Chanukah this year."

Itzik gasped, and the boy, responding, began to bawl.

"Calm down there, little one. Santa's right here." Reaching back and squirming in his chair, Itzik produced a clean hankie. "Blow," he said, holding it to the child's nose. The child blew with some force. "Now don't you worry about a thing. You ask Santa for Chanukah, you get it." He tried his best to sound cheery, but he could feel the fury rattling in the back of his voice. "You just tell me your address and I'll bring you the candles myself."

The boy had quieted down some, but did not answer.

"Upper West or East?" Santa asked.

The boy emitted a high-pitched "Neither."

"Not in the Village, I hope," Santa said.

"We'll be in Vermont for Christmas. We have to drive all the way there so we can go to his stupid parents' church." Right then, Itzik knew, in an already fading flash of total clarity, that the farce had finally come to an end.

"Church," he said, his voice booming. "Church and no Chanukah!" Itzik yelled, scooping the boy off his knee and getting to his feet. Itzik, glaring, held the child under his arm. The elf with the high-tops took the boy and stood him up on the platform as Itzik again yelled, "No Chanukah!"

This Buna would understand; hearing this she would understand why the whole thing, the job and the costume and the laughter, was a sin. It was blasphemy! And then he screamed, loud and long, because of the cramps in his legs and the sciatic nerve that felt as if it had been stretched and released like the hemp cord of an archer's bow.

"Where is this mother?" he called out over the crowd. Grabbing the boy and risking a pinch to the already inflamed nerve, Itzik lifted him by the arm off the ground. "Where is this father?" Itzik demanded, the boy dangling like a purse in his hand. He wanted this grinch of a man brought forth, presented to him in judgment.

The boy wriggled his way free. He took a cellular phone from his pocket and called his mother on the first floor.

Itzik, conscious of the phone, began to feel guilty for scaring the child. He was still furious but also ashamed. He lowered his eyes and found the throng of holiday shoppers and the startled tots, eyes wide, staring back. Itzik, seeking a friendly face, a calm face, found none. He knew he had crossed the boundaries of propriety, and he was far past the point where he could sit back down and nod toward the elf in the combat boots to set loose the next child in line. He grabbed the pompom hanging down from his head and yanked off his hat, revealing a large black yarmulke.

"This," he yelled from deep down in his ample belly, "is not a fit job for a Jew."

A woman toward the middle of the room fainted dead away without letting go of the hand of her wailing daughter. She fell atop a padded rope that pulled down the brass-plated poles, spreading panic through the already jittery crowd, which began to knock over the aluminum trees and towering candy canes. The elves scurried, cursing and shrieking, unprepared by their half-day course for such an emergency. And one elf, the undercover security elf, clasped the earplug in his pointy ear and began to whisper furiously into his green velvet collar, an action that brought on the entrance of two more elves, one big and black, the other smaller, stockier, and white as the fake snow.

The pair tackled the Jewish Santa, the impostor, only kept on by the store out of fear. It had been a bad idea from the beginning, authentic beard or not; a very terrible idea from the very first year. And they would have been rid of him, too, would have been rid of Itzik ten times over, if not for the headlock that management was in. The department store had only in September paid out two-point-three million dollars for giving the boot to HIV Santa, and it didn't have a penny more for Reb Santa or Punjabi Santa—didn't yet have an inkling about how to handle the third application from Ms. Santa that had, this time, been submitted by her counsel.

As Itzik was hustled away, his replacement, tuna-fish sandwich still in hand, was pushed in through a side door. The boy's mother fought her way in from the back of what had been the line. Wielding her shopping bags like battle-axes, she moved toward her son. She called his name with the force of a terrified parent, so loudly that it carried over the echoing hysteria of the crowd, so that Itzik heard it and knew to whom the voice belonged. Reaching the boy, she stroked his hair, and finding the throne empty and her son seemingly unharmed, she asked the question to which every mother fears the answer.

"Matthew dear, tell me the truth. Did Santa Claus touch you?"

They held him in a storeroom, in a chair neither gilt nor comfortable. The chair was in a clearing surrounded by towering walls of boxes that looked more precarious than the walls of Jericho on Joshua's sixth pass. Itzik sat with his suit undone, the patent-leather belt hanging at his sides along with his ritual fringes. The pale security guard, a bitter elf, chided him for his lack of professionalism in the face of duty, telling Itzik he was lower than the Muscatel Santas on the street—a travesty in red.

"Better than to hang up my beard on a hook every night," Itzik said. He waited with the elf for the chief Santa to arrive.

Chief Santa was as much of a shock to Reb Itzik as Reb Itzik was to all the children, for the wizard behind this Christmas empire was not fat or jolly or even a man, but a small thin-lipped woman, without the slightest paunch from which to laugh, whose feet had clearly never donned a curly-toed bootee.

She handed him an envelope.

"Check," she said, with such great force that Itzik half expected to see a waiter rush through the door.

"You," she said, the thin lips so white with tension that her face seemed an uninterrupted plane below the nose. "You are a disgrace to the profession! And as far as we, and all of our one-hundred-and-six satellite stores are concerned, you are no longer Santa Claus."

It's not as simple as that, he wanted to tell her. Granting wishes that you don't have to make good on is simple. Believing every child who says he wasn't naughty but nice also can be done with little effort. But telling the man in the red suit—the only one in your employ with a real belly, the only one whose beard does not drip glue—that he is not Santa Claus is another matter completely. That, this woman hadn't the power to decide; Reb Yitzhak from Royal Hills, Brooklyn, hadn't the power to decide. The only one who could make such a decision was Buna Michla herself, and she had said that Itzik would finish out the year. This was the truth, he knew, as well as he knew that, sciatica or not, he would be carrying Passover dishes up from the basement again in the spring.

Itzik considered what would be worse as he rode down the freight elevator. He leaned the satin box against an empty garment rack, the naked hangers banging against each other like bones. He pictured himself riding the subway the next morning with the apology Buna Michla had coached him on, or rejected and cleaning the pews in his costume with Buna standing over him. She'd see to it. Itzik was Santa until the end of the season, whether he lost his throne or not.

1997

NALO HOPKINSON

A Young Candy Daughter

THE SALVATION ARMY Santa Claus wasn't ho-ho-hoing, not any more. He was no longer singing a carol, and he had stopped ringing his bell. He stood on the busy street corner—a thin brown man wearing Saint Nick's heavy velvet-red-and-whites and sweating himself thinner in the tropical heat—and gaped into the brass pot he had hanging in a frame for people to put their coins in.

Only two people stood near him. The young woman's freshness of skin and mischievous smile made it impossible to guess her age. She could have been sixteen, or twenty-six. Her jeans were scandalously tight, and, he noticed as she bent to tie her child's shoelace, showed off her high bottom nicely. Under different circumstances, the Salvation Army Santa Claus would have been using the cover of his cotton wool mustachios and beard to sneak a better glance. The young woman was not so much beautiful as *pretty*. The Salvation Army Santa Claus preferred pretty; he generally found it to be friendlier. Hers shone through despite hair severely processed into rigid ringlets. Her stylized makeup job failed to homogenize and blanch her features. Instead of the sparkling gold chain around her neck, silver or platinum would have complemented her black skin better, but no matter. (The chain supported a pendant with the word "foxy" in gold, followed by a star.) If you were to search for a word for what glowed through her as it did, made you want to laugh with her, and dance, you would have come up with "joy."

The young woman smiled as she placed her hand on the head of the second person standing at the Salvation Army pot; a little boy? Girl? Difficult to tell. An even younger person. The child wore too-big jeans, rolled up at the ankles, with threadbare knees. Its hair was cane-rowed neatly against its head, in even rows that went from nape to neck. It wore a scowl, a Spider-Man t-shirt, and a gold stud in either ear. But earrings were no indicator of gender these days. The child had one foot on a skateboard, up-ending it at an angle. The child pulled a handful of candy out of the Salvation Army pot and, with a look of intense concentration, flung it in an arc away from its body. Other children at the street corner broke free of their parents and scrabbled to collect it. So did one woman, her feet bare and black-bottomed, her body burly only because she seemed to be wearing everything she'd ever owned, in dirty and torn layers one atop the other. She clutched two packets of tamarind balls and five peppermints to her bosom with one hand. In the other hand she held a purple lollipop. As she scuttled into a corner to eat the rest of her prize, she tore the lollipop wrapper away with her teeth.

The Salvation Army Santa Claus stared at the young woman. "It didn't have any sweeties in there before," he said.

In response, she only grinned. *Worlds in that grin; miracles. Somewhere, a leader was shot, and the wondrous creation that was a gull swooped down over the waves and caught a fat fish for its young.* "La'shawna," she said to the child—a girl, then—"people want more than sweeties to fill their belly."

The tomboy of a girl looked up at her, scratched her nose, and said, "So what I should give them?"

"I ain't know," her mother replied. "Some people eat meat but no provisions. Some people eat provisions but no meat. Some people only want a cold beer and some peace and quiet."

The little girl considered. The Salvation Army Santa Claus peered into his brass pot. As far as he could see, it still only held the few coins he had received for singing his carols and ringing his bell. Perhaps the child had put the sweeties in there herself? They were troublemakers, her and her pretty mother. He was going to have to run them off.

"All right," the child said. She tossed her chin in greeting to the Salvation Army Santa. "Mister, tell any hungry people to put they hand in your pot. Each one will find what they want."

"What?" The Salvation Army Santa scowled at the little girl.

"You eat lunch yet?" her mother said to him.

"What that have to do with . . . why?"

"You hungry?"

Her smile was infectious. He found himself beaming back at her. "Yes."

"Then put your hand in the pot, nuh?"

Feeling like an idiot, the Salvation Army Santa did as she suggested. His hand closed over something warm and yielding. A delicious smell came from it. His tummy rumbled. He pulled his lunch out of the pot and nearly dropped it in surprise.

The child laughed. "Mummy, check it," she said. "All he want is a patty and a cocoa bread!"

People were starting to gather round. The woman in all her tattered clothing was tiptoeing nearer. "Only the hungry ones will get anything," the child told the man.

"Come, darling," said the young woman. "We have to go. Plenty to do."

The girl let the skateboard slap to the floor. "What else we must do now?" she asked.

"Well, this nice man going to get more customers than he can handle. So now we have to visit every Salvation Army Santa we can find round here and make their pots into cook pots, too."

"That's a lot of work, Mummy."

"You started it, girlchild."

The little girl made a face and kissed her teeth in mild exasperation. She shook her head, but then she smiled. The smile had something of her mother's about it.

The little girl hopped onto the skateboard and rolled away slowly. She stopped a little way away and did skillful, impatient circles, waiting for her mother to catch up.

Cringing as though she feared violence, the tattered woman snuck her hand into the pot. The thing she brought out was wrapped in banana leaves, tied with string, and steaming. She cackled in amazement, a delight rare and miraculous. *Somewhere, children got a snow day. Somewhere else, a political prisoner died only minutes into his "interrogation," cheating his torturer.* A man stepped up to the pot and put his hand inside.

"Is not this easy, you know," the Salvation Army Santa said to the young woman.

She gave him an appraising look,

"Doing good, I mean," he explained.

She sighed. "I know. She still have plenty to learn, and sometimes I don't know what to tell her. When she help one person, she might be harming someone else." She gestured at the pot, where four people were elbowing at each other to try and get their hands inside. "Where you think all this food coming from?" she asked. "Is somebody hard labour." She clapped her hands to get the attention of the people squabbling over the pot of plenty. "Hey!" she yelled. Faces turned to her. "If allyuh fight, that food going to turn to shit in allyuh mouth one time."

The wrangling subsided a little. The little girl came whizzing up on her skateboard, dipped her hand into the pot, and brought it back out overflowing with penny sweeties, sweet and sour plums, candy canes and gummy bears; only the red ones. She flashed a triumphant grin at her mother, who said, "La'shawna, you have to have more than that for lunch!" The girl put two gummy bears in her mouth and zoomed away again.

The young woman sighed. "I have to go with she," she said. "Yesterday she turned an old man's walking cane into solid gold. He nearly break he foot when he drop it." She waved goodbye to the Salvation Army Santa Claus. Tentatively, he waved back. She began to run after her child. She stopped a little way off, cupped her mouth with her hands and yelled back at the Santa Claus, "Yes, the name is Mary. I ain't have no Joseph. But you nice. I could come back and check you later?"

He nodded.

She ran to catch up with La'shawna.

2004

List of Sources

Great effort has been made to locate all owners of copyrighted material. Any owner who has inadvertently been omitted will gladly be acknowledged in future printings.

Bret Harte, "How Santa Claus Came To Simpson's Bar," *Mrs. Skagg's Husbands, and Other Sketches* (Boston: James R. Osgood and Company, 1873), pp. 55–79.

Louisa May Alcott, "Kate's Choice," *Aunt Jo's Scrap-Bag. Cupid and Chow-Chow, Etc.* (Boston: Roberts Brothers, 1874), pp. 128–156.

Mark Twain, "A Letter from Santa Claus," Samuel Langhorne Clemens to Olivia Susan (Susy) Clemens, December 25, 1875, Hartford, Conn., in *Mark Twain's Letters, Volume 6: 1874–1875*, eds. Michael B. Frank and Harriet Elinor Smith. The Mark Twain Papers (Berkeley, Los Angeles, London: University of California Press, 2002, 2007), pp. 604–6. Copyright © 2002 by Richard A. Watson and the Chase Global Private Bank as Trustees of the Mark Twain Foundation. Republished by permission of University of California Press; permission conveyed through Copyright Clearance Center, Inc.

J. B. Moore Bristor, "Found After Thirty-Five Years—Lucy Marshall's Letter," *Christian Recorder*, Vol. 21, No. 52 (December 27, 1883), p. 1.

Mary Agnes Tincker, "From the Garden of a Friend," *Autumn Leaves* (New York: William H. Young & Company, 1898), pp. 150–74.

William Dean Howells, "Christmas Every Day," *Christmas Every Day: And Other Stories Told to Children* (New York: Harper and Brothers, 1892), pp. 3–22.

John Kendrick Bangs, "Thurlow's Christmas Story," *Ghosts I Have Met and Some Others* (New York: Harper & Bros., 1898), pp. 109–39.

Jack London, "Klondike Christmas," *Boys' Life*, Vol. 66, No. 12 (December 1976), pp. 40–41. Copyright © 1976. Reprinted by permission of the Irving Shepard Trust.

Stephen Crane, "A Little Pilgrim," *Tales of Whilomville* [The University of Virginia Edition of The Works of Stephen Crane, vol. 7], Fredson Bowers and J. C. Levenson, eds. (Charlottesville, VA: The University Press of Virginia, 1969), pp. 235–39. Copyright © 1969 by the Rector and Visitors of the University of Virginia. Reprinted by permission of the University of Virginia Press.

Paul Laurence Dunbar, "An Old-Time Christmas," *The Strength of Gideon and Other Stories* (New York: Dodd, Mead & Company, 1900), pp. 231–38.

Pauline E. Hopkins, "General Washington: A Christmas Story," *The Colored American Magazine*, Vol. 2, No. 2 (December 1900), pp, 95–104.

Jacob Riis, "The Kid Hangs Up His Stocking," *Children of the Tenements* (New York: Macmillan, 1903), pp. 21–27.

George Ade, "The Set of Poe," *In Babel: Stories of Chicago* (New York: McClure, Phillips & Co., 1903), pp. 115–22.

O. Henry, "A Chaparral Christmas Gift," *Whirligigs* (New York: Doubleday, Page & Company, 1910), pp. 223–230.

Charlotte Perkins Gilman, "According to Solomon," *The Forerunner* Vol. 1, No. 2 (December 1909), pp. 1–5.

Edward Lucas White, "The Picture Puzzle," *Lukundoo and Other Stories* (New York: George H. Doran Company, 1927), pp. 75–94.

Margaret Black, "A Christmas Party That Prevented a Split in the Church," *Baltimore Afro-American*, (December 23, 1916), pp. 2; and (December 30, 1916), p. 2.

Dorothy Parker, "The Christmas Magazines: And the Inevitable Story of the Snowbound Train," *Vanity Fair*, Vol. 7, No. 4 (December 1916), pp. 83.

Robert Benchley, "Christmas Afternoon," *Of All Things* (New York: Henry Holt and Company, 1921), pp. 193–99.

W.E.B. Du Bois, "The Sermon in the Cradle," *The Crisis*, Vol. 23, No. 2 (December 1921), pp. 58–59.

Ben Hecht, "Holiday Thoughts," *Chicago Daily News* (December 5, 1921).

Heywood Broun, "Bethlehem, Dec. 25," *Sitting on the World* (New York: G. P. Putnam's Sons, 1924), pp. 67–69.

Christopher Morley, "The Tree That Didn't Get Trimmed," *Essays* (New York: Doubleday, Doran, & Company, Inc., 1928), pp. 686–93. Copyright © 1925, 1927 by Christopher Morley. Reprinted by permission of John Woodruff, Executor, Christopher Morley Literary Estate.

Sherwood Anderson, "A Criminal's Christmas," *Vanity Fair* (December 1926), pp. 89, 130.

James Thurber, "A Visit from Saint Nicholas (in the Ernest Hemingway Manner)," *The New Yorker* (December 24, 1927), pp. 17–18. Copyright © 1927 Rosemary A. Thurber. Reprinted by arrangement with Rosemary A. Thurber and The Barbara Hogenson Agency, Inc. All rights reserved.

Langston Hughes, "One Christmas Eve," *The Ways of White Folks* (New York: Knopf, 1934), pp. 192–99. Copyright © 1934 by Penguin Random House LLC, renewed 1962 by Langston Hughes. Used by permission of Harold Ober Associates and Alfred A. Knopf, an imprint of the Knopf Doubleday Publishing Group, a division of Penguin Random House LLC. All rights reserved.

Damon Runyon, "The Three Wise Guys," *Collier's Weekly*, Vol. 92, No. 26 (December 23, 1933), pp. 7ff. Published in *Guys and Dolls: The Stories of Damon Runyon* by Damon Runyon, copyright © 2008 by American Rights Management Co., LLC.

Used by permission of Viking Books, an imprint of Penguin Publishing Group, a division of Penguin Random House LLC. All rights reserved.

Leo Rosten, "Mr. K*A*P*L*A*N and the Magi," *The Education of Hyman Kaplan* (New York: Harcourt, Brace & World, 1937), pp. 66–79. Copyright © 1937 by Houghton Mifflin Harcourt Publishing Company, renewed 1965 by Leo C. Rosten. Reprinted by permission of Houghton Mifflin Harcourt Publishing Company. All rights reserved.

John Henrik Clarke, "Santa Claus is a White Man: A Story of the Color Line," *Opportunity: A Journal of Negro Life,* Vol. 17, No. 12 (December, 1939), pp. 365–367. Copyright © 1939 by National Urban League. Reprinted with permission. All rights reserved.

John Collier, "Back for Christmas," *Fancies and Goodnights* (New York: Doubleday, 1951), pp. 157–162. Copyright © 1951 by John Collier. Copyright renewed 1979 by the Estate of John Collier. Reprinted by permission of Harold Matson – Ben Camardi, Inc.

Edna Ferber, "No Room at the Inn," *One Basket: Thirty-One Short Stories* (New York: Simon and Schuster, 1947), pp. 515–21. Copyright © 1947 by Edna Ferber. Reprinted by permission.

John McNulty, "Two People He Never Saw," *Third Avenue, New York* (Boston: Little, Brown and Company, 1946), pp. 129–39. First appeared in *The New Yorker* (December 23, 1944). Copyright © 1944 by John McNulty. Reprinted by permission of John McNulty, Jr.

Mary Roberts Rinehart, "The Butler's Christmas Eve," *Alibi for Isabel and Other Stories* (New York: Farrar & Rinehart, 1944), pp. 187–208. Copyright © 1944 by Mary Roberts Rinehart, renewed. Reprinted by permission of MysteriousPress.com.

Katherine Anne Porter, *A Christmas Story* (New York: A Seymour Lawrence Book/Delacorte Press). First appeared in *Mademoiselle* (December, 1946). Copyright © 1946, 1967 by Katherine Anne Porter. Reprinted by permission of The Permissions Company, LLC on behalf of The Katherine Anne Porter Literary Trust.

Abelardo Díaz Alfaro, "'Santa Clo' Comes to La Cuchilla," *Classic Tales from Spanish America*, trans. William E. Colford (Great Neck, New York: Barron's Education Series, Inc., 1962), pp. 206–10.

Ray Bradbury, "The Gift," *A Medicine for Melancholy* (New York: Doubleday & Company, 1959), pp. 183–85. Copyright © 1952 by Esquire, Inc., renewed 1980 by Ray Bradbury. Reprinted by permission of Don Congdon Associates, Inc.

Raymond E. Banks, "Christmas Trombone," *The Magazine of Fantasy and Science Fiction* Vol. 6, No. 1 (January, 1954) pp. 117–25.

Mildred Clingerman, "The Wild Wood," *A Cupful of Space* (New York: Ballantine Books, 1961) pp. 86–94. Copyright © 2017 by Cupful of Space LLC. Reprinted by permission of Mark Bradley, Cupful of Space LLC. Not to be reprinted without permission.

Shirley Jackson, from *Raising Demons* (New York: Farrar, Straus and Cudahy, 1957),

Index of Authors

This book is set in 10⅓ point Minion Pro, a digital typeface designed by Robert Slimbach in 1990 for Adobe Systems and inspired by Renaissance-era fonts. The name comes from the traditional nomenclature for type sizes, the smallest of which was diamond, followed by pearl, agate, nonpareil, minion, brevier, bourgeois, long primer, small pica, pica, etc.

Two sans-serif fonts are used for display. The titles and subtitles are set in Yana, designed in 2010 by Laura Worthington, an artist in Washington State who creates typefaces based on her own hand-lettering and calligraphy. The ornamental drop caps are Orpheus Pro, released in 2011 by Toronto-based typographers Kevin King and Patrick Griffin and inspired by the classic font of the same name issued in 1928 by German designer Walter Tiemann.

The paper is acid-free and exceeds the requirements for permanence established by the American National Standards Institute. The binding material is Brillianta, a woven rayon cloth made by Van Heek–Scholco Textielfabrieken, Holland. Text design and composition by Gopa & Ted2, Inc., Albuquerque, New Mexico. Printing and binding by Sheridan Books, Inc., in Chelsea, Michigan.